"I would recommend this book in a heartbeat. It's a wonderful fantasy book filled with tons of magic that will leave you wanting more. I am very much looking forward to the next installment."
The Nightly Book Owl

"I laughed, I ranted, I cried twice. It was a bit of an emotional rollercoaster for me but I thoroughly enjoyed it and look forward to reading the next book in the trilogy."
Leanne Crabtree

"If you're looking for a YA fantasy full of magic and mystery and intrigue and romance and wonderful, heartfelt characters that you could easily accept to be trapped under a mountain with, then don't just read *Stolen Songbird* – inhale it. Deliciously written in two POVs that are deep and personal and completely intertwined with one another, this book is at once like hot chocolate on a rainy day with a cat on your lap, and a shot of something wicked when you're feeling wired. There's nothing I even remotely disliked, and a list as long as most Welsh train station names of things I loved. *Stolen Songbird* was a dream to read, a dream to adventure through, and a nightmare to leave. I didn't want to wake up – and neither will you."
Jet Black Ink

"If you love fantasies, romance, and political intrigue, then you really need to add this book to your wishlist and tell all your friends you want it for your birthday, because Oh my gosh, it is my new favorite book of this year."
Book Marks the Spot

DANIELLE L JENSEN

Hidden Huntress

ANGRY
ROBOT

ANGRY ROBOT
An imprint of Watkins Media

Lace Market House,
54-56 High Pavement,
Nottingham,
NG1 1HW
UK

angryrobotbooks.com
twitter.com/angryrobotbooks
Hear my song

Coventry City Council	
STO	
3 8002 02232 165 9	
Askews & Holts	Aug-2015
TEENAGE 11-14	£8.99

An Angry Robot paperback original 2015
1

Copyright © Danielle L Jensen 2015

Danielle L Jensen asserts the moral right to be
identified as the author of this work.

A catalogue record for this book is available
from the British Library.

ISBN 978 0 85766 465 5
EBook ISBN 978 0 85766 473 0

Set in Meridien by Epub Services.
Printed by 4edge Limited.

For my mom, who reads the dreadful first drafts, the polished final drafts, and the many, many versions in between. Thanks for everything you do.

CHAPTER 1
Cécile

My voice faded into silence, though the memory of it seemed to haunt the theatre as I slumped gracefully, trusting that Julian would catch me, however much he might not want to. The stage was smooth and cool against my cheek, a blessed relief against the heat of hundreds of bodies packed into one place. I tried to breathe shallowly, ignoring the stench of too much perfume and far too few baths as I feigned death. Julian's voice replaced mine, and his lament echoed across my ears and through the theatre, but I only half-listened, my attention drifting away to fix on the all too real sorrow of another. One far out of reach.

The audience erupted into cheers. "Bravo!" someone shouted, and I almost smiled when a falling flower brushed against my cheek. The curtain hit the stage floor, and I reluctantly opened my eyes, the red velvet of the curtains pulling me back into an unwelcome reality.

"You seem distracted tonight," Julian said, hauling me unceremoniously to my feet. "And about as emotive as my left boot. *She* won't be best pleased, you know."

"I know," I muttered, smoothing my costume into place. "I had a late night."

"Shocking." Julian rolled his eyes. "It's tiring work ingratiating yourself with every rich man and woman in the city." He took my hand again, nodded at the crew, and we both plastered smiles on our faces as the curtain rose again. "Cécile! Cécile!" the audience shouted. Waving blindly, I blew a kiss to the sea of faces before dropping into a deep curtsey. We stepped back to let the rest of the cast take their bows before coming forward again. Julian dropped to one knee and kissed my gloved fingers to the roaring approval of the crowd, and then the curtain dropped for the final time.

The moment the fabric hit the stage floor, Julian jerked his hand away from mine and rose to his feet. "Funny how even at your worst, they still scream your name," he said, his handsome face dark with anger. "They treat me as though I am one of your stage props."

"You know that isn't true," I said. "You've legions of admirers. All the men are jealous, and all the women wish it was them in your arms."

"Spare me your platitudes."

I shrugged and turned my back on him, walking offstage. It was two months to the day since I had arrived in Trianon and nearly three since my dramatic exit from Trollus, and despite arriving with a plan I had thought was good, I was still no closer to finding Anushka. Julian's jealousy was the least of my concerns.

Backstage was its usual state of organized chaos – only now that the performance was over, the wine was pouring more liberally. Half-dressed chorus girls preened at Julian, their overlapping words barely intelligible as they rained praise upon his performance. I was glad for it – he didn't get the credit he deserved. Me they ignored, which was fine, because all I wanted was to be done with working for the night. Eyes on my dressing room, I wove through the performers until the sound of my name stopped me in my tracks.

"Cécile!"

Slowly, I turned on my heel and watched everyone scatter as my mother strode through the room. She kissed me hard on both cheeks and then pulled me into a tight embrace, her strong fingers digging painfully into the long livid scar where Gran had cut me open to repair my injury. "That was positively dreadful," she hissed into my ear, breath hot. "Be thankful for small mercies that there was no one of taste in the audience tonight."

"Of course not," I whispered back. "Because if there had been, you would have been the one onstage."

"Something you would be grateful for if you weren't so ignorant." She pushed away from me. "Wasn't she brilliant tonight!" she announced to the room. "A natural talent. The world has never known such a voice."

Everyone murmured in agreement, a few going so far as to clap their hands. My mother beamed at them. She might criticize me until she was blue in the face, but she wouldn't tolerate anyone else saying a thing against me.

"Yes indeed, well done, Cécile!" A man's voice caught my attention, and looking around my mother, I saw the Marquis strolling across the room. He was a bland man, as remarkable and memorable as grey paint but for the fact he usually had my mother on his arm.

I dropped into a curtsey. "Thank you, my lord."

He waved me up, his eyes on the chorus girls. "Wonderful performance, my dear. If Genevieve hadn't been sitting right next to me, I would have sworn it was her onstage."

My mother's face tightened and I felt mine blanch. "You are too kind."

Everyone stood staring mutely at each other long enough for it to become uncomfortable.

"We'd best be off," my mother finally said, her voice jarringly cheerful. "We're late as it is. Cécile, darling, I won't be home tonight, so don't wait up."

I nodded my head and watched the Marquis escort my mother out the back entrance. I wondered briefly whether he knew she was married to my father, and if he did, whether he cared. He'd been my mother's patron for years, but I hadn't known he existed until I came to Trianon. As to whether my family had been kept from that knowledge or my family had kept the knowledge from me, I couldn't say. Sighing, I made my way to my dressing room, closing the door firmly behind me.

Sitting down on the stool in front of the mirror, I slowly peeled off my stage gloves and picked up a short lace pair that I habitually wore to cover my bonding marks. The silver of my tattoo shone in the candlelight, and my shoulders slumped.

How much torture could a person endure before breaking? A knot of continuous pain sat in the back of my mind – pain laced with wild fear and anger that never diminished, never seemed to rest. A constant reminder that Tristan suffered in Trollus so that I could be safe in Trianon. A constant reminder of my failure to help him.

"Cécile?"

I twisted around, instinctively covering my bonding marks with my other hand until I saw it was Sabine, and then I let my arms drop to my sides. Her brow furrowed when she saw my face, and she came the rest of the way inside, shutting the door behind her.

Despite her parents' protestations, my oldest and dearest friend had insisted on coming to Trianon with me. She'd always been a talented seamstress and had proven to have a knack for hair and cosmetics, so I'd been able to convince the company to hire her as my dresser.

While I had been recovering, my family had told everyone in the Hollow that I'd gotten cold feet about moving to Trianon and fled to Courville on the southern tip of the Isle. But keeping my secret from Sabine had never been an option. After what she'd gone through during my disappearance, allowing her to believe that I'd let her endure all that hurt because of performance nerves would have been unforgivable.

"You weren't all that bad," she said, dipping a rag in some cold cream and setting to work removing my makeup before fastening my gold necklace back around my throat. "In fact, you weren't bad at all. Just not your best. Who could be under the circumstances?"

I nodded, both of us aware that it wasn't my mother's words troubling me.

"And Genevieve, she's being a right old witch to say otherwise."

Apparently my mother's whispered criticism had not gone unheard. "She wants the best for me," I said, not knowing why I felt the urge to defend her. It was a childhood habit I couldn't seem to break.

"You'd think that, you being her daughter and all, but..." Sabine hesitated, her brown eyes searching mine in our reflection. "Everyone knows she's jealous of you – her star's setting while yours is on the rise." She smiled. "It looks better onstage when it's you playing Julian's lover. Genevieve is old enough to be his mother, and the audience, well, they're not blind, you know?"

"She's still better than I am."

Her smile fell away. "Only because your passion has been stolen by what's happening to *him*."

She never said Tristan's name.

"If you sang how you used to before..." Sabine huffed out a frustrated breath. "You worked so hard for this, Cécile, and I know you love it. It makes me angry knowing that you're throwing your life away for the sake of some creature."

I'd been so angry the first time she picked this argument; hackles up and claws out in defense of Tristan and my choices. But I'd come to see events from Sabine's perspective. All that resonated with her was the worst of it, which made my decision to put aside everything to try to free my captors incomprehensible to her.

"It's not only him I'm trying to help." Names drifted through my mind. So many faces, and all of them relying on me. *Tristan, Marc, Victoria, Vincent...*

"Maybe not. But it's *him* who's changed you."

There was something in her tone and the set of her jaw that made me turn from the mirror to face her.

"You might be hunting this woman for the sake of *them*, but you've stopped living your life because of *him*." Sabine bent down and took my hands in hers. "It's because you're in love with *him* that you've lost your passion for singing, and I wish…" She broke off, eyes fixed on my hands.

I knew she wasn't attacking, that she only wanted what was best for me, but I was sick of defending my choices. "I'm not going to stop loving him for the sake of improving the caliber of my performance," I snapped, pulling my hands out of her grip, and a second later regretting my tone. "I'm sorry. It's only that I wish you'd accept that I'm set on this path."

"I know." She rose to her feet. "I only wish there was more I could do to help you find happiness."

Find happiness… Not find the witch. Sabine had been an integral part of my plan to find Anushka – her ability to ferret out gossip and information was second to none – but she'd been clear that she wasn't happy about doing it.

"You do enough by listening." I caught hold of her hand and kissed it. "And by keeping me in style."

We stared at each other, keenly aware that the awkwardness between us was new and strange. Both of us longing for the days when it hadn't existed.

"Come out with us tonight," she said, the words spilling from her mouth in one last desperate plea. "Just this once, can't you forget the trolls and be with us lowly humans? We're going to have our fortunes told in Pigalle. One of the dancers heard from a subscriber that there's a woman who can see your future in the palm of your hand."

"I'll not hand my hard-earned coins over to a charlatan," I said, forcing lightness into my voice. "But if she happens to have red hair and blue eyes and seems wise beyond her years, do let me know."

If only it could be so easy…

I lingered in my dressing room so that everyone would have the chance to go out into the foyer or vacate the theatre. I wasn't in the mood to entertain subscribers, and besides, I'd all but given up on finding Anushka on the arm of some wealthy nobleman out for a night at the opera. Or at parties. Or in private salons. All that behavior had earned me was legions of admirers and a reputation for stringing men along. I needed a new strategy, and I needed it soon.

Drawing up the hood of my cloak, I hurried out the back entrance of the theatre and down the steps.

"Took you long enough."

I smiled at Chris as he materialized out of the shadows. He was dressed in his work clothes, boots caked thick with mud and manure. "No loitering," I said, pointing at the much-ignored sign.

"I wasn't loitering, I was waiting," he retorted.

"So say all loiterers." I jumped down the steps and fell into stride next to him. "You have anything?" While Sabine had focused on researching the histories of the women I'd sent her after, Chris had been hunting down whispers of magic with the tenacity of one of the Regent's witch-hunters.

He nodded. Stepping into the shadows, he handed me a curved statue with a necklace of herbs twisted around its neck. "Let me guess," I said. "Fertility charm."

"Put it under our pillow and you are sure to give me many strong sons," he said, his voice full of wry amusement rather than the anticipation it had held when we arrived in Trianon.

I held it for a moment, then shook my head. "Anything else?"

He handed me a bracelet of woven twigs. "She called it witch's bane. It's from a rowan tree. If you wear it, a witch won't be able to cast magic your direction."

I frowned at the strange item, and then shoved it in my pocket. What nonsense. "How much did it cost you?"

He told me a number, and I winced as I dug the coins out of my pocket. I spent more than half my wages on potions and bobbles, and so far, it had amounted to nothing more than a strange collection of knickknacks. The few legitimate witches we'd discovered had known nothing about a mysterious redheaded witch or curses, and all had refused my request for tutoring in the arts.

"You discover anything new?" he asked.

I shook my head. "No one who looks anything like her. No

one with an unknown or questionable past. No one who's been inexplicably on the social scene for five centuries."

Chris sighed. "I'll take you home."

We strolled, the walkway drifting from light to dark as we passed in and out of the golden glow of the gas lamps. But when we reached the street that would take me home to my mother's empty townhouse, I stopped. I needed a change. "Let's go see if Fred is at the Parrot."

Chris looked surprised, but didn't argue as we continued down the street toward my brother's favorite drinking establishment. Sidestepping a brawl out front, we pushed our way into the busy tavern. Almost everyone inside was a soldier of some sort – not the sort of place artists such as myself were normally found – but everyone knew I was Frédéric de Troyes' little sister, and no one would bother me here.

"Cécile! Christophe!" Fred shouted when he caught sight of us. He released the barmaid he had his arm around long enough to order a round of beer and deposit the flagons in our hands. He resumed whatever tall tale he was telling the girl, then his eyes went back to me.

"Best I let you get back to work before the barkeep tosses me out," he said to the girl, waiting for her to go back to serving drinks before adding, "You look terrible, Cécile. You should be at *home* in bed."

I grimaced, knowing that *home* meant the Hollow, not our mother's townhouse. He was worse than Sabine, because not only was he adamantly against my hunt for Anushka, he was against my being in Trianon at all. "Don't start."

He set his drink down on the bar with a clank, casting a black glare at a group of men who jostled against me as they passed. The tension radiating from him told me that he was looking for a reason to scrap. Any reason at all. He was angry all the time now. At my mother, at me, at the world.

"You're not going to listen to a word I say anyhow," he muttered. "Might as well go on and do what you do."

Chris tugged on my elbow, drawing me towards a table at

the back. "Fred only wants to protect you, Cécile," he said. "He blames himself for what happened. For not being there for you."

"I know." His first reaction to hearing my story had been a vow to burn Trollus and all its inhabitants to the ground, and the verbal brawl between us when I'd told him my intention to do the exact opposite was probably heard three farms away. Not only did he not agree with my decision, he didn't understand it. And that made Fred angry. But then again, it didn't take much to set him off these days – and I knew that *that* had nothing to do with the trolls. Something had happened long before my disappearance. Something that had occurred when he'd first come to Trianon. Something that had to do with our mother. He hated her, and there were times I thought he believed I'd betrayed him by choosing to live and work with her in Trianon.

Sitting at the sticky table, I proceeded to drain my beer, hoping to wash away thoughts of my brother and everything else.

"Easy there," Chris said, sipping his brew at a more measured pace. "I take it something has happened, and it isn't Fred's perpetual sour mood."

"No." I motioned for one of the girls to bring me another drink. "Nothing's happened, and therein lies the problem." I took several long swallows. "Just another day gone by where I've made no progress finding her. Another day gone by where Tristan suffers God knows what sort of tortures, while I sing on stage to crowds of admirers. I hate it."

"It's the only way you can afford to stay in Trianon. And besides, I thought you liked performing?"

I squeezed my eyes tightly shut and nodded. "But I shouldn't."

"Cécile." Chris reached across the table and tried to hold my mug down, but I jerked it out of his grasp and finished the contents. He grimaced. "You know that he doesn't want you miserable every waking breath for his sake."

"How would you know?" I asked, digging money out of my pocket to pay for another drink.

"We've tried everything," he said, going with a different tactic.

"For two months you've run in the circles you'd thought she'd occupy and not seen hide nor hair of her. You have lists and lists of women whose backgrounds you and Sabine have checked, which yielded nothing but gossip. I've lost count of how many witches, real or otherwise, that we've talked to. None of them would help us."

"Most of them can't." During my recovery, I'd pressed my Gran into teaching me all she knew about magic. She'd taught me how to balance the elements, why certain plants had the effects they did, and how to time a spell casting at a moment of transition: sunrise and sunset, a full moon, and the solstices in order to maximize the amount of power drawn from the earth. She didn't know a great deal – and nearly all of it was relating to healing injuries and curing sickness, but I'd gained enough knowledge to know magic when I saw it.

"My point is," Chris continued, "that maybe you've done enough. Maybe it's time for you to move on with your life."

I set my empty mug down with a clatter, not bothering to keep the anger off my face. I expected this from Sabine, but not from Chris. For her, it was still half a fairytale, but he'd been to Trollus. He knew the stakes. "Are you actually suggesting I give up?"

"I don't know." He looked away. "He doesn't even want you to break the curse. Maybe it would be better for everyone if you stopped hunting."

"Better for humans, you mean," I snapped, my words slurring together. "How can you be so selfish?"

Chris turned bright red. Hands gripping the edge of the table, he leaned toward me. "If you want to see selfish, go look in the mirror. I'm not the one willing to sell the whole world into slavery for the sake of a love affair!" He stormed away through the crowd of patrons and out of sight.

I stared blindly at my empty mug, ignoring the dampness of spilled beer and wine soaking into the sleeves of my dress. Was Chris right? Was I being selfish? Two months ago, I set out to Trianon to hunt down and kill Anushka so that the curse would be broken. There had been no doubt in my mind that I was doing the right thing, and that certainty had been unwavering.

Or had it?

I wanted Tristan freed, that I knew. And my friends. Marc, the twins, Pierre, and the Duchesse Sylvie. Zoé and Élise. All the half-bloods, really. I wanted them free of the curse. But the others? I thought about Angoulême, King Thibault, and especially about Tristan's demon of a little brother, and a cold sweat broke across my brow. Them I would be well and truly content to keep locked up for eternity.

But that was the problem. If I released one, I released all, and the consequences would be on me. But so would the consequences of doing nothing.

Pain twisted in my chest, and I shoved my mug across the table. I missed him. Not only for reasons of the heart, but as an ally. Missed watching his formidable and tenacious intelligence at work – that mind of his that I so greatly admired. What I would not give for his ability to see to the heart of a puzzle.

The room spun as I looked around, making my stomach churn. I sucked in a deep breath to try to calm my senses and instantly regretted it. The stench of stale beer and sweat assaulted my nostrils and I gagged. "Bloody stones and sky." Clambering to my feet, I pushed my way through the revelers, eyes fixed on the front door and fresh air.

I wasn't going to make it.

I pushed harder, ignoring the complaints of those in my path. Reaching the door, I flung it open and staggered out into the cool air. Then I fell to my knees and retched up three flagons of beer into the gutter.

"I must confess," a voice said from behind me. "This wasn't precisely the posture I expected to find you in."

Wiping my mouth on my sleeve, I looked over my shoulder. A cloaked man stood a few paces behind me, face shadowed by his hood. "What do you want?"

"Only to deliver a message." His mouth widened into a smile. "To her Royal Highness, Princess Cécile de Montigny."

CHAPTER 2
Cécile

I rose unsteadily to my feet, the lace of my gloves catching on the brick wall as I grasped it for support. "Who are you?"

"A messenger."

"From who?" I asked, though I already knew.

"From his Majesty, King Thibault." The man inclined his head. "He sends his warmest and most heartfelt greetings to his absent daughter-in-law. Trollus hasn't been the same since your hasty departure."

"Are you here to kill me?" *Was this the moment of reckoning?*

The messenger laughed. "Kill you? Certainly not. If I'd been here to kill you, you would already be dead. I'm not one to delay the inevitable."

"Then why?" I asked, feeling not at all reassured. "And how is it that you can speak of them at all?"

"His Majesty would like..." he started to say, then Chris burst out the front door of the bar. "Cécile" he called, looking around wildly. His eyes fixed on me and the messenger. "Hey!" he shouted. "Leave her alone!"

He started to run toward us, but I held up a warning hand. "He's a messenger from the King."

Chris's eyes widened. "What does *he* want?"

The messenger eyed Chris like he'd expected him, his acceptance of Chris's presence making me uneasy, because it meant he knew who my friend was. "His Majesty would like to meet with Cécile."

"No!" Chris burst out, almost drowning out my question, "When?"

He smiled. "Tonight."

"Absolutely not," Chris said. "There is no bloody way I'm letting you go back to Trollus."

"Only to the mouth of the River Road," the messenger clarified. "The gates to Trollus remain closed to humans."

We'd known that. Although Chris's father, Jérôme, was still bound by his oaths and unable to speak about Trollus, he'd enough practice working around his oaths to explain that trade was now conducted at the mouth of the river, and only by the King's agents. The change effectively cut off our one source of news about what was going on inside the city.

Chris shook his head. "Still too close."

"It isn't your decision," I said, my mind racing. What did the King want? Would Tristan be there? Would I get to see him? Even the chance was enough to make up my mind. "I'll go."

"You can't," Chris hissed. "Tristan warned you never to come back. They'll kill you!"

I slowly shook my head. "No. If the King wanted me dead, I would be. He wants something else." And I was willing to bet I knew exactly what it was.

The messenger escorted us out of the city and into the countryside where horses waited tethered in the trees. Despite the hour, the guards at the gates opened them for us without question, no doubt motivated by gold mined in the depths of Trollus.

We moved at a steady pace, our path lit by the moon as it drifted out from behind dark patches of cloud. It was a good night for casting spells, the round silver disk in the sky magnifying the amount of power a witch could tap. Not that it would do me any good against the trolls.

It was the darkest hour of the night by the time we cleared the trees and came into sight of the bridge spanning the rock fall. Our escort did not follow us as we dismounted and slowly picked our way down to the water.

"What do you think they want?" Chris asked under his breath, holding my arm as I scrambled over some rocks. The tide was retreating, but it was still high enough that there was only a dozen feet of sand between the fallen boulders and the gentle waves. The stench of sewers was strong, the city releasing refuse only when the tide was high enough to wash away the evidence.

"I think they want out." Ahead, water poured out from under an overhang, the river carving a path through the sand down to where it met the ocean. Beneath that overhang was the entrance to Trollus, and further in, a single ball of light hovered, waiting. A reminder that here lay the gateway between worlds, the divide between reality and fantasy. A dream or, depending on who waited, a nightmare. Shoving my torch into the sand, I motioned for Chris to do the same, and then we cautiously made our way closer.

A small troll child sat cross-legged in the middle of the road. He looked up at our approach, revealing a younger version of Tristan. Except for the curve of his lips... those reminded me of his half-sister, Lessa. The face of angel, but the mind of a monster.

"Good evening, Your Highness," I said, stopping a healthy distance from the barrier and dropping into a deep curtsey. "Bow," I hissed under my breath.

Prince Roland de Montigny cocked his head and eyed us as though we were insects. "Good evening, Cécile."

Why was Roland here? Where was the King?

"It's hard to see you there, standing in the dark," he said. "Come closer."

I licked my parched lips. The barrier kept him caged, but I didn't want to go any nearer to the monster who'd nearly taken my life. Roland got to his feet. "Come closer," he said. "I want to look at you."

"Stay here," I murmured to Chris and, against all my instincts, walked toward the barrier. My heart raced and sweat trickled down my back. He was just a child, but I was utterly terrified of him. More so than even the King or Angoulême, because at least they were sane. No matter how calm and civilized he was pretending to be, the thing standing before me was not. He was mad, unpredictable, treacherous, and very, very dangerous.

"Closer," he crooned. "Closer."

My boots scraped along the ground as I inched forward, not certain precisely where the barrier lay. Abruptly, I felt the air thicken and I recoiled back a pace, heart in my throat. And like a snake whose prey has moved beyond reach, his little form relaxed, no longer poised to strike. He'd wanted me to come within reach so that he could finish what he started that fateful day in the Dregs.

I held up my hand. "You can see well enough from there."

Roland ignored my hand and my words, but his lips pulled back, revealing little straight white teeth. "Scared?"

Terrified.

"Where is your brother?" I asked. "Where is Tristan?"

Roland's grin intensified. "They dug a special hole for him in prison." He giggled, the sound of it high-pitched, childish, and horrifying. "He doesn't get out much."

He clapped a hand over his mouth, but the apparent humor was too much for him and his giggles turned into shrieks of laughter that echoed through the tunnel. I took a step back and nearly collided with Chris, who'd worked his way closer during the exchange. His face was pale. Though I'd told him about Roland, nothing could have prepared him for such a creature.

I turned back to Roland. "You find it amusing that your elder brother and heir to the throne is in prison?"

The boy's laughter cut off. "Tristan isn't heir any longer. I am."

I shook my head, not so much to deny he was telling the truth, but more at the sheer horror of the devil in front of me one day ruling the kingdom. Either way, my denial incensed him.

"I will be King!" he screamed, and flung himself at me. I leapt back, but my heel snagged on my dress and I toppled to the ground. Chris's hands caught my arms and heaved me far out of reach, but not out of sight of Roland throwing himself over and over against the barrier, his fists splitting open and healing in an instant, his blood splattering the magic that caged him and rendering it visible. The rocks shook and trembled as his power hammered against the curse, muffling his screams. But nothing could spare us the feral rage written across his face – an expression void of any form of sanity.

"Heaven help us," Chris whispered, our hands locked together as we watched.

The hammering stopped. Roland's face smoothed into composure, and turning, he bowed low to the troll-light coming down the road. "Father."

The King walked into view. "You're making a great deal of noise, boy."

Roland scowled. "She said Tristan was heir, not me."

"Did she now?" The King looked through the blood-splattered barrier and caught my eye. "Humans are liars, Roland. You know that. Now go back to the city. The Duke is waiting for you."

An answer that was no answer. There was hope for Tristan yet.

Roland shot me one last triumphant look, then sped off into the darkness.

"What do you want?" I asked, climbing to my feet. "Why did you have me brought here?"

"Oh, I think you know why," the King replied. Removing a handkerchief from his pocket, he wiped the blood off the barrier. He watched us with interest, but said nothing. I stared back until I could stand it no more. "Where is Tristan? I want to see him."

His chuckle drifted around me. "You'd make a poor politician, Cécile. You're far too honest about your desires."

"I thought all humans were liars?"

He shrugged. "True, but you are honest in spirit, which is

more than I can say for myself. Or any troll, really." His orb of light brightened until the tunnel shone like day. "One wants what one cannot have. And when one cannot lie, the ability to deceive becomes a far more meaningful talent. Something to be revered. But all this philosophizing is something better left to another day. I have what you want; and you, my dear, I believe to be capable of delivering what I want. What I propose is an exchange."

I shook my head rapidly. "I am not so stupid as to think it would be that simple, Thibault. Nor am I so selfish as to consider releasing you upon the world for the sake of one life."

Which was a lie. I considered it every waking minute.

The King tilted his head and nodded slowly. "Tell me, Cécile, what exactly is it about my release that terrifies you so?"

"Everything." My voice sounded high-pitched and strange. "You're a cruel, heartless tyrant. I've seen the way you rule – I know all about your laws. If I let you free, you'll slaughter every last one of us."

"Don't be foolish," the King interrupted. "The last thing I intend is to wipe out humanity. I *need* your kind. Do you expect the Duke d'Angoulême to pick up the plow to work the field? Or your dear friend, Marc, the Comte de Courville, to lay paving stones day in and out?" He waved a hand at me as though my fears were utter madness. "Do not stand there and preach to me that the Regent of Trianon does not have laws, or that his aristocracy is any less dismissive of their commoners than we are of ours."

He pointed a finger at me. "You call me a tyrant, but I can say that there isn't one individual in Trollus who goes hungry or doesn't have a roof over his head. Every last one of them is educated and employed. Can your regent claim as much?"

I bit my lip. "What about freedom? The Regent allows no slavery on the Isle."

The King made a face. "Why don't you go ask those starving in the Pigalle quarter how much their freedom is worth. Or those freezing to death in ditches along country roads." He rested a hand against the barrier. "You would be exchanging one aristocracy for another. Those such as your father would still raise pigs and sell them at market. Your mother would still sing onstage for those who could afford a ticket. For most, very little about their lives would change." He sighed deeply. "How much are you willing to sacrifice for your ungrounded fears?"

"Don't listen to him," Chris said from behind me. "He's only acting in his own interests."

"And you aren't, Christophe Girard?" The King spoke to Chris, but his gaze remained fixed on me. Gauging my reaction. "Don't tell me," he continued, "that you have not considered how you might benefit from keeping Cécile and my son separated."

"Tristan being freed is the least of my concerns," Chris retorted, but their words washed over me unheard. Were my fears unfounded? I closed my eyes and remembered the paintings Tristan had shown me, depicting what life had been like for humanity under troll domination. Remembered the drawings of humans begging for salvation after the Fall and the atrocities that followed. Would it be the same under King Thibault? Better? Or worse? I clenched my teeth.

But what he said next changed everything.

"I have no intention of going to war to regain my kingdom," the King said. "Power over the Isle will be ceded to me peacefully."

I felt my jaw drop open. "How can you claim such a thing?"

He gave a slight shake of his head. "That is for me to know – I would not care for my plans to be disrupted. That," he added, "might necessitate violence against your kind, which is something I wish to avoid. I've seen enough bloodshed, and I grow weary of it."

Of all the things I had expected him to say, *that* hadn't been one of them: an offer of a peaceful resolution from the mouth of one who could not lie. Yet I could not find it in myself to believe him. Still, I'd be a fool not to try to discover the rest of his plans.

"I've been looking for Anushka," I said abruptly.

The King nodded. "And tell me, Cécile, in what manner has your search differed from that of the thousands of men and women who have sought her over the past five centuries? Do you think we've not hunted down every rumor, searched every face, infiltrated even the most exclusive of circles? Do you think we haven't searched out birth records or found someone who could account for the childhood years of every woman with a hazy past?"

I opened my mouth, then closed it again.

"You are unique, girl, and so should be your search," he said softly.

He meant magic. The trolls had likely never sent a witch after her before; and if they had, there was no way she was as committed as me.

"I don't know how," I said, not bothering to keep the bitterness from my voice. "And no one will teach me." I had left all the grimoires in Trollus, and the handful of spells I could remember were useless in my search. I knew more than I had before, but that wasn't saying much.

The King reached into his coat, and my heart skipped as I recognized the cover of the book he removed: it was Anushka's grimoire. He held the book through the barrier, and I reached for it eagerly, but before I could grab it, he pulled it back. "First I want your word."

A small smile made its way onto my face. "Afraid I'll use her magic against you?"

He waved the bloody handkerchief back and forth. "I believe you lack one of the requisite ingredients. No, before I give you this nasty bit of work, I want your word that you will use it to hunt down Anushka. That you will stop at nothing to find her and bring her to me here."

"Cécile, don't!" Chris shouted. "If you promise him something, it will be binding."

"I'm not promising you anything until I see Tristan," I said.

"You'll see him when you make progress."

"I'll stop searching this moment unless you let me see him," I said, raising my chin in defiance. This might be my only chance, and I wouldn't give it up without a fight.

"I hoped you would be reasonable," the King said with a sigh. "But very well. Bring him!" he shouted back into the tunnel. Moments later, I could hear boots treading on stone, but also the sound of something heavy being dragged.

Chris gripped my arm. "Be strong. This isn't going to be easy."

As if I didn't know. For months I'd felt Tristan's agony as he was subjected to punishment at his father's order. Had watched the silver marks on my knuckles tarnish as his strength was sapped in ways my mind too easily imagined. But none of it prepared me for the sight of him being dragged barefoot and shirtless between armed guards, who flung him at his father's feet.

A sob tore from my lips as my eyes took in his gaunt frame, filthy and covered with dried blood. Three sets of manacles encircled his arms, manacles designed to hold in place iron spikes skewered through flesh and bone. Fresh blood oozed around the metal, falling in crimson droplets to soak the sand beneath him. The King reached down and pulled the hood off his head. Tristan remained unmoving, slumped against the barrier. A breeze rose off the sea, gusting by me to tug at his grime-caked hair.

Very slowly, he raised his face, eyes focusing on me. "Cécile," he croaked. "I told you never to come back."

CHAPTER 3
Cécile

Only Chris's firm grip on my arm prevented me from launching myself through the barrier. "Damn you to hell," I screamed at the King. "Who does this to his own son? How do you live with yourself?"

How could I live with myself knowing it was my fault Tristan was in this position, and that I'd done nothing about it?

"He's lucky I suffer him to live," the King replied evenly. "Tristan is guilty of treason of the highest level. He conspired against his father and his king. He instigated a rebellion that resulted in numerous deaths. He began a duel against me that very nearly cost me my life."

"You gave him no choice," I replied, my voice bitter.

The King slowly shook his head. "He always had a choice. He chose you. Now he must suffer the consequences."

Tristan slowly pushed himself up onto his knees, and I saw with relief that there was still a gleam of spirit in his eyes. He wasn't broken. At least, not yet. "Cécile, don't listen to him." His voice was rough from lack of use. Or screaming. "You need to go now."

"I'm not leaving you like this," I said.

Tristan grimaced. "Christophe, take her away from here. Far away. You promised to keep her safe, and this is far from it."

"He's right." Chris tugged on my arms, drawing me back. I

29

struggled against him, digging my heels into the rock and sand, but he was stronger.

"Let me go," I shouted.

Tristan's face tightened with concentration that mirrored the resolve I felt through our bond. "You gave me your word, Christophe," he said. "I expect you to keep it."

"Damn troll," Chris muttered. Ignoring my hammering fists, he flipped me over his shoulder and started out to the beach.

"Put me down," I demanded. I'd abandoned Tristan once, and I wasn't going to do it again. Clenching my teeth, I called upon the power of the earth, drawing it deep within me. "Stop."

The fire of the torch flared and bent away from the wind gusting in off the ocean, the river reversing its direction as the waves surged, flooding up around Chris's boots. The full moon gave me power enough to match Tristan in this, and I intended to use it.

Chris froze.

"You will not interfere," I said.

"Christophe!" Tristan shouted. "Take Cécile away from here."

Chris groaned and clutched his head, dropping me with a splash.

"You're going to break his mind," the King said, and when I regained my feet, I saw that he was watching with great interest.

Chris fell to his knees in the water, clutching at the rocks beneath. "Please," he groaned. "It hurts."

I relaxed my will, unwilling to let my friend suffer to prove a point. "Tristan, stop what you're doing to him," I said. "You've no right making decisions for me."

He glared at me, then gave a short nod. "Stay, then."

I turned my attention back to the King. "What do you want?"

"I've told you," he replied. "I want your word that you will do *everything* within your power to find Anushka and deliver her to me. And in exchange, I will allow you and Tristan to be reunited."

"Cécile, don't." Tristan rested a bloody hand against the

barrier. "You know what will happen if you break the curse. It won't just be us you set loose, the others will be free to walk in this world once more."

"She knows what you've told her," the King said, looking down at his son as though no longer quite certain how much Tristan had divulged. "What loyalty does she owe the Regent of Trianon? What has he ever done for her? Is keeping him in power," he said, turning his attention back to me, "worth the cost?"

Indecision racked me to the core. "He says he can take back the Isle peacefully," I said, my eyes flicking to the King. "He said he has a plan."

I felt Tristan's shock at my words, and he tilted his face up to look upon his father, who nodded. "It is the truth. When my plans are complete, Trianon will be ceded without violence against the citizens of the Isle."

Long moments passed, and then Tristan dropped his head. "It's a trick. Don't believe him."

"But, Tristan!" I desperately wanted the King's words to be true – desperately wanted there to be an easy solution to this hopeless situation.

"Please," Tristan pleaded. "Don't promise him anything. If you do, he'll own your will. Walk away from here and never come back."

I trembled, my mind racing through all of the possible options. Tristan couldn't see the future, he didn't know for certain that history would repeat itself. Was it not possible that the King really meant what he said?

"I'm begging you, Cécile," Tristan said, his voice shaking. "If you love me, you won't give him what he wants."

My eyes stung. "If I refuse," I said to the King. "What then?"

His face hardened. "Are you certain you want to know?"

"Yes." I had to tear the word from my throat, which was tight with terror.

"As you wish." An invisible hand of magic slammed Tristan against the barrier, making him grimace in pain. I could see him struggling, muscles straining as he tried to free himself. Fresh blood welled up around the spikes through his arms.

"No!" I screamed. "No, no, no. Stop, please don't hurt him!" I flung myself at the wall caging them in and ran up against magic as hard as rock. The King had erected his own barrier to keep me out. I whimpered as one of the guards revealed a whip studded with iron spikes.

"I'll ask you again, Cécile, is it worth the cost?" The King nodded at the guard, and the lash snapped wickedly across Tristan's shoulders, tearing open his skin. His face twisted, but his eyes locked on mine. "Don't do it. No matter what he does, agree to nothing."

The whip fell again. Blood splattered and Tristan clenched his teeth in agony. *He won't kill him*, logic told me, but logic was cold comfort in the face of Tristan's pain.

The King nodded, and the whip fell again. And again. Tristan bore it in near silence at first, but I felt his reaction to every fiery lash. And I felt him break an instant before the first scream tore from his throat. Still the whip fell.

It was too much.

"Stop! I promise. I'll find her." My words were garbled, falling over each other, but the King heard. The whip froze mid-lash and Tristan crumpled to the ground. Rivulets of blood trickled down his back, the iron-inflicted wounds refusing to heal.

"Whatever it takes?" the King asked. "And you'll bring her here? I feel inclined to hear how well the witch crows with her guts removed, although I'd accept her death in any fashion."

I nodded numbly. "I promise to do whatever it takes to find her and bring her here."

"Good girl." He tossed Anushka's grimoire through the barrier. It landed with a thud on the wet rock.

I ignored it, dropping to my hands and knees. "Tristan?"

His eyes half-opened and fixed on mine.

"I'm sorry," I whispered. "I couldn't bear it."

He turned his face away from me. He wasn't grateful – he was angry that I'd failed him.

"Take him back to the palace and have him cleaned up." The King watched with an expression devoid of emotion as the guards lifted Tristan between them and carried him up the River Road. Then he turned to me. "Best you get to work, little witch. You've a promise to keep."

CHAPTER 4
Tristan

Maintaining one's dignity while being dragged in chains through the city one had once been destined to rule, covered in weeks' worth of one's own filth, is difficult. That being said, I thought I had managed the deed well enough on the trip between my prison cell and the River Road. Not so on the return voyage. There had been no dignity in my screams; and while the streaks left behind by my tears of pain might have elicited the pity of some, they certainly earned me no respect. I did not deserve it.

I was the fallen prince. Twice a traitor, having betrayed both my father and my cause in a single moment, ensuring that I would remain an outcast for whatever remained of my life. All for a human girl who I loved above all things, and all, it seemed, for nothing.

My jaw ached as I clenched my teeth, half for the pain racking my body, but more for the remembrance of her expression. Horror and pity mixed together in her brilliant blue eyes, but all paling beneath the weight of the promise she'd made for my sake. The burden of a choice that should have been mine, but because I'd been too weak to endure my father's abuse, the choice had fallen on her instead. I hadn't even been man enough to look her in the eye and own my defeat – had instead turned my head away, feeling that not only had I failed her, I'd failed at everything I had ever set out to accomplish, at everything that I thought myself to be.

The guards dropped me, and I ground my teeth to keep from crying out. My eyes fixed on the familiar carpet beneath my knees.

"Leave," said a voice I would recognize anywhere. The guards grumbled, but their boots retreated from my line of sight and the door slammed shut behind me. It took a concerted effort to lift my head enough to see the troll standing in front of me. "Hello, cousin," I said, my voice hoarse.

"You look terrible," Marc replied, his disfigured face grim. "Can you get up?"

"I think I am content where I am." The carpet scratched against my cheek as I lay my head down. "Why am I here?" I asked as an afterthought.

"I've little notion – I was hoping you might provide some insight into why your father ordered your change of accommodation." Marc came toward me, and I rolled one eye up at the sound of metal keys clinking together, remaining motionless as he unlocked four of the six manacles skewering my arms. "Brace yourself," he said, and jerked one of the cuffs open. A wet sucking noise filled my ears, and I fainted.

When my consciousness returned some moments later, the manacles lay in a blood-crusted and rusty pile on the floor. The two remaining on my wrists stung, the cursed iron still itching and infuriating, but the relief of having the others removed was enormous. Having them in place was like having bands of metal wrapped around my chest, allowing me little gasps of breath, but never enough to satisfy my need. I greedily drew upon my magic, using it to prop myself up on my knees.

"Better? He ordered that I leave two in place."

I nodded. "Much."

"I had a bath ordered for you." He gestured to the steaming tub. "I hadn't reckoned on the injuries."

"Just as well." I slowly got to my feet. "I'm not much for conversation, I'm afraid. Send in my servants on your way out."

"I'm afraid you have no servants."

I turned from the bath to look at him. "What?"

"They all refuse to attend you."

"All?" The loss was surprisingly painful. "So I have only you."

He nodded. "And the twins, of course. But his Majesty ordered them to the mines as punishment for their actions. I believe he thought the low ceiling would trouble their backs, and perhaps it does, but I doubt he considered how well they'd take to the competition of it all. They do well enough down there."

I gripped the edges of the tub. "He'll only find another way to make them suffer. You should all forsake me – attempting to continue our friendship will only bring you trouble." I fumbled with my destroyed clothing, cursing my numb fingers. "You may go."

"Tristan, we knew what we were doing when we helped you free Cécile."

"Don't say her name," I snarled, glaring at the water. I swore I could see her eyes reflected in its depths. "Leave."

"I'm not leaving you in this state," Marc said. "You're injured – let me help you, at least."

You are helpless. Fury flooded through me, and I rounded on him. "I do not need your help," I screamed. The room shook as I lashed out with magic. Marc raised a shield, but the blow still sent him staggering. If it were not for the fact I was a fraction my usual strength, what I had done would likely have killed him. "Please leave."

He eyed me warily. "I'll not leave of my own accord. If you desire me gone so badly, you will have to order me properly. You have my name."

I sagged against the tub, my wrists screaming against the pressure. "Never again," I muttered.

"Then you will have to suffer my presence."

I didn't respond. Instead, I set to ridding myself of my filthy clothing. Taking a deep breath, I stepped into the steaming water and plunged down. It felt like hot pokers were sliding into my collection of injuries, but I relished the pain. And for a moment, it drowned the sense of *her* out of my mind. Ignoring my cousin's presence, I scrubbed away most of the blood and grime until the water was the color of rust, and then I rested my arms on the edges, breathing deeply.

"Are you going to tell me what happened?"

Ignoring the question, I watched fresh blood well out of the punctures in my arm and drip into the tub.

"Tristan!" Marc snapped and I looked at him in surprise. He was not one to raise his voice.

"Yes?"

"Your father has kept you locked in a prison cell for months, and then today, for seemingly no reason whatsoever, he has allowed you to return home. After a mysterious meeting at the mouth of the River Road. Why? Who did you go to see? What drove him to do this to you?"

I opened my mouth to answer, then closed it again, the words sticking in my throat.

"It was Cécile, wasn't it?"

I nodded mutely.

"Is she well?" There was more than a hint of concern in his voice.

"Yes," I said. "For now, at any rate." I swallowed the taste of bile that had risen in my throat. "He used me to exact her word that she would hunt down Anushka for him."

"A promise? Were there any loopholes?"

"Yes, but she's had no experience finding a way out of bargains and I've no way to get word to her." I squeezed my eyes tight, trying to drive away the memory of her expression as she pleaded that I be spared. "So she will either succeed, or he will ensure her failure drives her mad."

"And *if* she succeeds? What is your plan then?"

"I don't have one." Standing, I wrapped a length of toweling around my waist and retrieved a pair of trousers from my wardrobe, struggling into them. I discarded the idea of a shirt, the thought of the fabric rubbing against the open wounds on my back more than I cared to bear. Marc remained silent through all of it, but his unease was apparent in the way he cloaked his face with shadow.

"There will be no more plans, no more plotting," I said. "I've overestimated myself for far too long, and look at the results. There is nothing I can do but wait for the end to come."

"I can't believe you mean that," Marc said. "The cousin I know has never conceded defeat."

"Three months trapped alone in a hole changes a man," I muttered, sitting down cautiously on the chaise. "I've had a lot of time to think and to come to terms with my failures. To accept that I am, and have never been more than, a puppet in my father's machinations."

"You're giving up because he discovered one of your plans?" Marc's voice was incredulous. "Because of one lost battle you relegate yourself to the status of a puppet?"

"It's not that the battle was lost," I said, closing my eyes. "It's how it was lost." I swallowed hard. "If I had been betrayed or outwitted – that I could accept. But…"

He remained quiet while I searched for the words to explain my torment. "He knew that I loved her," I finally said. "And he used my love as a weapon against me. As a weapon against my cause. He took the one thing I had that was good, and he corrupted it." My shoulders slumped. "I love her, and there is nothing I would not do to save her, and for that, I loathe myself, because all my love seems capable of accomplishing is evil. And now he means to do the same to her. To make her choose between my life and the lives of countless others." I clenched my teeth.

"Her choice is already made." His words held a trace of bitterness. "Will you leave her to struggle on alone?"

"There is nothing I can do to help her." I stared at the floor, but all I could see was her face. "She was doomed from the moment she set foot in Trollus, perhaps doomed from the moment she was born. I thought I could protect her, but I was wrong." My fingers twitched slightly and drops of blood rained down on the carpet. "She will determine all our fates – the burden is hers. There is nothing I can do."

"How very fatalistic of you," Marc snapped. "If you can trouble yourself to move, there's something I want you to see."

Reluctantly, I rose and followed him out onto the balcony.

The city was mostly dark as it was the middle of the night, but scattered throughout the blackness were pockets of lights. I frowned. "What are they doing?"

"Building your structure – they started shortly after you were put in prison."

I blinked once. "Why? On whose orders?"

"Your father's." Marc leaned against the railing. "Shortly after your imprisonment, he announced to the half-bloods that he would fund the construction of your project if they provided the labor."

"Why would he do that?" I muttered, resting my elbows on the railing.

Marc shrugged. "It did much to restore his popularity with them. They practically sing his name in the streets these days."

"He never needed or wanted their support before." My eyes flicked between construction sites. Something wasn't right. "Surely his actions have cost him popularity with the aristocracy."

"Indeed they have." Marc shifted his weight slightly from one foot to another, showing his unease. "He almost never leaves the palace these days. When he does, he always goes with a full complement of guards. Your mother, too, is guarded at all times. He clearly fears an assassination attempt."

"He doesn't fear anything," I replied, scoffing at the very idea. "And his resumed control over the tree protects him – no one would dare it."

"He didn't resume control of the tree. He gave the task over to the Builder's Guild. They're taxed right to their limit in keeping it stable."

I sucked in a deep breath. "Bloody stones! What is he thinking?"

Since the moment a permanent tree structure had been established, the ruling monarch controlled it. Part of the reason was the immense amount of power it took to maintain, but the other part was the protection it gave the King. Magic didn't disappear the moment a troll died, but it dissipated quickly, making the death of a king a dangerous time in Trollus. Especially when the death was unexpected. Giving up control of the tree made my father vulnerable indeed.

"The reason he gave was that having the lives of all those in Trollus held in the hand of one troll had proven to be too much of a risk."

I cringed inwardly, remembering how when he had first imprisoned me I'd threatened to pull the tree down on all our heads should something happen to Cécile. "He's not wrong," I said under my breath. "But that risk has always existed – why change now?"

"His actions certainly bear consideration."

"As always," I said, my mind sorting through possible motivations. But I couldn't quite concentrate, because something about the construction going on in front of me was wrong. "They aren't following my plans," I said abruptly.

"I thought they seemed different." Marc's voice was mild. "Of course, I am no engineer."

But I was – and even though the foundations of the structure were only just being laid, I could tell it would never support the weight of Forsaken Mountain.

"I thought the half-bloods had your diagrams?" Marc said. "What reason would they have to deviate from them?"

I shook my head. "I promised them the plans once I had their names – but I didn't have the time to collect all of them, which gave me an out on my promise."

"No wonder they curse your name. You should have handed them over as a show of good faith."

"I didn't trust them," I muttered, remembering the moment as vividly as though it were yesterday. I'd collected as many names as I could before Cécile's terror had driven me back to the palace. Just before I'd reached the gates, Anaïs had found me and told me my father was alone with Cécile. I'd given her my plans and told her to hide them, then I'd gone inside to duel with my father. Anaïs would only have had a few minutes to hide the documents before she came through my window to fight. Which meant she'd hidden them nearby.

Retreating back inside, I went to the glass doors Anaïs had broken through. Below lay my private courtyard and the wall she would have come over to get inside. Opening the doors, I hurried down the steps, barely noticing Marc trailing along after me.

Cécile's piano still stood in the middle of the space, but it was covered in a layer of dust. I walked in a slow circle around it, then came to a halt at the bench. Stacks of music covered the seat, the paper as dusty as the piano. Wiping my hands on my trousers to remove the blood dripping down from my wrists, I began to sort through them, quickly coming up with what I'd been looking for. "Hidden in plain sight," I said, holding them up.

"Then what are the half-bloods constructing?" Marc asked, his expression grim.

"Were you present when he told them to build?"

Marc nodded, his eyes growing distant as he remembered. "His speech was long, but he concluded by lifting a roll of parchment into the air and shouting, 'Behold the plans for a stone tree.'"

I shook my head slowly, admiring his genius. "He gave them drawings of the tree as it is now. They're building something that is doomed to fail – and he knows it. And by keeping the Builders' Guild focused entirely on maintaining the magic version, he ensures none of them will have the time to do the calculations to determine that while the existing structure works for magic, it won't work for stone."

Marc blinked.

"You didn't think it took me two years to come up with plans identical to something I looked at every day, did you?" I asked, shaking my head. "I assure you, these plans" – I shook the parchment – "are drastically different for a reason. The question is, why would my father let me out, knowing that I would see through his deception?"

Marc shook his head slightly.

Turning round, I pressed a piano key, the note echoing out around us. "He wants me to do something." I pressed another key. "What does he *think* I'm going to do?"

"I thought you weren't going to do anything but wait to die?"

I shot him a dark look. "I haven't said I'm going to do anything."

"Of course not." Marc kept a straight face. "This is all just speculation."

"Indeed. Something to pass the time while I wait."

"To die."

"Or not." I scratched the skin around one puncture in my arm – it had finally scabbed over, but the healing itched terribly. "What does he want from me?" I murmured to myself.

"Perhaps he wanted you to lead him to where your plans were hidden," Marc said. "Maybe we've just given him what he wanted." We both looked around, but we were alone, and Marc's magic kept our conversation private.

"Perhaps," I replied, but I was not convinced. There was no evidence he'd even gone looking for them. "If that's the case, he lucked out, because I didn't know where they were."

Marc's brow furrowed. "Then who hid them here?"

"Anaïs," I said. "She hid them before she came to help me fight my father." I swallowed hard, remembering the sight of my friend impaled on the sluag spear. "She gave up everything for me," I said, closing my eyes. "She died for me."

I jerked them open again at Marc's sharp intake of breath. He stood rigid in front of me, unease on his face. "Tristan," he said. "Anaïs isn't dead."

"That's impossible." But even as I said the words, hope rose in my heart. Anaïs, alive?

"And not only is she alive," Marc continued, "she claims your father saved her life."

CHAPTER 5
Cécile

I jerked upright, my heart racing and skin damp with sweat. Shadows swam and loomed in the darkness of my room, and my eyes leapt between them, searching for the source of my fear. The only time I'd felt anything close to this was when I'd fallen and broken my light in the labyrinth. This was worse. In those twisting tunnels, I'd known why I was afraid, but now the danger was insidious and unknown. My senses tried to reconcile the terror with a threat, eyes twitching around the room of their own accord, spine stiffening with each gust of wind or creak in the floorboards.

The sheer curtains surrounding the bed blew inward, brushing against my face. I flinched, batting them away with one hand while pulling up my blankets to ward away the chill from the open window.

Nightmare.

Taking deep measured breaths, I clambered out of bed, dragging my blankets with me. Slamming the window shut, I flipped the latch. With trembling fingers, I turned up the lamp, but while the light drove away the shadows, the panic scorching through my veins only worsened. Because it hadn't been a nightmare. Everything that had happened was real, and with every blink of my eyelids, I saw the whip crack through the air, the blood splatter against the curse, the look in Tristan's eyes as he turned away from me. And echoing in my head, ceaseless and unending, were his screams.

"Tristan." His name came out as a gasp, and I dropped to my knees. My hands twisted like claws, nails clutching and snagging the fabric of my bedding, a scream threatening to rise in my throat. I clapped my hands over my ears and buried my face in my knees, trying to drown out the sound and failing because it came from inside my own head. The voice of reason shouted warning after warning at me, and I clenched my teeth and held my breath until my chest burned. What was done was done, and I would not improve either of our circumstances by panicking.

"Get up," I snapped as though my body was some sort of separate entity that I could order about. "Move." My knees cracked loudly as I straightened, my numb feet hardly feeling the floor beneath me as I paced shakily up and down the room. My mind raced, coming up with increasingly elaborate waking nightmares of what was happening to him now. Should I go? Should I take Fleur, gallop through the night, and try to sneak into Trollus? But even if I didn't get caught, what help would I be?

"Stop it," I said. "Quit thinking." As if such a thing were possible.

Stumbling over to my desk, I snatched up a page of lyrics. Eyes jumping from line to line, I softly sang, my voice breathless and terrible. "Again!" I said, trying to mimic my mother's voice. "That was dreadful."

Starting again, I sang louder, pushing everything into my voice. It was raw and wild, but like a hammer to a blade, I used it to temper my emotion into something useful, something I could control.

The door swung open, and I broke off mid-note, my hands grasping for the bedposts to keep my balance. But before I could regain an ounce of composure, my mother strode in.

"Cécile!" she snarled, but I cut her off before she could start into me.

"Mama!" I flung myself against her, burying my face in the

fur collar of her coat. She smelled like perfume, cigar smoke, and spilled wine, but I didn't care.

"What's happened?" she demanded. "Has someone hurt you?" Her strong arms pushed me back, face pale as she examined me. "Well?"

What to say? The truth was impossible – even if I could tell her, after the way I'd just acted, I'd sound like a raving lunatic. "I woke up afraid," I mumbled, looking away for shame of how childish I sounded.

"A bad dream?" From the tone of her voice, my mother agreed with my assessment of my behavior.

Wiping tears away with the back of my hand, I nodded.

"Stars and heavens, you will be the death of me!" She pressed the heel of her hand to her forehead, and only then did I notice how disheveled she was. Her hair was loose of all its pins and the kohl rimming her eyes was smeared. "For a dream you wake the neighbors. Ahh!" she grimaced. "Not just the neighbors, half the dogs in the city were caterwauling along with you."

"I'm sorry."

"You're a fool of a girl." She shook her head, her eyes blurry with something – likely wine, though it could have been absinthe. Or worse. Her hand reached for me so suddenly that I had to stop myself from jerking away. "You've been crying."

Warmth filled my chest, my heart convinced I'd heard a note of compassion in her voice.

"You shouldn't, you know. Some girls look pretty when they cry and can wield their tears like a weapon against men. But you aren't one of them. Instead of wrapping them around your finger, you'll send them running."

The warmth fled, and my mutinous bottom lip began to tremble.

Her shoulders slumped a little. "Heaven knows, that's why I never shed a tear in public." Letting go of my face, she took my arm and pulled me toward the door. "It's freezing in here. If you catch cold, you won't be able to sing. And if you can't sing…"

Her mouth pressed out in a little pout. "Well, the neighbors might well be pleased."

I steadied her arm as we walked down the stairs together. "Build up the fire a bit," she said. "I will make us something hot to drink."

I mindlessly stirred the coals and added wood to the fire, my mind all for Tristan and what could possibly be going on in Trollus. Where was he now? What were they doing to him? And worst of all, what was I going to do about it? The promise I'd made his father felt like it was crawling through my veins, a separate living thing that had found its way inside me against my will.

"Sit with me."

My mother had returned to the great room with two steaming cups in her hands, the faint smell of mint and chamomile drifting through the air. I settled next to her on the well-padded settee, tucking my chilled feet underneath me to warm them. She waited until I was settled to hand me a cup, and for a long time we both silently watched the fire. It felt comfortable and warm, and for the first time ever, the austere townhouse felt almost like home and Genevieve almost like a real mother. I clung to the feeling, letting it drive away the black thoughts threatening to overtake me.

"Where were you?" I asked. The water clock showed the time as five in the morning. I hadn't slept for more than an hour. That I'd fallen asleep at all was astonishing.

"The Marquis' salon." She tucked a lock of hair behind her ear, revealing her profile. In the firelight, I could see little crinkles were starting to form around her eyes, black little lines where the kohl had caught in them. "Some gentlemen he conducts business with are here from the mainland, and he wanted them well entertained."

I hesitated, a question that I'd been dying – but also afraid – to ask burning on the tip of my tongue. "What exactly does that mean?"

She turned her head to look at me. "What," she asked, raising one eyebrow, "do you think it means?"

"That you sing?" I ventured, because that was what I hoped. I might have been born in the morning, but not yesterday morning. I'd heard the gossip and the rumors, and though he'd never outright explained his dislike, I believed that was why Fred refused to have much of anything to do with her.

"Sometimes." She set her steaming cup down on the table. "But mostly, I talk."

Not what I'd expected her to say. I took a large mouthful, burning my tongue. "About what?"

"Everything. Anything." She pushed out her bottom lip. "Women of the nobility, or at the very least, of quality, are limited by propriety in what they can discuss. I am not." She pointed a finger at me. "Neither are you. And that makes us far more desirable company than any of their wives."

I started to look away in discomfort, but she caught my chin. "That is why I sent tutors for you in the Hollow, Cécile. Because for you to succeed in this world, you must not only be beautiful, you must be educated, clever, and above all things, you must be interesting."

Her eyes searched my face, and I got the impression that I was supposed to say something. Except I didn't know what. All these things she thought I should be were fine qualities, but I didn't like the idea that their only purpose was for the entertainment of rich men.

"The Marquis keeps us in very fine style," she continued. "He pays for all this," she gestured around the house, "and for everything you have, for everything you know." One finger coiled around a lock of hair, her eyes intent. "But I am not getting any younger, and soon he will tire of me and look for a replacement. *You* could be my successor."

I pulled my chin out of her grasp and looked at the fire, everything becoming clear. That was why she'd wanted me educated, trained, and brought to live with her in Trianon. Not because she wanted her daughter close, but because she wanted insurance that she'd be kept in the style to which she'd grown accustomed. To live off the coin I could secure by being *interesting.*

"The Marquis must not have much regard for you if he'd put you aside for aging," I said coldly. I watched, waiting for her eyes to light up so that I'd know my barb had sunk deep.

Instead, she smiled and lifted her chin. "Such is the nature of men, Cécile. They will keep you only so long as there isn't something better within their reach; then they will discard you. Best you hear that from me now than learn it the hard way later."

The smoke from the fire made my eyes burn and water as I took in her words. "Papa didn't discard you."

The room seemed to shrink, sucked in and made small by the silence.

"Is that what you think?" she whispered. "Is that what he told you?"

The truth was, my father never spoke much of it at all. It was Gran who'd told us the story of how we'd come to be in the Hollow, but I knew as well as I knew the back of my own hands that my grandmother was no liar. It was my turn to lift my chin. "Are you saying it happened differently?"

She rose abruptly to her feet, tripping on the hem of her skirt as she walked swiftly over to the sideboard. I heard the clink of glass and a splash of liquid. "I should have expected that you'd believe his side of the story."

My heart skipped a little. Was there more to it than what Gran had told us? When I was a child, I'd daydreamed that my mother had only allowed us to be separated by necessity – that secretly, she'd always wanted us to stay together as a family. Time and much evidence to the contrary had beaten those dreams out of me, but what if my child-self had been right? "It's the only side that's ever been told to me," I said, trying to keep my greed for the truth out of my voice. "But if there's more to hear, I'll listen."

"What's the point?" she asked. "I told your brother, and look how well it served me."

Fred knew? And hadn't told me? "I'm not my brother," I said, irritated that he'd be so petty.

"No," she agreed, her voice soft. "You've always been the most loyal of my children. My favorite."

I watched her elbow move as she lifted the glass to her mouth, but the only sound was the crackling of the fire. I felt tense with anticipation, perhaps more than the situation warranted. What would she say? Would her story paint a different picture of our lives? Would it change the way I felt about her?

"I was sixteen and a fool when I met your father." She set the glass down but didn't remove her hand from it. "He'd left Goshawk's Hollow, gone to the continent for a time, then returned to Trianon." She turned around, and I did not fail to notice the streaks of damp on her face or the redness of her cheeks. "He was looking for a bit of excitement." She gestured at herself, flicking her hand up and down. "He found it at the opera house."

I winced, discomforted about thinking of my parents *that* way.

"I was certain I was in love. Thought the sun rose and set on him, and that we'd be together forever." She drained her glass. "My mother warned me otherwise, but I wouldn't listen. And by seventeen, I was married and pregnant with your brother." Her lip trembled, and she bit it furiously, trying to keep her emotions under control.

"It was fine, at first. Your father worked in the city, and I worked for the opera company when I wasn't too big with child." Her shoulders twitched. "He knew how much I loved singing onstage, and he promised never to keep me from my passion." One fat tear ran down her face.

"But after your sister arrived, we received word that your grandfather was ill. Your father went back to be with him when he died, and when he returned, everything was different. All he talked about, all he cared about, was that farm. What *I* wanted wasn't important anymore." She shook her head sharply. "He insisted we move to the Hollow, but I refused. I'd grown up in the city. Everyone I knew and cared about was in the city.

The thought of leaving made me miserable. I thought he'd come around, that he loved me enough to stay." She drew in a ragged breath. "I was wrong."

She was crying now. My mother, who never cried, was snuffling and sobbing. "I wanted to keep you three, but he wouldn't let me. He convinced me that I couldn't do it, that we'd be destitute, that my babies would starve." The words came out between gulps of air, and she wiped a hand under her nose. "My own mother went missing when this was all happening, and everything was madness and misery, and I… I let him take you."

An oppressive weariness fell upon me, and my mind struggled with how the same story could paint an entirely different picture when told from another point of view. She wasn't denying that she'd chosen herself and her career over being with us, but now I could see it from her perspective. Could understand how difficult it had been for her.

"It was so hard after you left. My heart was broken, and I had no money. I could barely afford to feed myself, and eventually, I came to believe your father was right. I couldn't take care of my babies, and you three were better off with him. Better off without me." A fresh swell of tears stormed down her cheeks. "I'm sorry, Cécile. You deserved a better mother." Her eyes met mine. "I do love you, and I always have. I hope you know that."

I wasn't blind: I knew she was selfish, but no one was perfect. Everyone had flaws. She'd been put in a situation where there were no easy choices. I well knew how that felt. What it was like knowing there would be horrible consequences no matter what path I took.

"I love you too, Mama." Rising, I swayed wearily, my feet feeling like lead as I walked over to wrap my arms around her. I was so tired. She guided me back to the settee, and I settled down, feet tucked up and my head on her lap. Her hands gently stroked my hair, and she sang, her voice hitching and catching a bit from crying.

My head was fuzzy and numb, my tongue thick in my mouth. So tired, so tired.

"Where were you, Cécile?" Her voice was soft. "Where were you all those months?"

I wanted to tell her, to trust her, but Tristan's emotions were growing again in the back of my head. Unease. Everything merged, and I couldn't tell if he was worried, or whether I was. I shifted, tried to rise, but my limbs felt weak. My mother smoothed my hair down my back and I settled.

"I thought I'd lost you," she said. "I thought you were dead, or that maybe you'd hated the idea of coming to stay with me so much that you'd run away."

"No." The word was muddled, but I needed her to know that wasn't it. That I *had* wanted to be with her. "Didn't… didn't go by choice."

"Who took you?"

My teeth clenched together, the fire in the hearth seeming to blaze brighter than the sun. It hurt my eyes. "A boy from the Hollow."

"Where did he take you?"

I squeezed them shut. "Under the mountain."

"For what purpose?"

Everything was fading into black, a darkness foreign and stained with uncertainty. I fought it, trying to stay awake, to feel the heat on my face, and my mother's touch. "He sold me to them. To the trolls."

She stiffened, but I hardly felt it. My senses were numb. Everything was slipping.

"What did they want from you?" The question, insistent, buzzing and loud. Demanding to be answered. I was falling, falling, falling, but the words still slipped from my mouth.

"To set them free."

CHAPTER 6
Tristan

I carefully tightened the handkerchiefs I'd tied around the manacles on my wrists, in a likely futile attempt to keep blood from soaking into the cuffs of my shirt. I had an extensive wardrobe, but eventually, I was going to have to undertake the process of laundering my clothes, and I had read somewhere that bloodstains were challenging to remove.

Dropping my fingers from the handkerchief, I scowled at the paving stones as I meandered through the nearly empty streets of the Elysium quarter, the massive homes brilliantly lit but quiet compared to the rest of Trollus. I'd been inside most of them at one time or another, but their doorways now seemed foreign and unwelcoming, and I found myself clinging to the shadows, glancing over my shoulder like an intruder up to no good.

Though our connection was muted by distance, Cécile's mind had practically sung with tension since the moment she'd awoken. It was the feeling of someone crossing a precariously narrow bridge: unwavering focus mixed with a hint of fear, and above all, the incredible need to reach the other side. The sensation was not unfamiliar – it was much like what I, or any troll, felt after making a promise. But it felt utterly alien coming from her, as did the aggressive impatience that flared within her with increasing frequency. She seemed... *changed*.

The arched entrance to the Angoulême manor appeared as

I rounded the corner. There were two women standing guard, and I retreated back down the street before they could see me, leaning against a wall to wait. Anaïs would have to pass by this way eventually.

The true power of a promise was not something humans gave entirely enough thought to. Those who knew of us seemed to consider the binding nature of our word a weakness only partially tempered by our ability to twist speech to suit our purposes.

What they did not understand, at least not until it was far too late, was that there was a certain reciprocity to the magic. If a human made a promise to a troll, the troll was quite capable of binding the human to her word, should he feel inclined. If the troll was willing enough to make the effort, and the promise impossible enough to fulfill, the human could be driven to the point where she would not sleep or eat – to the point where her mind cracked or her heart stopped beating over the stress of her continued failure. And I had no doubt my father was willing to make the effort in order to reach his goal.

I considered how he would use the leverage he had gained over my human wife. He would not drive her so hard as to kill her, not yet, anyway. He was patient – he'd keep pressure on her for months, slowly stripping away her mind until all that would be left was a shell with one purpose: to break the curse. Even if she survived it, she would no longer be the Cécile I knew and loved. I had to keep that from happening, but the only sure way to stop it was to kill my father, and that solution was fraught with more complications than I cared to count. Which was half the reason I was standing here in the shadows.

The other half was something else entirely.

I waited a long time until I was almost sure I'd missed her, when suddenly a familiar form came around the bend and started up the set of stairs I lurked next to. "Anaïs," I breathed. She hadn't noticed me, so I watched her walk, shoulders back and head high, like the princess she had almost been. She was beautiful, there was no denying that. But it was a loveliness that came from flawlessness, every feature perfect in a way that made her seem almost created by design. It was the beauty of the fey. A face echoing all those who had come before, much as was my own.

Anaïs froze mid-step, eyes scanning the shadows until they latched on to me. Lowering her foot, she stared, face expressionless.

Until recently, I'd barely gone a day without spending time in her presence. With the exception of Marc, she was my oldest and closest friend. And without a doubt, she was my most loyal accomplice. Her history was my history, our lives interwoven as only those who were childhood friends could be. I knew everything about her, all her stories and secrets, and she knew me equally as well.

As our eyes locked, I remembered what I had told Cécile before the sluag attack – that Anaïs and I had never been more than friends. Technically, that was true. But it was also a lie. Anaïs was the first girl I'd lusted after, the first I'd ever kissed, the first of many things. But I'd never loved her, not like *that*.

Almost as though she could sense my thoughts, Anaïs bolted up the last few steps and started down the street toward her home.

"Anaïs," I called, hurrying after her. "Anaïs, wait!"

She ignored me, and in another few steps, she would be in sight of the guards at the gate.

"Anaïs, please." I broke into a run. "I need to talk to you."

She slid to a stop and rounded on me. "I suppose that's the key word, isn't it? *Need?* Did you ever talk to me because you *wanted* to?"

I opened my mouth to speak, but she raised a hand. "I don't want to hear it, Tristan. I don't want to hear you. I don't ever want to see your face again. I'm tired of you using me."

"Anaïs." I closed the distance between us, my pleasure at seeing her alive tempered by the fury in her eyes. She had never looked at me like that before. "We've been friends our whole lives; how can you say these things?"

"Friends?" she scoffed. "Friend is just a label you give your favorite tools. I see that now. You only pretended to care so we'd assist with your plans."

"You know that isn't true." I searched her face, looking for a trace of something that wasn't anger. "I care about you. I…"

"Right." She rolled her eyes, but I could see her hands were clenching her skirts. "The only person you care about, the only person you love, is *her*. And sometimes I wonder if that isn't just out of some sense of self-preservation on your part." She laughed wildly, and it sounded strange and off-key in my ears. Not a laugh I'd heard before. "Except that can't be right," she said, her shoulders shaking. "Because you loathe yourself, don't you? You despise your very nature." The corner of her mouth turned up. "Well, now you are in good company, because with the exception of that imbecile, Marc, there isn't a soul in Trollus who does not hate you."

She was the last person I'd ever expected to turn on me. Had I not known her as well as I thought? Or was what I'd done worse than I believed? "If I don't care about you, then why was I so happy to learn you had survived? Why am I here now?"

"I really don't know, Tristan." Her eyes filled with tears that spilled down her cheeks. I hadn't seen her cry like this since Pénélope died – she always said she hated public displays of emotion. "You left me there to die. Left me there even though you knew…" Her voice cracked, and she wiped the dampness from her face.

"Even though I knew what?" I asked, though the answer had already oozed up from the depths of my subconscious.

She swallowed hard before answering. "Even though you knew I could be saved. You knew that witches could heal trolls from iron wounds, because Cécile healed you." She sniffed, squeezing her eyes shut. "Your father had a witch in Trollus, but you didn't stop to think of me. You just took her and left." Her eyes snapped back open. "After everything I'd done for you, you left me to die. If not for your father, I would be rotting in a tomb. He only stabbed me out of desperation – he never had any intention of harming me."

The moment replayed through my mind. She was right – I hadn't even stopped to consider that her life could be saved. My one and only concern had been getting Cécile safely away from Trollus.

"I didn't know where he was keeping the witch," I said. "If I had known…"

"If you had known, you still would have chosen Cécile over me."

Denying it was impossible.

"I'm sorry," I said, searching her face for some sign that this was an act. A strategy she'd employed while I was in prison to protect herself from punishment. But there was nothing. "I have no right to even ask for your forgiveness."

"Then spare me and don't," she hissed, wiping her hands on her dress. I fixed on those hands, her usually perfectly manicured nails bitten down to the quick. "If you want to make it up to me, stay far away."

Words were incapable of undoing what I had done to her. What I hadn't done *for* her. But part of me couldn't reconcile the Anaïs standing before me with the girl who had calmly ordered me to take Cécile and go. *Anaïstromeria, no more tears.* My last command to her echoed through my mind, and I fixed on the damp streaks marring her face.

"If that's what you want." My voice sounded strange and distant.

"It is." She spun around, lavender skirts lifting enough for me to see her matching flat shoes. A sense of wrongness shot through me, slicing through the fog of guilt. Something was amiss, something about her wasn't right. I watched her stride away, the ghostly echo in my memory of clicking high heels drowned out by the slapping of flat soles.

"Anaïstromeria," I said under my breath. "Stop."

She kept walking.

"Anaïstromeria, turn around." My fingers dug into the stones of the wall I leaned against, mortar crumbling. "Anaïstromeria, come back to me." If she'd been half a world away, she would have heard. Such was the power of a true name.

It was only the dead who could not hear.

CHAPTER 7
Tristan

"What are you doing?"

I did not let my attention waver from the five white shapes bobbing about in the basin full of bubbling water. "Making lunch."

"Boiled eggs?"

I slowly lifted my gaze to meet Marc's, all but daring him to make a comment, but he wisely refrained.

"Did you see Anaïs? Would she speak to you?"

I snorted softly, and the water in the basin went nearly all to steam in an instant. "She isn't Anaïs." I poured cold water over my eggs to cool them, then set the basin aside.

"I know she seems different," Marc started to say, but I interrupted him.

"Someone is posing as her, but Anaïs is dead."

My cousin sat down heavily on a chair. With one hand, he pushed back his hood, his light extinguishing as he did. "How is that... Are you certain?"

"She was wearing flat shoes," I said, as though that would explain everything.

Marc lifted his head. "Tristan..."

There was concern in his voice, so I quickly added, "Her nails were bitten, and her laugh was off key. She isn't our Anaïs." I picked up an egg and stared at it. "Whoever she is, she's my

58

father's accomplice, and the plot was planned well. She claimed he saved her life, which means that he must have arranged to somehow do so. With a witch." I set the egg down. "He had a witch in Trollus the entire time." He had planned *everything*.

I looked up at his sharp intake of breath, certain he was about to accuse me of having lost my mind to be making such accusations. "I called her by name, and she did not answer, so I know it isn't her. Anaïs is dead."

Marc slumped forward, burying his face in one hand. His shoulders twitched once, then again.

You inconsiderate bastard. I directed a few more choice words at myself for realizing too late that while I had months to come to terms with my grief, Marc had not. His relationship with Anaïs had been tense since Pénélope had died, but they were still close, in their own way. Family too, if by marriage and not by blood.

"Victoria will be devastated."

His words were thick with emotion, and they sparked multiple realizations within me. No one, with the exception of Cécile, my father, me, and now Marc, knew that Anaïs was dead. No one grieved for her. None of the death rituals of our people had been given to her, none of the words spoken, none of the songs sung. Much had been done to our friend, and much was still being done to her memory, and my father was the cause of all of it.

But the sight of Marc's stifled grief kept me silent. Anaïs's death was as much my fault as my father's. I might not have put the spear through her chest, but the impostor hadn't been wrong when she said I'd done nothing to save her. She might still be alive if only I'd tried harder, if only I'd tried bringing a witch to Trollus, if only…

"I'm sorry." The words were clipped.

"You had to make a choice," he finally replied. "You chose. Now you have to live with the consequences" – he squared his shoulders – "and not squander what was paid for in blood."

The consequences: not only Anaïs's life, but those of dozens of others. The punishment my friends endured for helping me. The sacrifice of years of planning. The destruction of the half-bloods' hope for freedom. All to save one life.

A life that was once again in jeopardy.

"And there is always vengeance."

A charge of eagerness surged through me, ideas and plans swirling about in my head. "There is that."

"Do you know who the impostor is?"

"No," I said, picking up one of my eggs, carefully cracking it and peeling away the shell. "But I intend to find out."

We spent the rest of that day in mourning, first delivering the news to Vincent, who took it badly, and then later, when the mining shifts changed, to Victoria, who took it worse.

In quiet voices, Marc and I debated who could be impersonating Anaïs. The list was short. For one, Anaïs had been one of the most powerful trolls living, and there were only a few women with enough raw power to fool those close to her. Two, the troll would need to have known Anaïs well enough to imitate her voice and mannerisms. And three, it had to be someone who could go absent for days at a time without it being noticed.

"Her grandmother?" Marc suggested. "Damia's always been something of a recluse."

I frowned, bending my mind around the idea of the Dowager Duchesse posing as her granddaughter. "If anyone could manage it, it would be her. But…" It didn't feel right. Whoever it was, she was in collusion with my father, and those two hated each other. "I don't see how she or Angoulême could profit from this sort of deception." I shook my head once. "I don't think it's her."

"Then who? Who could it possibly be?"

I tilted my head from side to side, listening to my neck crack. "I have no idea." Not only that, I had no idea how she was doing it. Creating the illusion was easy enough, but keeping it in place day and night, never letting it slip. That was no mean feat. It wasn't only a matter of walking around and looking like

Anaïs, it was a matter of becoming her. A fragile act that could be destroyed with one direct question: are you really Anaïs? Because no troll could say yes.

The door swung open, and our voices cut off as Vincent stepped inside, his face drawn and exhausted, his hair coated with grey dust so that he looked twenty years older than he was.

Vincent coughed once. "Took some convincing, but he agreed."

My blood started to race, and I stood up, feeling the need to act. "When?"

"Tonight." Vincent met my gaze. "But he had one condition."

"Anything." The word was out before I thought through what meeting Tips tonight would actually entail.

Despite his exhaustion, Vincent must have noticed my slip, because he winced. "His condition was that the conversation take place in his territory."

I forced myself to nod, the movement jerky. "Fine. I'm in no position to argue."

But bloody stones and skies did I want to, because Tips's territory was the one place in Trollus that I never went. The one place that I hated above all others.

The mines.

CHAPTER 8
Cécile

"Don't you have a bed?" A sharp poke in the ribs pulled me out of my dreams, and I opened one bleary eye to regard my brother. His face was only inches from mine, full of a mixture of curiosity and amusement. "Your breath stinks," he informed me.

"Shut up." I tried to bury my face in the settee, but the fabric was stiff and unyielding, and all the action accomplished was making my nose hurt.

Why was I asleep on the sofa? Memory of the night before came crashing down on me, from the events at the mouth of the River Road, to my mother stumbling in drunk, to her tearful justification of her abandonment of us. And then...

I sat upright, the motion making me dizzy. When the stars cleared, my eyes fixed on the empty teacup on the table. "She drugged me!"

One of Fred's eyebrows rose.

"Mother," I muttered, arranging my nightclothes so that I was decent.

My brother laughed, but he didn't sound all that amused. "Sounds about right. She probably got tired of pretending to be a parent."

I grunted in agreement, but Fred wasn't through. "I'm fairly certain that's where my predisposition for strong drink came from – that she fed me whisky as a babe to stop the squalling."

"Don't start." I shivered. The fire had all but gone cold, and the great room was freezing. "I really don't understand why you hate her so much. You might not agree with the choices she's made, but it isn't as though she's harmed you."

It was the wrong thing to say. Fred's face darkened, and he tossed two letters on my lap. "One for you from father. Another for Sabine from her parents that you'll need to read for her." He turned and walked toward the door. "She's far from harmless, Cécile, but maybe the only way you'll learn is the hard way."

"Wait!" I called after him, but he kept walking. Stumbling off the sofa, I scuttled around so that I was between him and the door. "I'm sorry. Stay for breakfast."

He glared at me.

"Please?" I pantomimed a sad face. "I hardly see you."

"I have work to do." He picked me up and set me to one side, but this was a well-worn routine of ours. "Please!" I mock-pleaded.

"Don't got time for you."

I flung myself at his knees, wrapping my arms around one leg so that he dragged me forward with every step. "Please!"

"Let go. What sort of reputable lady acts this way? You're behaving like a child off the streets of Pigalle."

I clung tighter.

He stopped walking long enough to rub the bottom of his boot on my hair.

"We've got bacon," I said, trying not to laugh and hating that laughing was even possible after last night. "And apricot marmalade."

He switched directions and started toward the kitchen, dragging me along with him. I let go after a few steps, and getting to my feet, trailed after him. Our cook was working away, and was only now setting the bread dough aside to rise. My mother didn't keep live-in servants. She said it was because of the cost, but I expected it was more a matter of privacy.

"What hour is it?"

"Almost noon," Fred replied, sitting down at the table. He was wearing his uniform, with both a sword and pistol buckled at his waist. He had always been tall, but at nearly twenty, he had finally filled out his frame. He looked quite dashing, I thought, bending to examine the badges of rank adorning his chest.

"My brother will be joining me for breakfast," I said to the cook, taking the seat closest to the fire. My mother would have insisted we eat in the dining room or the parlor, but the farm girl in me wouldn't let go of the kitchen.

"Yes, mademoiselle." She did not look up from her dough. My mother did not encourage familiarity with the servants, and she was a difficult woman to work for. The maids changed so often, I could scarce keep track of their names for trying.

"I saw Chris this morning," Fred said quietly, buttering a piece of yesterday's bread. "He told me your reclusive *friends* from the south are stirring up trouble."

I sighed and nodded, wishing for a moment that I'd never told him the truth. But keeping it a secret from my family had never even occurred to me, even if I could have pulled it off.

Other than my family, only Sabine, Chris, and his father knew the truth. Gran's magic hadn't been strong enough to heal my injuries entirely and we'd been forced to come up with a tale to explain them. She told everyone that I'd been attacked by a madman, and only by the grace of God had the Girards been in town to rush me home in time for me to be saved. It was a truth and a lie in one, a fact I was reminded of every time I undressed and saw the six-inch red scar running the length of my ribcage. It was a mark I'd bear for the rest of my life.

"You haven't told *her* anything?" He jerked his head up toward the second level where my mother was presumably still abed, keeping an eye on the cook while he did it.

"Are you mad?" I hissed. "Of course I haven't. Telling her anything would be as good as telling the whole Isle. All she knows is that I got cold feet and spent the summer in the south. Nothing more." And she never pried into the details. I wasn't sure if it was because she didn't care, or if her own secret-keeping tendencies caused her to respect mine. Either way, it worked in my favor.

"That's good. She's a way of using information to her advantage." His eyes were distant. "Though it might be better if the whole damned Isle did know."

Tension sang down my spine. "Fred, you promised to keep it between us."

"I know." He tracked the cook as she moved behind me. "But I don't like it. I think we should do something. Go on the offensive when they aren't expecting it."

I winced. "You wouldn't have a chance against them. How many times must I explain this to you?" I glanced over my shoulder. "They've got magic," I mouthed.

He snorted, his lips pinching together. "Something else then. Cut them off. Starve them." He leaned closer to me. "I've met the Regent's son, Lord Aiden. He's young, not more than a few years older than me, and he's a man of action. He often walks with the men. He'd grant my request to speak privately, and I could tell him…"

"No!" I heard the cook stop moving, so I lowered my voice. "No, Fred. You can't. Most of them are good, decent folk. They don't deserve that. And there's…"

"Tristan?"

It was strange hearing his name on my brother's lips. I looked away. "Yes."

Fred's hands clenched where they rested on the table. "*Him* I'd like to have a word or two with. Stealing my little sister and performing godless magic so that I don't dare strike at him for fear of hurting you. Bastard!"

The cook made a comment under her breath about soldiers and foul language, making Fred's scowl deepen.

"Well, then, there you have it," I whispered. "Fine if you have no care for starving innocent people, but at least have a care for your own sister's life."

He gnawed on his bottom lip, eyes narrowed to slits. "You're an idiot and a fool when it comes to judging character, Cécile. Always have been. Refusing to see the black side of folk even when it's right in front of your eyes."

Was this about the trolls or our mother?

I pressed my palms against the table, and met his gaze. "You don't know them, Fred. You don't know him."

"I don't have to!" He stood up, knocking the table hard. "I can't listen to this. I need to go."

Fred started to go to the door, but then came back and enveloped me in a fierce bear hug. "I love you, Im-be-Cécile," he mumbled into my hair. "But you're blind when it comes to those you love. You need to open your eyes."

I listened to the heavy tread of his boots, hoping that he'd reconsider and come back. But he was gone.

The clock in the great room struck the hour, pulling me from my thoughts. *Bong, bong, bong,* it sang softly, and I counted the beats up to twelve. "Do you know when my mother plans to rise?" I asked the cook.

"She rose at a decent hour, mademoiselle," the cook said with a little sniff. "She departed several hours ago, but she left you a note. It's on the front table."

Frowning, I went out to the front entry and found a folded bit of paper with my name on the front.

Darling, I hope you are feeling much improved this morning. Please meet me at the opera house at noon today – I have wonderfully exciting news to share with you.

I glanced at the water clock, then back at the note. "Stones and sky!" I swore, then bolted to the stairs.

CHAPTER 9
Cécile

I was late, but my mother was later.

We had grouped in the foyer de la danse, a grand room reserved for the premiere ballerinas and the gentlemen subscribers who admired them. It was a golden place, pilasters rising up to the graceful arches of the frescoed ceiling and mirrors reflecting the light of the massive chandelier hanging in the center.

Portraits of famous dancers and sopranos ringed the room, their intricate frames clutched by gilded cherubs. It was, in a way, a history of the Trianon opera, for while this building was relatively new, the portraits dated back to when the company was in its infancy some two hundred years prior. It reminded me of the gallery of the Kings in the Trollus library, and made me wish I'd taken the time to see the gallery of the Queens. History told through faces and clothing, the skill of the artist whispering a story with oil and brush.

I stared at the portrait of my mother hung in a place of privilege on one wall and wondered what secret truths, if any, it told about her. Moving almost of their own accord, my fingers brushed against the golden locket hanging at my throat, even as my eyes fixed on the one painted around hers.

"Cécile?"

I blinked. Sabine was staring at me with a frown on her face. "Sorry," I said. "What was that you were saying about Julian?"

She'd been telling me about my co-star's antics the night prior, but I'd barely been listening.

She frowned. "Has something happened?"

I nodded. "Chris and I had a little adventure. I'll tell you about it after."

"Bad?"

I gave her a grim nod. We were practiced in speaking in code when we weren't alone, but this conversation needed to wait.

I shifted on the velvet banquette, pulling off my shoes and tucking my feet underneath me. I needed to change the subject before anyone took note of our conversation. "Does anyone know what this is about?"

"I do," Julian said from where he sat perched on his own cushion. He looked as fresh as someone who has had a night of uninterrupted sleep, although from what Sabine had been saying, he hadn't gotten any more than I had.

"Do you intend to share what you know with us?" I asked.

He shook his head and grinned. "It's Genny's news to tell."

I winced inwardly at his familiarity, remembering all too clearly how she had rejected my father's use of the very same nickname. They were very close, Julian and my mother. Uncomfortably so, at times.

She had "discovered" him years ago, an orphan singing on the street corner for coin, and had taken him under her wing. Then she'd made him a star. Unbeknownst to me, or to any of my family other than Fred, he had been living with her for the past four years. He'd been ousted the day I arrived in Trianon because it would have been improper for us to live under the same roof, and anyone with two wits to rub together knew that he resented me for it.

I glanced around the room to see who'd been invited. It was all the principal members of the company, plus a few from costuming and set design. A select group, which indicated we'd be performing outside of the theatre. "A private performance for some nobleman?" I asked, hoping to take the wind out of Julian's sails if I guessed correctly.

His grin widened, white teeth gleaming. "Better."

I slouched down. Whatever. It didn't matter what or for whom. Adding another performance meant more rehearsals, and I didn't have time for that. I needed to be out looking for Anushka. The need to be out on the streets doing *something* was like an itch that couldn't be scratched.

But my mother had set conditions when I'd come to Trianon, and the primary one was that I perform often and that I perform well. Failure would see me evicted from her house before I could blink, and I had no other skills for supporting myself in Trianon. Even if I did, none of them would give me the sort of access to all the levels of society that singing did, which meant that I had no choice but to indulge my mother's wishes.

I closed my eyes, feeling the pressure of the promise I'd made to the King. It wasn't anything like a promise made to another human. I had barely gone a moment without thinking about how badly I needed to find her. My hunt had monopolized my thoughts since I'd left Trollus, but now it was much worse. *Obsessive.* I needed to find her, but the question was how? I had already done everything I could think of to find her – short of walking through the streets, screaming her name, and hoping she might deign to show herself.

And I hadn't the slightest idea how to use magic to improve my chances. None of the spells in the grimoire mentioned anything about how to find someone, and it was my only resource. I needed a teacher, and not just anyone would do. I needed someone who understood the dark arts.

The room went quiet, and I opened my eyes to see my mother swaying across the floor. She settled down on a banquette in the middle of the circle, always the star of the show.

"Thank you all for coming," my mother said, pausing to blow steam off the cup Julian had handed her. "I have very exciting news that I'm finally able to share." She paused again for effect. "I am so pleased to announce that the Regent's wife, Lady Marie du Chastelier, has commissioned our company to stage and perform a masque for her annual winter solstice party."

Most of the company exchanged confused glances, but history of the arts had been one of the things I'd studied in Trollus. I cleared my throat. "Haven't masques been out of fashion for, I don't know, two hundred years?"

My mother raised one tawny eyebrow. "What is old is new again, *dearest*."

There was nothing she hated more than having her ideas contested. She always had to have her way.

"What's a masque?" Sabine asked.

"It's a performance," Julian interjected, "in which all the important ladies of the court will be a part. Lady Marie intends to spare no expense." Rising to his feet, he retrieved sheets of paper and distributed them to the group. "I will be playing the devil," he said, handing me a page. "Genny will play Vice and Cécile will play Virtue."

I scanned the pages, my interest in the idea briefly pushing away Thibault's compulsion. But only for a moment. The lively murmurs of the group buzzed like a hive of bees, but I didn't join in. All I could think about was how I didn't have time for this. I rubbed my temples with my fingers, but nothing seemed to reduce the tension in my skull.

"Attention, attention!" my mother trilled. "I also have one more announcement to make."

Conversation ceased and heads swiveled back around, everyone curious about what else Genevieve might have up her sleeve. Even once she had our attention, she took her time, slowly smoothing the lace overlay of her dress while she fed off our anticipation. "This is bittersweet," she finally whispered.

The whole company leaned forward.

"I…" She hesitated, the corners of her mouth tipping slightly downwards. "I've decided that the Regent's court masque will be my final performance."

I felt my mouth drop open. No one in the room spoke a word, such was our collective astonishment. *Genevieve, retire?*

"Years ago," she continued, reveling in our shock, "I made

the decision to put my career ahead of my family. I know you all, as artists, can understand why I made the decision, and it has been a rare moment I've had cause to regret it."

Her words stung, undoing all the goodwill from the night prior I'd barely realized had built up. I remembered all too clearly the number of times I'd sat waiting for her on the lane leading toward our farm on the day of a promised visit. A visit that only rarely materialized.

Before I'd moved to Trianon, I'd always made excuses for her, imagining her reluctantly prioritizing her performances – when in her heart, she really wanted to be visiting me. I knew better, but even so, her ability to manipulate my emotions never seemed to diminish. Fred was right: I was an idiot. My cup hit the saucer with a sharp click, and she glanced my direction.

"But," she said, her eyes not moving from me, "I feel that I have reached the peak of my career. I have sung all the great roles and performed for all the most powerful and influential people on the Isle. There is nothing more I can achieve onstage, and I would rather retire now than witness my own decline."

"You can't!"

Everyone in the room jumped and turned to look at Julian, who was on his feet, face drained of color. "You can't leave!"

My mother's brow creased. "I won't be *leaving*, darling. I will merely be stepping off the stage so that I can focus on Cécile's career. It is time for her portrait to be hung on these walls."

Julian rounded on me, his expression filled with venom. "This is your fault. Your coming to Trianon ruined everything. I wish you had died in Courville."

I flinched, half expecting him to attack me, but instead he stormed out of the room.

"Julian, darling! Wait." My mother scampered to her feet and ran after him.

Everyone turned to look at me. "I didn't know," I said, holding up my hands. "I am as shocked as the rest of you."

Half a dozen conversations ensued, everyone interrupting each other as they speculated about whether Julian would forgive my mother, why she'd really decided to retire, and what the Regent's masque would be like. I said nothing, only stared down at the papers in my hand. My head began to steadily pound as though I were being punished for my momentary distraction, the pain making the words on the page blur. The ache beat in a rhythm that seemed to repeat the words "find her" over and over again. Climbing to my feet, I hurried out into the corridor, then around the corner until I stood in the stage wings.

From the pocket of my dress, I withdrew the grimoire, the feel of its repulsive cover somehow soothing my head. Opening the clasp, I flipped through the spells. Despite its current unhelpfulness, it felt good to have it back in my possession once more. Glancing around to make sure I was alone, I focused my attention on Tristan. He seemed so far away, the knot of emotion I associated with him small compared to how it had felt when I was in Trollus, but I could still sense his pain and anger.

Anger at you.

"You all right?"

I turned to see Sabine.

"Your dream is coming true. Lead soprano for the most famous opera house on the Isle." Her smile was half-hearted. "Or at least, what used to be your dream."

It still was, and that was what made it so hard, because I had to willfully push it aside. It was a dream that needed to remain that way. "It's a demanding position. I don't have time for it, and the last thing I need is my mother turning her full attention on me." But declining wasn't an option. She had a plan in her mind, and if I disrupted it, she'd send me back to the Hollow in an instant. She'd rather see her plans destroyed than ever consider a compromise.

Sabine hesitated, then held out a glass of what looked like brandy. "You look like you need this. For fortitude."

"Thanks." I accepted the glass, although the thought of drinking it turned my stomach.

"Your mother's given me a list of tasks that I need to get started on," she said. "But maybe we can meet after and you can tell me what happened."

"I'll come find you," I said. But instead of leaving, she stood watching me, a faint look of expectation on her face. "You should get to work on your list," I said. "Julian's reaction will have put her in a foul mood."

"Right." She hesitated for a heartbeat longer, and then left me alone. Pressing my forehead against the coolness of the wall, I took a deep breath. Would nothing ever go right for me again? Problem after cursed problem seemed to stack up every which way I turned, and I had no solution to any of them. I didn't even know where to begin looking for solutions.

And then I got handed something I actually wanted – a chance I'd longed for most of my life – and I couldn't even bear to be happy about it. What did it matter if I were a star soprano when the man I loved was being tortured at the hands of his father. When I'd locked myself into a binding promise to find a five century-old witch with a grudge. When my brother was threatening to find a way to starve my friends caught in Trollus...

Part of me had felt a thrill of excitement when my mother had made her announcement, because singing is what I'd always wanted to do. I loved it so, so, so much. But how dare I even consider such a life when so much of what mattered to me was in danger?

Imagine what your life would have been like if you'd never gone to Trollus...

I shoved the thought away. "Imagine what you wouldn't have if you hadn't gone," I hissed at myself. "Imagine who you wouldn't know. Imagine who you wouldn't love." But my words were cold comfort.

Back in the foyer, everyone was pretending to be reading the script, but I could see the furtive glances cast between the sullen and red-eyed Julian and the tight-faced Genevieve. Nothing would get done until the two of them reconciled, and I needed to be out and away from here looking for Anushka.

Squaring my shoulders, I approached Julian. "You can't really believe she means to go through with it," I said, leaning against the wall next to him.

He silently crossed his arms, eyes fixed on the floor.

"It's probably only a ploy to increase the excitement over the masque. Genevieve de Troyes' final performance," I said, lowering my voice in mimicry of our stage manager. "Six months from now, she'll probably be opening some grand new opera from the continent, and I'll be back as her understudy."

Julian snorted softly, unconvinced.

Nibbling on my lip, I stared into the depths of the brandy I still held. "She would have told you before anyone else if she really meant it," I said. "She confides so much in you – more than even me, and I'm her daughter. The reason she's upset is probably because she thought you'd see through to the heart of her little plot."

"Why should she confide in you?" he muttered. "She hardly knows you to trust you."

My spine stiffened, and I bit down on a retort that the distance between us was far more her choice than mine. But doing so would not help speed this process along. "I know," I said instead. "I'm envious of you in that."

The corner of his mouth twitched, and I knew my ploy had worked. And frankly, everything I'd said felt true. I didn't believe for a second that my mother had really decided to give up her career in favor of mine – she needed to be onstage like she needed air.

"Envy is unbecoming." He plucked the glass out of my hand. "But I'll take your peace offering. For now." He swallowed the brandy with one gulp and grimaced. "My God, where did you get that? Tastes like it has been sitting behind a plant pot for a month."

"I…" But before I could finish, a draft rushed through the room, and the dregs of the brandy beaded together, rising up the sides of the glass to perch on the rim. Julian's eyes went blank for instant, and when they refocused, they were confused.

"I don't really know why I care," he said, then frowned. "Cared. What matters is asses in seats. No one wants to see an old woman playing a young woman's part. Truthfully, I'm glad she decided to retire. It would have been embarrassing to watch her fight her eventual decline. This is our livelihood, and having you star will put money in our pockets." He set the glass on the table, and the beads of brandy collapsed inward, pooling at the bottom once more.

I opened my mouth and then closed it. There was nothing in Julian's expression or tone to suggest he intended his words to hurt. They were emotionless. Cool. Logical. Strangely out of character.

I picked up the discarded glass and sniffed it, a faintly herbal smell filling my nostrils along with the charge of something more. My skin prickled and my headache faded, because a charlatan couldn't have made this potion.

This was magic; and what's more, the spell had been intended for me.

CHAPTER 10
Cécile

I found Sabine in the storeroom filled with costumes. At the sound of my footsteps, she turned, and I caught the bright glow of expectation in her eyes. It faded quickly at the sight of my expression.

"Julian took it upon himself to drink the brandy you gave me," I said. "Not an entirely surprising thing for him to do; what made it interesting was what happened to him afterward."

Sabine paled.

"I think we'll skip the part where you deny the very obvious fact there was a potion in that brandy," I said, my voice shaking with anger. "And past the part where you obviously intended to magic me out of love with my husband. Let's go straight to the point where you explain to me why, knowing that I've spent months hunting for witches who could help me, you decided to keep the fact you'd found one a secret?"

"I wasn't keeping it from you," she blurted out. "I only met her last night."

"And instead of telling me straight away, you decided to take advantage of the information yourself? Anything else you've been keeping from me?" *Had she lied to me all along?*

"No!" She reached for my hand, but I stepped back, crossing my arms. "I only wanted to help you. To give you a chance to live..."

"By stealing away the most precious thing in my life?" I snarled out the words. "You want to know where Chris and I were last night? We went to see the troll king. And he tortured Tristan in front of me until I gave my word I'd find the witch for him. A binding promise. I could no sooner turn from this path now than an addict from her absinthe."

Sabine's face crumbled and she pressed a hand to her mouth. "Oh, Cécile. I'm so sorry."

"Spare me," I said, furious that Tristan would suffer so much for humanity, and this was how he was repaid. "Tell me the name of the witch and where to find her."

"I can take you to her myself."

Her voice was desperate with the need to make amends, but what she'd tried to do to me wasn't something I'd forgive lightly. "So you can sabotage me further?" I shook my head. "I'll go with Chris. At least him I can trust."

Tears flooded down Sabine's cheeks. "You know I'd never do anything to hurt you."

"I *thought* I knew that," I said. "Tell me her name."

Her breath hitched. "They call her La Voisin – the neighbor. She's got a shop in Pigalle."

The words sang through me; and for a moment, they chased away my anger, fear, and even my love for Tristan in order to make room for the single-minded purpose of my hunt. I clenched my teeth and dug my nails into my palms to regain control of the compulsion, but it was like trying to stop a wave with my bare hands. "Let's hope she can help me, and some good might come from this."

Chris and I walked swiftly through the narrow and muddy streets of the Pigalle quarter, the only light coming from between the homeless huddled around piles of burning trash in the alleyways, their emaciated forms hidden by layers of rags. The buildings were pressed tightly together, windows boarded over and wooden frames weak with rot. Every so often, we passed a building that had collapsed from an earthshake, its bones picked away for wood to burn until nothing remained but the foundation.

The air was filled with the smell of the harbor fish markets, but Pigalle itself smelled like too many people stuffed into too small a place. Human filth, waste, and desperation. It made me think about what the King had said to me on the beach. It made me think he was right.

"This isn't a safe part of town to be in, especially after dark," Chris muttered, eyeing the brothel on our left, shrieks of laughter coming from its open doors.

"Why do you think I didn't come alone?" I whispered back.

"How do you know this La Voisin woman isn't a charlatan like all the others?"

"I felt the magic, and even if I hadn't, I saw what the potion did to Julian," I said. "One minute, he was devastated about my mother's pending retirement, and the next, he couldn't have cared less. Impassioned one moment, pure cold logic the next."

"And Sabine meant for you to drink it?"

Angry heat prickled along my skin, but I shrugged it off. "I don't want to talk about it."

"All right," Chris said, rolling his shoulders uncomfortably as a group of dockworkers staggered by. "So it's possible we could be walking toward Anushka herself?"

"I doubt it." I laughed humorlessly, although that had been my original hope before I'd thought it through a little more. "Do you really think the woman who cursed the trolls to an eternity of captivity lives in the slums of *Pigalle*?"

"Good point," he said. "So what are we doing here then?"

I bit the inside of my cheeks and said nothing, because I wasn't precisely certain what I expected to gain from this mysterious witch. "A way to find Anushka." *A way to kill her.*

"I think this is it," Chris said, stopping in front of a short wooden building that was squeezed between two run-down boarding houses. Lines of laundry hung between windows of the taller buildings, dripping dirty water on the witch's abode. The front of the building had no windows, only a narrow, unmarked door.

"Charming," Chris muttered. I swallowed hard, knocked once, and opened the door.

It took a long moment for my eyes to adjust to the dim interior, and even longer for them to take in the chaos filling the room in front of us. The walls, what I could see of them, were jammed with shelves full of herbs, stones, and small statues. There were bottles containing creatures suspended in fluid, some animals, some I didn't care to identify. The tables and cupboards littering the center of room were piled nearly to the ceiling with papers, books, bolts of fabric, more herbs, crystals, and unlit lamps, turning the room into a maze that I didn't look forward to navigating. A small dog ran around a stack of books, barked at us once, and disappeared again.

"Hello?" I called out. "Madame?"

No one responded, so I picked my way through the maze of clutter, Chris following behind. "Hello?" I called out again.

"I guess there isn't anyone home," Chris announced. "We should go – it smells like dog piss in here."

"Souris likes to mark his territory," a voice said from behind us. We both jumped. Chris collided with a stack of papers that proceeded to rain down around us as we took in the woman who seemed to have materialized out of nowhere.

"Are you the one they call La Voisin?" I asked.

"That depends," the woman said, eyeing me up and down. "What do you want?"

What did I want? I stared at the woman in front of me, taking in her brilliant red dress and greying blonde hair pulled back into a tight bun, debating what to say. There was a haughtiness about her not suited to Pigalle – something about the way she held her head that suggested she hadn't always lived in poverty.

She tilted her head and looked at Chris, who was gathering up the papers behind me. "Pregnant?"

Chris jerked upright, banging his head against an open drawer. "No," I said quickly. "Nothing like that."

"What then? Spit it out, girl."

There was an intensity about the woman that made me

nervous, and I could all but feel the power in her words. This was the woman who had made the potion, I was certain of it.

"You gave my friend Sabine a potion. One intended to make a person fall out of love and into logic." I watched her expectantly, but she turned away.

"I deal with herbs, girl, and medicines. What you're talking of smacks of witchcraft, the practice of which sees a woman burned at the stake." She looked over her shoulder at me. "People fall out of love every day without the help of magic. Half the time they fall back in love in a matter of days."

"Not that quickly and not for no reason," I snapped, feeling my temper rising for no reason other than she was thwarting me, standing between me and my goal. "She told me it was you who made it for her, so you can quit playing coy."

The corner of her mouth turned up. "I'm many things, but coy isn't one of them."

"I need your help," I said, trying another tactic. "I've nowhere else to go."

She laughed. "I doubt that. Ladies with fancy clothes and clean fingernails don't need anything from the poor folk of Pigalle. Go back to your parties and gossip."

"Please, hear me out." Far more force went into my words then I intended, a breeze rising and drifting around the shop, the flame of the lamp flaring bright.

Her eyes glazed, but only for a second. "Well, well, well," she said, realizing what I had done. "Apparently there is more to you than meets the eye."

The sound of horses outside caught everyone's attention. Boots thudded against the frozen ground, accompanied by the jangle of steel.

"The city guard!" she hissed.

In one swift motion, Chris reached over and turned the bolt on the door, locking the men out.

And us in.

"La Voisin!" One of the men pounded on the door. "Open up."

"What do they want?" Chris whispered.

I didn't need to ask. There was only one reason for the city guard to be banging at a witch's door. "Is there another way out?"

She shook her head. "They'll be watching the back." Closing her eyes for a heartbeat, she inhaled deeply, pressing a hand to her chest. "This way."

On silent feet, we followed her through the clutter-filled shop into a small living space in the rear. There was another exit, but just as the witch had suspected, there was motion outside that door as well. Pushing aside a threadbare rug, her slender fingers caught hold of a notch in the wood, which she tugged on to reveal a trapdoor. "Down," she whispered, pointing at the cellar below. "Stay silent. It's me they're here for."

The trapdoor closed above us.

At first, I could do nothing more than stare at the bits of light filtering through the gaps in the floorboards, my attention all for the sharp thuds of the woman – the witch – striding toward the front door. What did they want from her? More to the point, what would they do to her? My heart was loud in my ears, and I wished there was a way to still it so that I could better hear the voices of the guards drifting through the thin floor. "Accusations... witchcraft... warning... the flames." My stomach twisted, and even though my palms were clammy, I took hold of Chris's hand.

Boots thumped across the shop, each one sending a spike of ice down my spine. What if they searched the place? What if they found us down here? I glanced around the dark cellar space, and my heart sank. The shelves were lined with oddities that made those upstairs look tame, the table held a silver basin and a ball of crystal, but most damning of all, I was certain, was the stack of books on the table. It wouldn't matter what explanations we gave if they caught us; our complicity was ensured.

The guard stopped right over the trapdoor, the thin rug concealing whatever small glimpses we might have had of him. "No one back here," he announced loudly. "Let's go. It smells like dog piss."

There was a commotion at the front of the shop, and I heard La Voisin shriek, her heels drumming against the floor as they dragged her. She was keeping us safe, and I didn't even know her real name. My heart tried to hammer its way out of my chest, and I all but swore I could smell smoke, hear the crackle of flames. That's what they'd do – they'd burn her at a stake. All because of a hunt the trolls started, and that I hadn't managed to finish. I had to help her.

"Be bold, Cécile," I whispered to myself, trying to ignore the shake in my hands. "Be brave."

"What?" There was alarm in Chris's voice.

I held a finger up to my lips. Pushing by him, I went up the first few rungs of the ladder and cautiously lifted the trapdoor an inch. The only sight I could see was the woman's dog cowering under a chair. La Voisin was still shouting away out front, drowning out any noise I might make. And with any luck, the guard who had been out back would have gone round to assist. Lifting the trapdoor the rest of the way, I climbed out, holding it open for Chris. "This way," I mouthed, pointing at the back door.

Luck was with us when I peeked out, as the tiny yard was devoid of life. We swiftly exited, and Chris grabbed hold of my wrist, dragging me toward the stone fence dividing the yard from the adjoining properties. "No," I whispered, tugging free. "You can go, if you want. But I'm helping her."

He swore quietly under his breath, but didn't try to stop me as I squeezed through the narrow space between the witch's shop and the boardinghouse next to it. The night was black as pitch; Pigalle was not graced with gas lamps to light its streets as the rest of Trianon was. I prayed it would be enough to hide me as I emerged from between the buildings. There were shockingly few onlookers on the street – no one was willing to fall afoul of the law – but I could see faces looking out from windows and entranceways.

Three uniformed guards were struggling with La Voisin, who was screaming like a banshee that she was falsely accused while clinging to the doorframe with one hand. Two of the young men struggling with her were strangers to me. One of them was not.

"Frédéric de Troyes," I snarled, "I daresay, if our father saw you allowing a woman to be treated this way, he'd disown you and never look back."

My brother twisted around to stare at me, his eyes wide with shock. "Cécile? Stones and sky, why are you here?"

"For tea." I shot black glares at the two other men, and while they didn't let go of the woman, they ceased their attempts to drag her off the door.

"Tea?" Fred's voice was strangled. "In Pigalle? After dark?"

"A special tea," I clarified. "That only she makes. And I'm here after dark because it was the only time Chris could bring me."

Fred's eyes flicked over my shoulder and latched onto Chris. "You better have a good explanation for this, Girard."

I rolled my eyes and walked closer. "Oh, stop that and let the poor woman go. Mother will thrash me if I don't bring back the tea to soothe her throat, and half a dozen of the dancers begged me to retrieve some ointment for their poor heels."

"Go home, Cécile." My brother's cheeks were flushed red with anger. "Pigalle is no place for a girl like you. This woman has been accused of witchcraft and…"

"God in heaven," I swore, cutting him off. "If she could fix all the ailments troubling the girls at the opera house with witchcraft, she'd be the richest woman in Trianon for it. But clearly not." I gestured at the ramshackle buildings. "Let her go, Fred. This is nonsensical."

"Who's she?" one of the guards asked.

"My sister."

A lascivious grin split the other man's face. "Oh, the opera girl."

I didn't like the way he said it. Neither, apparently, did my brother. Snatching a fistful of the guard's uniform, Fred dragged him forward until they were face to face. "Watch your mouth when you're talking about my sister, you hear?" Then he shoved him away, and looked back at me.

He knew I was lying. He knew I wasn't here for tea. But he wasn't a fool, and there was no way he'd blunder forward without first discovering why I'd chosen to defend this woman. *Trust me*, I silently pleaded. *Trust me this one time.*

A scowl imprinted on his face, he jabbed a finger at La Voisin. "Last warning, woman. I hear another whisper that you're dabbling in things you shouldn't be, and your feet will be dangling above the fire. Understand?"

"Yes." She gave me a long look before hurrying back into the shop.

"Meet me back at the barracks," Fred ordered the other two men. Both drifted toward their horses, their brows furrowed and eyes full of questions. But they obeyed, and for the moment, nothing else mattered.

Fred stood stock-still, head lowered and eyes fixed on the muddy street. The muscles in his jaw were clenched tight, his hands balled up into fists. When the sound of hooves faded into the distance, he lifted his head. "You better have a good explanation for this."

It was an effort to look him in the eye. "I need her help."

He barked out a laugh. "Her help? Need a love potion? Your fortune read?" Taking hold of my shoulders, he shook me hard enough that my teeth rattled together. "Curses, Cécile, what's wrong with you?"

"Let her go, Fred."

"Piss off, Girard." Fred shoved Chris hard, and my heart skipped at the thought that he might do worse. But it was me he was angry at. "Not only did you make a fool of me in front of my men, you forced me to ignore orders. Orders that came from the very top. Do you have any idea how much trouble I might end up in if I can't talk my way out of this? Do you even care?"

I bit my lip, my throat burning. "I'm sorry. I wouldn't have done it if I hadn't thought it was absolutely necessary."

"Absolutely necessary?" His shoulders shook with silent hysterical laughter. "Absolutely necessary in this fantastical world you've created for yourself?"

"It isn't a fantasy. You know that."

"Wrong!" he shouted, flecks of spit hitting me in the face. "I know what you've told me. But there isn't any proof!"

"She isn't lying," Chris said, the tension in his shoulders mirroring my own as he eyed those still watching us. "I've been there myself."

"Shut up!" Fred was shaking now, his eyes wild with anger. "You were gone for months. Months with no word from you, and everyone thought you were in a shallow grave somewhere. And then you return half-dead and spouting this impossible tale for your family and countless lies for everyone else. I don't even know who you are anymore."

"Fred..." I needed to fix this, to make him understand that everything I'd told him was true. That what I'd done tonight was necessary. But only soundless air came out, because I didn't know what to say. My chest burned with the hurt of his disbelief. He was my older brother, my defender – my lifelong threat against anyone who gave me trouble. The only person I'd thought capable of rescuing me in those dark early days of my captivity in Trollus. And he was turning on me.

He held up a hand. "I don't want to hear any more of your delusions." His finger twisted out, jabbing at the shop next to us. "This. This is real. And far more dangerous than you seem to realize."

I opened my mouth to tell him I knew exactly how dangerous it all was, but he cut me off. "Do you even know who La Voisin is?" He leaned close. "She was a lady's maid to Marie du Chastelier, the Regent's wife. She should have found herself burning for what she did, but instead she was exiled from court. But that doesn't mean they've forgotten. And it certainly doesn't mean they aren't watching. The very fact I'm here tells you as much."

Ever and always the stakes grew higher, enemies cropping up at every turn while my allies fell away. My veins felt as though they ran with ice and that I would never again know warmth. His words terrified me, but I'd made my choice on the beach when I'd made my promise to the troll king. "I have to do this."

His shoulders abruptly slumped, the tension flying from his jaw, leaving it sagging. Defeated. It made me wish for his anger to return. "I could lose my position for this. I could go to prison for this." His voice lowered, making me strain to hear. "But worst of all, what you've done might well bring the Regent's gaze down upon you, and if they discover what you are, you'll die for it." He took one step back and away from me, and then another. "This is the last and only time I help you with your delusions, Cécile. I don't want to see you anymore."

"Fred, don't say that." I tried to go after him, but Chris pulled me back. "Let him go. He doesn't mean that – he only needs time to cool off."

I wasn't convinced, but I let Chris hold me still. Because I didn't know what words existed in the world that would make things right. It ate at my heart to watch my brother ride away. He was one of the people I loved most. One of the people I should be trying to protect. Yet I'd done the exact opposite, endangering his career and maybe even his freedom, all while destroying the trust he had in me.

My tongue was sour with guilt, but underneath it, creeping its way up through my innards, was something worse. Tristan had warned me that releasing the trolls would be the downfall of humanity, forcing me to see the faces of my friends and family as those who would suffer first. And what was this, if not a precursor of what would happen should I succeed in my hunt? It was an omen, as dark and ugly as I had seen, and yet there was no turning back.

Because over and over in my ear, I heard a voice. Louder now, like the call of a hound who has caught the scent of his quarry.

Find her.

CHAPTER 11
Tristan

Trollus seemed overly bright as Marc and I walked toward the entrance to the mines. I moved without really seeing, the details of the comings and goings of my city sliding by in a blur. As we rounded the corner and the wide steps leading down to the mines materialized ahead of us, my legs seemed to forget their purpose, and I tripped, stumbling to a halt.

"Are you sure you want to do this?" Marc said under his breath.

No. "Yes." My voice sounded far away. "This conversation needs to be had."

Marc hesitated, shooting me an uneasy look. "It can be had elsewhere."

"I'm not so sure that's the case." My intense distaste for the mines was an extremely well kept secret, in that only Marc, the twins, and Anaïs knew anything about it. And the only reason they knew was because when I was ten, Anaïs had dared us all to sneak down. Pride had been enough to get me down there, but it ran out before I could get back out again. Then claustrophobia had taken over, and I couldn't have gotten out faster. It had taken all four of them to control me long enough to ride the lift out, and I could tell Marc wasn't looking forward to repeating that experience. Neither was I.

"I'm not a child to be governed by my illogical fears," I

muttered more to myself than to him, forcing my feet to start moving toward the deceptively quiet entrance.

The mines were even louder than I remembered. The shifts had changed two hours ago, so the corridors were almost empty, but I could hear the dull throb of explosions from deep in the earth and the crack of rock as it was crushed to remove the ore. The heat was intense, the air thick with the magic needed to melt the gold down so it could be poured into various molds.

I mechanically followed Marc toward the lift shaft, the dust in the air sticking to my tongue and filling my lungs. There were two guild members sitting on stools near the shaft, their heads bent over a deck of cards. Both jumped up as we entered the room, eyes widening when they recognized me.

"We've business in the mines," Marc said to them.

The two exchanged unhappy glances, and part of me hoped they'd deny us access. A big part. If I couldn't go down there, then Tips would have to meet me somewhere else. It would be better that way. I wasn't at my sharpest, and if there was ever a conversation where I needed focus, this was it. *Why was it so cursed hot in here?*

"As you like, my Lord Comte," one of the men said, and the platform rotated over the shaft, my stomach contents bobbling as it shifted under our weight.

"Ring the bell when you're ready to come back up, my lord."

The platform dropped out from underneath us.

I flung my arms out to keep my balance, my teeth clamping together to prevent a dignity-compromising yelp from filling the air.

"Bastards," Marc swore, glaring up as we hurtled down the shaft, the gleaming girders lighting our passage. But it wasn't the speed of our descent that bothered me, it was the amount of rock piling up above our heads.

The lift stopped, and I stumbled off.

"You're late." Vincent sat on a crate a few feet away, his arms crossed. "Are you sure it was wise you coming down here, Tristan? I know this is not your favorite place."

"It seems a long time since wisdom guided my actions," I said, squaring my shoulders. "Let's get going."

"Good." Vincent's voice sounded unfamiliar and sour. "You took forever getting here, and I've a quota to meet." Not waiting for a response, he started down one of the narrow tunnels leading under the mountain. Marc and I exchanged weighted looks before starting after him, his lone shape hunched over beneath the low ceiling.

This was Vincent and Victoria's punishment for having helped me, spending day after day, night after night, in the mines. It was hard, dirty, and dangerous work, but it hit me then that the work wasn't the punishment. My father had separated them.

The twins' mother had died in childbirth, and their father had passed only days later from the shock of it. Victoria and Vincent had been raised by half-blood servants with only each other for family. They had always been inseparable, never going more than a few waking hours apart. Now, they'd be lucky to see each other for a quarter-hour each day. It was the worst thing he could have done to them. The twins were broken, Anaïs was dead, and Marc...

"How did he punish you for helping me?" I asked quietly.

Marc took a long time to respond. "I was fined."

There was something about his tone that told me there was more to it than a fine, but Marc was not one you pressed.

Vincent stopped abruptly and I nearly collided with him. Turning round, he fixed me with a stare. "They came to his house and took all of Pénélope's things away. All her art. All his portraits of her. Everything."

My father knew everyone's weaknesses. And Pénélope was Marc's. No one knew that better than me.

We'd all known her life would be a short one. I'd been furious when he'd bonded to her, no part of me understanding why he'd tied himself to someone who lived at death's door. I'd thought it was a selfish act on both their parts, and while I'd said nothing to Marc, Pénélope hadn't been so fortunate. It had been the last conversation we'd had.

She hadn't died swiftly, but rather after days of ceaseless bleeding that had diminished her, drained her, until not even her fey nature could delay the inevitable any longer, and her light had gone out. I'd lurked in the corner, and even now, I could hear the loud thud of my heart in my ears, beating with dreadful anticipation as I'd planned how to keep my cousin alive after she died.

I'd kept him bound for what seemed an eternity, each day hoping that he'd come to his senses, but it never happened. So I forced him to promise that he'd live. When Marc had told Cécile about that promise, he'd made it sound as though I'd done some grand thing. In reality, it was one of the worst decisions of my life. That he'd trusted me long ago with his true name was the only reason I'd been able to salvage the situation, because using it gave me not only the power to control what he did, it allowed me to control what he thought. What he felt. What he remembered…

"I…" I started to say, but Vincent was already hurrying down the tunnel. Marc had his head lowered, face hidden by his hood.

"I'll get it all back," I blurted out. My father had stolen everything Marc had left of the girl he loved, and my cousin hadn't said a word. Hadn't complained once. And I hadn't asked.

"It doesn't matter, Tristan," he said. "They're just things. They aren't her."

"It does matter," I argued. "It's because of me that he took them, so I'll get them back."

"It's fine."

"It's not fine." I was angry now. "It is in no way fine that I never asked what he did to you. I didn't even think…" I ground my teeth together. "I've been selfish. Lately. Always, maybe. That needs to change."

"Then change," he said, walking faster to catch up with Vincent. "But don't concern yourself about Pénélope's things. There are other matters more pressing."

The conversation was over. Marc did not like to talk about

Pénélope. Even when she'd been alive, he'd been close-lipped about her, as though what was between them was private and precious, not to be shared. The only person I'd ever seen him willingly discuss her with had been Cécile. She had a way of getting people to talk that I didn't. She was empathetic. I was... judgmental.

Breaking into a trot, I hurried to catch up with my friends.

It didn't take as long to reach Tips and his gang as I thought it would. From the way Cécile had described it to me, they worked a couple of hours' walk from the lifts, but no more than a half hour had passed when we reached them.

Tips must have felt our power, because he was watching our direction rather than where his crew was working.

"Vincent," he said with a nod. Vincent didn't reply, only went over to where the half-bloods were rooting around in piles of blasted rock.

"My Lord Comte." Tips bowed low to Marc. Then he turned to me. "I've been looking forward to this."

His fist flew forward, catching me hard in the cheek. I staggered back, more out of surprise than pain. With one hand, I touched my face and my fingers came away bloody. Tips's fingers glinted with metal, and for a swift, angry moment, I thought he wore iron. Then I felt the itch of my flesh healing and realized it was only silver.

"I've been wanting to do that for months," he said, a cocky grin smeared across his face.

"Satisfied?" I demanded, my voice colder than I intended. *You deserved that and more.*

"Not even close."

We glared at each other, seemingly at an impasse before we even started.

"This passage is supposed to be closed," Marc said, breaking the standoff. "It's dangerous."

Tips's eyes flicked his direction. "Was," he corrected. "Lord Vincent's got the knack for shoring things up."

I didn't really hear the last bit. All that registered in my head was that the rock overhead was unstable. Sweat trickling down my cheek, I searched the ceiling above us for cracks, my magic manifesting, ready to form a shield in an instant. Whatever Tips and Marc were arguing about went unheard, my ears peeled for the sound of moving rock.

"Bloody stones, what do you think you're doing!" Tips's voice caught my attention.

"Is this passage stable?" I demanded, hating the way my voice sounded.

"Stable enough." Tips cocked his head, and then he started laughing. "You're scared. *You*, the most powerful troll alive, scared to be in the mines."

"I'm not…" I broke off with a scowl. "I don't like it down here."

"Poor pretty prince." He rubbed the corner of his eye like he was wiping away a tear. "You realize that makes no sense. You've lived your whole life under a mountain of rock. I've seen you go into the labyrinth, which is a far worse place than here, and come out looking like you've just been for tea with your mother. It's ridiculous for you to be afraid."

"It's actually perfectly logical," I retorted, hating everything that was coming out of his mouth.

"A rock on the head is a rock on the head." There was laughter in his voice, and he leaned on his crutch, looking at me like I was the most amusing thing he'd seen all year.

"I can hold up the rocks in the labyrinth and those above the city," I snarled at him. "But this is too much. Even for me."

Everyone and everything went silent. Swearing, I swung a fist into the wall and instantly regretted it when dust rained down on my head and pain lanced through my arm. Why had Marc said anything about the passage being unstable? He had to have known it would throw me off, make me say things I'd regret.

"Well, I suppose that does make a bit of sense." Tips's voice broke the silence.

I only scowled, refusing to say anything that would implicate me further.

"Although I suppose I shouldn't be surprised," Tips continued. "You have to be in control of everyone around you, so it makes sense that you'd want control of *everything.*"

Was that so wrong? It was. I knew it was. I heard the thud of Tips's wooden leg retreating back toward his crew and knew I needed to say something. Why had I come down here? Because I didn't want to squander the only good that had come from the choices that I'd made? Or was it to make amends for those choices? Both, I decided. It's both. "Wait."

Tips stopped walking.

"I'm sorry for what I did," I said, stumbling over the words. "I'm sorry for deceiving you, but I had to…"

Tips whirled around and limped back toward me. "You didn't just deceive us, boy," he snarled, jabbing a finger into my chest.

"I…"

"Shut up and listen."

The only person who'd ever spoken to me this way was my father.

"You didn't just deceive us, you blackmailed us, you used us, and you killed us." Flecks of spit landed on my face. "And the worst part? We would have helped you if you'd only asked. That girl saved my life when my leg got crushed. And she saved the lives of countless others when she went up against that menace you call a brother." His finger dug deeper into my chest. "Me and everyone else? We would have given our lives to save her, if you'd only trusted us enough to help. But you couldn't let us give our lives, you had to take them."

What could I say? Everything he said was true, but I could so easily remember the deep, numbing terror I'd felt knowing that Cécile would die if I didn't take the right actions to save her. "I had to be sure," I said. "I couldn't risk doing it any other way."

"You mean you had to be in control."

"I…" I wanted to argue with him, to justify and explain the necessity of what I'd done. I wanted to point to the fact that my actions had worked – that Cécile had escaped Trollus, and that she was alive and well. I wanted to make him see that not trusting anyone – other than myself to do what needed to be done – was different than needing to be in control. But mostly I hated that word. Control. Controlling. It made me think of my father and how everything had to be his way. How everyone needed to think and act exactly as he did.

If the shoe fits…

Reluctantly, I nodded.

"Good boy." He patted my cheek, and I found myself too astonished at his audacity to move out of the way. But my astonishment swiftly turned to anger. What did he want from me? I'd apologized for what I'd done. I'd conceded my own personal failings. I'd let him say what he needed to say with no fear of consequence, and for that, he treated me like a spoiled child? Ignoring the burning sting of the iron in my wrists, I drew on my power, intent on putting him back in his place.

He knows his place, you idiot. Grinding my teeth, I listened to the warning little voice in my head. *He knows you can crush him like a fly, but he doesn't care. All attacking him would do is prove his point.*

Tips must have felt the flux of magic, because the condescension fled from his face and he took a half step back. "I don't suppose it matters much to you, though," he said. "Cécile's away from Trollus, and she's safe. In the end, that's all you really wanted."

Inclining his head slightly, he started to back away, the conversation over in his mind. But it wasn't over in mine. I'd faced my dislike of the mines for reason, even if it was only now coming together in my mind.

"Cécile isn't anywhere near safe."

Tips froze, and his crew quit pretending to work, their eyes fixing on me.

A few months ago, bloody stones, maybe even an hour ago, I would have told them only what they needed to know. Only what was necessary to secure their support. But things had changed. I had to change. I was no longer heir to the throne of Trollus. I was no longer the leader of a revolution. I was prince of nothing.

But I had a new weapon, one that I'd never used much before: the truth.

"My father," I said, "coerced Cécile into making him a promise she is unlikely to be able to fulfill. He's leaning on her mind, and if I don't find a way to stop him, he's going to either kill her or drive her mad."

Tips winced, but I wasn't through. With painstaking detail, I explained exactly what had happened at the mouth of the River Road.

Tips's face was grim by the time I finished. "Maybe she'll succeed and deliver Anushka," he said, but the doubt in his voice hung between us. The half-bloods knew as well as anyone how thoroughly the witch had evaded capture.

"Maybe." My eyes flicked to Marc, but his face was unreadable. "But I can't count on it."

Tips leaned on his crutch, his gaze distant and unfocused as he considered everything I'd told him, and I searched his face for any sign of what he might be thinking. "I hate to hear of anything bad happening to the girl," he finally said. "But I don't entirely understand what you expect us to do about it."

I exhaled softly. "Other than catching Anushka, there are only two ways Cécile can be freed of the burden of her promise. The first is that my father no longer desires or cares if she fulfills it, which is something entirely unlikely to occur. The second is..."

"He dies."

"He dies," I agreed.

Tips absently rubbed one shoulder, his eyes on the floor. The muscles in his jaw moved beneath his skin, tightening and relaxing as he thought. After a long moment, he looked over his shoulder at his friends. They were silent, but made no effort to hide their apprehension.

Not good.

"I hate your father," Tips said, the words harsh and clipped. "I hate him to the very depths of whatever soul I have. We all do. But…"

"But…" I pressed, even though I knew what he was going to say.

His shoulders lifted and fell with an apologetic slump. "He's given us everything we asked for. Better treatment. The plans for the stone tree and the gold to build it." Tips lifted his face, meeting my gaze with steady eyes. "He's delivered everything you offered us, everything you failed to give. We'd be mad to side with you against him." The corner of his mouth turned up and he snorted angrily. "It makes me sick to say it, but it's the truth."

I bit the insides of my cheeks. I'd expected this, but that didn't make me any less angry. Every which way I turned, my father had schemes designed to make me and everyone else dance to his tune. Even this… he'd known I'd see that the structure the half-bloods were building was doomed to fail. He'd known that I'd feel compelled to do something about it. I was walking down a path he'd laid for me with no idea of where I'd end up. Part of me wanted to keep the information between Marc and me until I'd figured out what my father was up to, but that strategy had served me poorly in the recent past.

"He's given you nothing," I said. "The plans my father provided are not mine – they are false. Even if he allows you to complete the structure, it won't hold for more than an instant. Take away the magic, and Forsaken Mountain will finish the destruction it started five hundred years past."

Tips's mouth dropped open, and his crew exchanged horrified glances.

The dullness fled from Vincent's eyes. "That bastard!" he swore, voice loud enough to make dust rain down. "He's a blasted sly old fox."

I could think of a few more choice words to describe my father than that, but now wasn't the time.

"But…" Tips's mouth moved, forming words, but no sound

came out. "They're detailed," he finally blurted out. "They've got calculations... lists of materials. They're in your hand!"

I shrugged. "I've no doubt he was meticulous in ensuring that the plans he gave you appeared authentic. But I assure you, they are not."

He squeezed his eyes shut. "I've seen them – they replicate the magic structure perfectly."

"Which is precisely the problem. Stone and steel aren't strong enough," I replied, trying to think of a way to explain it to them. Spying a large boulder in a pile of rubble, I gestured for Vincent to retrieve it, then I created a narrow column of magic. "Balance the rock on the column." He did so, and everyone stared at the combination without comprehension. I sighed. "Now balance it on Tip's crutch."

Vincent picked up the rock, then hesitated. "It'll break."

"Indeed it will," I agreed. "But what if you had three crutches, and arrayed them so that the weight would be evenly dispersed?"

"That would work." Vincent chuckled and nodded. "Now I see. Magic is a stronger material."

"And more flexible," I added, pleased to see the understanding on everyone's faces. And their growing anger.

"We're a blasted bunch of idiots," Tips snarled. "Fools, snatching the low-hanging fruit without worrying that it dangled from our enemy's hand. He'll pay for this, mark my words."

I could not deny my elation. I had the half-bloods – at least some of them – back on my side. I held up a cautionary hand. "We cannot act in haste."

Tips's brow furrowed, and the rest of his crew made angry exclamations demanding instant action.

"He'll have predicted that this conversation would occur," I said. "He'll know I'm down here by now, and he will be expecting us to take certain actions."

"Which actions?"

"I don't know." I sucked in a deep breath. "But I do know he will have planned for all contingencies."

Tips crossed his arms. "So what do we do?"

I cast my gaze around the tunnel, meeting the eyes of every one of the young men and women. "We need to figure out his endgame, and we need to sabotage it."

The mine echoed with shouts of agreement, but Tips was quiet. "I'm hearing a lot of 'us' and 'we' coming from you, Tristan, but what makes you think we want you as our leader again? You betrayed us once to suit your purposes, how are we to know you won't do it again?"

The tunnel grew deathly quiet.

"You don't," I said, squaring my shoulders. "Which is why I'm not asking to be your leader – I'm asking for you to let me help us accomplish this coup as comrades. As equals. And..." I hesitated, the cynical, logical part of my brain screaming that what I was about to do was absolute lunacy. That I would have cause to regret this action countless times in the future. But I needed their trust. No... I needed to prove that I could be trusted.

"I..." My throat felt tight, as though my very nature was trying to strangle the words forming in my mind. "I, Tristan of the Royal House of Montigny, do swear that I will never again use or speak the true name of a half-blood, or" – I glanced at Marc – "full-blooded troll for the rest of my days."

My vision blurred, and I could feel myself lose control of the power of their names. It was still there, like a sword lying motionless behind an impenetrable shield of glass, forever out of my reach. I felt rather than saw a shudder run through Marc, Vincent, and the mining crew as my power over them was relinquished. Only Tips seemed unaffected, which was strange. Very strange indeed.

"A grand gesture," he muttered, seeming to sense my scrutiny. "One we all appreciate."

I leaned back on my heels, not taking my eyes off him. "Some more than others, perhaps." A bead of sweat trickled down his face. He licked his lips, looking anywhere but at me. A dark and ugly suspicion grew inside me, an inkling of an idea that, if proven true, would rattle Trollus to its very core. *Not possible, not possible!*

I flicked my attention to the other half-bloods, but they showed no signs of Tips's nerves. Perhaps they didn't know? He *was* more human than any of them – it was possible the talent was unique to him, and if so, bringing it out into the open could be his undoing. And I needed him.

"I would speak with you alone," I said softly enough that only he and Marc could hear.

Tips wiped the sweat off his brow. "No…" he replied, the word sounding like he'd torn it out of his chest. "Anything that needs saying can be said in front of my crew. I trust them."

With his life? Because if what I suspected was true, his life would be very much in jeopardy. I'd have to speak to him about it later.

"I accepted your criticism of my previous actions. Of my… *duplicity*," I said instead, leaning heavily on the word. "And have since dealt with you honestly and in good faith. I would have the same from you, should we agree to conspire together against my father."

"A fair demand." Tips closed his eyes for a long moment, and I watched his throat move as he swallowed hard. "We'll need a moment."

I nodded. Tips crutched over to where his crew stood, said a few words to Vincent, who started in our direction. Then one of the half-bloods erected a flimsy shield and they all began to talk in earnest.

"Why did you do it?" The words all but exploded out of Marc's lips.

"Without free will there can be no equality, and while I held the power of your names, your will was always within my control."

"But at what cost?" he demanded.

There was a wild tension about him, and I could feel the heat of magic ebbing and flowing through the tunnel. "How much it cost me?" I asked, then paused, realizing the true source of his anger. "Or how much it cost you?"

Marc spun away from us and slumped against the tunnel wall, his face entirely hidden by shadows. "It is all undone." I had not heard such despair in his voice in a very long time. Not since the days following Pénélope's death.

Vincent caught hold of my arm, concern making him squeeze hard enough that it hurt. "What's happening to him?"

I'd never considered this consequence. No troll I'd ever heard of had given up the power of another's name, so I'd undertaken the task without complete understanding of the ramifications. And they'd been far greater than I'd anticipated. I hadn't only given up the power to command them in the future, I'd undone the power of any commands uttered in the past. And there was no one that affected more than my cousin.

"We've decided." Tips's voice drifted down the tunnel toward us.

"Cursed timing," I swore, exchanging a panicked look with Vincent.

Tentatively, I reached out and rested a hand on Marc's shoulder. "I'm sorry," I said under my breath. "I didn't know this would happen."

He didn't respond, but the rock he was gripping with one hand began to crumble.

"Your Highness?" There was heat in Tips's tone. "Lost interest in us already?"

I ignored him. Marc was more important. "Does your word still hold?" I hissed.

His hood jerked up and down once, and a modicum of relief flooded through me. "Can you hold yourself together while I finish this? After, I'll think of something."

He didn't respond.

"Marc!" I clenched his shoulder. "Answer me."

Slowly, he turned his head so that I could see one eye. It was coated with a thin layer of blood, the vessels breaking under pressure and reforming in an instant. I wanted to recoil away from that gaze, but I didn't let myself.

"You chose," he said, his voice thick with animosity. "Do not squander what you have gained."

His words were a punch to the gut, driving away my breath. Was this always to be my destiny? Hurting those who mattered most with my failed efforts to make the right choices? "I'm sorry."

"Get on with it."

I turned numbly back to the half-bloods, only a lifetime of practice allowing me to wipe away all traces of what I was feeling. Tips and his crew were watching us with interest, aware that something had occurred during their discussions, but uncertain what.

"What is your decision?" I asked, finding it hard to care with my cousin rapidly losing his mind behind me.

Tips didn't hesitate. "We're with you." He gestured at his crew. "All of us." They nodded in agreement. "But as for the rest of the half-bloods… That will take time. They aren't the most trusting these days."

My relief at his words felt small and inconsequential. "Until we know more about my father's plans, we dare not act," I said. "We've got time. Best we keep this between us until we think of a strategy."

Tips nodded. "Now that we've got that settled, you should make yourself scarce. Our cooperation means nothing if we don't make quota."

"Until then." I nodded at the half-bloods, and a few of them bowed awkwardly. Tips did not. He, at least, would take our equality seriously. And frankly, I had bigger concerns.

"Get him out of here," Vincent said quietly. "And think of a solution."

"I will," I muttered. Marc was already facing down the tunnel, but the air was thick with magic that coiled unguided, brushing against me, the walls, the ceiling. I touched the manacle on my left wrist, ignoring the stab of pain while I cursed the steely handicap. Was the punishment worth taking them off? I might end up with more than just the two in my wrists. What good would I be to anyone then?

"Let's go." Marc's voice sounded strange and unfamiliar. Angry. Dangerous.

I'd be punished for taking the manacles off, but if I left them on, there was a real chance I might not get out of these tunnels alive.

CHAPTER 12
Cécile

"You're out late."

I jumped, my mother's voice acidic in my ears. She stood next to the roaring fire, face cast in shadows, a glass of brandy in her hand. "Feeling a bit dramatic this evening?" I asked, hanging my cloak on a hook. "Besides, aren't you supposed to be dining with Julian?"

She took a sip of her drink. "He was otherwise occupied."

"At least he's recovered from your announcement," I said, flopping into a chair. "I was more than a little concerned he'd quit the company for spite."

"Quitting isn't an option for him."

There was enough venom in her voice to make me re-evaluate the severity of the situation. I'd long known that Julian was enamored with her, but surely the emotions were not reciprocated? He was the same age as my brother. "Did he say something to you?"

She took another swift drink. "He said a good many things."

I grimaced, knowing that if he'd repeated what he'd said to me to her, she would not have taken it well.

"Enough of Julian." Setting down her glass, she drifted across the carpets, coming to a stop in front of me. "Where were you this evening?"

"Here and there." She had never cared where I was before,

other than to suggest I spend more time entertaining subscribers after performances.

"Here and there," she parroted my words back, and I knew I was in trouble. "Perhaps I need to be more specific, Cécile. Why were you in Pigalle?"

I gaped at her, my mind scrambling for a lie even as it raced for a possible explanation of *how* she knew.

"Don't bother trying to squirm your way out of it, my dear," she snapped. "Your brother was here, which would have been a shock in and of itself, but he insisted on giving me an earful about letting you run wild through the slums. What could possibly even interest you in that trash heap they call a quarter?"

I had no good answer. There was nothing in Pigalle that should appeal to a girl like the one I was supposed to be. But if I didn't give her an answer, she'd go hunting for one, and the absolute last thing I needed was Fred telling her the whole truth because he was angry with me. "I…"

"You…?" Her cheeks were flushed with alcohol and anger. Why, tonight of all nights, did she have to start taking an interest in where I spent my time?

"I was getting my fortune told." The words came out in a tangled rush. "Some of the girls were talking about it, and I wanted to see what my future held."

She straightened, her head tilting slightly as though considering whether I might possibly be so foolish as to lie. "No one can see the future."

"I know," I blurted out, getting to my feet because I couldn't sit still. "It was all nonsense. I'm sorry I went. It won't happen again." I wanted to go upstairs to my room, to hide and let this day be over, but she stepped into my path.

"These next few weeks are going to be very important for you, you know."

Important, yes, but not in the ways she imagined.

"I need you to understand that I'm setting you up so that you will have a grand future." Her eyes delved deeply into mine, but I wasn't sure what they were looking for. "I need you to be ready to take over my role, my place, my position."

"You're being dramatic." Did she really mean to retire? "It isn't as though you are dying."

Something flicked across her gaze, but was gone again in an instant. "Of course not. But the young inherit. That is how it has always been, and it is how it will always be. I need…" She broke off, then huffed out a breath of air. "I need you to go to your room. And every night you aren't performing, I expect you to be back in this house before dark. Am I clear, or must I go over the terms of your continued presence in Trianon once again?"

"Perfectly clear." Agreeing with her was easier than arguing. She was never at home at night anyway, so it would be easy to sneak out when and if I needed to. Twisting past her, I trotted toward the stairs.

"You'll be accompanying Julian and me to the castle in the morning to meet with Lady Marie and the rest of the ladies who will be performing in the masque. I want you dressed in your finest and on your best behavior."

"But…" I'd had every intention of going back to Pigalle in the morning to speak with La Voisin.

"No buts." Her voice was sharp. "You *will* do as I say, or you will find yourself back on the farm."

Gooseflesh prickled across my skin, and the idea of disobeying her abruptly felt like an especially bad idea. She did not make idle threats. "I'll be ready."

The chill didn't abandon me until I was up in my room, ensconced in front of the fire and a thick blanket wrapped around my shoulders. I stared into the flames, trying to put my thoughts in order.

The moment felt surreal, which was strange, given that sitting on the floor of my bedroom wrapped up in my own thoughts was the most normal thing I'd done in recent days. I'd ridden out into the dark of night with a stranger. Made a bargain with the king of the trolls. Tracked down a witch in the most dangerous quarter of Trianon. Confronted the city guard. In all of those moments, I'd felt so present and alive, but now, sitting alone in front of the fire, I barely felt like myself.

Maybe because I wasn't. Maybe because I'd changed.

Covering my eyes with my hands, I mumbled, "I don't know who I am anymore."

"You are Cécile de Troyes, star of the opera stage and Trianon's new favorite ingénue."

Every muscle in my body jerked at the sarcastic voice. It was one thing talking to myself, quite another to have myself answer back. Spreading my fingers ever so slightly, I peered through the narrow cracks between them. Eyes stared out at me from the flames.

Squeaking, I fell backwards, tangling in my blanket.

"Oh, stop that."

The voice was familiar. Cautiously, I crawled on hands and knees back toward the fire, my body tense and ready to bound away again at the slightest hint of a threat. "La Voisin? Is that you?"

"Please call me Catherine." Disembodied though it was, her voice seemed calm.

I was anything but. I'd seen so many incredible things, but this... If she could do this spell, that meant I could learn to as well. A thousand possibilities blossomed in my mind of the ways I could make use of it. Maybe it meant I could talk to some of my half-blood friends in Trollus. Maybe it meant I could see Tristan. "How is this possible?"

"Magic, obviously." The eyes in the flames blinked at me. "You've very distinctive hair, and you lost a few strands in my shop today. You should be careful about leaving behind pieces of yourself – they can be used."

The eyes disappeared and reappeared with an eerie blink.

"You did me a good turn today, getting me out of that spot of trouble with the guard," she continued, not waiting for me to answer. "Come by the shop tomorrow, and I'll help you as best I can."

I opened my mouth to speak, but the flames flared up high, and as suddenly as they had arrived, the witch's eyes were gone.

CHAPTER 13
Tristan

I left the manacles on. Not because I was afraid of the punishment for removing them, though I was. And not because I was cocky enough to believe I could easily best him. The reason I left them on was that I refused to believe that even in these dark hours I had any need to defend myself from my cousin. Which perhaps made me a fool, because just as only my father's death would release Cécile from her promise, only my death would set Marc free.

I followed him through the mines, every blast of the miners' magic making me jump as I struggled to come up with a solution for what I had done. For the unintended consequences.

But there was none.

Before long, Marc's swift walk turned into a run, and even though his crooked legs made his stride uneven and strange, it still took everything I had to keep up with him. He was taller and faster, and the distance between us began to grow. Scenario after scenario ran through my head, each worse than the last. I'd only seen him like this once, and I'd fixed him before I'd had the chance to see how far madness would drive him. I didn't know Marc like this. I could not guess what he was capable of.

"Marc, stop!" I shouted between gulps of breath.

He ran faster.

"Marc! Marc, listen to me!"

I might as well have been howling into the wind. We were very nearly at the base of the shaft where the lift would be waiting to take us up. I had to stop him, speak to him, try to contain him, because fixing him was no longer within my power. Desperate, I flung out a rope of magic, catching him around the ankle seconds before he rounded a bend. I heard a thud and a string of curses, then silence. Sliding to a halt, I walked cautiously around the bend.

Marc stood in the middle of the tunnel, sword drawn. "What makes you think I want to listen to a word you say?"

I stopped, keeping a wary eye on his sword. My fingers itched to draw my own blade, but my gut stayed my hand.

"Why did you do it?" he demanded.

"As a show of trust," I said. "And to put everyone on equal footing."

"As if any of us could ever be your equals." He spat the words, the tip of his sword shaking. "And you know that isn't what I meant."

"I know." I inhaled deeply, trying to find some measure of calm. This had little to do with my choice to relinquish power over names and everything to do with the choices I'd made two years ago. "There is no grand explanation. I didn't want Pénélope's death to kill you. So I did the only thing I could think of to keep it from happening." I pressed a weary hand to my face, blocking out the light of the girders lining the walls and remembering the black day when Pénélope had died.

"Whether I lived or died wasn't your choice to make." He lifted his sword, tensing as he readied to strike. "It wasn't your choice!" His voice echoed, repeating over and over as though the tunnels themselves desired to have their point made. He looked feral, eyes red and muscles pulling his deformed face into the mask of madness that I remembered so well because I had been its instigator. Forcing a promise from him that set his mind to battling itself, half desperate to die and the other compelled to live.

"I know," I said. "I didn't understand then what forcing you to make the promise to live would do."

At least not until it was too late. And then it had been a wild scramble to correct what I'd done, ordering him by name not to think of his loss, of his pain, or his misery. It took days to carefully craft the layers of commands needed to maintain his sanity without being so cruel as to eliminate Pénélope from his thoughts entirely. Orders that had remained in place until I'd relinquished control over the names of him and the half-bloods. And now all that remained was that ill-thought promise that could not be undone by anything but death and a mind once again at war with itself.

"I do not know myself." He flung his sword against the ground and pressed the heels of his hands to his temples, squeezing hard. "Two years I've lived under your control. Two years I've been not who I am, but who *you* wanted me to be. I should have died with her. I should have died with her." He kept repeating himself, and his words made me shake with sudden fury.

Heedless of the spikes skewering my wrists, I swung hard, catching him in the jaw. He stumbled back, and I bent double, swearing as blood splattered the floor. "Why should you have died?" I shouted through the pain. "To prove that you loved her? Because you thought you'd betray her by living? Because you thought that was what she wanted?" I straightened slowly, the stench of blood and iron thick in the air. "She wanted you to survive her death – I know that, because she told me herself!"

"I have no reason to live without her."

I spat on the floor. "Nothing to live for? What of your family? Your friends? Your cause? Does none of that matter to you anymore?" I stormed forward until we were eye to eye, inches apart. "Before Anaïs. Before the twins. Before the half-bloods, there existed an idea between you and me about how we could change our world for the better. This has always been as much your cause as mine."

He looked away first. "Don't stand there and pretend you'd be any better if Cécile died. I watched you throw away everything to save her."

"Because she could be saved! I'll not claim that what I did was right, but at least it had purpose. Your death has none. It won't bring Pénélope back. And if Cécile were to die and I survived long enough to listen, I'd hope you'd say the same thing to me."

I balled my fists until my wrists screamed and forced me to relax them. "There is more to my life than just her. There are other people I care for. Causes that matter." I drew in a deep breath. "She walks as close to the line of death as Pénélope ever did, and there are times I question why we do this to ourselves. Why we tie our fate so closely to one person that everything we are, everything we do, hangs upon them. It seems a cruel thing that we lose not only the one we love most, but also the opportunity to endure. To finish the things we've started."

My anger fled, and I suddenly felt bone-weary. "I do not know what her death would do to me, whether I'd have the will to carry on." I concentrated on the pain in my wrists, trying to focus my thoughts. "I cannot imagine life without her, but at the same time, I hate the thought that what we've started in Trollus might go unfinished. It seems such a wretched waste."

Neither of us said anything for a long time, the activity of the mines the only sound to break the silence.

"I'm sorry for the pain my choices caused you," I said. "But I cannot seem to regret them." Pushing past him, I started toward the lift.

"That's it?" he shouted after me. "You're just going to wash your hands of what you've done and leave my mind to turn as twisted and broken as the rest of me?"

I stopped, but I didn't turn around. I was afraid that if I looked at him, I'd lose my nerve, the fragile confidence I had in the truth my own fears had revealed to me.

"It's not up to me anymore, Marc," I said. "If you find reason inside yourself to live, your will and your word might cease to be at odds and your mind once again be whole. Or you can pine away for death and let the madness grow until my father orders you put down. The choice is yours."

My feet didn't want to move, but I made them. Step after step until the stone slab of the lift lay beneath them. And as it started to rise, I prayed to fate and the stars that I hadn't made another choice that I'd have cause to regret.

CHAPTER 14
Cécile

The carriage jerked and bounced over the ruts in the road, bruising my bottom and making my teeth clack together. Winter was approaching, the ground hard with frost and the air laced with the scent of coming snow. I pulled my cloak tighter around my body as I watched the faces of those we passed, wishing my eyes would light upon the one I sought, even as I knew that I would never be so lucky.

But then my eyes did catch sight of a familiar face: Esmeralda. She stood with a group of sailors, gesturing angrily, and although there was little chance of her glancing up to see me, I leaned back so that my face was obscured by the curtain. And felt cowardly as I did. I was supposed to have helped Zoé and Élise – all the half-bloods – but there were times when I thought all I'd done was make things worse for them. I'd distracted Tristan and altered his focus, and I knew he'd sacrificed them to save me when I'd been hurt.

No humans were allowed into Trollus anymore, so Esmeralda had lost her only contact with her nieces. All because of me. There was no apology capable of making up for that – the only thing that could would be breaking the curse and winning the girls' freedom.

I sighed, pushing my regrets to the back of my mind. I'd barely been able to sleep last night, my mind so full of the possibilities that one short conversation with La Voisin – Catherine – had opened up for me. The least of which was the chance I might be able to communicate with those in Trollus.

Tristan had been up to something last night, and his wakefulness had contributed to my own insomnia. It would help so much to be able to talk to him just once. To explain what had happened and what I'd discovered. I bit my lip, thinking about how that conversation would go. Perhaps not as well as I'd like. I knew that he did not support my actions, and given the chance, he'd probably tell me to stop. To give up.

But I couldn't.

I shivered, and then slid the window shut so my mother and Julian would think the chill was finally getting to me. We were on the way to the Regent's castle for our first rehearsal with the ladies who would be part of the performance; and as she had commissioned the performance, the Regent's wife, Marie du Chastelier, was certain to be there. Twelve of the most important women in Trianon, and who knew how many others there to keep them entertained.

It was an incredible and unique opportunity, but my enjoyment was tempered by another thought that had occurred to me last night: this was not a social circle I'd met in the foyer of the opera. These women were a level above me, and it might be possible that Anushka was among them.

"Have you given any consideration to the list of operas I provided you?" Julian asked. "Given it will be Cécile's debut as lead soprano, it's important we make the correct choice. A fresh new act for a fresh new face."

He's still under the effects of the potion. The thought nudged me, sending a trickle of discontent through my veins. I hadn't spoken to Sabine since I'd confronted her, but I was finding it hard to stay angry with her. What she'd tried to do was wrong, but her actions had a good intention.

"I'll keep your suggestions in mind." There was a trace of sarcasm in my mother's voice, but Julian didn't seem to notice.

"It needs to be something avant-garde, maybe a little scandalous..."

"And its selection is not our priority," my mother interrupted. "The masque is."

"But we need to stay ahead of our competition!"

"Drop it, Julian," I muttered, then tuned them out and stared down at my hands. My chapped fingertips peeked out from blue lace half-gloves, nails bitten down to the quick. When had I started doing that?

Over the rattle of the carriage, I heard the sound of rushing water. A glance out the window confirmed we were on the bridge leading to the walled castle gates. The Regent's castle was built on an island in the middle of the Indre River, the thick stone walls rising up from the swift rapids. The only access to the island was the bridges, one to the north bank and one to the south, both with heavily fortified gates. I'd never been inside the walls before, and despite myself, I was eager to see what the castle would be like.

The carriage stopped, and moments later, a guard looked in the window at us. My mother lifted a hand in greeting, and he waved us forward. I caught a quick flash of the walls as we passed through the gates. They were dull grey with a faint hint of green lichen in the mortar cracks, but the impression they gave me was of strength and practicality. The castle had been built with defense, not beauty, in mind, although to the best of my knowledge, it had never been attacked.

My eyes flicked over the outbuildings as we slowly passed by, all of them squat and sturdy. I wanted to get out and go look at them – to see what sort of activities went on within the confines of the walls. But the ground was wet and the delicate shoes my mother had insisted I wear were unsuited for traipsing through stables and smithies.

The carriage drew to a halt; and seconds later, a liveried footman opened the door, holding out an arm to help me descend. Lifting my skirts up with one hand, I slowly turned in a circle, trying to take in everything I could while Julian helped my mother out of the carriage. The castle itself was little more impressive than the outbuildings, ugly and low to the ground, with the exception of two towers rising up above the whole. Everything was a dull grey, the only flashes of color the two flags flapping in the cold breeze coming off the sea.

"Come along, Cécile." My mother caught Julian's arm before he could walk away, and they started up the steps to the entrance. I followed, my heels clicking against steps worn smooth by years of traffic and weather. Two uniformed guards swung open the doors, which were thick oak banded with pieces of steel. I noticed steel-bracketed holes in the stone, and looking up, I saw the pointed spikes of a portcullis that could be lowered to further protect the entrance.

The inside of the castle seemed as barren and grey as the exterior, the narrow hallway we walked down dark despite the multitude of lamps. There were no windows that I could see, making the place seem tight and close as a coffin. Impenetrable. It should've felt safe, but all I felt was cold.

After walking for what seemed like an eternity through a maze of passages, the servant leading us stopped at a closed door, knocked, then stepped inside to announce us. A wall of warmth and light hit me as I stepped into the room, making me blink. A massive fireplace burned against one wall, but the light came from two ornate candelabras hanging from the ceiling. Thick carpets covered the floors, and tapestries concealed the ugly grey walls.

The room had the same narrow windows I'd seen from outside, but these had panes of beautiful stained glass that spilled a rainbow of color across the two dozen women filling the room. Not that any of them needed it – every one of them was dressed in a different hue, their gowns elaborate contraptions of silk, satin, and velvet. My eyes passed over them swiftly, but none had red hair or bore the haughty chiseled features of Anushka.

Though I had never seen her before, I immediately picked out the Regent's wife, the Lady Marie du Chastelier. Her aubergine gown was no more elaborate than many of the others, but if my time with the trolls had taught me nothing else, it had taught me to recognize the gravitas that so often came with rank. Young or old, every woman in the room was keenly aware of her, all of them waiting for her to recognize us before acting themselves.

Lady Marie rose and came toward us. I kept my face lowered, watching her through my eyelashes. She was somewhat older than my own mother, her brown hair silver at the temples, and while not beautiful, she was attractive in a stately sort of way. She wore a strange necklace made of wood, and a sprig of crimson berries pinned in her hair. They looked real rather than wax, but I couldn't imagine where they had come from at this time of year.

My mother dropped into a deep curtsey at her approach. "My lady."

"Genevieve." There was no inflection in her voice, but I sensed immediately that Lady Marie did not much like my mother as she walked by her without stopping. A flicker of annoyance passed over my mother's face as she straightened.

Julian bowed and I dropped into a smooth curtsey as the most powerful woman in Trianon approached us. She went to him first, raising a hand to cup his cheek. "You must be Julian."

He nodded. "Yes, my lady."

"You have a great many admirers here," Lady Marie said, a warm smile crossing her face. "Try not to break too many hearts."

Julian ducked his head. "I think it is my heart that will be at risk, my lady." The words were too smooth, making them sound disingenuous. Rehearsed.

"How charming," Lady Marie said, but there was the faintest hint of sarcasm in her voice. Then she turned to me.

My knees ached from holding a curtsey, but I did not rise until I felt her fingers catch the bottom of my chin. "Cécile de Troyes," she murmured, her voice thoughtful. "I've seen you perform before, and I confess, you seem much taller onstage." Her smile was gone. "But you're only a little doll, aren't you?"

She wasn't the first to say so, but it was still difficult to keep my dislike of the comparison off my face. Dolls had no minds – they were pretty things to be played with, and I'd had quite enough of that in my life. "Appearances can be deceiving, my lady," I replied, meeting her gaze. "The heels I wear onstage are quite high."

One of her eyebrows rose, and for a moment, I feared I had overstepped. But then she chuckled. "Indeed they can be."

Our conversation ended with the arrival of the masque composer, Monsieur Johnson, who amused the ladies with his foreign accent and dress as he herded them down the hall. Julian and I were left to trail after everyone as we went to where the stage was under construction. Other hangers-on swelled their ranks, and my eyes flicked over their faces, searching, searching for that sly gaze.

And found nothing. Finding her here on display had been a foolish hope.

Leaning against a wall, I watched the ladies swarm around, their questions – about the costumes, music, and dance steps – filling the air. Even though the set was only in the beginning stages, I could tell it would be magnificent. Both of them, for Monsieur Johnson was explaining that there would be a change during the break between acts. The darkness of Vice – my mother's role – was what they were constructing now, and I watched her move amongst the giggling ladies as she explained their parts. Julian walked with her, his face more relaxed as he adopted the persona of the devil meant to tempt them.

"You watch them as I do."

I jumped, Lady Marie's sudden appearance at my elbow startling me out of my thoughts. "Pardon?"

She chuckled, and to my astonishment, leaned her own shoulders against the papered walls. "You're watching the girls like you're looking for something within them, but you're uncertain what. I often find myself doing the same."

It was her I was watching now. Was I so obvious, or did she know more about me than she was letting on? "I'm curious to see how they will perform," I said, watching her face for any sort of reaction. "I hope my scrutiny has not upset any of them – it is merely habit."

The corner of her mouth turned up, but she kept her eyes on the scene in front of us. "I doubt it. They are all used to scrutiny. More so, I think, than you are." Her eyes went to mine and away again. She knew I was lying.

I swallowed. "Why do you watch them, my lady? What is it you are looking for?"

"I'm not sure." Her smile fell away, and she shook her head once. "That's a lie. I do know what I'm looking for, or, rather, whom."

Though I desperately wanted to press her, I knew it was not my place.

"My son, Aiden," she eventually said. "It is near time he was wed, but he stubbornly refuses to consider any option put to him." She sighed. "One day, he will be the ruler of all the Isle, and he will need a strong and intelligent woman by his side in order to do it. That is the purpose of this masque – to put all his options on display for him. He needs to choose well, for the woman will carry a greater burden than anyone realizes."

It sounded so crass when said that way – as though all these young women were animals on an auction block. Although in fairness, it was certainly no worse than how I'd been selected. At least they were willing.

"My brother is under his command," I offered timidly, uncertain why she was revealing this information to me. "He speaks very highly of Lord Aiden."

"He would." There was heat in her voice. "His command is all that he attends to now – it is as though he has no time for anything other than military pursuits." As abruptly as her anger arrived, it vanished. "Though that was not always the case. At one time, it seemed his entertainments would consume him. But this last year he's changed – become melancholy and brooding, prone to disappearing for days at time. I hardly know him." She huffed out a breath, and waved her hand as though to dispel the tension of her words. "Young men, Cécile – they are impossible."

I ventured a smile. "Perhaps during our performance, he'll

realize that the one he's looking for has been here the entire time."

"Perhaps." She straightened and stepped away from the wall. "Sometimes what we are looking for is right in front of us, but more often, I think, one must look long and hard, for she will not reveal herself so easily."

Her words echoed in my ears, and I bit my tongue to keep from reacting.

"Your mother is performing for us tomorrow night, as she has done so many times over the years," she said, her eyes searching mine. "Although I understand you will soon be taking up her torch, and it will be your voice gracing our dinner parties."

"I can't find it in myself to believe she truly intends to retire," I said, tension rising up my spine as it dawned on me that this woman was far more familiar with me than I was with her. Fred had said that contact with La Voisin would bring the attention of those in power down upon me, but what if it already was? Lady Marie du Chastelier had no reason to care who I was, no reason to seek out my attention. No reason, unless she knew I had a darker purpose for being in Trianon beyond performing onstage.

"Believe it," Lady Marie said. "Genevieve's time on the stage is over, but I've no doubt you'll make a wonderful successor. Your talents, it would seem, are endless."

"I'll do my best." My words sounded breathy, and a bead of sweat ran down the back of my leg. She was not talking about my voice...

"Are you quite well, dear?" She touched my arm, and every muscle in my body twitched. She frowned.

Get control of yourself!

"Sorry!" I took a deep breath, trying to control my pounding heart, but it did no good. "My apologies, my lady. I'm overwhelmed – I didn't expect this."

Lady Marie's frown melted away, but that did nothing to ease the tension singing through my veins. "Such an innocent little thing you are. Hard to believe, given whom you've been spending time with..."

"Please excuse the interruption, my lady, but Monsieur Johnson is asking for my daughter."

My mother had appeared out of nowhere, and was now standing next to me. *She knows about the trolls*, my mind screamed, but I forced a smile onto my face.

"By all means, take her," Lady Marie replied, eyes fixed on Genevieve's, expression flinty. "After all, that is why she is here." Her gaze went to me. "We'll be watching every move you make, Cécile. Be sure of it."

I bobbed a shaky curtsey, allowing my mother to lead me away. A droning like that of a swarm of flies filled my ears, and I could all but feel her eyes burning into my back.

"What did she want?" My mother's breath brushed against my ear, her voice low. "What did she say?"

"That she might like for me to perform for them in the future." My tongue felt almost too numb to form the words correctly.

"Excellent." Her voice was low and full of satisfaction. "She and her predecessors have long supported the opera. I'm pleased Marie intends to maintain the relationship."

My head jerked up and down, but my mind shouted something quite different. Marie knew I was a witch and she knew about the trolls, I was sure of it. But then why invite me to perform? Why not lock me in a dungeon or burn me at the stake like every other witch the Regency caught? What did she want from me? How much did she know?

We'll be watching every move you make... We'll be watching... We'll... As the words repeated themselves, a theory began to form in my mind. An idea that should have sent me running as fast and far as my feet would take me. But instead a wicked anticipation like nothing I'd felt before fueled my stride.

I've found her.

CHAPTER 15
Tristan

"Item fourteen!" The auctioneer's voice echoed through the market, voice magnified by a simple but effective trick of magic. I watched, but I didn't see. I listened, but I didn't hear. It was merely a place to be while I thought.

I'd heard nothing since leaving Marc in the depths of the mines. That meant the worst had not happened – he hadn't sunk so low as to wreak vengeance upon Trollus, nor found some way to contrive to end his life. Which didn't mean he was well, and certainly didn't mean he'd forgiven me, but I'd take it. My problems were stacked high enough that even small blessings were a relief.

Something struck me in the backs of my calves, and I turned to see a troll woman limping slowly away. It had been her cane that had hit me, and I did not think it had been an accident. Sure enough, she glanced over her shoulder, expression far from apologetic. I recognized her as the sculptor called Reagan. She was a nasty-spirited creature, but had gained a certain notoriety for the Guerre sets she made for the upper classes.

"Female, age twenty-six, scaled at five." the auctioneer shouted, the number catching my attention back to the stage. Half-bloods scaled at more than a four were rare to see at the auctions – their sales were normally conducted privately. That the woman was being sold here indicated something about her was undesirable.

"House born and trained!"

But no mention of which house, which meant they did not care to be associated with her. One of the auction workers snapped a lash of magic at the woman's feet, and she jumped before following the instruction to walk the length of the stage and back. To my eyes, she looked normal enough. No obvious deformities, twitches, or signs of madness. She kept her face lowered, as any house trained servant would, but I was close enough to see the tears dripping off her chin.

"Reads and writes in four languages! Takes dictation with an excellent hand."

Which meant nothing to any of the buyers here. Her power made her too expensive for bourgeoisie who might use her skills, and whatever she'd done made her unpalatable to the upper classes. The Miners' Guild would take her, I was sure of it.

"Proven breeder."

And there it was. An indiscretion, and it would not matter whether it was voluntary or not.

"We'll start at fifty!"

The bidding began fast and furious, but my attention snapped away from the proceedings as I felt a familiar and impressive amount of power coming up behind me. Turning round, I came face to face with my brother. On his arm was the impostor, and behind her, the Duke d'Angoulême.

"Your Highness." I inclined my head slightly. He had always been fond of any show of subservience or reminder that he was a royal. And it was always best to placate him – to do otherwise invited disaster, and with my manacles on, I was in no position to do anything about it. I ignored the impostor and Angoulême.

"Tristan." Roland's eyes gleamed bright and unblinking, but he didn't seem to be of a mind to make trouble.

The impostor glared at me, clearly waiting to be acknowledged. "You should show courtesy to your betters," she snapped.

I flicked my gaze to her. "That's true." I did not move and said nothing more. Roland tittered softly, shifting from one leg to another. "He's right, lady Anaïs," he said. "For all he's done, Tristan is still a Montigny, and that makes him better than you."

The mask of Anaïs's face seemed to quiver, and my pulse quickened the second I thought the illusion might fracture enough to reveal who was underneath. But she regained control, inclining her head to Roland. "Of course you are right, Your Highness. I meant only that Tristan owes more courtesy to the future king of Trollus."

That hadn't been what she meant at all. I glanced at Angoulême, but his arms were crossed, eyes on the woman on the auction block.

Roland was rubbing his chin with one gloved finger. "That's true, Anaïs." He dropped his hand to the child-sized sword hanging from his waist. "Bow."

Fighting back a sigh, I did so. "Forgive my lapse, Your Highness."

My brother smirked. "You are forgiven."

I had thought the impostor would be pleased to see me so lowered, but when I straightened, I found she wasn't looking at me, but rather at the girl on the platform. Nevertheless, her expression was pleased. "Will you watch with me, Highness?" she said, tugging on his arm.

"I suppose." Roland grudgingly allowed himself to be led closer to the platform, the crowd parting for him, all eyes nervous.

"Are you sure it's wise having him near this many half-bloods?" I muttered to Angoulême.

"He won't do anything I don't want him to."

It was a strange thing to be so certain about. I eyed Angoulême curiously, wondering when he had last spoken so forthrightly. Indeed, he hardly seemed to be paying any attention to me at all, the blank expression he wore clearly driven by some other cause.

"Sold!" the auctioneer shouted. "For two hundred three gold pieces to the Miners' Guild." The Anaïs impostor clapped her hands once, the outburst strange enough that even Roland eyed her uncertainly.

Angoulême closed his eyes for one, two, three heartbeats, and when they opened, they were full of an emotion I'd never seen on his face. It dawned on me why he was here, and why he was ignoring me.

"How long do you suppose she'll last down there?" I asked quietly, watching the crying half-blood trip off the platform. "House born. House trained. Nearly as pampered as the ladies she served."

Angoulême slowly turned his head to meet my gaze. "What makes you think that is any concern of mine?"

I shrugged one shoulder. "It certainly seems to concern her." I jerked my chin in the impostor's direction, finding myself unable to even call her by Anaïs's name.

"Yes." He turned to look at the pair. "I suppose I have that much to thank you for, Tristan. Your betrayal has well and truly turned Anaïs from your cause. She is now every bit the daughter I had hoped for. And more."

He didn't know it wasn't her. The impostor had managed to fool even Anaïs's own father. How blind was Angoulême that he couldn't see the impostor for what she was? I opened my lips to say as much; to, in one fell swoop, foil whatever it was my father was planning. "What..." I broke off. As much as I wanted to reveal the impostor, doing so without understanding my father's intentions might be a mistake.

She and Roland walked back up to us, but Angoulême ignored them. "What..." He raised one eyebrow at me. I decided to go another route.

"What happened to the child?"

Angoulême's face went purple with fury. "Unlike your father," he spat, "I do not suffer such abominations to live."

Out of the corner of my eye, I saw the impostor jerk as if she'd been slapped.

The puzzle pieces fell into place, and in that instant, I knew who'd stolen Anaïs's life.

CHAPTER 16
Tristan

Lessa.

"Anaïs, come!" Angoulême turned on his heel and stalked away, not waiting to see if she and Roland followed.

I bowed low again to my brother, forcing a hint of irritation onto my face to hide my astonishment. How had our father convinced her to play this part? As far as I knew, she hated him. He'd abandoned her to the law and fate without a second thought – letting her live a life of servitude while the rest of her blood were served. But perhaps she hated Angoulême even more? His views on the half-bloods made my father's look moderate, and she'd lived in his household for almost her entire life. Perhaps what my father had offered her was a chance for revenge?

Were there no limits to his power? Even now, after everything that had happened, the extent of my father's machinations still amazed me. He seemed able to predict every move that not only I, but everyone else made. He had a plan for every possible circumstance, and the strategies he had in place seemed endless. He had an endgame for every game, and the entire city, perhaps even the entire Isle dancing to his tune. If I didn't hate him so much, I'd almost admire his genius.

I watched the auction with glazed eyes, half my mind noting the half-bloods being marched across the stage and sold to the highest bidder, while the other half puzzled through my problems, all of which affected those who mattered to me most. No matter how I laid the puzzles out, I could not seem to solve a single one. No allegiance was certain. No motivation obvious. And at the center of everything was my father, and it seemed to me that in order to solve any of these puzzles, I needed to solve him.

And to do that, I would need help.

"I was wondering when you'd bother to visit. Seems to me you've been too busy learning to boil eggs and darn socks than to visit your poor old aunt."

"It is good to see you too," I said, waiting for the Duchesse Sylvie's guard – who had reluctantly announced me – to leave. "And you are neither old nor poor."

One of her eyebrows rose. "Dear, then?"

"Dear to me," I replied, bowing low. "But it would seem I have fallen out of your favor if you have knowingly left me to dine on the results of my scavengings. It is I who am the poor one."

"Still a smart mouth on you. Élise!" She shouted the half-blood's name at the top of her lungs, despite the fact the girl stood only a few paces away. I had been relieved to see she was well and that my aunt had taken her back under her wing after my ill-fated coup.

"Fetch His Highness something to eat. I'll have some of whatever you bring, so mind you only spit in his portion."

"Yes, Your Grace." Élise curtseyed deeply. "I'll ensure you have separate plates."

Apparently I had a few more apologies to make.

Élise hesitated before leaving. "Would Her Majesty…"

My aunt silently shook her head, waving her off. *Strange…*

I circled the chaise my mother sat upon so that I might see her better. Part of me wished that I had not. Mother's normally serene face was lined with tension, the muscles in her jaw clenched so tightly that they bulged. Her eyes fixed on some unseen thing, her pupils dilated wide and her brow furrowed. Her hands sat in her lap, kneading each other so hard that red marks rose and faded on her flesh. "Mother?" I asked hesitantly. I had never seen her like this, not ever.

If she heard me, she showed no sign of it.

"Mother?" I started to reach for her, but a coil of my aunt's magic caught my arm.

"Have a care, Tristan. She is of an ill temper."

Was this my doing? Was she upset with me? Of all those I'd worried about angering with my actions, my mother hadn't been one of them. Never mind that her mind was not entirely in this world, she had never been cross with me in all my life. And there had certainly been times I'd deserved it.

You attacked your own father, a voice whispered inside my head. *You almost killed him. She might have died, and your aunt along with her. What did you expect?*

Not this.

Cautiously, I moved into her line of sight, keeping my magic ready to defend myself if need be. She'd never tried to harm me, but that didn't mean she wouldn't. It certainly didn't mean she couldn't – weak women did not become queens of Trollus. "Mother?" Every inch of me singing with tension, I tentatively touched her shoulder.

She flinched, and I jerked my hand back, hardly noticing the jolt of pain in my wrist. *Please don't let it come to this,* I silently prayed. *Please don't let her have turned on me.*

"Tristan?" Her eyes focused on my face, all the tension and fury washing away in a flood. "You're here!"

"I am." I tried to smile, but my face felt incapable of it. "Are you angry with me?" The question came out before I even knew I was thinking it.

"Why should I be angry with you?" Her face managed to be guileless and unreadable at the same time.

My mouth went dry, and I struggled with what to say to her. "Because I have not been a good son."

Her eyes drifted, and not for the first time, I wondered what it was she saw. What she heard. What she thought. There was a rumor that my mother's mind was half through the door to Arcadia, and that it walked through the lands of endless summer, which lent her serenity. It was a pretty thought – far better than to believe she was just another victim of the inbreeding and iron slowly poisoning us all.

It also provided a potential explanation for how the fey were able to communicate with my aunt. It was they who provided the foretellings: though they could not come to this world, it did not mean they could not watch. I wondered what they had seen that made them believe my and Cécile's union could end the curse. I wished I could ask them, but even if I could, I knew they'd give me naught but riddles in response.

A shudder abruptly ran through my mother, and her face twisted back into the unfamiliar mask. "Leave me be."

"But…"

"Leave me be!" I recoiled from her shrill shriek, stumbling over my own boots as I backed away.

"Let her be, Tristan." My aunt's voice sounded weary. "Come and sit with me."

On numb feet, I made my way back around and sat down. The dozen mirrors in the room reflected an image that betrayed nothing of how I felt. "What has happened to her?" I demanded. "Who has done this to her? Was it me? Is this my fault?"

Aunt Sylvie regarded me for a long moment. "How is Cécile feeling?"

"Never mind Cécile," I snapped. "Tell me what is wrong with my mother!"

Her head tilted slightly, her eyes boring into mine. "I always liked her, you know. Little spitfire of a thing. Not one easily led, so I imagine she's not pleased about the yoke your father managed to place around her neck."

I opened my mouth to demand she answer my questions and to quit changing the subject, but realization dawned, and I clamped my teeth shut. "Physically, she is well," I finally said. "But these last days she has rarely been herself."

"Her will is at odds with his compulsion."

I nodded slightly. "A ceaseless tension."

"Do you feel it?" She asked the question as though it were the idle curiosity of one who had never been bonded.

"At its worst, it seems it is not her mind that suffers, but my own."

She sniffed. "How taxing."

And there it was – I had answered my own question. The emotions my mother was feeling were not her own – they were my father's. My mind skittered and tripped over the implications – not only was something angering him terribly, it was bad enough to affect my mother. For the first time since my imprisonment, I started to wonder if perhaps my father wasn't as in control of Trollus as I had thought.

"It is better than not knowing," I said, settling back more comfortably in the chair, pushing aside my concerns so that my mind was wholly on our double conversation. It was always this way with her – she would not tell me outright anything that would betray my father's confidence. I didn't know – and would never ask – if she did this out of courtesy to my mother or because he had forced a promise from her at some point in the past. Ultimately, it didn't really matter. The information I needed would be hidden in everything she did or said; it was up to me to extract it and put it together.

"Is it?" She tugged at the sleeve of her dress. "I should think that it would at times be worse – knowing how someone was feeling, but not the cause. You've been what now, three months parted?" She shook her head. "Strange how time manages to both accumulate and fade."

She did not know the full extent of what troubled my father, but whatever it was had been mounting since my incarceration. Time was of the essence.

"It seems like longer," I said. "I miss her terribly."

One eyebrow rose in acknowledgment of my uncharacteristic frankness, but she did not seem surprised. "Do you still wish to play?" She gestured at the Guerre boards sitting in their rack, but it was not the game of which she spoke.

I said nothing for long enough for my silence to be significant. "I *will* play," I said. "But only because there is no other worthy opponent."

"It's in your blood," she replied.

The four primary boards floated off their rack, the pieces lifting out of their boxes. They were new, I noticed, elaborately carved out of black onyx and white marble. Undoubtedly Reagan's work. "Shall we start where the game was left off?"

I nodded, my pulse quickening as I watched to see how she would place the players.

The pieces circled the boards. Kings and queens. Princes and princesses. Warriors, spies, tricksters, nobles, assassins, half-bloods, and tiny humans went round and round. "You play the white."

It wasn't a question, but I nodded for the benefit of those who spied on us.

White pieces rained down onto the carpet, accompanied by only a few black. "You're losing," she said.

"But I haven't lost."

"Not yet." Her voice was cool, eyes unreadable as the players settled into their places. The black players were thick on the board – not representing her, but my father. Only a handful of white remained. The king, four warriors, and one human. I stepped closer to look at them, recognizing my own face carved onto the king, and those of Marc, Anaïs, Victoria, Vincent, and Cécile. I touched the piece representing my wife, marble curls hanging down her back and an amused smile on her face. Instead of the cudgel usually wielded by a human piece, she held an open book out in front of her.

"Is the game laid correctly?"

"No," I said quietly. "I lost her." I pointed to the female warrior, hair blown back in an imagined wind, sword raised in defiance. The piece floated off and settled gently on the table, her onyx twin rising to settle itself amongst my father's players. "No." I snatched the piece off, my eyes searching until I found a female spy on the carpet. "Her." I set the piece next to the black king.

"Are you certain?"

"Yes. There is no doubt."

Crystal clinked, and two glasses of pale wine made their way over. I accepted mine, holding it absently with a filament of magic while I considered the board. Plucking a male half-blood off the carpet, I set it next to Vincent's piece. *Tips.*

"But you lost this one, no?" She lifted Marc's hooded warrior and started to set it aside.

"Not yet!" My voice was too loud, too heated. I forced myself to relax. "His fate is yet uncertain."

"Hmm." She sipped at her wine. "I will have to take your word on that."

Ice ran through me. Had something more happened to Marc that I didn't know about? If she knew for certain that he was lost, she wouldn't have let me keep the piece, but I did not like the doubt in her voice.

"We are in agreement?"

"We are." It all looked so hopeless, laid out like this. My father stood next to his queen and a tiny crowned prince, surrounded by all his other key players. I had only four allies, all of which were in some sort of jeopardy.

"A bleak position you are in, Your Highness," she said. "What are the options for the white?" Her tone was lecturing, as though she were still teaching me the game. But she wasn't. The question was legitimate.

"Political positioning." In the game, it was a risky move that involved maneuvering your king into a specific position among your opponent's players. If done correctly, you could replace every one of the players within range with your own pieces. But if you executed your strategy poorly, you could lose your most powerful player.

"Do you see a strategy that would have them in the position to listen?"

"Some of them." I moved Tips's piece to the second board.

"Only the weaker players would be in position to hear. It isn't enough to win."

I no longer saw the half-bloods as weak, especially as a group, but she was right. "Agreed." I cracked my neck from side to side. "Assassination."

"You have no assassin."

"True." I nudged my own piece. "But I have a player who could manage the task."

She sniffed. "Risky, and even if the black king fell, the crowned prince is still in play. You would not have won."

I looked at the tiny representation of Roland, half-imagining I could see the madness in his onyx gaze. "I know. It would take more than one assassination."

"Perhaps."

I turned my attention from the pieces to my aunt. She obviously thought there was another option, but nothing on her face told me what it was.

"You should enjoy your wine while we still have it," she said, sipping hers. "It will become a dear thing if circumstances continue as they have."

"A fair point." And an obvious one. What was she getting at? Even though it was tasteless to do so, I lifted the glass to my lips using my magic and took a long swallow. My wrists hurt like the fire of the damned after my scuffle with Marc, and even the weight of a wine glass was enough strain to make me feel sick. I did not care to admit it, but the manacles were starting to have a marked impact on me. The tips of my fingers had turned slightly blue and my hands grew stiffer by the day. If they remained on much longer, the damage might be permanent.

Taking another mouthful, I lowered the glass.

My aunt's lip curled and she clucked loudly. "The next thing will be elbows on the table at dinner. Your father would have a fit if he knew you were behaving so."

As if my father cared about my manners. What was she implying? That he'd be upset that the torture devices I wore under his orders were harming me? Surely not. If anything, he would be glad that they were finally having their desired effect. "I think it might please him."

"Do you now?" Her eyes flicked to the board, where all the answers lay. I walked in a circle around the four boards, examining my father's pieces instead of my own. Familiar and expected faces graced the players; expected at least, until I encountered my own. In onyx, I was still a prince, but the piece sat on a square rimmed with steel, which meant that it was not lost, but unplayable. There were several other pieces set up in a strategy to free it, but they were still many moves away from their goal. Leaning closer, I saw tiny grooves on the black prince's brow where a crown had once sat.

And might sit again.

If I was interpreting the game correctly, my father still considered me one of his players. He had strategies in place to return me to my rank as crown prince and heir, but only on his terms. The piece was onyx – it was his. To regain my position, I would have to be his puppet.

I stepped back to my place across from her. "That piece will not come back into play. I still maintain that the only strategy the white has left is to regain those players" – I gestured at the half-bloods – "with politics, and then maneuver to assassinate the black king."

"And it might work," she said, "if it did not play in so well to the third player's strategy."

Third player?

Two more boards lifted from the racks off to the side and came over to join our four. With them came another case of players, of which she selected several pieces to set on the boards, none of which were half-blood or human. The pieces were made of garnet, the red jewel glittering in the light.

Angoulême.

"Your new Guerre set is well made," I said, stalling. It was perfectly made for the purposes of this conversation, but it would have taken months for an artist to craft. How had she known it would be needed?

Setting my wine glass down on the table, I lifted the onyx spy representing Lessa-as-Anaïs, and set it down next to the garnet duke. My aunt nodded slightly, and Roland's onyx piece floated over to join them, garnet warriors lining up around him to show the piece as captured.

"Correct?" she asked.

"Yes," I said, but the memory of Roland walking with Lessa and Angoulême troubled me. He had certainly not been under guard, and he had not looked discontented with his position. Quite the opposite, in fact.

"Then if the white follows through with your suggested strategy..." Marble half-bloods replaced onyx and the black king toppled off the boards, his crown detaching to float over and replace the simple circlet on Roland's head. "The red now controls the black players, and they are all now aligned against the white."

Which put me in a worse position. I inhaled, then let the air out slowly. "The white could rescue the new black king."

"Are you sure?" Her face sagged, crinkling in a way I'd never seen before. The black crown lifted off the onyx Roland's head, and he floated away. His garnet twin lifted out of its case, coming to rest on the board, the black crown settling on his head.

"No," I whispered. "That cannot be. It cannot..."

The shattering of glass interrupted me, and what I'd been about to say ceased to matter as every mirror in the room exploded, the air filling with a million shards of razor-sharp glass and the sound of my mother's piercing scream.

CHAPTER 17
Cécile

The chaotic noise of the musicians warming up filtered through the door of my dressing room, adding to the air of tension found backstage before any performance. I was on tenterhooks too, but for different reasons: I was convinced Marie du Chastelier had some sort of association with Anushka, and that she knew who I was. That I was working for the troll king. That I was hunting her.

The idea had tickled at my mind that despite the lack of resemblance to the portrait I'd seen, that maybe she *was* Anushka. But the more I thought about it, the more I knew that couldn't be the case. Marie was too visible – she was the daughter of a minor but exceptionally wealthy noble family. Her birth and childhood were a matter of record, witnessed by many.

Anushka likely altered her appearance with hair dye, cosmetics, and magic, but she couldn't disguise herself as an infant or a child. She'd been in her twenties when she'd cursed the trolls, and though she'd found a way to stop herself from aging, she still remained a woman grown. It would have been necessary to disappear and start new lives continually, or those around her would notice that she never aged. Taking on roles where her face would be well known would have been impossible – the risk of being discovered by the trolls or persecuted for witchcraft would be too great.

Unless those who would persecute her were actually protecting her. I chewed my lip, thinking. If the Regent and his predecessors knew about the trolls, and I had my suspicions that they did, given they maintained the title of regent rather than adopting that of king, it was in their best interest to help Anushka keep the trolls contained. Which meant they'd do anything they could to keep her safe.

And yet Lady Marie had selected me to perform in her masque, had invited me into her home. Was it a matter of keeping her friends close, but her enemies closer? Or had the hunter become the hunted? Clichés, but my gut told me that at least one, if not both, were apt.

Sabine jerked hard on my hair. "Ow," I muttered, grimacing at her in the reflection of the mirror.

She was braiding my hair so that it would fit under the cheap brown wig of the minor role I played tonight, her blonde ringlets bouncing each time she jerked a strand of my hair into place. It was the first time I'd seen her since our confrontation over the potion she'd given Julian, and there was an uneasy silence between us. She kept her eyes fixed on the back of my head, refusing to look into the mirror lest she accidentally meet my gaze, and it gave me the opportunity to scrutinize her without her noticing.

She had changed.

I could not say whether it had happened while I was in Trollus or since we had come to Trianon, but my friend looked older. The full cheeks of childhood had melted away to reveal delicate features, and while she was not beautiful in the way Anaïs was, Sabine was the sort of pretty that appealed to men and women alike. Her blonde hair was always neatly coifed, and her skill with a needle and thread ensured that even with her limited budget, she was always well dressed. But that wasn't what was bothering me.

My brow furrowed as I juxtaposed my memory of the girl with the reality of the young woman standing behind me.

Sabine had always been a people-pleaser – she liked doing what made others happy, even if doing so caused her grief. During my recovery from my injury, she'd visited me every day, helping Gran take care of me and tolerating my moody silences with the patience of a saint. When I announced my intention to go to Trianon, she'd insisted on accompanying me despite the fact she'd never shown any interest in leaving the Hollow before.

"What?" Her voice was sharp, and I flinched. Apparently I wasn't the only angry one.

"I was thinking about how you've changed."

"I didn't have much choice." She jammed the wig down on my head, forcibly shoving wisps of red hair underneath it.

"What do you mean?"

She was quiet for a long time before speaking. "Everyone thought you were dead." There was a hint of unsteadiness in her voice. "Do you have any idea what it felt like knowing that my best friend had died because of me?"

I could not have been more blindsided if I'd been smacked in the face with a fence post. "What?" I spluttered. "That's nonsense. What could you have done?"

"Exactly." She was shaking. "I could have ridden with you. Or made you wait until Fred reached the Hollow. Something. Anything." Her words were choked, like she couldn't get enough air into her chest to get them out properly. "But instead I let my fears get in the way, and I lost you."

I felt sick to my stomach. Tristan had told me how badly she'd taken my disappearance, but I'd thought it was only grief. I'd never considered that she might blame herself for what happened. Worse yet, what she'd thought had been her decision hadn't been. I had assumed she'd refuse to ride with me and compelled her choice, even if I hadn't known what I'd been doing at the time. Even if I had died some accidental death, it wouldn't have been her fault. It would have been my own.

But would it have changed the course of events if she had ridden with me? Would her presence have kept Luc from kidnapping me and dragging me under the mountain? No,

I decided quickly. At best, he would have waited for another opportunity to snatch me away, and at worst... A vision of Sabine lying dead on the ground filled my eyes, and I blinked it away furiously. It was better that events had happened as they did. "Sabine, I didn't give you the cho..."

She held up a hand, cutting me off. "And then you came back, and I was happier than I'd ever been in my whole life. You were alive." She pressed her palm to her forehead as though to force down a memory. "And when you told me what had happened, I hated them so much. Hated them for what they had done to you, to your family. To me."

Her arms dropped to her sides. "But you didn't hate them. Quite the opposite, you were in love with one of them." Her eyes met mine in the mirror. "And I don't understand it, Cécile. They hurt you, took away everything from you, and even though you escaped, it seems like you'll never be free of them. They've stolen your future, robbed you of everything you had a passion for – and so how can you blame me for trying to at least liberate your heart from their clutches."

I didn't blame her. Nor could I quite explain to her that I'd gained as much as I'd lost while I was in Trollus, without making it seem that I valued one life over another. I *had* been hurt. I'd made sacrifices. But I did not feel bereft.

"I..."

A knock sounded on the door, and a second later, Julian leaned inside. "It's time," he said, his eyes shifting between us. Sabine pushed past him, and with a sigh, I followed.

My mother was waiting outside the door, her brow furrowed as she watched Sabine weave her way through the chaos of backstage. "That girl has a spirit for stirring up trouble," she said, turning to the two of us. "It may be time for her to find employment elsewhere."

My skin flushed hotly, and I jabbed a finger against my mother's chest. "Leave. Her. Alone."

Genevieve's eyes widened in surprise.

"I mean it, Mother," I said, glaring up at her. "If she leaves because of anything that you've done, I'll quit. And not just the company – I'll walk away from you, and I won't look back."

Not waiting for her to respond, I stormed through the corridors to the foyer. There were still a handful of young gentlemen watching the dancers finish their warm-up, but most had retreated to their boxes as the performance was about to begin. A few of the girls gave me curious glances, but no one troubled me.

Was it an idle threat, or had I meant what I said to my mother? I wasn't sure. My eyes flicked over the portraits of the famous women who had graced the stage and my stomach clenched at the idea of willingly giving up my dream of standing amongst them. I mouthed the names written on little plaques beneath the paintings in a silent plea for guidance. My mother's I ignored, but I paused when a familiar name passed my lips. *Lise Tautin*. My grandmother.

I touched the spot on my throat where the necklace she was pictured wearing usually hung, but it was in my dressing room. I had no memory of her – she'd gone missing when I was very young. Her hair was blonde and her eye color indistinct, yet I could see my mother in the arch of her cheeks and the coolness of her gaze. But I didn't have time to give it much thought before I was caught up in the exodus from the foyer. Finding my spot among the chorus, I watched as ballerinas dressed as harem girls exited the stage, their shoes making soft little thuds as they ran past me. It was time to go on.

Adjusting the basket across my elbow, I linked arms with one of the girls, and then we strolled out onto the set staged as an exotic spice market, warm with the heat of the audience rather than the desert sun. I sang and skipped and spun, the words rising instinctively to my lips as I matched the volume and sound of the other girls. The audience was a faceless blur, the colors brilliant, the lights bright as we set the scene.

Then my mother walked onto the stage, her voice dominating the theatre. She sang, and the rest of us were silent, relegated to the backdrop. The girls of the chorus tempted her with their wares, jewelry, spices, and all manners of delicacies. Then it was my turn. I stepped in front of her, holding out my basket of wax fruit for her to see. Still singing, she selected an apple, which I pretended to refuse payment for. As I retreated to the backdrop, something caught my eye.

A flash of light. Motion in the Regent's private box. No one was allowed to sit in there unless accompanied by the Regent or his family. *I'll be watching every move you make...* Marie's voice whispered across my thoughts. Was she alone, or was Anushka with her?

I wanted to stare, but that would mean breaking character, so I couldn't. One of the other girls caught my arm, spinning me away, our voices chorusing my mother's. My spine prickled. Even though I was in the middle of a stage, countless eyes upon me, I felt as though I were being stalked. It was all I could do to keep smiling, singing, and dancing, because I wanted to run. Every chance I had, I glanced toward the box, but it was too dark to say who sat within.

The scene ended, and we all danced offstage. I needed to go change my costume, but instead of going with the other girls, I hesitated in the darkness of the wings. My sweating fingers clutched at the basket handle, and I stepped as close to the stage as I dared go without being seen by the audience. The Regent's colors hung below the railing, as they always did. The box itself was dark, but a single gloved hand rested on the railing. Why were they watching me? What did they intend to do?

Fingers dug into my elbow, pulling me back. "What are you doing?" Sabine hissed. "You need to change."

I let her lead me backstage.

"You're sweating like a pig," she informed me, wrinkling her nose as she unfastened the merchant costume's buttons.

"Pigs don't sweat," I said absently, barely noticing as she rolled her eyes. I needed to see who was in those seats. I was certain it was *her*, but I needed to be sure. And if it was her, then what? Confront her? No. Whether I was right or wrong about her association with Anushka, that wouldn't go well for me.

"Did you mean it?"

Sabine was fussing with my skirt, only the top of her head visible. "Pardon?"

"What you said to your mother, did you mean it?"

There was an intensity in her voice that told me it wasn't an idle question. I bit down on the inside of my cheeks. Had I meant it? Part of me screamed that it didn't matter – there was the accomplice to a five hundred year-old murderer sitting in the wings watching me. But a bigger part of me refused to let fear rule my actions. "I meant it," I said, wiping my hands on my skirts. "If she fires you, I'll quit."

"But she's your mother." I could only see the top of her head, but I knew her well enough to know that she was shaken.

"Only when it's convenient for her," I said, catching one of her gold curls with my finger. "And you've always been my best friend. I understand why you did what you did, Sabine. But I need you to understand that I need to do this."

We stood quietly together for a moment before Sabine whispered, "You should go." She didn't look up, and I knew she wouldn't, so I left.

The rest of the performance was an exercise in torture. I made countless little mistakes, and my eyes kept drifting to the box. I felt on display. Vulnerable. But there was no denying the anticipation in my heart. I needed to see who was in those seats. I would have one good opportunity to get a glimpse when we took our bows at the end of the performance, one moment when I could stare out into the audience without reproach.

The wait seemed interminable, but finally the curtain fell with my mother feigning death in Julian's arms. I stood in the wings, my heart beating faster and faster. The trepidation wasn't all my own – something was happening to Tristan, but I couldn't think about him now. I would only have one chance, and I didn't dare miss it. The other girls were whispering, but I barely heard them. The audience was cheering, shouting my mother's name. They were on their feet. The other girls of the chorus ran forward, and I went with them. Would it be her I saw? Did I want it to be?

Stopping in my appointed spot, I took the hands of the girls to either side and dropped into a deep curtsey. We rose and stepped back. I looked up.

The Regent's box was empty. Whoever had been there was gone.

CHAPTER 18
Tristan

The Guerre boards dropped to the ground, and I threw up a shield to block the flying glass. My aunt did the same, attempting to protect my mother, but it was a wasted effort. The magic that had shattered the mirrors was stronger, and the outward force coming from my mother tossed aside my aunt's magic with ease. Razor-sharp shards cut into my mother's skin and shredded her clothes, but she barely seemed to notice. Her face was slick with blood and contorted with irrational fury, the like of which I had only seen before on Roland. The comparison terrified me, because it meant that she couldn't be reasoned with. Only force would stop her.

Motion in my peripheral vision caught my attention. Élise stood in the open doorway, a tray of food lying in disarray at her feet. "Move!" I shouted, but it was too late. My mother had already rounded on her, eyes seeing yet unseeing.

I leapt between the two, the blow directed at the half-blood girl making my shield quake and sending me staggering back. I collided with Élise, and both of us tumbled into the hallway. A second later, another blow impacted the walls, only the thousand years of magic layering them keeping everything from collapsing down on top of us.

I clambered to my feet, hauling Élise up with me. "Run," I ordered her. "Find my father and tell him what's happening."

"What are you going to do?"

"I'm going to stop her."

I grimly wrapped bands of power around the manacles on my wrists, and before I could lose my nerve, jerked them apart. The pain almost drove me to my knees, but with it came relief as my magic surged, no longer limited by the toxic metal. Steeling myself, I stepped back into the room.

The air was thick with dust and smoke, but it was still possible to see the chaos my mother had enacted upon the room. Everything was destroyed, furniture little more than splinters, paintings and tapestries ablaze. The ceiling had partially caved in to reveal the dark cavernous space hanging above the city. I searched the room for my aunt's light, but there was only the orange glow of fire. My eyes stung, and I coughed on the thickening smoke.

The blow came sharp and sudden, but I was ready for it. Again and again she struck; and through the haze, I caught sight of her coming toward me. My aunt hung limply from her back, and I prayed she was only unconscious, the alternative too terrible to contemplate.

"Mother!" I had to shout over the exploding collisions of our magic. "It's Tristan."

But she didn't seem to hear or recognize me, her mind wholly concerned with inflicting wrath and ruin. The mere act of protecting myself from her assault was exhausting, and I did not see how it would be possible for me to cut her off from her magic. She was too strong, and she was wasting no power on trying to protect herself, forcing me to deflect the collapsing rubble away from both of us. All she cared about was destroying me, and that she might lose her own life in the process didn't seem to matter.

I needed my father's help, and I needed it soon – or she was going to pull the entire palace down. And without the walls to contain her, there was the very real chance she might damage the magic of the tree and put all of Trollus in danger. If she did, then I'd be forced to hurt her to stop her, and that I didn't want to do.

Holding her back was akin to containing a storm. Magic ceaselessly buffeted and slammed up against me, employing no strategy, only mindless force. Smoke and heat blew into my face, rubble piling up beneath my feet and threatening to trip me up. I didn't know how to stop her. If it had been a duel, I could have killed her easily, but stopping her without hurting her seemed impossible. If I hit her too hard, I might harm her, but if I didn't hit her hard enough, it would only infuriate her more. All I could think of was keeping her focus on trying to hurt me and minimizing what collateral damage I could.

Please hurry. I couldn't remember the last time I'd desired my father's presence, but I needed him now. He'd know what to do.

The walls of the adjoining rooms fell in around us, and the floor beneath my feet began to shake. The whole wing of the palace was going to collapse.

"Matilde!"

My mother's head jerked up at the sound of my father's voice, and as abruptly as it had begun, it was over. She looked around in bewilderment, seemingly unable to comprehend that she had been the cause of the destruction. "What has happened?"

"Move." My father shoved me aside, striding through the rubble. With the sleeve of his coat, he wiped the blood off her face, his expression surprisingly anxious. "Are you hurt, darling?"

She shook her head, tears turning pink as they ran down her cheeks. "I was so angry. So angry." She pressed one hand to her forehead, and my heart ached watching her struggle to remember, her shoulders beginning to shake as the little pieces fit themselves together. "Tristan?" She choked out my name.

"He's fine." My father turned his head to look at me as though to prove to himself that I was unharmed. "He's fine," he repeated again, pulling her close. "Sylvie?"

"I was looking to redecorate anyway," my aunt replied. Her words might have been blasé, but not even my mother missed the tremble in her voice.

She broke into racking sobs, and collapsed against my

father's chest. A shimmer of magic appeared around my aunt as she walled herself off from them. I should have left or done the same, but instead I sat down in the rubble and dust, watching my parents.

"I'm sorry, love. This was not your fault – it was mine." He picked bits of broken rock out of her hair, tried fruitlessly to smooth away the dust, before resting his cheek against the top of her head. "I'm so sorry to have put you through this. I will make everything right."

And he was sorry, I realized. He was always kind to my mother, but never before had I seen any proof that he might actually care for her. That he might even love her, and that maybe I wasn't entirely the product of politics and social maneuvering. I held my breath, afraid that even that tiny motion might draw attention to me and disrupt what I was witnessing. I didn't want it to end, because seeing proof that he cared for my mother meant there was a chance he cared something for me.

Metal clinked against metal. Turning my head, I saw that my ruined manacles had risen from the rubble and even now hovered in the air. Heat radiated from them, magic melting and reforming the metal until they were whole again. They settled on the ground, and when I looked up, he was staring at me, silver eyes unreadable. "The next time I see you, those had better be back on or I'll put four more in their place." Without another word, he took my mother's arm and helped her through the debris and out of sight.

False, black, painful hope.

I rested my forehead on my knees, trying to shove away the old hurts behind their stone walls.

"Your Highness?" It was Élise's voice, quiet and tentative. I didn't move – it seemed like more effort than I could manage.

"Tristan?" A hand touched my shoulder.

Part of me wanted to shrug it off, to tell Élise, all the half-bloods, and everyone else in this cursed city to deal with their own problems. Except that what I'd told my aunt had been true – there was no one but me who could credibly oppose my father. And not just my father, but Angoulême.

I considered the clues my aunt had provided. The black-hearted Duke had control over my younger brother – had somehow managed to trick Roland into revealing his true name to him. Now that the idea was in my head, it seemed so obvious. *He won't do anything I don't want him to.* The words Angoulême had said to me at the auction repeated in my head, as well as those that had gone unspoken: *He will do everything I tell him to do.* If my father died tomorrow, Roland might be the one crowned king, but it would be Angoulême who ruled.

Whether I willed it or not, I had to play this game.

"What happened to anger Her Majesty?" Élise's voice cut through my thoughts.

"To her? Nothing." I lifted my head to meet her gaze. "That was my father's rage you witnessed, so the question we need to ask is what angered him? Or who?"

"We?" She pulled her hand away from my shoulder. I didn't say anything, seeing in her distant expression that she'd addressed the question not to me, but to herself. She was quiet for a long time before speaking. "I felt what you did. You can't tell me what to do any longer."

"Yes, I can," I said. "Only now it's your choice whether or not to listen. Will you?"

She didn't hesitate. "I will."

I expelled the breath I hadn't realized I was holding. Apparently her allegiance mattered more to me than I had realized. We'd known each other a long time, and there was a reason I'd chosen her and Zoé to watch over Cécile. They were loyal and brave to a fault.

As if reading my mind, she asked, "How is she?"

"Well enough, for now." I stared at the holes in my wrists, the blood running freely. "But she made a promise to my father to do whatever was necessary to find Anushka, and we all got a little demonstration just now of how thin his patience is running."

"Then she's in danger?"

I nodded. "We're all in danger. Cécile, you, me. Everyone. And I'd bet all the gold left in Forsaken Mountain that it's going to get much worse before it gets better."

"Will it get better?" Her head drooped, and a lock of dark hair fell across her face. "There are times when it all seems so hopeless."

How well did I know that feeling.

"I don't know," I admitted. "It's possible that no matter how hard we fight that we will still lose. But..." I stared out at the city through the broken walls of my home, the jagged pieces of marble rising up like some great monster's teeth. "I do know that if we do nothing, our defeat won't be just a possibility, it will be a certainty."

Élise lifted her chin and pushed back her hair. "Then we fight."

"We fight," I echoed, my eyes picking up the movements of those who had crept back to see what sort of damage my mother had inflicted. This conversation could not go on much longer.

"What about Cécile?" Élise lowered her voice, having noticed our watchers as well.

"She's far from powerless, and if anyone can discover a way to find Anushka, it will be her." My stomach clenched at the words, and I desperately wished keeping her safe were a possibility. Only I knew that even if it were, Cécile would never stand for being kept out of danger while her friends were in the thick of it. "We have to trust that she will hold up her end, and focus on holding up ours."

"Let her fight the human problem while we combat ours?"

I gave her a tight smile. "Exactly."

A half-dozen of my father's guards were coming through the rubble, their expressions grim. Élise saw them too. "The King was already on his way to find your mother when I encountered him, but I'm certain he was coming from his study."

"We need to find out who he was with," I murmured.

"Or if he received a letter. He does not usually allow anyone in his private chambers."

"A valid point." We were running out of time. "Can you do it?"

"I can try." She started to rise, wisely deciding she should be away before the guards were upon us.

"Will you do something for me, Élise?" I asked before she could go. At her nod, I reached down to pick up the still warm manacles lying in the rubble. I gave her a forced smile. "You can consider it revenge for what I did to you and your sister."

She recoiled back a pace. "Even if I desired revenge upon you, this wouldn't be it."

"A favor, then?" My bare hands began to itch where they touched the metal, and it took a concerted effort not to drop them. "Because if you don't do it, one of them will. And I daresay, they won't be half as gentle about it."

Élise clenched her teeth and squeezed her eyes shut. "Fine. I already know what I want from you in exchange."

"Anything."

"When you are king, I want you to change the laws so that half-bloods can be bonded. To… to anyone they choose."

Such a small request, in the scheme of things, but when one had lived a life enslaved, even small victories mattered. "If I make it that far, I will see it done."

"Thank you." She took the manacles from my hands. "Are you ready?"

I laughed. "No." But I held out my arms anyway. My father had made his move, and soon, I would make mine.

Let the games begin.

CHAPTER 19
Cécile

Fleur's hooves made little crunching sounds as they punched through the ice-coated puddles of the muddy streets. I'd sneaked silently out of the house at dawn, running all the way to the stables to meet Chris.

Now, I was glad that I'd let him convince me go by horse to see Catherine that morning. Pigalle was always dangerous, but it felt even more so now that I was caught between opposing forces, both of whom were watching me closely via their agents. The King's messenger, I knew, would be keeping tabs on my progress; but now that I was nearly certain that Marie was in league with Anushka, I expected her to try to stymie me at every turn. Which begged the question: Why hadn't she tried to kill me yet? Unfortunately, even a night of lying awake thinking had yielded no answers.

Sliding off Fleur's back once we reached Catherine's shop, I looked up at Chris. "You'll be back in an hour?"

He nodded. "Don't even think of leaving without me." Wheeling the mare around, he started down the street at a brisk canter. I watched him ride out of sight, then I knocked once and entered.

"I was wondering when you'd show up." Reaching past me, Catherine turned the bolt. "Let's not have a repeat of last time."

I followed after her, careful not to step on the little dog who insisted on sniffing the hem of my skirt. "You're much quieter this time," I said to him, patting his head.

"He only barks at strangers." Catherine moved silently through her shop, collecting bits of herb, bark, and bone in a plain cooking pot. Holding a bit of kindling to the fire, she carried all the materials to the front of the shop. Sitting on the floor with the pot on her knees, Catherine closed her eyes, mouthing a series of words. Then she dropped the flaming bit of wood into the mixture. Green fire flared up into the air, and she repeated the words one last time.

"What was that spell?" I asked.

Her eyes flicked up to mine. "Something to repel. Anyone who comes near will believe he smells something unbearably repugnant – the bone was from a skunk. It won't drive away anyone very determined, but neither will it raise the suspicion of magic."

I wanted to ask her to teach it to me – to fill my head with all these little spells that I might one day find myself needing. But there were more important questions that needed answering.

She puttered around the shop, adjusting bottles and arranging papers. She was nervous, I thought, but who wouldn't be in her situation? I was half-surprised she hadn't fled the city, but then again, maybe she couldn't afford to. Judging from the threadbare hem of her dress – the same she wore the last time we met – she had little money to spare. This shop and its contents might well be all she had, and giving that up, even if her life was at risk, was no small thing.

"Which side did you inherit from?"

I jumped, Catherine's voice startling me. "Pardon?"

She raised one eyebrow, then picked up her dog. "Your affinity with the earth's power – it's an inherited condition."

"I know…" I pressed fingers lightly against the long scar running down my ribs. "My grandmother. But she isn't…" I searched for a word, "… practicing. She's a healer of sorts, but she only uses plants, herbs, and the like. She taught me the basics."

"Then she is practicing."

"Really, it's a shame my sister wasn't the one who inherited the gift," I babbled. "She's much more interested in such things."

"It tends to fall to only one a generation," Catherine replied. Souris lifted his head, jumped to the ground, and hurried into the back. She watched him go, then asked, "What about your mother?"

"Oh, Gran is my father's mother," I corrected, following with a burst of nervous laughter. "My mother... No, my mother isn't a witch. At least not in the sense of magic." I laughed again, feeling unable to suppress it, the sound filling the room. "I didn't mean that. She can be dreadful sometimes, but she isn't..." I sucked in a deep breath and counted to five. "The magic comes from my grandmother."

Catherine's dark eyes seemed to bore into me. "You've a very loud voice."

I winced, feeling the skin across my chest and cheeks burn. "Sorry. Hazard of my profession." Apparently she wasn't the only one who was nervous.

"Indeed." She sat across from me at the table. "Why don't you go to her with your questions?"

I bit at my lip, praying I appeared more confident than I felt. "Because she doesn't know anything about the sort of magic I'm interested in."

"What sort of magic is that?" Her foot made a little drumming noise against the wooden floorboards.

"Blood magic."

Her foot stopped tapping.

"Curses, in particular," I added, before I lost my nerve.

"What makes you think I know anything about such things." She extracted a bottle of green liquid from her pocket and took several mouthfuls.

I lifted one shoulder and let it fall. "It's a long way from the Regent's court to Pigalle."

A muscle in her cheek twitched. "Far enough that perhaps I learned my lesson not to dabble in such things." It was as much admission as I was going to get that she was familiar with the dark arts.

"I'm not interested in casting a curse," I said. "I'm interested in breaking one."

The muscle in her cheek twitched again, but otherwise, she looked unsurprised at my question. "You can't," she said, then sighed. "Although that isn't precisely true. You can end a curse by ending the life of the witch whose will binds it."

"There is no other way?"

She hesitated for a heartbeat. "No. None."

Her reluctance made me feel uneasy. She was withholding information. "Why?"

Catherine took another mouthful from her bottle, refusing to look me in the eye. "A curse is an act of will, a desire, which is cemented by the magic of a sacrifice. It will continue until she no longer wills it, or until she dies."

I straightened in my chair. "Does one need a name to curse someone?"

She huffed out a heavy breath. "I should think the witch would know the name of the individual she was cursing, but I suppose it isn't necessary. Its only purpose is to create a focus."

I considered her words for a moment. "So the witch who cast the curse is capable of breaking it?"

Another hesitation. "If she no longer willed it, then it would cease to be."

I held my breath. There was something she wasn't telling me. I could not say exactly how, but I felt in my gut that the other woman was holding information back. But why? What cause or care could she have whether I tried to break a curse that, for all she knew, had naught to do with her. Unless...

Her foot tapping resumed. The air in the shop was cool, but tiny beads of sweat were forming on her forehead.

"That's unfortunate," I said. "But perhaps there is something else you might help me with."

"Oh?" Her eyes flicked to the door, then back to me.

"That spell you used to contact me through the fire, can you teach it to me?"

She settled into the chair. "That is a simple spell – all you really need is something of the person you wish to contact and fire on both ends. There are some plants you can put in the fire to fuel the magic, but a witch of even moderate ability has no real need of them."

"What do you mean, something of them?"

Catherine shrugged. "A strand of hair. A fingernail. Blood." Her eyes met mine. "It sometimes works if you have a possession belonging to the person. Something important. But not always."

My heart sank. I most certainly had nothing *of* Tristan's. I didn't even have anything that belonged to him. I sighed – the notion that I might be able to contact him had been foolish anyway. He wasn't human – the earth's magic didn't know him. What's more, there was no fire in Trollus.

But I did have Anushka's grimoire. If I used it to contact her, I'd see her face. What more proof would I need? "What's the incantation?" I asked.

She laughed, her tone mocking and amused. "You really know nothing, do you?"

My cheeks burned. "I don't recall saying otherwise."

"I suppose not." She pursed her lips. "The incantation – what you say – matters not. What matters is that your thoughts are focused on what you desire to occur. Some find it easier to focus their minds by speaking words. By making a ritual of the spell. Some don't."

"I see. And after you focus your thoughts, you…"

"Consign the hair, fingernail, or whatever it is you are using to the flames."

I winced. That was going to be problematic. I'd only have one chance, and what if she wasn't near a fire? Then I'd have lost her grimoire for nothing.

"Magic requires something to be given up," Catherine said, as though reading my thoughts. "Only the dark arts require nothing from the practitioner, because blood magic is all about taking that which is not freely given. That's why using blood for even one spell is a slippery slope." Her hand slipped unconsciously into her pocket to retrieve the bottle of absinthe. "It always catches up to you in the end."

As it had obviously caught up with her. Nibbling on the tip of one of my curls, I considered how to phrase my next question. "I've heard that you were once Lady Marie's maid."

Catherine's face smoothed into the expressionless mask of someone trying to hide a reaction. "That's no great secret."

"Were you dismissed because she discovered you were a witch?"

She barked out a laugh. "Hardly. That was half the reason I was in her employ."

I blinked, surprised to have my suspicions so easily confirmed. The Regent, or at the very least, Lady Marie, was apparently not as opposed to witchcraft as the laws would suggest. Which only cemented my belief that she was helping Anushka hide from the trolls. "I'm performing at her solstice party," I said. "She's shown an interest in me, and I was starting to become concerned that it was because she knew…" I trailed off when Catherine blanched.

"You must go now." She leapt to her feet, knocking her chair onto its back.

"But I've only just arrived. You said you'd help me."

"That was before I knew Marie was watching you." Snatching hold of my arm, she hauled me with surprising strength to the front of the shop. "Don't come back."

"What is wrong?" I demanded, unwilling to leave with so many questions left unanswered. "What happened to cause her to turn on you?"

"I meddled in that which I should not," she said, twisting the bolt and shoving me out before the door was half open. "I will not make the same mistake twice."

The door slammed in my face, and I stood staring at it like a fool, trying to think of what I should do.

"Well, that didn't go well."

I whirled around in time to see Chris stepping out from the narrow space between the two buildings. "You were listening."

He had the decency to look embarrassed. "The back door was unlocked."

"Well, I suppose that saves me having to explain our conversation." I followed him over to where Fleur was tethered.

"Catherine's not going to help you, Cécile. She's afraid."

"I know." I squinted up at the sky, judging the time. "But she's got answers, so I'm going to have to think of a way to get her to talk."

"Maybe not." He held out his hand, revealing a mat of hair pinched between his fingers. "You'd think she'd know better than to leave a hairbrush laying around."

"Christophe Girard, you are brilliant," I breathed, taking the hair from him and carefully tucking it away in my pocket, mentally flipping through Anushka's grimoire as I thought of ways to use it.

Glancing up, I saw that Chris's face was tight and he was studiously examining his boots. "What's wrong?"

"I took something else."

I raised one eyebrow. "What else could you possibly have taken? I was in there for only a few minutes."

He grimaced. "I took it before. When we were hiding in the cellar, I saw those books sitting on the table and I took one."

My other eyebrow rose to join its mate. "You stole it?"

"I was going to put it back – that was the reason I snuck in. But then I heard her talking and I knew she wasn't going to help, so…"

"So you kept it?" I struggled and failed to keep the eagerness from my voice. Part of me was annoyed that he hadn't told me he'd taken it in the first place, but a larger part knew he wouldn't have kept it from me without good reason.

"Here." He extracted a small, well-worn book from inside his coat. "I couldn't read much of it, but I recognized enough to know that it's a nasty bit of work."

Glancing surreptitiously around, I flipped through the pages.

It was full of spells, blood magic. And the instructions were both graphic and specific. I swallowed hard, remembering what Catherine had said about this sort of magic: *Using blood for even one spell can put any woman on a slippery slope, and – it always catches up to you in the end.* I'd heard her warning, but when my eyes landed on a spell on a particularly dog-eared page, I knew I was going to disregard it.

CHAPTER 20
Tristan

"So these are them?" Tips unfolded my plans across the scarred table, his face tightening as he noted the substantial differences between them and what my father had provided. I could see he was calculating the wasted months of work, and the effort that would be needed to pull down all the stone and begin anew. The emotional toll it would have on those who had already endured much loss.

"What's that?" he asked, pointing at a red smear across a series of calculations.

I leaned forward. "Jam. Raspberry, if I recall correctly."

Tips snorted. "The plans your father gave us didn't have any food stains."

I shrugged. "That should have been your first clue they were fake."

He stared at them for a long time, slowly flipping through the large pages of parchment as though he were memorizing every last detail. I let him take his time, leaning back on the rough chair and closing my eyes. I was tired. Sleep had eluded me last night, making it three nights in a row that I'd gone without rest, and I needed it. Badly. My mind felt fuzzy, and the coming days would be unforgiving of any mistakes.

Except every time I closed my eyes, I was plagued by the disasters that had happened. That could happen. My mother trying to kill me, my aunt hanging unconscious from her back. The feral expression I'd last seen on Marc's face, and my fear that madness would take him.

And Cécile.

My imagination was a ferocious thing, and I could well imagine the worst of disasters befalling her, all with me powerless to do anything to help. I had no way of discovering how she fared or what she was doing. No humans were allowed past the River Road gates, so even if my contacts had information, I had no way to meet with them. No way to pass a message to Cécile, either.

But worse were the other thoughts. They were daydreams, I supposed, although I tortured myself with them day or night. Unrealistic fantasies of a future where Cécile and I actually had a chance. Where she was with me every night. Where she was mine in all ways and all things. Where I could be the man she deserved. How could I possibly sleep when there was a chance to remember the smell of her hair? The clear blue of her eyes when she looked up at me. The way she arched her neck when I kissed her throat. I'd suffer a thousand sleepless nights to be lost in those waking dreams.

"So what's the plan?" Tips said, interrupting my thoughts. "Do we make it known that we've been duped? Another uprising? We aren't prepared for it, but when this comes out, it might happen whether we like it or not."

Opening my eyes, I tipped my chair forward and carefully set my arms on the table. Blood was seeping through the cloth I'd wrapped around the metal, and I could faintly hear the drip, drip of droplets landing on the wood. "I think we've something else to discuss first."

He rolled up my plans and set them aside. "You're referring to when I lied about my true name before you sent us all off to be slaughtered."

"Less about the name and more about the lie," I replied. "Specifically, how is it possible you *can?*"

Tips rolled his shoulders and shifted on his chair. "It's a fair bit harder than speaking the truth, but it can be done. Gets a bit easier with practice."

"Explain."

His eyes flicked to mine, then away again. "It's like when you've got something that needs saying, but you don't want to say it for whatever reason. Throat gets tight, tongue gets dry, and it seems like your whole body is fighting to keep the words inside. But you force them out anyway."

I thought about his analogy and nodded. "Can everyone with human blood do it, or only..." I tried to think of a polite way to phrase the thought, "Those whose blood is primarily human?"

He snorted softly and shook his head. "Those like me, you mean?"

"Yes." There was no point to beating around the bush.

"It's hard to know," he said, resting his elbows on the table. "It ain't something that's discussed much. But I do know a few who are mostly troll who can lie through their teeth, and a few with less magic than me who couldn't bend the truth to save their lives." He hesitated for a long moment. "I think the potential to lie comes with the human blood, but that it's something else that makes a half-blood actually capable of doing it."

"Willpower?" I suggested.

"Might be." He sighed. "Or just plain obstinacy. When we catch a young one lying, we all but beat the desire to do it ever again out of their skulls. It's a dangerous game to play, and if they got caught by the wrong person, it wouldn't be just their life on the line, it would be the lives of every half-blood. It's our greatest secret – we've killed our own just to keep it from coming out. Full-blooded bastards would all but shit bricks if they found out we'd been lying to their faces all these long years." He winced. "Not that I mean you..."

I waved him off. "You're right. It's an advantage you have over us, and there isn't a troll in the city who wouldn't begrudge that fact." I cracked my neck from side to side, considering what he'd told me. "Lady Anaïs is dead," I finally said. "She was killed helping me subdue my father the night I broke Cécile out of Trollus."

Tips's eyes widened. "That ain't possible. I've seen her since with my own two eyes!"

"Not her," I said. "Someone pretending to be her. I wasn't certain how the impostor was managing it until your little slip, but now I know for certain it's a half-blood wearing Anaïs's face."

Tips's breath hissed out between his teeth. "Only one who could manage it," he said. "And that's your sister."

"Half-sister," I muttered, "But yes. Lessa. She's powerful enough, and she lived in the same household as Anaïs for all of her life until Cécile tricked Damia into giving her to my father. And no one notices the presence or absence of a half-blood servant, no matter how powerful. Add in her ability to lie, and she's the perfect person to take over Anaïs's life. So perfect, it almost seems planned." A sick feeling rose in my stomach the moment the words came out. "He knows."

"What? Who?"

"My father," I said, my voice every bit as grim as I felt. "He knows you can lie. Your secret isn't a secret, at least not from him. I'd bet my life on it."

Tips blanched. "That can't be possible. He'd never stand for it if he knew. Your father already hates us – if he'd found out half-bloods could lie, we'd all be dead by now."

"He doesn't hate you," I said absently, staring at the wall behind Tips. "Hate is something he reserves for those with whom he has personal grievances. And he'd never act so impulsively if he thought he could put the information to use." A plan was beginning to form in my head. It was risky and rash, nothing I would ever have tried in the past, but it might just work.

"I'm afraid to ask," Tips muttered.

"Think of it this way," I said. "He knows you can lie to him, but you don't know that he knows. Not only can he use it against you, he can use you against his enemies by taking advantage of the fact that *they* don't know either."

Tips raised both eyebrows, giving me a dour look. "This is why I hate dealing with the aristocracy – you're all mad."

I grinned. "It's brilliant."

"Right."

I leaned forward. "Have you told anyone I caught you out?"

Tips winced. "Not yet. Haven't found the courage to tell them I slipped up."

"Excellent." I would've clapped my hands together if they didn't hurt so much. "I've an idea. It's more than a bit mad, and if it goes poorly, we might both lose our heads. But I think it'll work."

"And I must be mad to listen to you, but I'm going to anyway." Tips leaned on the table, his eyes bright. "Tell me what you've got in mind."

CHAPTER 21
Cécile

My mother wandered past me to look out the window, leaving a cloud of perfume in her wake. "You will stay in tonight, I trust," she said, letting the drapes fall back into place.

"I will," I said. "I think a cup of tea and a book are what I need." I coughed quietly. "My throat has been a bit sore, and I don't care to overdo it."

She frowned at me. "I hope you aren't coming down with something – you've seen how much work the Regent's masque will be."

"I'm sure it's nothing." I glanced at the clock. I'd told Chris to come to the back door at seven, but hopefully he'd be wise enough to ensure my mother was actually gone before he knocked. "Where did you say you were going?" I asked, looking blindly at the book in my lap.

"The Marquis is accompanying me to the palace for my performance. After that, we'll have to see. It seems anyone who is anyone is having a party tonight."

"Seems like poor planning on their parts," I muttered. I really didn't care about my mother's social schedule – what I cared about was her leaving so I'd have the privacy to try this spell.

A knock sounded at the door. "That will be my carriage." She picked up her thick velvet cloak. "I hope you enjoy your rest, darling. I will be late, if I'm home at all." Bending down she kissed my forehead, then stroked my cheek. "There is no one more important to me than you, Cécile. I hope you know that."

My traitorous heart warmed, then I squashed the feeling away, reminding myself that the last time she'd expressed herself this way, she'd been in the process of drugging me. "Good luck tonight, mother."

I waited until I was certain she was gone, then I threw off the robe covering my dress and hurried to the back door. Chris was waiting, a roll of parchment in one hand and a caged chicken in the other. "She's gone?" he asked.

I nodded. "Come in before the neighbors see you."

Once he was inside, we set to hurrying about the house closing all the curtains. I was taking no chances that someone might see us – at best, I'd be exiled from the city. And at worst... the smoke coming from the fireplace took on an ominous feel.

"Where do you want to do this?" Chris asked, holding up the cage and eyeing the chicken. "It will be messy."

I grimaced. "The kitchen would be the best, I suppose."

Following my terse instructions, we set up all of my supplies on the kitchen floor, along with a bucket and rags to clean up what would be a large amount of blood. I took the map Chris had brought and laid it out flat, then carefully began committing it to memory as well as I could.

"What are you doing?" Chris whispered.

"The map needs to be reflected in my mind's eye," I said. "Otherwise this won't work."

Catherine had devised the spell I intended to use to find missing loved ones. It was a noble cause, unlike my own, but cause meant little when it came to the effectiveness of the spell. All I really needed was a possession belonging to the missing, in this case, Anushka's grimoire, a map, and the raw power of a death. So little, and yet, so much.

When I was comfortable I could accurately visualize the map, I set a basin between it and me. Then I opened the chicken's cage and pulled her out. She clucked quietly in my arms, used to being handled. Chris handed me a knife, and I swallowed a wave of nausea. "I'm not sure I can do this."

"You've killed chickens before, Cécile. Lots of them." Chris's words were steady, but his face was ghostly pale.

"For eating," I muttered. "Not for... this." I petted the hen on her head and she clucked at me. No amount of farm living could prepare me for this.

"I could pluck her after and we could, umm, roast her up?"

I gagged and shook my head. The idea of eating my ritual sacrifice was too much.

"Or, or, I could pluck her, and give her to someone who needs the food." He nodded encouragingly at me.

"Yes," I said, swallowing down what had threatened to rise up. "We can do that."

My grip on the knife was slick with sweat. The chicken started to struggle in my grip, as though sensing my tension. "I can't hold her steady," I muttered, the knife and the chicken sliding in my grasp.

"Just get it over with," Chris said. "Do it now."

"I can't, I can't," I said, struggling to get the angle right. My hands knew what they were doing, but my mind was at war with itself. Walking down this path would change everything for me. It would change who I was.

Do it! The voice in my head was full of wicked glee. Was it me, or was it the King?

"I'm sorry." The words came out in a rush as I sliced the knife across the chicken's neck. Blood splattered everywhere, adding to the wetness of tears already dripping down my cheeks. I held the dying creature over the basin with shaking hands, letting the blood flow even as power flooded into me, then handed her to Chris.

Retrieving the candle, I held the flame to the crimson contents of the basin, part of me praying that it would go out and the spell would fail, even as I knew it wouldn't. Fire leapt up in the bowl and we both jerked back. I could feel magic rising all around us, but it had a dark, malignant edge to it. What I was doing was a corruption of the earth's power. What I was doing was evil.

"I can't go back," I whispered. And before I could lose my nerve, I plunged my hand into the flaming mixture. It was hot, but it didn't burn. Slowly, I lifted my hand from the basin, flames licking out from my fingers. With the grimoire in my free hand, I held my bloody hand over the map and closed my eyes, visualizing the city.

"Tell me where Anushka is," I said loudly, and focused my thoughts. I felt power gush from my fingers, filling the air with heat. The blood splattered loudly against the paper, but I kept my focus. "Tell me where Anushka is." The magic surged, and I smelled a faint hint of smoke, then it was over.

I opened my eyes. Chris was on the far side of the kitchen, his back against a cupboard. He stared at me with wild eyes, the dead chicken clutched to his chest. "Did it work?" His words were shaky, and I could tell he didn't want to come closer. He was afraid of me. I was afraid of myself.

Wiping my hand on my stained dress, I picked up the candle and leaned over to look at the map.

There were tiny burn marks on the parchment, barely more than pinpricks. But where I had expected one, there were nineteen. "I don't think it worked," I said, my breath coming in escalating pants as I stared at the blood-spattered map. "It didn't work." I slammed my fist into the floor, skinning my knuckles. "How could it not have worked?"

Chris was at my side in an instant, his eyes raking over the results of the spell. "Bloody stones and sky," he swore. "All that for nothing!"

"What am I doing? What have I become?" I sobbed, unable to contain the flood of disappointment and disgust I felt toward myself. "How did I become a chicken-killing practitioner of the dark arts? An agent for a king set on conquering the whole world? How did I get here? How did I become so evil?" The questions poured out of my mouth until the need to breathe silenced them.

"You're not evil, Cécile," Chris said softly, patting me on the shoulder.

"Then why am I doing this?" I demanded.

"Because you love Tristan," he said. "And you couldn't stand to see him hurt."

"That doesn't make it right."

"No." He sighed heavily. "It doesn't make it right, but I'm not sure that it's entirely wrong either." He moved in front of me so that we could see each other's faces. "I'm just a farmer with a good eye for horses. I'm not a scholar or a philosopher, or any of those sorts, but if you ask me, most people aren't tough enough to put a bunch of strangers ahead of their loved ones. And quite frankly, I'm not sure I'd want to know the sort of person who would."

"Tristan would," I said, wiping my nose on my sleeve. "It's what he wanted me to do."

Chris gave me a little shake. "He put your life ahead of everything and everyone – I know for a fact that he sent lots of those half-bloods to their deaths in order to get you out of Trollus alive. And rightly or wrongly, he did it because he loved you too much to let you die."

Pulling a slightly grimy handkerchief out of his pocket, he wiped my face. It came away bloody. "It seems to me, that no matter what we do, no matter what choices we make, there isn't a happy ending waiting for us at the end of the long road." He squared his shoulders and pushed me upright. "But that doesn't mean we give up. It doesn't mean we stop fighting."

He got to his feet. "I'm going to take this chicken down the road to a family I know could use it. Why don't you start cleaning up in here?"

I clung to Chris's optimism as I set to wiping away the blood splattered across the kitchen, but my heart wasn't in it. I hated what I was becoming. Every day, I lied and deceived those closest to me. Every time I practiced magic, I broke the law. I was attempting to find a way to unleash a terrifying force onto the world. And for what? To save the life of the one I loved? I cringed at how selfish it seemed, but no matter how many times I played the events at the mouth of the River Road over in my mind, I could not fathom doing anything different.

Gathering up the bloody rags, I tossed them into the fire. Pulling off my ruined dress, I tossed that in too, before donning my discarded dressing gown. Then I stood in front of the fire, my focus all on Tristan while I watched my dress burn into ash.

He was excited, which wasn't an emotion I'd felt from him in a long time. What was he up to? What was he planning? What would he think of what I had just done?

"You doing all right?"

I jumped. Chris had come back into the house without me even noticing. "No. I don't know," I said.

He gave me a sympathetic look, then picked up the discarded map.

"Just burn it," I said, turning back to the fire. "It's useless."

Chris made a noncommittal grunt. "That's interesting," he said.

"What?" The brightness of the fire was making my eyes sting, but I refused to blink.

"One of these burns is marking the castle."

My heart skipped, my thoughts instantly going to my theory about an alliance between Marie and Anushka.

"What about the others?" I asked, coming around to look over his shoulder. "Do you recognize any of the other locations?"

His finger trailed over the surface of the map. "I'm not sure about all of them, but at least ten of these marks are in cemeteries."

I met his gaze. "She's been staying alive all these long years. Maybe this is how."

"I think we should go look," Chris said. "After everything we went through tonight, it seems stupid not go check out what the map is showing us."

Anticipation prickled my skin. "You're right."

"Go put on something warm," Chris said, his cheeks reddening with excitement. "I'll get our horses – we have a lot of ground to cover tonight."

•••

The wind blasted bits of snow and sleet against my cheeks as we trotted through the quiet streets, the gas lamps dripping melted snow into their pools of light. Those few who were out kept their heads down and hoods up – their pace that of someone intent on putting a roof over their head and hands before a hearth. I could not recall a time when I'd felt the wind so frigid, the air biting gleefully at any skin that happened to be exposed. I pitied the poor folk in Pigalle who had no homes to flee to, and prayed that the cold snap would end swiftly.

My mind swirled as I tried to come up with justification for the nineteen marks on the map, but barring me having messed up the spell, there was no explanation other than that there were nineteen other lives tied to hers. Maybe nineteen victims.

Chris reined his horse in at the gates to the Montmartre cemetery. "What do you think we'll find?" he asked, dismounting.

"I have no idea." But I did know something was here; the earth was drawing me forward, leading me toward one of the spots my filthy bit of spell casting had revealed. Reins in one hand, I pushed open the iron gates and winced at the loud squeal of rusted hinges. "This way."

The Montmartre cemetery was below street level, giving the impression it was sunken into the earth. Leaving the horses tethered near the entrance, I led Chris down a set of steps and began to weave my way through the tombs, the statues gracing many of them casting eerie shadows in the light of our lantern. The narrow pathways were slick with ice, and twice I nearly fell, catching myself with the wing of an angel once, and on a marble epitaph the second. Both times I jerked my hand away, feeling as though I'd somehow desecrated the memory of those entombed within.

"Here," I said. "It's this one." My feet, of their own accord, had led us to a plain tomb that time had worn smooth. I carefully brushed the snow away from the faded etchings and held the light up to reveal a name and two dates. "Estelle Perrot," I murmured.

"Do you recognize it?" Chris asked, leaning over my shoulder.

"No," I said. "I don't. But there are two other locations in this cemetery."

Ignoring the icy cold of the wind, I let my feet take me on to a newer section of the yard. The tombs here were more ornate and the writing clearer. I stopped in front of a statue of a hooded woman sitting on the marble top, her head bent. " 'Ila Laval. Your sun set far too early,'" I read from the engraving, then reached up to brush some snow from the statue's arm. "I have no idea what this means."

"Is there really a body in there?" Chris asked, resting a hand on the top of the tomb. "Couldn't it be a false grave? A way of her changing lives without anyone the wiser."

"There's something in there," I said, not because I thought he was wrong, but because I could sense it in my bones that the tomb contained more than just empty space. "But I suppose there's only one way to find out."

We both stared at the statue for a long moment, then Chris set down the lantern. Bracing his feet against the granite of the next tomb, he shoved against the lid. It didn't budge. Digging the heels of my boots into the slippery ground, I threw my weight against the slab as Chris pushed. Stone ground against stone, loud even over the wind, but the top of the tomb inched sideways, then it stuck. No amount of pushing moved it any further.

Panting hard, I retrieved the lantern and tried to angle the light into the narrow crack, but I couldn't see anything. "Hold this," I said, passing it to Chris. Then I took a deep breath, and slowly eased my hand into the narrow gap. My pulse throbbed loud in my ears, my breath coming faster and faster as I eased my arm deeper into the tomb.

"Anything?"

I shook my head. The stone scraped tight against my skin, but I pressed my weight down and my arm abruptly slid in another few inches, my fingers punching through ancient fabric and into a ribcage.

A shriek forced itself from my lips, and I tried to jerk back, but I was stuck. Chris grabbed me around the waist and heaved me up, but the fabric of my dress bunched and caught. I tried to pull my fingers from the skeleton, but my wrist wouldn't bend enough, and the body shifted and moved with my jerky motions. "Get me out!"

He lifted me clear off the ground and pulled. Fabric tore and pain lanced through my arm, but then we were both tumbling back into the snow.

"What was it?" he demanded, eyes on the gap as though he expected a creature to rise up through it.

"A body." My voice was shaking, and I rubbed my sore arm with my other hand.

Chris's eyes shifted to me, and he was quiet for a long moment before saying, "City living has changed you."

I flushed at his sarcasm, climbing to my feet.

"Write the names and dates down," Chris said, going to the far side of the tomb to push the lid back into place. "Maybe once we find them all, we'll see a pattern."

I nodded uncertainly as I scribbled the names and dates on the back of the map with a pencil. "Let's go find the rest."

As the night progressed, we found tombs or graves matching all but two of the markings. One lay far to the south of the city, and the other was the location within the castle walls.

It was nearing the stroke of midnight when we pulled our horses up outside the Regent's castle. Or at least as near to the castle as we could get. The Indre River roared its way down to the ocean, the bridge leading over it to the island gated, and the walls on the far side guarded by men, marked by the glowing braziers they used to keep themselves warm.

I'd gained entrance so easily yesterday, but tonight the castle's fortifications did their duty. "She has to be here," I said through chattering teeth. "Every other location has been a corpse – it has to be her."

"It's not proof," Chris said, shaking the map in my face.

"There's the mark located outside the city that we need to investigate, and besides, for all we know, there could be another corpse hidden somewhere in the castle."

The snow spun and danced on the wind, the tiny white flakes mesmerizing. She was in there. I knew it.

"Cécile!" Chris shouted my name. Disorientation made me dizzy, and I shook my head, trying to clear it.

"Get away from the gate!" someone shouted. I looked up and saw a soldier in one of the guard posts pointing at us. Though I had no memory of moving, I was now most of the way across the bridge, the guards in plain sight. Fleur shied toward the edge of the bridge, and I clung to her frozen mane, afraid if I lost my seat I'd topple into the icy waters below.

Then Chris was next to me, hands reaching for the reins of my spooked horse.

"Sorry," he shouted. "She's drunk. I'll take her home. We don't want any trouble."

"Get away from the gates or I'll have you both thrown in the stocks for the night." He and one of his fellows started toward us.

"Stars and heavens," I swore, snatching up the frozen reins and digging my heels in. This was the last thing I needed. "Come on," I shouted at Chris over the wind, and together we cantered through the city, our horses' hooves sliding on the slick cobbles. When we reached my mother's street, I pulled my horse to a stop. Her ears were pinned, and she sidled uneasily beneath me, snorting out puffs of mist.

"What happened to you? You looked as though you were in a trance."

I tucked one numb hand into the pocket of my dress, trying to warm my fingers enough to use them. "I'm not sure. I was so certain she was within the walls, and then..." I broke off. "The promise took hold of me."

Sliding out of the saddle, I handed Chris the reins. "Are you certain you're all right to be alone?" he asked. "What if it happens again?"

"I'll be fine," I said quickly, wishing I felt half as confident as I sounded. "I need to get back before my mother realizes I'm gone."

Wrapping my cloak tightly around me, I started walking down the street.

"Cécile!"

I turned back.

"Be careful. If she was willing to kill all those women, then…" I knew what he'd left unsaid. *What's to stop her from killing you?*

What *was* stopping her from killing me?

I nodded, and broke into a quick trot down the road to my home as Chris went off in the opposite direction. These dead women, whoever they were, had some connection with Anushka. And if I wasn't missing the mark, I bet it had something to do with how she was achieving immortality. If I could only figure out the connection between them all.

Despite my exhaustion, I broke into a run. It wasn't just the cold driving me along – I sensed someone was watching me. My skin prickled, my eyes searching the street ahead and behind, but the darkness and the thick snow made it hard for me to see more than a few yards in any direction. Letting go of my cloak, I fumbled in my pocket for the small knife I kept, clutching it tight.

It was no small amount of relief when I reached home. Fumbling for the key, I had to try three times to get it in the lock, my hands were shaking so badly. I kept waiting for someone to come up and grab me, right when I thought I was safe. When the door finally swung open, I staggered in and slammed it hard behind me.

"Where have you been?"

My heart froze in my chest. Slowly, I turned around to face my mother. "What are you doing home so early?" I asked weakly.

"Answer my question," she barked.

I stared at the floor, my mind racing. I had said I was staying home all evening, but even if I hadn't, I had no good reason to be out past midnight in a blizzard. "Frédéric," I started to say, but she interrupted.

"Your brother is on duty at the palace. I saw him myself, so don't even try to say otherwise." She loomed over me. "And you certainly weren't out with your fellows in the company, no!" she scoffed. "No, that would be far too out of character for me to believe. Your lies are what is in character."

I stepped back as she flung her hands up. "For weeks you've been sneaking off, never telling me the truth about where you go. You deceitful, ungrateful little…"

"What do you care?" I shouted. "You've never cared before where I went, so why now? What difference does it make if I'm out with Christophe instead of with *Julian*?"

Her face darkened, blue eyes narrowing. "So that's it then?" She made a face. "I smell the horses on you now. A little roll in the hay with the stable boy?" Her face twisted and she spun away from me. "You're going to ruin your life, Cécile. What was the point of you ever leaving Goshawk's Hollow if you let a *farmer* get you with child?"

I flushed a dark red. Did I let what she was thinking stand? It was better than her finding out I was practicing blood magic in her kitchen and roaming the many city cemeteries in the dark of night, wasn't it? Better than her finding out that I was trying to release legions of mythological creatures who were currently cursed to their underground city. "What's wrong with Chris?" I demanded, pushing my way past her and into the great room.

"He's a farmer. He hasn't got any money."

I rounded on her. "Father was a farmer."

"Exactly," she snapped. "And look how well that worked out for me. Being forced to choose between my family and my career. I'm warning you, darling, don't go down the same path. Choose someone who won't force you to make sacrifices."

I stared coldly at her. I knew all this, of course, but hearing it out of her mouth was still astonishing. "Like the Marquis?" I said. "If rich is what counts, mother, you chose well."

Her eyes narrowed. "The Marquis is my patron, girl. He pays for all this, supports the company, keeps us in favor with the Regent. And in exchange, all he asks is that I entertain him and his friends."

"Of course, Mother," I said. "Everyone knows that all he's interested in is your…" I drew the pause out, "… voice."

She slapped me so hard that I staggered backwards. "You know nothing," she shrieked, then lunged at me.

I shoved her backwards. "Leave me alone!" I was angry – too angry – and the dark power of death still flickered inside of me, adding weight to my words.

She stumbled backwards, her eyes glazing over. "It's my life," I said, clenching my fist. "Not yours."

Snatching up my skirts, I bolted upstairs to my room. Flinging the door open, I was confronted with a wall of cold air. The window was open, snow blowing in and dusting the carpets with white. Hurrying over, I slammed the glass shut. Then I stopped in my tracks, goose bumps rising up on my flesh. I hadn't left the window open before I left. Slowly, I turned around.

A single candle burned on my desk, and on the mirror above it – written in smears of red – were three words: *Tick, tock, Princess.*

CHAPTER 22
Tristan

The sounds of a mob growing began to permeate the walls of the palace not long after curfew broke at shift change, though from the sounds of things, none of the day crew had gone down into the mines. It was a sure sign of their fury that they'd dare risk not meeting quotas. Despite knowing this would happen, having this much anger directed at me still made me uneasy. I'd been wrong to think that being ignored was the most horrible sort of punishment. This was far worse.

Someone hammered on the door to my rooms, and I jumped, for a moment thinking that the mob had somehow breached the palace gates and was even now coming for my head. "Come in."

The door opened, and Guillaume stepped through, a smile plastered across his face. I hadn't seen him since Cécile left Trollus, and I would have preferred to keep it that way. "His Majesty has ordered your presence in the throne room. Now."

I followed him out into the corridor, where I found six more guards waiting. "This isn't necessary," I said. "I'll go voluntarily."

"Excellent," Guillaume replied. "But we're still going with you. Not to make sure you go, but to make sure you get there alive."

I blinked. "I hardly need protection."

"His Majesty thinks otherwise. There are half-bloods aplenty within the palace, and all are seeking your blood."

"As you like."

They marched arrayed in a circle, their magic creating a shimmering dome that pressed in around me. I'd never needed guards to protect me before; but then, until recently, neither had my father. Dark times indeed that we were worried about an outright attack.

We marched through the vaulted marble halls toward the throne room, the din from outside growing worse with every step I took. The doors to the great chamber swung open, but no one bothered to announce me. Pushing past Guillaume, I stepped inside, taking in the countless figures on either side of the path leading to the throne. My father held audiences early, and the throne room was packed with those wishing to air their grievances and those who were keen to watch.

The hall grew silent as I was noticed, everyone turning to watch me as I walked swiftly toward the throne. The half-bloods' faces were all enraged, the aristocracy seemed curious, and everyone else appeared... worried. My father sat on the throne, the golden crown perched on his head, his expression unreadable. I met his gaze for a second, then bowed low. "Your Majesty."

"Tristan." My father shifted and stretched one leg out in front of him. "A grievous charge has been laid against you."

"Is that so?" I glanced over my shoulder, and smiled at the gathered group of half-bloods. The move was mostly to see if Tips was in the crowd, but it wouldn't hurt to stir them up. "I'll have to add it to my already impressive list of accomplishments."

It worked. They all began shouting, tossing insults and threats in my direction, until my father held up his hand to silence them. He was not so easily baited. "I've been told that sometime during the night all the work completed on the stone tree was destroyed, the foundations pulled apart and scattered throughout the city. Blame has been laid at your feet. What say you to the charges?"

"That I'm guilty," I said. "I took apart their precious bit of work, and I confess, I took no small amount of satisfaction in doing so."

The hall exploded with noise, a few booted feet taking off out of the room, no doubt to spread the word that I was guilty as charged. It wouldn't be long before everyone in the city knew with surety that it was me who had undone nearly three months of hard labor. Had undone the only hope they had for removing their reliance on the aristocracy. I was more than certain that we'd be able to hear their reaction from here.

But it wasn't their reaction I was interested in, it was my father's.

"Punish him!" someone shouted. "He needs to pay for what he's done!"

"Silence." He didn't shout. A king didn't need to.

The throne room grew quiet, which only made the escalation of noise outside the palace all the more noticeable. A guard skirted up the edge of the room, hurrying over to my father's arm when he was noticed. I heard bits of his whispered report. "They're threatening his life... hate him... will try to tear him apart if he leaves the palace... still praising your name." My father sighed and waved him away as though his report were of no more concern than a backed-up sewer drain. But I didn't miss the twitch in his fingers where they rested on the arm of the throne.

My heart skipped.

"I would have thought you'd be pleased to see your dream becoming a reality." His voice was mocking.

"What they were building out there did not much resemble my dream," I said. "Those were not my plans."

I vaguely heard the whispered speculation about what my words meant, but none would guess I was being literal. My father's fingers twitched again, then he pressed his palm hard against the gold arm of the throne. *Now, now, now,* I silently screamed.

"He did it out of spite, Your Majesty." Tips's voice echoed up into the dark and cavernous heights of the hall. "Tried to turn us against you again, and when we rejected him, this was his revenge."

One of my father's eyebrows rose, but there was a glimmer of uncertainty in his gaze. "Back to your old tricks so soon, my son?"

I said nothing, remaining still and motionless.

"You." He jerked his chin in Tips's direction. "Come forward."

The half-blood's wooden leg made sharp thuds as he strode toward the throne. I drew sharply on my magic, pulling in every ounce I had at my call as though I intended to silence Tips before he could speak some damning words. To make everyone believe the half-blood was enough of a threat that I'd kill him in front of my father rather than let him speak.

The throne room filled with screams as the spectators sensed the swell of magic, and everyone bolted, stumbling over each other in a mad rush to reach the exit.

My father's power hit me like a tidal wave, slamming me to the floor and containing the surge of heat and pressure. I struggled against him, fighting as hard as I could. But the iron did its duty.

A boot slammed down between my shoulder blades, and I grunted, struggling to breathe beneath its weight.

My father grabbed me by the hair and jerked my head far enough back to hurt. "Killing him will not absolve you of your guilt."

"Neither will letting him live." My tone was flat.

My father let go of my hair, but the boot stayed put, his weight and power holding me motionless against the floor. "Get back here, you cowards!" he bellowed, and if I could have sucked in enough breath, I would've sighed with relief. I needed an audience.

Out of the corner of my eye, I watched those who had run slink back in, aristocracy at the forefront. Despite their fear, they moved smoothly, flowing in an oddly coordinated mass, all eyes fixed on the two of us. With them came the clunk of Tips's leg, his pace reluctant as he played his part.

"Tell me of the conversation that passed between you and His Highness," my father ordered, once everyone had settled in.

"Yes, Your Majesty." Tips's voice was hoarse with all-too real nerves. "He came down into the mines not two nights after you released him from prison. Tracked down me and my crew and set to telling us that we'd been duped. That the plans you'd given us for the stone tree weren't what he designed, and that even if we completed them, that the structure would never hold. Said you'd knowingly given us false plans."

Whispers broke out through the throne room, too many and too quiet to clearly make out.

The weight between my shoulders shifted. This is what he'd thought I'd do – reveal that the plans he'd given the half-bloods were false and not of my making. He was ready for that move, but not, I thought, for the half-bloods turning against me for it.

"The lady you know as Anaïs d'Angoulême gave me those documents herself," my father said. "She swore they were the plans for a stone structure drafted by Tristan, entrusted to her for safekeeping. You all" – he gestured at the surrounding aristocracy – "were witness to that conversation."

There were murmurs of agreement, but I barely heard them. In one fell swoop, I had the confirmation I needed that he was in league with Lessa and that he was using her ability to lie to his advantage.

"And we've no cause to doubt her, Your Majesty," Tips replied. "But well we know His Highness' ability to twist words. We trusted him before, and all that gained us were the deaths of friends and family. I told him it wasn't happening again, and that we'd learned our lesson about turning traitor."

The truth, if not all of it.

"I'm pleased to hear it." The irony in my father's voice was unmistakable. "Tristan, do you deny this conversation took place?"

"No." I forced the word out loud enough for everyone to hear.

"But Your Majesty, there's more," Tips said, raising his voice so that he could be heard over the growing noise from outside. "He wouldn't let it be. He sought me out again yesterday, and tried to convince me to turn against you and accept his leadership. Made all sorts of promises of what he'd give us if we helped tear you off the throne and make him king. I told him that we wanted nothing more to do with him, and that we'd all go to the grave before seeing him on the throne."

The lie.

"Tristan, do you deny this second conversation took place as well?"

I hesitated, breathing in shallowly, once, twice, three times before I spoke. "That is what the half-blood said." Which he had. That he'd been lying through his teeth when he'd said it did not change the fact the words had come from his lips. No one in the room would doubt that I'd confirmed Tips's tale except my father, who had used the same ruse a time or two himself.

My father froze, his weight so steady on my back that I wondered if he was even breathing. I couldn't see his face, but I knew the wheels were turning. He knew Tips was lying for me, and that I'd put him up to it. And if Tips was lying for me, how many others were?

Something exploded outside and my father flinched, losing his balance enough that he stepped off my back. I desperately wanted to turn my head to see the look on his face as the belief I'd brought every half-blood in the city back to my cause settled into his mind. That all of them were actually oblivious to my machinations and really did want me dead didn't matter in that moment. All that mattered was that *he* thought they followed me. That he, in discovering that I knew the half-bloods' ability to lie, had become so wrapped up in his own web of duplicity that the probable became improbable, the truth a lie.

He was silent, and I could all but feel his mind working as he considered how to proceed. Calling Tips out for lying was out of the question. Not only would it bring to light that he'd known of the half-bloods' ability and kept it from his people, it would strip away a tool he'd long used to his advantage. His only choice was to play along, acting as though he believed Tips's words as much as anyone else in the room.

"What is it you want?" he finally asked.

"We want him punished," Tips said, slamming the bottom of his crutch against the marble floor. The rest of the half-bloods in the room crowed their agreement until my father made some motion to silence them.

"Should I throw him back in prison and leave him there to rot?" my father asked. "Or is that not extreme enough? Should I take off his head and put an end to his traitorous ways once and for all?"

"A sweet revenge for many," Tips said. "But some of us are less rash. He's no good to us dead or in prison."

"How is he good to you at all?" A question to which my father dearly wanted an answer.

I heard Tips swallow hard and I held my breath. This was the moment of reckoning.

"Prince Tristan undid in a night's work what it took us three months to complete," Tips said. "If you really want to see Trollus free from its dependence on magic, then you'll best punish him by making him use his research and plans to fulfill your vision. That is what we want as reparations for the hurt we have suffered. Order Prince Tristan to build the stone tree for us. And make him promise to do it right."

Stunned silence filled the throne room. No one had expected Tips to demand *that*. Not the aristocracy or the bourgeoisie, and certainly, *certainly*, not the half-bloods. My heart thundered in my chest, and sweat coated my palms. *Please let it work.*

My father began to laugh. At first, only a soft chuckle, but the sound gathered and grew until it filled the long hall. "What a pragmatic request, miner," he finally said, his voice still shaking with mirth. "I cannot say I expected it."

He nudged me with one foot and the weight of the magic holding me lifted. "Get up."

I climbed warily to my feet, not taking my eyes off him for a second. His expression terrified me. He knew I had tricked him, knew that I was plotting against him. But he looked pleased.

Which didn't make any sense. He had no clear way out of the trap I'd set for him. He knew Tips was working with me, but he didn't dare out the half-blood for his lies. He knew that commanding me to build the tree was what I wanted, but that if he didn't, he'd be all but confessing to the thousands of angry half-bloods outside the palace that he'd duped them. The half-bloods he wrongly believed I'd already recruited back to my leadership, when in actuality, they probably all hated me more than they ever hated him.

He'd figure my trick out eventually, but that didn't matter. What mattered was that right here, right now, he believed the majority of the city followed my orders.

Say something. My skin alternated hot and cold. Everyone in the room faded away; the sound of the mob barely a whisper in my ear. All that mattered was my father.

"You will do what the half-blood asks," he said, his voice loud enough for everyone to hear. A slight smile crept into his eyes. "As… punishment, for your actions."

Relief filled me, and it was a struggle to keep from showing it. I think I did not quite manage it, because the smile moved to his mouth. I stayed quiet long enough to make our act look real, then nodded. "As you command, so shall it be, Your Majesty."

"We want his promise!"

I started at Tips's voice. This wasn't part of our plan. I turned just in time to see magic that was not my own crush the half-blood against the marble floor.

"Do not make demands of your betters," my father snapped, his vehemence surprising me. Tips had been making demands this entire time, and my father had not seemed to care. What about me making a promise was different? It was a question that required more thought, but I didn't have time for it now. After everything that had happened today, the half-bloods were going to need more than a little reassurance that I was to be trusted, and I had every intention of giving it to them.

I cleared my throat. "I, Prince Tristan de Montigny, do so swear that I will build a stone tree for you, which, when it is complete, will protect Trollus from the weight of Forsaken Mountain without the use of magic."

My father snapped around to face me, his eyes bright with astonishment and anger. "You're a fool to bind yourself so." He muttered the words under his breath, and only I was close enough to hear them.

"That remains to be seen," I said softly, refusing to let myself wonder if he was right.

"Let it be known that His Highness has given his binding word!" he roared. Twisting on his heel, he strode up to the throne and settled down on it hard enough that the massive chair inched backwards. "Get back to your trades," he snarled at the crowd. "And you." His eyes settled on Tips. "Get back to the mines. It would be a shame after all of this if you were to miss your quota."

A not too subtle reminder that he was still King of Trollus, and that we all still lived and died by his word.

I had no escort back to my rooms, although I was as much in danger as I had ever been. It would take time for Tips to disperse the truth behind what had happened this morning, and despite knowing I worked for their freedom, many would resent being used once again. Even now, after this victory against my father, I still had so few allies. Only Tips, his crew, and Élise. Marc was still an unknown, holed up in his home and refusing any visitors, and the twins were limited by their banishment to the mines. I needed to find a way to help my friends, but as yet, I didn't know how.

The smell of food tickled my nose as I stepped into my rooms, a laden and steaming tray revealing itself as I expanded my pool of light. A note written on my aunt's stationery sat on the corner of the tray.

Because you are still dear to me.
S.

P.S. I had Élise bring this for you, and as such, I cannot vouch for what it might contain.

My pulse accelerated. Sitting down at my desk, I scanned the contents of the tray, searching for a hidden message from Élise. Nothing. No note, no symbols, no clever arrangement of food. "Bloody stones," I muttered, and started eating, because if nothing else, I was starving. Shoving half a roll into my mouth, I started on the bowl of soup, spooning the thick liquid into my mouth as fast as I could swallow it. Tipping the bowl with magic, I started to scoop up the last mouthful when my eyes caught sight of one word scored into the bottom of the dish.

Élise's mission had been to discover who or what had provoked my father into such a fury that my mother had nearly torn the palace down and cost me my life. And she'd done it.

Anaïs.

CHAPTER 23
Cécile

"Under no circumstances is she to leave the house today, do you understand? She has no rehearsals or performances or appointments, so don't believe any lies she might spin."

"Yes, Madame."

My mother repeated her instructions to the cook and maid, albeit with different phrasing. But the message was the same: short of the house burning down – and perhaps not even then – I was not to cross the threshold. Scowling, I rolled onto my back and stared up at the canopy of my bed.

It wasn't as though I couldn't sneak out. It would be easy enough to compel both women not to interfere, but both of them would lose their jobs if my mother discovered they'd let me go without a fight. Better to use a non-magical route. I was an experienced tree climber, and the sturdy trellis running down the house would not trouble me in the least.

But not getting caught was quite another matter. I'd ignored my mother's orders and today's internment was my punishment. But if I did it again, I knew she would and could do much worse to me. Chain my feet together, or hire guards to stand outside my door, or drug me to sleep every night. Her creativity knew no bounds.

The maid had been in a quarter-hour past to bring me a tray of breakfast, and sunlight beamed in between the drapes she had tossed open. The food was slowly growing cold, but the smell of it made my stomach roil, and the thought of eating was more than I could bear. My head throbbed unbearably and my whole body ached from riding around in the freezing cold. I felt like I was falling sick, but I knew better. Even without the message left on my mirror, I would have felt the urgency. Something had happened. Something had changed. The troll king was no longer content to wait. If he ever had been.

Tick, tock, Princess.

Rolling over, I buried my face in the pillow. When I'd first seen the red writing, I'd thought it was blood. It had turned out to be only my own lip stain. But while the medium of the message was more innocuous than I'd originally thought, its meaning was no less nefarious. Not only was I running out of time, the placement of the message and the casual use of my own cosmetics slapped me in the face with the knowledge that the King could reach me anytime and anywhere. I might be free of Trollus, but I was not free from danger. I wondered if *anywhere* was safe.

My thoughts swiftly returned to the results of my spell the prior night. And the spell itself. It had been so easy – no worrying about whether the nature and balance of the ingredients was correct, or if I was using the elements best suited to the task. No fear the power that manifested would be insufficient.

And it had felt good.

I shivered, worming my way deeper under the covers. Certainly, it had been hard to kill the chicken, but more than that, I remembered the euphoric influx of power. Power that had lingered in me long enough to shout my mother into submission when I'd returned home, hours after casting the spell. It had been a revolting act. But it had also been intoxicating. Addicting. Digging my bitten fingernails ineffectually into my palms, I mumbled, "Don't think about it."

Better to think of the results.

All but two of the burn marks on the map we'd proven to be deceased women. The one mark within Trianon we couldn't find had been located in the Regent's castle, and I knew for certain that Marie had been there last night, and I was certain Anushka had been in her company. My own blasted mother had performed for her. Chris would argue that it was still no proof. That we needed to investigate the mark outside the city. Yet even before I'd heard his argument, I was already dismissing it. It would only be another grave out in the middle of a field or a forest.

She could have left Trianon, Chris's phantom voice echoed in my head. *If she knows you're after her, perhaps she has fled.* I brushed the voice of my friend aside – my gut told me that Anushka would not flee from me.

But what about the trolls?

"Bloody stones, shut up!" I swore.

"Mademoiselle?"

Tipping my head, I peered out of the depths of my covers with one eye. The maid stood in the doorway, one eyebrow arched. "Not you," I said. "The... the neighbors are being loud."

"It is quite late in the morning," she said pointedly, her gaze flicking to my untouched tray.

"I'm sorry," I said, eyeing its contents again. My stomach did flip-flops. "I'm feeling under the weather. I don't think I can eat a thing."

A soft little sniff told me exactly what she thought of my malaise. "Will you be wanting lunch?"

"I'll let you know," I said, still eyeing the wasted food. "For now, I'll rest."

I waited for her to leave, then I dragged a chair under the door's handle so she wouldn't be able to sneak up on me again. Retrieving a pencil and a piece of stationery from my desk, I went back to my bed and got under the covers again. From under my pillow, I extracted the blood-smeared map with its hastily scrawled list of names and dates, and I carefully began to copy them out in order.

They spanned the past five centuries; the oldest tomb had been so weatherworn that we'd barely been able to make out the names and dates. Chewing on my fingernail, I carefully calculated the age of each woman at her death. No pattern. I calculated the years between their births. No pattern. I began calculating the years between their deaths. Eleven years. Nineteen years. Thirty-eight years. I flung my pencil down with annoyance, not bothering with the rest.

The dead women were connected to how Anushka was managing immortality, I was sure of it. But how? Killing them would certainly give her a glut of power, but it wouldn't last more than a few days, and nothing I'd read suggested that such behavior would prolong life. If that were the case, other witches would have discovered it and capitalized upon it. She had to be doing something with the power, but no matter how far I stretched my mind, I couldn't think what. A witch couldn't heal herself, and what was immortality if not a cure for old age? It didn't make sense. She had to be doing it another way.

I picked up the grimoire Chris had stolen and began going through the pages. Flip, flip, flip. The pages rasped against my blanket as I turned them, and then I stopped.

The grimoire was full of spells combining regular magic and blood magic to manage certain afflictions of the body, but only now was I noticing a theme among many of them. Potions to keep hair dark, creams to wipe away wrinkles, and tonics to keep skin firm. While the spells would do nothing for the subject's longevity, a combination of them would certainly replicate the appearance of immortality – the individual using them might well drop dead of old age, while appearing to all who looked on as though they were in the bloom of youth.

I rested my chin on my wrists. Catherine had been Lady Marie's maid. I suspected Marie was helping Anushka, so wasn't it possible she had enlisted Catherine, and maybe others before her, to help maintain her immortality? If one could use magic to combat the exterior signs of age, couldn't one do the same for the interior degeneration? It would be complicated, and the spells would need continual renewal, but it might be possible. The only certain thing was that she'd need the help of other witches to do it.

My heart started to beat a little faster. Maybe that had been the reason for Catherine's fall from grace – that she'd refused to help Anushka with her foul magic any longer.

I wondered how much Catherine knew. Whether Marie and Anushka had entrusted her with their secrets, or whether they'd only used her for her skills. Catherine had said Marie dismissed her for meddling in business she shouldn't have, which could well be Anushka's relationship with the trolls.

Snapping the book shut, I rolled onto my back. One question remained, itching and nagging at me, demanding to be scratched. If Anushka knew who I was, who I was working with, and that I was on her trail, why hadn't she tried to kill me yet?

The canopy of my bed seemed to swim above me, and I shut my eyes, trying desperately to think objectively about why she was keeping me alive. Was she toying with me, like a cat does with a mouse? Was she garnering some perverse sort of amusement watching me chase after her like an ignorant fool, waiting for the entertainment to play out before she ended my life? It seemed a reckless way to behave, but maybe after five hundred years of life one developed a different perspective on risk? Or was there something about me she thought was of use?

The door handle rattled. "Cécile? It's Sabine."

Tumbling out of bed, I hurried to the door and pulled the chair out from under the handle. "What are you doing here?"

"Helping you." Backing me into the room, she shut the door and put the chair back under the handle. "I crossed paths with your maid on her way to the market, and she told me Genevieve has clamped down on your 'midnight gallivanting' and 'scandalous behavior,' whatever that means." Kicking off her boots, she climbed onto my bed. "So I'm here to help you with whatever you need."

I perched on the covers next to her, not sure what to make of what she'd said. "Sabine…"

"I know," she said. "What's changed?" Her fingers plucked at my bedspread, her expression contemplative. "I suppose I thought time would change things back to the way they used to be. To the way *you* used to be. That you'd forget about them, and... Tristan. That the trolls would cease to exist if we stopped paying them any attention. Or at the very least, that we could go back to a life where they didn't affect us." She winced. "Now that I'm saying it, it seems so childish."

I pulled the covers over my feet. "Maybe. But sometimes when you want something badly enough, it doesn't matter if it's realistic. Or right." She'd never been to Trollus – until I'd told Sabine the truth, the trolls were nothing more than children's stories to her, so I could imagine how she would think shutting the book and putting it away would mean they'd cease to exist.

She nodded. "The thing was, once you told me about them, I started to see signs of them, or at least their influence, everywhere. I began to remember things that happened in the past that I found strange in the moment, but then forgot about. The way Chris's father would buy all the excess from the farms around the Hollow to sell in the Courville markets, but never seem to know what was going on in the city. The way merchants would stop in at my parents' inn for lunch on their way to Trianon, but then pass back through in less time than it would take to make the whole journey, wagons empty."

She blew a breath of air through her teeth. "And since we've been in Trianon, it's even more noticeable. I've watched merchants from the continent unload their ships' holds into wagons, bypass the Trianon markets, and head south, but there is no market between here and Courville for a hundred bolts of silk, and if their destination was Courville, why wouldn't they sail there directly? Obviously because it's intended for Trollus."

I gaped at her in astonishment. Not because what she was saying didn't make sense, but that she'd noticed all these comings and goings and I hadn't. I knew I wasn't the most observant, and that I'd a tendency to walk around with my head in the clouds, but it was alarming that I'd miss something so obvious.

"All these merchants know about the trolls," Sabine continued. "But more importantly, no one interferes with them. No one asks questions. Which means others either know about them too, or they've been paid off. Hundreds of people must be aware the trolls exist, but they remain a secret from most everyone on the Isle. The only way that's possible is that they are more in control than anyone realizes."

"You're right," I said, because though I may not have considered the practical aspects of trolls' control over the Isle, I knew no one was beyond the King's reach. "Sabine, do you know what a regent is?"

She shrugged. "Like a king?"

"It's the title given to the individual who is temporarily head of a kingdom in place of the monarch."

"But the Isle doesn't have a monarch."

I lifted one eyebrow, and watched understanding settle on her face. "I think the first regent was put in his position by the trolls after they were cursed, but only because they thought it would be temporary until Anushka was tracked down and killed."

A crease formed between Sabine's eyebrows. "But then... wouldn't it be in the best interest of the Regent *not* to find her? To keep the trolls contained, and thus keep control of the Isle?"

I nodded. "That's exactly what I think the Regency has been doing throughout history. On the surface, they've made it look like they are helping search by legalizing the witch-hunts, but in reality, they've been harboring the one witch who mattered most. I don't have any proof, but I think that might have something to do with Catherine's fall from grace – that she got too close to the truth."

"Catherine?"

"La Voisin," I clarified, so used to her knowing everything that I'd forgotten she didn't know the outcome of my meeting with the witch she'd discovered.

Sabine's frown stayed in place as I explained Catherine's connection to the Regency and the reasons for my speculations, growing deeper when I told her about the spell I'd done with Chris the prior night. "So even though she might not understand how important Anushka is, Catherine might still know her identity?"

"Not that she's likely to tell me anything," I said with a grimace. "She's terrified of the Regency."

"Too bad none of your books has a spell for plucking knowledge from someone's head," she said, giving Anushka's grimoire a poke.

An idea burst in my mind like a firecracker. "Sabine," I said. "You're a genius."

The cook had given me a strange look when I'd appeared downstairs in my dressing gown, but she hadn't interfered when I'd gone into the pantry to retrieve a sprig of rosemary. Back in my bedroom with the drapes drawn and my door jammed, I'd carefully torn the page containing the spell for the skin cream out of the grimoire. After I'd copied the contents of the page out on a piece of stationery under Sabine's watchful eye, I carefully rolled up the original, wrapped a strand of the hair Chris had stolen and the sprig of rosemary around it, and held the package over my washbasin full of water.

I understood better now than I had before why the spell worked as it did: the piece of paper with the spell on it focused on the memory I wished to extract, and the hair acted as a link to Catherine, while the rosemary improved and strengthened the clarity. Water was the element of choice because memory and thought were fluid and transitory, ever changing.

"You've done this before?" Sabine asked.

"A variation of it," I replied, examining my work. "Magic doesn't work on trolls, but it does work on half-bloods." The spell had been intended to find lost items, but I'd adapted it before when I'd used it on Élise in order to extract the memory of when she'd last seen the clove oil I'd needed for the injury I'd sustained during the earthshake. Catherine had told me that the incantation used was merely a way to focus on the desired outcome, so I was sure it was possible to change the spell again to suit my purposes.

"But if magic doesn't work on them, why does a curse?"

I bit my lip. Her question was one I'd pondered at length

before. "I don't know. But hush now, I need quiet for this."

Staring at the rolled-up paper, I focused my thoughts. I wanted the strongest memory associated with the spell, but more than that, I wanted to know whom it had been for.

"When did you cast this spell?" I whispered, then dropped the package into the water. "And for whom did you cast it?"

Touching the surface of the water, I felt power surge through me while the roaring sound of a river flowed out of the basin. The paper spun round and round, then as though it had suddenly tripled in weight, it plunged to the bottom.

Sabine gasped, and I almost did, too. That hadn't happened before.

My pulse fluttered in my neck, and it was a struggle to maintain my concentration as the water turned dark and murky. There was movement, but I felt as though I were spying on a scene taking place in the darkest of nights. Whispers of sound teased my ears, but I couldn't decipher what they were. Leaning closer to the water, I peered into the basin, trying to pick out something familiar.

"What's going to happen?" Sabine asked.

"Watch."

Crimson splattered up from the depths, and we both jerked back. The surface of the water caught and held the red liquid like a pane of glass, but I knew what it was. Blood, but from who or what, I could not say.

"Eternal youth, eternal youth, eternal youth." The words started quiet as a thought, but then grew louder and louder until I was sure everyone in the house could hear the voice. Catherine's voice.

Then abruptly as it had begun, the voice went silent. The bowl of water turned pristine white.

But the memory wasn't over.

Slowly, the whiteness faded like clouds clearing on a summer sky, and an image appeared. A woman – Catherine – was walking through the corridors of the castle, the skirt she was kicking out in front of her infinitely finer than what she wore now. I could hear her heels against the stone, the swish of the fabric of her dress, although the quality of the sound was strange. She paused in front of a door, looked both ways, then entered into the room.

"I have it." Catherine spoke, the words echoing as though she stood at the end of a long corridor.

"It took you long enough." The voice of the woman who spoke was distorted, and Catherine was staring at her feet, so I couldn't see who it was.

"This is the last batch." Catherine's voice shook. "I can't keep doing this – what if I get caught?"

"Be more afraid of what will happen to you if you stop!" There was a flurry of motion, and the other woman snatched up the jar Catherine was holding and spun away. She finally looked up, but the other woman was wearing a hooded cloak.

"Turn around," I breathed at the image. "Who are you?"

"It's getting harder and harder to hide the bodies," Catherine pleaded. "This is dark magic, mistress. There is always a cost."

"I don't care." The woman whirled around, revealing the cruel beaked mask she wore. It concealed all her features, making it impossible to tell what she looked like or even how old she was. "There is no cost too great. Not for this. I must endure."

The image vanished, and the basin was once again filled with ordinary water and the sodden bundle of paper, hair, and herb, the magic fading away. Sabine met my eyes. "Do you think that was her?"

I nodded slowly. "The way she said the last bit, *I must endure,* there was something about her phrasing. Not that her beauty or youth must endure, but that she herself must."

"It could mean nothing. She could just be a woman desperate to maintain her youth."

"Or it could mean everything." Pushing the basin back, I got to my feet. "I need to see Catherine and convince her to tell me what she knows."

"She's no more likely to tell you anything now than she was before, Cécile."

"I'm not so sure about that," I said. "The desire for revenge is a powerful motivator, and I think I can appeal to that."

"All right, but there's still one problem."

"I know," I said. "I need to find a way to get past my mother."

CHAPTER 24
Tristan

I frowned at the column of rock rising up before me, then scribbled a series of calculations, pen held with an invisible hand of magic. It had taken me a bit of practice to learn to write this way, but necessity had demanded it. Even if I could manage to grip a pen with my numb fingers, my shaking would have rendered whatever I tried to write illegible. I glanced down at my hands, knowing without removing my gloves that my fingers looked grey and lifeless, the skin surrounding the spikes through my wrists black with iron rot. I was ill and exhausted, my constant use of magic draining me and leaving my body susceptible to the toxic metal.

In the heat of the moment in the throne room, I'd made my promise to Tips without considering the ramifications. And now I was suffering the consequences. To build the tree, I needed to be alive; but the darkening bonding marks on my hand spoke of the deterioration of Cécile's strength, which, along with the spread of the iron rot in my wrists, was evidence that my days were numbered. Which drove me to work harder.

I couldn't stop, not to eat or to sleep; and the continual drain on my power allowed the rot to worsen. Which made me work harder still. I was caught in a spiral, and unless something changed, the result was inevitable.

I might have fought the compulsion to build continually a

little harder, but there was one other problem: I liked the work.

Liked wasn't even a strong enough word – I loved it. Loved transforming the vision in my mind into something tangible. Loved that I was creating something permanent. Loved that this was a problem I was solving, unlike the others on my very long list.

I still had no notion of what Lessa had said to my father to set him off so badly. She was effectively my father's spy in Angoulême's home, so it might well have been some information she had discovered. Possibly something to do with my brother, the idea of which made me very nervous.

Or it could have been something Lessa had done to anger our father herself, though I couldn't imagine why she would do that. They were allies in this, but that didn't mean he wouldn't dispose of her if necessary. I'd avoided her like the snake she was, but I'd seen her enough in the distance to know she was alive and unharmed. Part of me wished she were dead.

"Your Highness?"

I turned to see the crew of half-bloods I was working with standing next to the massive block of stone they'd carefully cut and prepared. "Ready?"

They nodded, their eyes wide with excitement. I wondered how many more blocks I'd have to lift before the euphoria of watching the tree come to life diminished. For them and me both.

Widening my stance for balance, I coiled magic around the stone and lifted it up into the air, the heels of my boots grinding into the cobblestones. Magic magnified my strength a thousandfold and more, but it still came from me. I'd knocked myself over before trying to lift something while I wasn't balanced; and the last thing I wanted to do was fall on my ass in front of everyone. Taking a step back, I brightened the light so I could see and gently set the stone on top of the column. One of the crew scrambled up the scaffolding, recklessly hanging off the structure to make certain the stone was square and level.

"It's perfect, Your Highness," she called down to me, and the others cheered.

"Good," I called back wearily. "I'll see you in a few days."

Fetching my hat and coat, I started walking toward my next scheduled stop, eyeing each construction site as I went. In two weeks, we'd more than quadrupled the progress they'd made over three months, but the amount of work left was daunting. The half-bloods had little time to spare to the effort, as most of their hours were spent working for the Guilds; but many of them were willing to forgo sleep in order to get another block of stone cut, another few yards of height on their columns.

They were warming to me, as well. I wasn't sure if it was the progress we were making together, or if Tips had worked some sort of magic, but I hadn't had to deal with one of them trying to kill me during the last twenty-four hours. Or maybe they were just waiting for me to finish the work before doing the deed.

"I'm telling you, fool, it shifted during the night. Look! Look!" Pierre's shrill voice pierced my ears, and I picked up my pace to see what had upset the man so much that he'd ventured from his home.

"There!" he shouted when he caught sight of me. "Someone who understands. Your Highness, please talk some sense into these imbeciles."

The three Builders' Guild members he had just insulted looked too weary to care. I recognized all of them, though I didn't know their names. One looked normal enough, but the strained wheeze of her breath suggested her affliction was internal. The other two were more obviously marked, one with an extra set of arms and the other with smooth skin where his eyes should be.

"There was a tremor in the night," Pierre said, shaking his fist in the air. "A small one, but enough that the rocks may have shifted. Yet all they do is walk to and fro, filling the tree with power. They aren't checking for changes. They don't understand it. They'll kill us all." His eyes were wild, watching the blackness of the cavern above us as though he expected a rock to drop and hit him directly.

"Pierre, calm down," I said. "I can't get involved – my father specifically commanded me to leave the Guild to its business." I flicked my attention to the three trolls. "He's right, though, you know. You cannot treat this structure as static. It wasn't built that way."

"It seems fine," the wheezy one replied, gesturing skyward. "It looks fine."

"*Looks*?" I repeated, looking pointedly up at the blackness. "You can't manage the tree by looking at it. You have to do it by feel." I muttered a few choice curses and then tossed my coat and hat on the back of Pierre's wheeled chair. "Warn me if anyone comes."

Reluctantly, I peeled off my gloves. Setting them aside, I put my hands into the nearest column of magic, feeling the warm vestiges of my own power flow over my fingers. I closed my eyes, letting my magic drift over the ceiling above, each rock a familiar old friend. There were a few small changes, but nothing of great concern. I started to pull away from the tree when the blind guild member approached. "Will you tell me how you do it, Your Highness?"

"By feel," I said, glad that it had been him who had approached because he couldn't see the damaged state of my wrists and hands. "You must memorize how each and every rock is placed so that you will know instinctively if something has shifted. Then you must judge how the weight and balance has changed and modify the canopy to compensate."

The man smiled, resting a hand against the column. He was quiet for a moment, then he said, "Northwest sixty-three and sixty-five are lower, but barely."

"Yes," I said, frowning at him. "But you already knew that, didn't you?"

"I did." He turned his head toward where Pierre was arguing with the other two guild members. "But it was an excuse to speak with you."

Curiosity flared in side of me. "About?"

"I knew what the half-bloods were constructing would never

work," he said softly. "I could hear where they were building, and it didn't feel right. And I wasn't the only one. Others noticed it too." He wrung his hands together. "We knew he'd tricked them, but we'd be fools to say anything against your father."

I hesitated. "Why are you telling me this?"

"Because we want you to know that it isn't only the half-bloods who will rise up against your father to put you on the throne." He turned his face back to me, and even though he had no eyes, I could have sworn he was seeing me.

"The guilds are full of your supporters – full-bloods who believe you are the key to our survival. That you will be the one who sets us free."

A thousand thoughts chased each other through my mind, but I couldn't think of a single thing to say.

Pierre's whistle stole away the moment. "Visitors," he hissed, jerking his chin in the direction of the bobbing light coming swiftly down the street.

I rose, backing away from the tree and letting my light dim in the foolish hope that whoever approached wouldn't recognize me.

A boy near to my age skidded to a stop in front of us, his uniform marked with the Builders' Guild emblem of a hammer and chisel. "News from the palace!" His eyes widened when he saw me. "Begging your pardon, Your Highness." He started to bow, then stopped, his eyes flicking between his elder fellows for guidance.

"Don't hold back on my account," I said, leaning against the wall. "Tell us the news."

"It's about your brother," he said. "Prince Roland."

"I know who my brother is." My voice was light, but if I'd had hackles, they would have risen. "What about him?"

"The King has announced his betrothal."

I grimaced. He wouldn't be bound to anyone until he was at least sixteen, but I still pitied whatever girl had been chosen. The idea of anyone being emotionally tied to my insane, sadistic little brother made me sick. "To whom?"

The boy licked his lips, looking anywhere but at me. My unease grew – something wasn't right. What was my father up to? "Spit it out," I snapped, ignoring how he jumped, eyes bright with fear.

"It's just that I don't think you're going to like it very much, given that you… and her…"

The lights of those around me began to spin. *No, no, no!* "Tell me who!"

The boy swallowed hard. "To Lady Anaïs, Your Highness. Prince Roland has been betrothed to the heiress of the Duchy of Angoulême."

CHAPTER 25
Cécile

"Please let me go out," I begged, flinging myself onto the sofa where my mother sat reading.

She turned a page and didn't look up. "No. I don't trust you not to go running toward trouble."

"You're driving me mad," I muttered. And she really was. It had been over a week since I'd stolen Catherine's memory, but I'd been able to do nothing about it thanks to my mother. The only time I was allowed out of the house was for performances or masque rehearsals – none of which Marie had attended – and she never let me out of her sight for more than a moment. Compelling her with magic might well get me free of her for a few moments, but the effects were fleeting and I knew no way of permanently altering her thoughts. Nor was the idea of doing so particularly conscionable.

As it was, rare was the moment when I was alone with her, and I was not sure if I could compel two people at once. I'd been forced to satisfy myself with setting Sabine and Chris to keeping an eye on Catherine, but that wasn't progress. I was becoming desperate enough to try anything, and well I knew how desperate people made mistakes. "Are you going to keep me locked up like this forever?"

"Just until after the masque, darling. After that, I've no concern over what you do."

The masque, the masque, the masque. It was all she cared about, acting as though it were the most important night of my life. There was no arguing with her, and no, I'd discovered, getting around her. The trellis running along the side of the building had been removed, a lock was installed on my window, and when I'd picked that in an attempt to escape, she'd had the cook's husband nail the window shut. My door was bolted from the outside at night, and whenever we went anywhere, she kept a firm grip on my wrist to keep me from running off.

Any and all attempts to look for further clues toward Anushka's identity had been thoroughly and effectively stymied. But my need to hunt her had not. I hadn't slept for days, and I'd started throwing up everything I ate. A quick glance in the mirror showed hollow cheeks and shadowed eyes, but my color was high. I should've been exhausted, but instead I felt jittery, like a child who has consumed too many sweets.

"It's weeks away." And I wasn't sure I'd last that long without progress. I felt as though I was being consumed from the inside out.

"Barely enough time to prepare," she said, staring blindly at her book. "But the date is set."

I scowled at her, though she wasn't paying any attention. She was obsessed with this stupid performance. "Any longer and I might throw myself off a bridge," I muttered.

Her eyes flicked my direction. "Don't be morbid."

"Says the person trying to kill me."

Julian snickered from where he sat perched on a chair. My mother shot him a withering glance, but it didn't seem to affect him in the least. The spell remained in effect, the contempt he used to hold for me replaced by his wholehearted enthusiasm for my rise to lead soprano. He might well have fallen out of love into logic, but that was not the same as falling into intelligence. If he didn't learn to mind his tongue, I suspected he might find himself cut from the coming season entirely. For his sake, I hoped it wore off soon. "I'm bored," he announced. "I want to go out."

"Then go," my mother said.

"I've no one to go with."

An idea crossed through my mind. "I could go out with you, Julian. It would be a fine thing for people to start seeing us together before the start of next season, wouldn't you agree?"

His eyes brightened at the idea.

Genevieve set down her book. "You're not going anywhere without me until after the masque is over. I'll not have you ruining everything."

I opened my mouth to argue, but Julian beat me to it. "Don't you trust me to keep an eye on her?" he asked. "After all, *I* know how important the masque is" – his eyes went to me and then back to my mother – "to both of us."

I silently applauded his tactic while watching my mother's profile for any sign of what she might be thinking. But her face was as smooth and unreadable as a troll's. "Back by midnight," she said, and snapped her book open again.

I grinned at Julian and he winked.

While he went outside to hail a hackney cab, I changed into a dark blue dress, braided my hair so that it hung over one shoulder, and shoved what I needed into a satchel. Kissing my mother on the cheek, I hurried out into the chill air where my co-star was waiting. Taking his arm, I scrambled up into the carriage.

"Le Chat?" Julian asked.

I shook my head. "After. There's somewhere we need to go first."

One dark eyebrow cocked. "Oh? Where's that?"

"Pigalle."

His other eyebrow shot up to join the first. "*Pigalle?* Curses, why would you want to go there?"

"There's something I need," I said, waiting for him to argue, but he only shrugged and gave the instruction to the driver.

"You won't tell her where we went, will you?" I asked as the horse started trotting down the street. "She'll lock me up for the rest of my life if she finds out."

Julian tilted his head from side to side in a parody of extreme thought. "I suppose not. It wouldn't really do for me to have a prisoner for a co-star. But in exchange for my deception, I expect you to pay for all my libations tonight."

"As much as you can drink."

"Then off to Pigalle we go." He clapped his hands together. "Which isn't something I'd ever thought I'd say."

"Wait here," I said to Julian as I slipped out of the hack. "I won't be very long."

It was very dark in Pigalle, the moon little more than a sliver in the night sky, but I still looked up and down the street to see if anyone was watching, before going to the door and knocking. Moments later, I heard footsteps, and the door opened.

"I told you never to come back!"

Catherine tried to shut the door to her shop in my face, but I threw my shoulder against it, forcing my way in before Julian could take notice. "I have questions that need answering."

"I don't care. You need to leave." The sticky scent of absinthe was heavy on her breath, and she was unsteady on her feet.

"I'm not going anywhere until you tell me what I need to know."

"I have nothing to say to you."

Pulling her grimoire out of my satchel, I held it up. "I think you do."

Catherine's eyes bulged as she recognized the book. "Thief!" she shrieked, lunging at me as though to claw my eyes out.

I dodged her drunken swipe at my face easily, but prudence made me retreat a few paces lest she try again. "Here," I said, holding the book out at arm's length. "I'm giving it back."

She snatched it out of my hand and clutched it against her chest. "You're going to get me killed."

"That isn't my plan," I said. "I haven't told anyone about those spells, and I have no intention of doing so. If you help me."

"Is that a threat?"

I didn't answer. I didn't have to – her imagination would do my dirty work.

She glared at me for a long time, then the heat left her eyes and her shoulders slumped. "I suppose it doesn't really matter anymore. They know I've consorted with you."

She was talking about the Regency. I wanted to press her for details, but my time was limited and I needed to extract everything she knew about the masked woman. Wary of another attack, I gently took her by the arm and led her to the back table. When I had her seated with the dog on her lap, I took the chair across from her.

"There's a spell in that book for the making of a cream that wipes away age. I know you made it for a woman who at least once appeared to you hooded and wearing a mask, and that you perhaps cast other spells for her as well."

"I don't know what you're talking about."

"There is no point in denying it, Catherine. I pulled the memory from your own thoughts."

I braced myself, expecting my admission to elicit another attack, but no anger flowed into her eyes. Only resignation. "I had no choice but to help her."

"Who was she?" I asked.

Catherine shook her head. "I don't know. She always appeared in some sort of disguise, and she took steps to alter her voice so that I couldn't identify her."

I swore silently. "Do know anything about her? Any clues to who she might be?"

"No." The other witch gently stroked her dog's back. "She approached me the first time nearly ten years ago – had heard I could make creams and lotions that would wipe the years off a woman's face. She had the money to pay, and there was no harm in it. The spells I was using at the time were harmless combinations of herbs and earth. But they only worked so well. And they most certainly could not stop the passage of time."

"So you turned to the dark arts?"

"I had no choice." Her mouth twisted. "She told me that if

I did not do what she wanted, she'd arrange for the Regent to discover I was a witch. That she'd see me burn. So I did it." A single tear ran down her face. "It was difficult procuring the… the sacrifices I needed. And difficult disposing of the bodies. I was terrified I'd be caught, and I could feel myself changing. I felt corrupted, as though some insidious substance had got into my veins and was slowly working its way through my body. I can only imagine what they were doing to her mind with the quantities in which she used them."

"Did she ask you to make any other potions? Perform other spells?" It was a struggle to keep the anticipation from my voice.

"Only the creams."

My anticipation burned away leaving disappointment in its wake. I'd been so sure there'd be others – spells to somehow prolong Anushka's life. Was my theory entirely wrong? Clearing my throat, I said, "So you stopped. Told her you wouldn't make her potions any longer?"

"I tried." She scrubbed a hand across her red-rimmed eyes. "But she wouldn't hear of it, and I was afraid to cross her. Nor could I go to Marie, because she would never have forgiven me for abusing my position."

"You said before that she knew you were a witch?"

Catherine nodded. "Her son, Aiden, was a sickly child. She approached me and brought me into her household as his nurse at great risk to herself, given the Regent's views on witchcraft. I involved her in my spells to help him, because the bond of blood between parent and child holds an intense amount of power. No one but Marie knew I was a witch until…" She broke off.

"Until?" I leaned forward in anticipation.

"Some four years ago, the masked woman left me a note asking for me to meet her. Of course I went, but instead of her usual request, she asked for something different."

"What did she want?"

"A love potion."

I sat up straight in my chair. If this woman was Anushka, why would she ask for that? The creams and such I understood – she couldn't affect herself with magic, so she needed another witch's help. But she was more than capable, and by my reckoning, quite practiced at making love potions herself. "To use on whom?"

"The Regent."

My jaw dropped. The Regent? But that made no sense at all – if Marie was allied with Anushka, why would she allow such a thing?

"I was loath to do it. Marie had never been anything but kind to me and spelling her husband would be the ultimate betrayal, but the woman did not hesitate to remind me how quickly the flames would lick at my toes if it were discovered I was performing black magic." She sucked in a deep breath. "And I knew that if she used the potion her identity would be revealed to me and she'd no longer be able to blackmail me so easily. But…" she broke off, hands clawing into fists.

"It didn't work?" I asked.

"Oh, it worked. The Regent fell in love, but not with her." Her shoulders trembled. "He fell in love with me. Me, whom he had never so much as conversed with in all his life. Me." She pointed at her face.

Catherine was by no means an unattractive woman, but she was no great beauty and many years past her prime. Which is not to say an affair couldn't have taken place if the Regent had been charmed by her personality; but if it was as she said and they had never spoken, that seemed unlikely. "What a disaster," I murmured. "How did it happen? Did you make a mistake in the spell?"

"I'd never made an error before, and I've never made one since," she said, eyes flashing. "Certainly not in this. I'd made dozens of similar potions before and countless after."

I wanted to point out that everyone was fallible, but keeping my mouth shut seemed the more prudent course. Besides, I didn't think she had made a mistake – I thought she'd been framed. "So what do you think happened?"

"I don't know." She pressed long fingers to her forehead as though the memory pained her. "It was horrible. When I realized what had happened, I tried to flee, but he sent soldiers to bring me back. Professed his love for me in front of countless courtiers, with seemingly no regard for the repercussions. Not only had he fallen for the wrong person, the potion was far more potent than I'd ever intended, and it impacted everything he thought, every action he took.

"Marie, as you would expect, was in a frenzy over it. He cared not for how he was hurting her, and the depression that ensued made her physically ill." Catherine shook her head. "I cast the spell days before the summer solstice, but the spell held the power of one cast at the very moment of the season's transition. I thought it would never end. The effects of these potions normally fade over a matter of days, but it lasted for weeks. Everyone suspected what had been done, but of course, it couldn't be proven. Not that that really mattered – women have been burned for less."

"Did Marie out you as a witch?"

"No," she whispered. "Not even then. I told her everything, but how could she possibly forgive me? The spell may have gone awry, but the fact remained that I'd intentionally created a potion for her husband to make him love another woman."

"What happened next?"

"The Regent's son, Aiden, was particularly incensed. There was no doubt in his mind that I was a witch and was the cause of his father's irrational behavior. He hated me for the hurt caused to his mother, and demanded time and time again that I be put to death. And once the potion's effects finally began to fade, the Regent was of the same mind. But Marie pleaded with him to have mercy on me, and he satisfied himself with taking everything I had and evicting me from his household. Marie spoke with me once after my sentencing, and made me swear to stay far away from anyone she was close to. My life would be forfeit if I ever came back."

"Did you ever see the masked woman again?" I asked. Anushka had obviously wanted Catherine dead, but Marie had interfered. Had she known it was Anushka who'd requested the love potion? And why would Anushka do such a thing to her ally? There were so many unknowns.

"Not since the night I delivered it to her."

"And you have no idea who she was? No clues that might narrow down her identity?"

Catherine lifted one shoulder, then let it slump. "Not really. She was of average height and build, and she moved easily, so I do not think she was past her middle years. Her clothes were of fine cut and material, and she always met with me in the castle, but never anywhere that would suggest her identity."

"Nothing at all?" I pressed. "No mannerisms or tics you recognized from any of the women at court?"

"None. She was very careful to keep her identity a secret."

I hesitated. "Was there ever any suggestion that she might be a witch herself?"

Catherine grew still. "Why?"

I stared silently at her until she sighed.

"She gave no such indication."

"But you would have known, yes?" I pressed. "You knew I was."

"Only because you drew on the earth's power right in front of me," Catherine replied. "Which is something she never did. What cause have you to believe she might have the talent? Do you know who she is?" She leaned forward, eyes searching mine.

"If she were a witch, she could have substituted her own potion for yours," I said, choosing not to answer her question in its entirety. "What better and more sure way to get rid of you, with no one ever suspecting her. Not even you."

Catherine said nothing, but her cheeks rose to a high color. She had long since ceased petting Souris, but I could see her hands balling into fists where they lay on her lap. Her anger gave me the answer to my question. I could not even imagine how I would feel, having thought for all those long years that I had ruined my own life with a simple mistake, only to discover that it had been orchestrated by another.

"We could find her," I said softly. "You and I, together."

Her eyes flicked to mine. "Revenge?"

I shrugged. "At the very least, you could discover the truth."

"Why would you help me?" she asked, suspicion in her eyes. "What interest have you in this?"

"A very personal one," I said. "Because I believe the witch whose curse I wish to break is the same one who orchestrated your fall from grace." I purposefully refrained from telling her that I suspected her former mistress knew the witch's identity.

All the color fled from her cheeks, but before I could garner much more than surprise from her expression, she dropped her head. "Marie warned me to stay away," she said. "I need to think hard about the consequences of doing otherwise before I take any action."

I wanted to demand that she decide now – the promise all but forcing the words from my lips, but I clamped them shut. Better for her to come around to the idea herself than for me to try to bully her. She'd be a stronger ally if she acted of her own accord. "Very well," I said, rising to my feet. "If you decide you want to discover the identity of the woman who ruined your life, send me word."

CHAPTER 26
Tristan

He had gone too far.

Brushing aside the guards as though they were little more than flies, I flung open the doors to the throne room and then bound them shut behind me with enough magic to ensure we wouldn't be interrupted.

It was disgusting. An abomination.

The heels of my boots thudded against the marble as I strode toward the throne, the lamps flaring up as I passed, my power looking for an outlet as it filled the room.

He had to be mad – what else could drive him to make such a match?

My father was alone in the room, and he did not bother to look up at my approach, which infuriated me all the more. There was a table spread in front of the throne, laden with enough food to feed two dozen men; but of him, all I could see was the top of his head as he bent over a steaming platter.

"You great gluttonous pig." The words were out before I could even think, the icy coldness of my voice at odds with the fire burning through my veins.

The hand holding a leg of chicken paused in its rise, but still, he did not look up. "Have you no shame?" I hissed. "All your people suffer food rations, and here you sit, shoveling all you can fit and more down your gullet."

213

His gluttony was not what I was really angry about, but it would serve. I wasn't ready to put words to the real reason, though it hung between us like the stench of a sewer.

My father set the chicken leg down. And then he raised his head.

He looked as weary as I had ever seen him, eyes drooped and shadowed, lines I had never noticed before marring his skin. "Tristan," he said, leaning back on the throne and resting his elbows on the arms. "I have very, very few pleasures in life. I will not begrudge myself this one. Not as long as I am king." He tilted his head slightly to one side. "Unless, of course, that is why you are here?"

Reaching up over his head, he lifted the crown from where it was casually hooked over the back of the throne. "Finally come to take it? Here." He tossed the golden circlet over the table. "Have it."

It landed with a loud clank against the stairs of the dais, bounced once, then rolled across the floor before coming to a stop at my feet. I stared at it, astonishment chasing away my anger and giving me a moment of clarity. A moment was all I needed to realize what had happened.

I looked up. "It's frustrating, isn't it, when your pawns don't play by your rules?"

He stared silently back at me, but I needed no confirmation that he understood. I knew now what Lessa had done to provoke his wrath, the knowledge solid in my mind as only the truth was. "This is Lessa's doing. She has her own endgame in mind."

Very slowly, he nodded. "How long have you known?"

"That Anaïs was dead, or that it was my own sister who had stolen her place?" I didn't wait for an answer. "I knew it wasn't Anaïs within moments of speaking with her. Lessa is not so fine an actress as she thinks."

"Fine enough to fool the girl's own father."

I laughed, the sound harsh. "Angoulême never bothered to know Anaïs. He saw her only as he imagined her to be."

"And now she *is* as he imagined her to be."

I grimaced. "Even so."

"And how did you know it was Lessa?" He sounded genuinely curious, as though this were all a game with no lives at stake.

"There are few with power enough to manage it," I said. "Fewer still who could go so long without their absence noted. And only *one* capable of this level of duplicity."

His eyes gleamed. "I was curious as to when you would figure out the half-bloods' talent. Did they tell you directly, or did one of them slip up?"

"A slip, of sorts." I searched his face, trying to gauge him and failing. "And you? How did you discover that those with human blood can lie?"

Emotion flashed across his face, too swift for me to identify, but enough for me to know I'd struck a nerve. The light behind him dimmed. "Lessa's mother. She lied to me. I caught her. I killed her."

There was much, much more to that story than anyone knew. "What was the lie?"

My father shook his head once. Even in this rare moment of honesty between us, some things he would not tell, so I started down another path. "What did you do with Anaïs's... body?" It was still hard to say it, hard to relegate my friend to an inanimate corpse.

He snorted derisively. "Of all the questions you might ask, you choose a sentimental one like that? Why do you even care?"

I hoped all the powers in this world and the next would strike me down if I *stopped* caring. "Humor me."

Something in my voice wiped the mockery away from his. "Fire. Hot enough to burn away any trace that she ever existed."

I bowed my head, not bothering to hide my grief. It was part of what made me different from him, and I wanted him to see it. I thought he would say something – mock me for my sentiments. Tell me that they made me weak. He didn't disappoint.

He leaned back and rested his head against the gold throne.

"Everything had come to pass as I had anticipated. You had foolishly allowed your emotions to guide you and played your hand. Attacked me when you thought I intended to harm Cécile." He sighed. "If you thought clearly and logically, you would have known that I'd never allow harm to come to that girl. She is more precious to me than perhaps even to you, which is why I had the witch they call La Voisin brought to Trollus the moment she was injured. Once I had her assurances that Cécile could be saved, I decided to take advantage of the situation as it had presented itself. You acted predictably. Your sister did not.

"Lessa was supposed to prevent Anaïs from interfering, but for her own reasons chose not to." He grimaced. "Lessa came into your rooms moments after you left with Cécile. And in that moment, I thought I was done. That all my plans, and plots, and work, and hardships had been for naught. And for a moment, I wished that you..." He broke off. "But instead of killing me, she dispatched your loyal little friend. And then she offered me a bargain."

I didn't care about the bargain: I cared about what he'd been about to say. That I'd... *what?* What had he wished I'd done?

"The bargain was this: I let her take over Anaïs's life in exchange for her becoming my spy in the Angoulême household."

"Why would she want such an existence?" I asked. "She'd be living a lie. Living every day with the fear of discovery, and knowing that if she was discovered, that her life would be forfeit." Even as I asked the question, I knew the answer.

My father shrugged. "She clearly thought the risks worth the reward."

Better to live a lie than to live a slave.

I shifted my weight, too many thoughts filling my head. This was not the sort of conversation he and I ever had. He was treating me almost like I was his... I pushed the thought away. We were not equals. It was all tricks. Always tricks, with him. "If she killed Anaïs first, then you were released. You could have killed Lessa where she stood, but you did not. Why?"

"Bastard half-blood or not, she is my daughter."

"Which makes you no less likely to kill her than anyone else who stands in your way."

His fingers twitched ever so slightly. "Think what you'd like. But to answer your question, I made the bargain with her because I considered it to be to my advantage. Not only would I gain a spy in the home of my greatest adversary, I would gain a most powerful ally."

"Because Anaïs was the heir to the Duchy of Angoulême," I said. "Lessa could dispatch the Duke and inherit it and all of his powerful alliances."

"Just so."

I nodded slowly. "It was a good plan."

"Indeed."

I shifted my weight to my other leg. I didn't feel well. "Lessa was the cause of what happened with Mother, wasn't she?"

This time it was my father's turn not to hide his emotions. His fingers clenched on the arms of the throne, and I could see a vein rise in his forehead. "Wretched creature wasn't satisfied with becoming a duchesse, she wanted to be a princess."

"She wants to be Queen." My father met my gaze, and for a heartbeat, we were in perfect understanding. "Does Angoulême know Roland's *name*?" I asked, knowing in my heart already that it was the case, but wanting confirmation from my father's lips. Wanting, though I hated to admit it, some reassurance that he had a plan that would fix things.

"I have strong reason to believe that is the case."

I expected his anger to rise at the admission, but the throbbing vein in his forehead disappeared, and he averted his gaze, looking over my shoulder at the door. Was it possible that he was upset about what was happening to my brother? Was it possible that he cared?

My heart thudded loud in my ears. Dare I say it? Was it the correct move? "You could undo all these troubles," I said, my desire to keep the hope from my voice making it sound toneless. "You could reinstate me as heir."

A smile grew on his lips, growing wider and wider. But it wasn't an expression of happiness or pleasure, and I knew nothing had changed. I became painfully aware that I was dressed only in shirtsleeves, dusty and sweaty, that my coat and hat were still hanging on the back of Pierre's chair. And my gloves still sat on the wall next to the tree, leaving my weakened state glaringly obvious.

His eyes met mine. "They say nothing worth having comes easily, Tristan. If you want the crown, you're going to have to take it."

The golden circlet still lay at my feet.

I wanted to snatch it up.

I wanted to run as far away from it as possible.

Swallowing the burn in my throat, I reached down, forcing my numb fingers to pick up the symbol of my father's power. The weight of it made my wrist scream, but I had a lot of practice in keeping pain from showing. In one, two, three steps, I was up on the dais, and I slammed the crown against his chest. "I'll take it when I'm good and ready, and that's a promise." The weight of my word sank into me, horrible, wonderful, and binding.

Letting go of the crown, I spun on my heel and started down the steps toward the door, and not once did I look back.

The antechamber was full of my father's guardsmen and women, and they all tensed when I swung the doors open, a few peering past me to see if my father had survived our encounter. None of them looked as though they had put any great effort into trying to get past my wards, which led me to believe that my father had forewarned them not to interfere. Which led me to believe that he had predicted my arrival after his announcement. I wondered if his seeming ability to see the future would ever stop amazing me.

The guards parted to let me pass, and I stalked through their midst, eager to be away, when a scent that didn't belong caught my attention.

Horses.

I stopped in my tracks and took one step backwards. If not for the smell, I might not have noticed the man leaning against the wall, his dark cloak blending into the shadows. A guard stepped between us.

"Move," I said.

The guard licked his lips nervously, staring at my feet. "The King has ordered that he not speak to anyone while in Trollus, my lord."

I didn't respond, only stood silently, waiting. The guard moved out of my way.

The human didn't straighten from his slouch against the wall at my approach, only watched me with the interest of someone who has nothing better to look at. He was somewhat shorter than me, but something about him made him seem larger than he was. A certain mien that made me suspect that he was someone of importance in the human world.

His clothes confirmed my suspicion, his fur-lined cloak of the finest wool and boots polished to a high shine. A sword hung from his waist, and I did not fail to notice the corner of the emblem stitched onto his breast. An officer in the Regent's army, and unless I missed my mark, part of the Regent's court as well. But I didn't really care about any of that. He was human and he was here, which meant that he was working for my father.

"Who are you?" I asked.

He straightened out of his slouch. "I might ask you the same question."

"You'd be the first."

He laughed, but there was no humor in it. "I suppose it's difficult to maintain anonymity when one is trapped in a cage."

My smile was all teeth. "For some more than others."

"In a cage and in the world, Your Highness." He bowed, but it was sardonic. For a second, I thought he was mocking my fall from grace, but I quickly realized it was more than that. He was mocking our claim to any sort of authority. It wasn't just me being censured, it was my father. *Who was he to be so bold?*

"You seem to manage," I said, taking a jab at his sense of self-importance to see if he would bite and reveal his identity.

He only inclined his head. "We all have our talents. Now if you'd please excuse me, I have important matters requiring my attention, and I do not care to linger in this hole longer than I must." He started to brush by me, but I caught him before he could go more than a pace. Not with my hand, as I might otherwise, but with magic.

I all but felt his skin crawl, his shudder visible to the eye. "How is she?" I asked, keeping my voice low.

He turned his head, looking me up and down before snorting softly. "Better than you, it would seem," he said. "And yet worse. The woman I have watching her says she has turned to the dark arts."

Blood magic. My stomach tightened at the idea of Cécile killing anything, and I almost regretted handing my father back the crown when I might have murdered him where he sat.

"I know what it is she seeks and how," he said. "And as much as I know it is against her will, if I were master of my own, I would see her dead before I would see her succeed."

Like a giant fist, my power contracted, forcing a wheeze of pain from the man. Only the small thread of control I had left kept me from squeezing the life out of him. From his own lips he'd admitted he could not harm her. My father owned his will, and this man hated him for it. Which meant there was a chance he'd help Cécile if he thought it in his best interests. Or he might be so bound by oath that he'd turn around and deliver the information back to my father. Did I risk giving him knowledge that might help her? It might be her only chance. Drawing in a ragged breath, I released him.

He staggered back and away from me, colliding with the guards. "You and yours are a scourge on this earth," he hissed. "If Cécile falls like so many before her, it will not be because of anything I have done. Her death will be on your hands."

Shoving the guards aside, I leaned close so that we were eye to eye. "I think that if you let her die because of what you have *not* done, you will find that guilt is not such an easy thing to escape." Hands were snatching at me, pulling me back and away. And I could feel my father coming in our direction; this man of enough importance to him that he'd interfere himself.

I had only a second. Jerking out of their grip, I whispered, "There is a loophole in the promise she made. Tell her to think on it."

The human's eyes widened, but there was no time to say more. I could only pray that I'd delivered Cécile an ally, not an enemy.

CHAPTER 27
Cécile

I spent the entire night sitting in front of the fire, hoping Catherine would contact me through the flames and tell me that she'd help; but all I'd got for my efforts were bloodshot eyes, smoky hair, and the realization that the other witch might be too afraid to provide me with assistance. If I hadn't heard from her by tonight, my plan was to try the map spell again to see if the mark at the castle moved. It was a sure way to prove that it was Anushka, but I'd been avoiding using it again mostly because I so badly *wanted* to. The need to feel that flood of power lurked inside me, and I was afraid of how much worse the feeling would be if I gave in to the temptation.

Although I might not have a choice.

We were rehearsing in the foyer de la danse, because the stage in the room was much closer in size to the one we'd perform on at the castle than the massive one in the main theatre. A dozen young girls from the dance school played the roles belonging to the ladies of the court, their tarlatan skirts jutting out from their hips to reveal legs muscled from hours of training. The steps were no challenge to them, but their eyes gleamed with the excitement of holding the attention, however briefly, of the most influential members of the company.

I watched dubiously while crewmembers rigged a swing that

would suspend me above the rest of the cast through the second half of the masque.

"And you will swing gently back and forth," Monsieur Johnson explained to me. "The Queen of Virtue, smiling down upon her beautiful subjects."

"I can't smile while I sing," I said, giving the swing a hard jerk with one hand to ensure it was secure.

"Smile with your eyes," he exclaimed. "With your posture. With your very soul!"

From behind him, my mother rolled her eyes, and I had to bite my lip to keep from laughing. I was back in her good graces after my venture out with Julian, who had dutifully returned me home before midnight, and, to the best of my knowledge, not breathed a word about where we had gone. "My soul will be beaming, monsieur," I said. "I will not disappoint."

He clapped his hands together, then ran off to herd the rest of the cast into the wings.

"What a silly little man," my mother murmured, yanking on the ropes. Seeming unsatisfied, she took hold of the swing with both hands and lifted her feet so that she was suspended off the ground. "If it holds my weight, it will hold yours," she said. "Although maybe we should attach a wire to you just in case."

"It will be fine," I said, sitting down on the plank.

"Please hold on tightly." She pulled my hair out from where it was tucked behind my ears. "If you were to fall and injure yourself, it would be a disaster."

"I won't fall," I assured her.

She did not look convinced.

"How do you feel about tomorrow?" I asked. Tomorrow was closing night for this particular production run, and Genevieve's final public performance.

"It matters less than you might think," she said, bending down to kiss me on the forehead. "I'll be living through you every time you step onstage."

Pulleys creaked, and I lifted up into the air until I was at the same level as the massive crystal chandelier hanging in the center of the room. Kicking my feet, I began to swing back and forth.

"Too much vigor," Monsieur Johnson shouted. "You look like a child at play, not a queen."

I slowed my momentum.

"Uncross your ankles!"

I did so.

"I didn't say spread your legs," he shouted. "You're Virtue, not some Pigalle harlot!"

My mother snarled something I couldn't hear and the man blanched. "Please keep your knees together, Mademoiselle de Troyes," he said, tone contrite. "Otherwise the audience will see up your skirts."

He nodded to the musicians, and they began to play. Taking a few swift breaths, I inhaled deeply, and then I sang.

For the first verse, I was alone on the stage, but then the dancers made their way out from the wings. They did not make it far before Monsieur Johnson called a halt. "Softer, mademoiselle," he said to me. "This is not the theatre."

We started and stopped another dozen times, while the man shouted instructions and criticism, keen to have perfection from the professionals before he brought in the untutored ladies of the court. The rough plank of the swing was hard, and my bottom grew numb even as my back began to ache.

Would the mark on the castle move if the spell were performed again, I wondered. And what would I do if it did?

"Again!"

The map spell had given me clues to how Anushka was achieving immortality, but I was at a loss of what to make of them. I was certain the mark at the castle had been the living, breathing witch, but that didn't bring me much closer to discovering her identity. I was sure Marie knew who she was, but I was just as sure she wouldn't volunteer the information, especially to me. If I could get a strand of her hair, it was possible I could take the knowledge from her mind with magic, but getting the hair would be no mean feat, given I hadn't so much as seen her since our first meeting.

"You call yourselves the best? This is a disaster! Again!"

We finally made it all the way through the first piece without interruption and were rewarded with grudging praise. Turning to my mother, Monsieur Johnson began to speak in earnest, and I gave off swinging. My back ached fiercely, and I swallowed away the malaise swimming in my stomach.

What linked the dead women? Why had Anushka chosen them among all the other souls living on the Isle? It was possible they were entirely random, but my gut told me otherwise. If there was a pattern, it was possible I could predict who was next, and that had to be worth something.

Leaning backwards, I cracked my aching back, my eyes drifting over the paintings of women hanging to the left of the stage. Their hairstyles and clothing were old-fashioned and strange to me, but what caught my eye was something all too familiar. My heart lurched, and I jerked upright, twisting on the swing to stare at the painting of a young woman.

Letting go with one hand, I touched the necklace at my throat, twin to the one the artist had rendered. But that paled in comparison to the fire of exhilaration that seared through my veins as I took in the writing on the plaque beneath it.

I'd seen that name before.

CHAPTER 28
Cécile

"This way," I whispered, trotting toward the foyer's entrance. Chris hurried after me, ladder slung under one arm.

"What happens if we get caught in here?" he asked. "Aren't there guards patrolling?"

"Sabine's distracting him, and besides, we're not doing anything wrong," I said, easing the door shut. "But I'd rather not have to answer any questions about why we're here, so keep your voice down."

In truth, my bigger concern was what my mother would do if she knew I'd sneaked out in the middle of the night. With my luck, she'd probably start chaining me to the bed every evening. But it was worth the risk. There was no other time I could reasonably drag a ladder in here to look at the rest of the paintings, and I needed to confirm whether my suspicions were correct.

While Chris set up the ladder, I circled the room with my lamp, examining all the portraits that were at eye level. I had the map and my neatly written list of names, and I compared the little engraved plaques below each painting as I went. "Estelle Perrot," I murmured, lifting the lamp so I could better see her face. "I found one."

Chris hurried over. "She's wearing your necklace," he said.

"I know. So is Ila Laval. She's in the one to the left of the stage." I gestured in that direction, but of course it was too dark to see. "My mother told me it's a family heirloom."

We were both quiet, the implications of *that* hanging heavily between us.

"Who are all these women?" Chris finally asked, touching the gilded frame.

"Mostly ballerinas," I said, making a note next to Estelle's name. "But some of them are sopranos."

"Like you."

I nodded, moving on to the next portrait. There were dozens in the room – the task was going to take forever.

"Cécile?"

I heard the question in his voice, but I wasn't ready to talk about the realization that was twisting through my stomach. "I know," I said. "Let's finish this, and then... And then we'll discuss what we've discovered."

We circled the room, then went around again with the ladder. But even the effort of clambering up and down the rungs wasn't enough to drive away the chill that prickled my skin every time we found a portrait matching a name on the list.

Only when I was certain we'd examined the name and face of every one of the two hundred years' worth of paintings did I finally sit cross-legged in the center of the room, my skirts pooled around me and the annotated list on the wooden floor. "Help yourself to a drink from the cart," I said, my eyes fixed on the undeniable truth on the paper. The last ten names on my list were represented by portraits in the foyer, and every last one of them was wearing my necklace.

Which meant all of them were my ancestors.

"Here." Chris handed me a glass, and with a shaking hand, I took a large swallow. The brandy seared down my throat, but did nothing to steady my nerves.

"She's killing your maternal line," he said, sitting across from me. "But why?"

I set my drink down on the floor, the answer coming to me even as he asked the question. "Blood." I sucked in a breath of air through my teeth, seeing the verity of the trolls' prophesy. "The connection of a blood tie can be important to some spells, because it is a link between people. That's how she's doing it."

"But that means…"

"It means that all these women are her descendants. And," I swallowed down the burn of brandy rising back up in my throat, "That means so am I."

I clenched my fists so hard my pencil snapped. I'd thought the prophesy meant I'd do something, that it would be my and Tristan's actions that would bring an end to Anushka's life. But that wasn't it at all. What it meant was that I was a future victim. I didn't have to do anything – my very existence ensured she'd one day come after me to maintain her immortal life. All the trolls had to do was hold on to me and wait.

All this time, I'd thought there was something special about me, something making me uniquely capable of ending the curse. And what a fool I was to have thought so. Any of Anushka's line would have been sufficient. Only chance had made it me.

Chris had picked up the end of my broken pencil and was counting on his fingers, then writing down numbers between names. "There's something of a pattern," he said. "There's a few times she breaks with it, but for the most part, the deaths are usually nineteen or thirty-eight years apart. Can't say what the significance of that is, but it does look as though she's picking one off almost every generation."

"My grandmother's name isn't on our list."

Chris picked up the map and unrolled it, pointing to the burn mark we hadn't investigated. The one on the road to the Hollow.

Taking the pencil, I carefully wrote my grandmother's name and the year of her death. It was nineteen years after the last name on my list. By the odds, the soonest Anushka could be expected to kill again was nineteen years later. I did the math. "We have six years before she's likely to strike."

"It could be less," Chris warned.

"Or longer." I wondered how Thibault would take it when I told him he could have another twenty-five years to wait before

Anushka came after me. I did not think it would sit well with him to know that he'd be a doddering old man when he finally won his freedom.

Except it wouldn't be me she came after.

Leaping to my feet, I snatched up the lamp and went over to where my mother's portrait hung. It was many years old, from the prime of her youth, and before she'd given me the necklace. With a shaking hand, I reached up to touch the gold paint on the canvas. I wasn't the next target, my mother was.

"Are you going to tell the trolls it's Genevieve she'll go after?"

"N... N..." I tried to force the word *no* out, but it kept sticking on my lips, the desire to do what was needed to fulfill my promise feeling almost as necessary as breathing. "If I tell them, they'll kill her in the hopes of ending Anushka's immortality, and with it, the curse. If it were me, it would be different. Being bonded to Tristan keeps me safe from the King. He might well drag me back to Trollus to keep me out of the witch's reach, but he won't kill me."

Chris looked unconvinced, but I knew that despite how horribly Tristan's father treated him, he'd never risk killing him. Thibault did the things he did because he believed Tristan needed to be a certain kind of man to rule the trolls. And while I'd never condone or truly understand his abuse of his son, I was certain that the King would do everything in his power to keep Tristan alive.

The sound of Sabine's laugh trickled through the walls, echoed by the deeper sound of the guard. We both hurried behind the curtain at the far end of the room.

Just as I dimmed the lantern, the door opened, and two sets of footsteps came inside. "I told you that you were imagining those voices," Sabine said. "There's no one here unless the opera house has ghosts."

"What's this ladder doing in here?"

"They're probably making space for Cécile de Troyes' portrait. You did hear that she's to star in next season's production?" It was only because I knew her so well that I heard the nervous edge to her voice. "Now didn't you say you'd show me the salons out front? I've been dying to see them."

"For a pretty girl like you, I can show you anything you like."

Sabine giggled, and I rolled my eyes on her behalf, but a sigh of relief still escaped my chest when the door opened and shut again. "Let's get out of here."

Leaving the ladder where it was in case the guard came back, we moved silently through the dark corridors of the theatre and out the crew entrance.

"Sabine will meet us here," I said, extracting a pair of warmer gloves from the pocket of my cloak. "We need to think of a plan – of some way to protect my mother."

"Cécile?"

I jumped, colliding with Chris as I spun around. "Fred?"

My brother stepped out of the shadows, his black horse trailing along behind. "What are you doing here at this hour?"

What was he doing here? "I don't see how it's any of your business," I said, my voice sharper than I intended it to be. "You made it clear you wanted nothing more to do with my *delusions*."

He grimaced. "I didn't mean it. I was angry, and... You're my little sister, Cécile. There isn't anything I wouldn't do to keep you safe."

Tension I hadn't even realized I was carrying slipped out of my shoulders, relief filling me. Losing my brother's goodwill and trust had bothered me, and having him back on my side meant a great deal. A spark of light in the darkness. "I'm glad to hear it."

"Can I walk you home?" he asked. "There's something I need to talk to you about."

I didn't want to go home. Sneaking out had been hard enough, and I needed to talk to my friends about what we'd learned tonight. But I also didn't want to turn down my brother's tenuous peace offering, so I nodded.

We started to the main street, and Chris made to follow, but Fred rounded on him. "Can't I talk to my sister alone without you listening to every word we say?"

Chris stopped and held up his hands in defense. "Sorry, I just…"

"It's fine," I said, catching my friend's eye. "Wait for Sabine. Make sure she gets home safe. I'll meet both of you at dawn for that ride we were talking about."

Chris retreated back to the crew entrance without argument, but there was no missing the hurt in his eyes. I waited until Fred and I were out of earshot before saying, "If it wasn't for the fact I knew you two used to be best friends, I'd never guess it for how you treat him."

"I've been in Trianon for almost five years," he replied in a low voice. "Things change. People change."

"And that gives you the right to treat him worse than you would a stranger?"

"I don't trust him."

I nearly stopped in my tracks. "Whyever not?" There was no one more trustworthy than Christophe Girard. He didn't have a dishonest bone in his body.

"Because I don't understand his motives." Fred pulled the hood of his cloak up. "Why's he helping you with this mad plan of yours to free those monsters? What's in it for him?"

"He's helping me because he's my friend," I said, trying to shove down my rising temper. "And they aren't monsters."

"Right. It couldn't possibly be because they've provided him some sort of incentive of the golden variety."

"No." I shook my head sharply, refusing to even consider the notion.

"Cécile…" He broke off as though his frustration with me were too great a thing to articulate. "It's what the trolls do. It's how they control the Isle – by buying everyone off and paying assassins to kill those who interfere with their schemes."

"Because you know so much about them now?"

"More than you might think." He stopped, pulling his horse around so it blocked the wind. "Cécile, I spoke to Lord Aiden…"

"You what?" Fury chased away the chill of the air. "Fred, you promised to keep quiet."

"Would you listen?" He bent down so that we were eye to eye. "He approached *me*. He already knew everything about them and about you. Told me that the Regency has always known about them, but they can't move against them for fear of what the trolls' agents will do. Whole families have been assassinated in the worst sort of ways for even the smallest of slights."

I swallowed, looking away from him.

"They know that none of this is your fault," Fred continued. "They want to help you. Lord Aiden says there's a way to get you free of the promise you made to find the witch. You could be done with all of this, and you could go home. If you'll only speak to him…"

"No." My voice sounded harsh and unfamiliar, the malignant power of my oath taking control of my mind, turning my thoughts dark and violent. "You will not interfere. And neither will they."

Fred took a step back, bumping into his horse. "Cécile?"

I looked down, realizing with horror that my little knife was in my hand, blade extended. "I'm sorry," I whispered, letting it slip from my fingers and into the snow. "I'm so sorry, Frédéric. You need to stay away from me."

Spinning around, I hurried in the opposite direction, my breathing ragged. I was not in control of myself – that I'd been willing to harm my own beloved brother was proof. And it made me doubt every decision I'd made and action I'd taken since that fateful night on the beach. How much of this was what I wanted? How much was what the troll king wanted? Fear careened through my heart, because I was no longer certain of what I was capable of. Because I was starting to wonder if there was no line I couldn't be driven across.

An arm wrapped around my head, and a damp cloth reeking of herbs and magic clamped across my face.

"I'm sorry, Cécile. I'm so sorry for this," my brother whispered into my ear. "But it's the only way I can help you."

Then there was nothing.

CHAPTER 29
Cécile

I awoke, not with a start, but in a slow and arduous climb to consciousness. Footsteps thudded over my head – but it took a few moments of blinking at the gapped floorboards to realize I was lying on the dirt floor of a cellar, my feet and wrists bound and a rag stuffed in my mouth. I tried to spit it out, but the effort made me gag, which made my eyes water. My nose started running, and breathing became a challenge, little bubbles of snot forming, breaking, then dripping down my cheek. It was horrible, but so very fitting.

My brother had betrayed me.

That he believed he was acting in my best interests didn't ease the hurt, because he'd still taken away my freedom to make my own choices and my ability to do what I believed was right. I was Tristan's only hope, and he was the half-bloods' only chance at a better life, and I felt in my gut that I'd been so close to making a breakthrough in my hunt. Now everything was lost.

Above, I could hear the sound of weight shifting on a chair, and the measured step of another person pacing across the floor. Neither of the people spoke, but then the *tick tick* of a dog's toenails caught my attention, and I knew where I was. Lifting my head as much as I could, I peered into the darkness of the cellar, the familiar table and shelves stacked with oddities faintly visible in the dim light. My heart sank: this was Catherine's cellar. It had been her magic that had allowed my brother to subdue me. Another betrayal.

I wondered if she had been duping me from the beginning – whether it had been no coincidence that she'd crossed paths with Sabine and that I'd ended up on her doorstep. Had it all been an act to lure me in and gain my trust, and if so, did that mean my brother had been involved from the beginning? He'd said the Regent knew everything, but why go through such an elaborate process when they could just as easily have arrested me and forced the information out?

Fred had said they wanted to help me get free of the trolls, which certainly implied a desire to keep them contained. But if that was what the Regent wanted, why not just kill me and be done with it? What possible reason could he have for keeping me alive?

The rear door to the shop opened and slammed shut, heavy boots thudding across the floor.

"My lord. I expected you sooner." I tensed at the sound of my brother's voice, my ears peeled for the reply. It was Lord Aiden he was speaking to, I was sure of it.

"I had to ensure I wasn't followed. The moment the trolls realize she's missing, they'll have every agent on the Isle looking for her. Did she have the book on her?"

"It was in her bag with some other papers. Lists of names and dates."

"Good. Without it, we have nothing. Catherine, I assume you've taken precautions to ensure she can't use magic to contact her friends?" His voice was familiar. I knew it – had heard it before. But where?

"She's bound and gagged," the witch replied in an emotionless voice. "The spell will keep her asleep for some time yet, given how small she is."

"It won't hurt her, will it?" Fred asked, and I scowled around my gag, wondering if he'd considered *that* before he'd used it on me. "Why are we keeping her here anyway? You said you'd help my sister, not keep her captive in some hovel in Pigalle. Why aren't you keeping her in the castle?"

"Too many eyes, and it is not your place to question my decisions," Lord Aiden snapped, and in the change of tone, I recognized his voice. Lord Aiden was the King's messenger. A thousand pieces fell into place, and suddenly the King's confidence in his plans to take the Isle all made sense. He controlled the man who would inherit the Regency. And yet that very man was double-crossing him, so it would seem his confidence was misplaced.

"You need to report to duty, de Troyes. Her friends will be looking for her, and you're the first person they'll go to. Make sure your story is convincing."

"I don't care to leave my sister tied up in a cellar."

"If you value her life as much as you claim, you'll do just that," Aiden replied. "We must move quickly as it is if we are to find this witch and extricate your sister from the trolls' power. We cannot raise their suspicion." He didn't know who or where Anushka was…

Fred was quiet, and I prayed that he wouldn't leave. That he'd reconsidered what he'd done. But he didn't. "Take care of her," he muttered, and the door opened and slammed shut.

Disappointment carved out my guts, but I forced myself to concentrate on the conversation that ensued between Aiden and Catherine.

"Is the book what she was using to track Anushka?" he demanded once Fred was gone. "The troll king gave it to her on the beach – it was clearly of some significance."

"It's significant if it really is hers," Catherine replied. "It's certainly old enough, and the fact it's written in a northern tongue is no small coincidence. But I won't know until I cast the spell."

"Do it now. We can't waste any more time."

"Not without my pardon." Catherine paused. "Those have always been our terms, my lord. I want my life back. I want your mother to know the truth."

"Leave my mother out of this. She knows nothing of the trolls, and I intend to keep it that way."

That wasn't true. Of a surety, Marie knew about the trolls and Anushka, but I wasn't sure if he was unaware of that fact or was lying. I'd assumed all of the Regent's family was in this together, but maybe I was wrong. Maybe they were as self-motivated and deceptive with each other as Tristan's family was.

"Your mother is involved in this, whether she wills it or not. Though she must be living under another identity, Anushka is involved with the court. It was her who gave the potion to your father, and though we must needs keep her alive to keep the curse in place, that doesn't mean she can't be punished."

"My mother doesn't keep company with witches."

"She kept company with me. She keeps company with Cécile."

Aiden was quiet for a minute. "She'd not knowingly harbor Anushka – it's too much of a risk. If the trolls ever discovered we were working against them... No, my mother cannot be involved. You will not speak to her of this, and neither will I."

"You haven't told your parents, have you?" Catherine's voice was amused. "They have no idea how caught up in the King's web you really are. Nothing more than the troll king's errand boy. After generations of regents so carefully toeing the line between keeping the trolls placated and imprisoned, you hand them the keys to the realm for the sake of your greed."

"You overstep yourself, La Voisin. The gratitude I felt for you in my youth was used up a long time ago. And besides, if my plan works, I'll have accomplished something that no other regent has..." He broke off. "Did you hear something outside? If that's de Troyes lurking about..."

Above, there was a flurry of footsteps and the sounds of a struggle overhead. A familiar voice shouted, "Let me go." *Sabine*.

Lord Aiden was swearing as he struggled to subdue my friend, and I held my breath, afraid he'd hurt her. "Open the cellar. We'll have to keep her here for now."

The trapdoor flipped open, and I closed my eyes so they wouldn't realize I was awake. Boots thudded down the ladder, then Sabine was tossed forcibly next to me. She sobbed raggedly around the gag, and I recognized a garbled version of my name. Only when the trapdoor shut again did I open my eyes and nudge her with my knees.

Faint light trickled through the floor, but it was enough to see her face soften with relief. I jerked my chin upwards. *Listen.*

"Do you see now why time is of the essence?" Aiden said. "The girl won't be the first to come looking – no doubt the stable boy is lurking about as well, and he's had contact with the trolls before. He'll go to them for help."

"Pardon first. Then I'll cast the spell, and we'll learn the identity of the witch everyone so desperately seeks. You need me far more than I need you, my lord. You cannot *exploit*" – she spat the word out – "Cécile without my help. Remember that."

"Why would you care?" Aiden asked. "She's naught but another tool in their arsenal."

"I pity her," Catherine replied. "The trolls took her against her will and then manipulated her sentiments so that she'd agree to this bargain. You forget that I saw her when she lay dying in Trollus – she has suffered enough."

He laughed. "I think you give her too much credit, Catherine. She cares a great deal for the prince, that much is certain. She considers many of them her friends. She *wants* them freed."

"I don't think she does. Not deep in her heart," Catherine said. "Because if she did, the trolls would already be loose."

"Are you suggesting she has sabotaged her own hunt?"

"I don't believe her oath would allow her to do so, but regardless, that's not of which I speak."

My pulse sounded loud in my own ears, every muscle tense with anticipation of what she would say. I'd known she'd been holding back information about curses, and it seemed now I was about to discover what. I only prayed it would not be too late.

"Think of what they did to her. They didn't treat her badly or keep her a prisoner in a cell. They married her to a handsome young prince. They made her a princess, and did what they could to make her love him. I knew within an instant of meeting that creature of a king that he was far more clever and complex than you gave him credit for."

"What of it?" Aiden demanded. I wanted to know the same thing, but at the same time my stomach clenched at the idea my emotions had been manipulated. Had the King really known I'd fall for Tristan? That he'd fall for me? Worse, had he actively manipulated us into it?

"The curse is an act of will," Catherine replied. "Will, fueled by an intense desire to see something done and cemented by magic." A chair scraped a bit on the floor, and I could all but see her leaning closer to him. "And it can be broken by will; by an intense desire to see the curse ended driven like a hammer with the force of magic."

I felt numb. Rolling forward, I rested my forehead against the damp earth of the cellar, unable to meet Sabine's questioning gaze. The idea that my role in the prophesy was to be bait had been bad enough, but this was worse. That the King had predicted bonding me to Tristan would make me fall for him, and that my love for him would give me the power to break the curse? I didn't like that. It made me feel sick and even more used than I had before. It made me feel as though falling in love with him hadn't been my choice, but part of a plan much greater than I knew.

"An interesting notion," he said after a minute. "But how she feels about the trolls is of little import. What matters is that the troll prince loves her. It was he who told me there was a loophole in the girl's promise in a desperate hope that I would help her. And I will, but it will come at a cost to him."

Oh, Tristan. Tears dripped off my nose into the dirt.

"Her promise to the troll king was thus: *I promise to do whatever it takes to find her and bring her here.*" His laugh had a hysterical edge to it that made me cringe. "Cécile never went into Trollus. *Here* is the sand she was standing on when she gave her word, and that sand exists outside the barrier."

Of course Tristan had heard the loophole in my promise even while he'd been suffering torture. All his life he'd been twisting words and undermining their meanings. He'd figured out the one way I could win free of my promise without breaking the curse, and he'd tried to give it to me. Now this man intended to use the information against him.

"So you intend for us to find Anushka, bring her to that spot, and then let her escape unharmed." Catherine's voice was toneless, but I knew she was angry. She wanted revenge for what Anushka had done to her, but that wasn't part of Aiden's plan.

"It will be a sweet thing to see the look in that devil of a creature's eyes when he realizes he's been outwitted." He stood and paced slowly across the floor. "You see, Catherine, you need not fear for Cécile's welfare, for she is the most precious thing in all the world, because with her in my possession, I'm in control of Prince Tristan."

No, no, no!

"The half-bloods have rallied behind him again, and there are whispers that a great many others wish to see him on the throne. Mark my words, he intends to kill his father and take the crown. And there is nothing I would like better." He spat out the last words. "With Thibault dead, I'll be free of the foolish promises I made to him in my youth, and with Cécile in my care, Tristan will have to do what I say. I will control the trolls."

From a troll tyrant to a human tyrant.

"What of Anushka?" Catherine pressed again. "What will become of her?"

"I'll let her go," he replied. "She's survived on her own this long, I expect she can live a few generations more."

"She deserves to be punished."

"It doesn't matter what she deserves," Aiden said. "She's all that keeps us safe from the trolls, and that makes her untouchable. Angering her would be madness."

Catherine said nothing, but I could imagine his words were a bitter tonic to swallow, because they were the truth.

"You'll have your pardon after our plans come to fruition," Aiden said. "With what we will accomplish, my father will have no choice but to grant the request. We'll need you to keep Cécile in check."

Silence.

"Very well," Catherine said. "I'll do as you ask, but there are materials I need and preparations that must be made before I can cast the spell. Deal with her other friend, then come back an hour before sunset, and we will begin."

"I'll be here. And don't even think of crossing me, witch." The rear door opened and slammed shut with enough force to make the shop shudder.

An hour before sunset... That was all the time I had to escape. All the time I had to steal back the grimoire and find Anushka myself. Because if I failed, the cost to everyone I cared about in Trollus would be far worse than they ever dreamed possible.

CHAPTER 30
Tristan

The half-bloods had fallen slightly behind, so I took a moment's worth of time to return to my rooms to change the bandages on my wrists. The corridors of my home seemed to swim around me, and I stumbled more than once on the smooth marble floors, my feet feeling like stones attached to my legs.

I had one of my sleeves up and a bandage half unraveled before I realized I wasn't alone.

"Hello, Tristan."

Tucking the bandage back into place, I slowly turned. Lessa, wearing her Anaïs-mask, was sprawled across my bed, head resting on one hand. "Get. Out," I said.

She pushed her bottom lip out into a pout. "So hasty!"

"Get out," I repeated. "Or I will make you leave, and I won't be gentle about it."

A cruel little giggle escaped from between her lips. "Are you so sure you can?" Sitting up, she slid off the bed and came toward me, stopping about a pace away. "I daresay, you aren't looking in the peak of health." Her eyes flicked to my manacled and bandaged wrist and up again. "It must be dreadful to feel so abused."

I stared silently at her. Did she know that I was aware of her true identity? Or was she still going to attempt to pretend to be Anaïs? "What do you want from me?"

Lessa smiled, the curve of her lips familiar in a way that made me want to tear the magic off her face. "We'll get to that." She closed the distance between us so that we were only inches apart. My skin crawled, but I refused to give her the satisfaction of driving me back.

"You're in quite a predicament. One that might very well send you to your death if I don't help you."

"I don't want your help."

She tilted her head back and laughed. "But you might need it. Cécile made a promise to the King to find Anushka. There is nothing he desires more, and his obsession will force her to the grave if she does not succeed. You promised the half-bloods you'd build a stone tree for them, which frankly, requires you to be alive. Except that you know Cécile's time is short, which means *your* time is short, and you are driven to work day and night without rest, which is driving you to the point where you'll burn out your power. Especially given the iron rot that is consuming you. Such a sordid circle of things: the King's desire creates Cécile's obsession, which drives your addiction to your work. Work that the King does not care to see completed, which makes him want the curse broken all the more. Around and around we go." She walked in a slow rotation behind me and back to where she had started. "Spiraling down until someone dies."

"Make your point."

"It doesn't have to be you and Cécile who die." She tilted her head. "It could be him. He is, after all, the instigator."

As if I hadn't thought of that every waking minute for days. "Wonderfully traitorous solution, but unfortunately, killing my father would only delay the inevitable. As I'm sure you're well aware, my brother is heir to the throne, and I cannot imagine he'll suffer me to live long after he is crowned. Any fool could see your little ploy is self-serving."

"It could serve us both." Her voice was soft, persuasive. "No one wants Roland to be king, least of all me."

"Yet you are betrothed to him." Just saying the words made

me feel sick. "And I think you are wrong to say that no one wants him to be king. I believe the Duke wants that very much indeed."

"Betrothals can be broken, alliances reforged. He might be persuaded to see you as king if" – she traced a finger down my chest – "you could be persuaded to take a new wife."

Revulsion held me frozen in place even as my mind recoiled from what she was suggesting. She had to be sick, her brain warped by iron-madness or worse. No amount of ambition could drive anyone toward this. "You are insane." I choked the words out before stepping out of reach. "What sort of twisted creature are you to want such a match?"

The smile slowly melted from her face. "You were not opposed to it so very long ago."

Enough of this. "With Anaïs, perhaps, but not with you." With clawed fingers of magic, I tore the mask off her face, sending her staggering. "Never with you."

Regaining her balance, she snapped her head up to look at me, teeth bared with the fury of a rabid animal. The air in the room went searing hot, the vases and lamps shattering under the pressure. The whole wing of the palace shook and trembled beneath my feet, sending books toppling off their shelves and knocking paintings from the walls.

Instead of trying to stop her, I laughed in my sister's face. "What do you suppose Father will do to you if you kill me?"

The shaking stopped and Lessa's face resumed a false expression of composure. "I don't want you dead."

"Liar."

She huffed out a breath and rolled her eyes. "Is that how it's to be? Because I can lie you'll not believe a single word I say?"

"No," I said. "I'll not believe a thing you say because I don't trust you."

The room began to cool before she answered.

"Believe me or not, it's the truth. I don't want you dead, I want you to see reason." She lifted a foot as though she intended to walk closer, then wisely lowered it again. "Don't you see?

United, we could have everything. Together, we could kill Father, and believing his daughter would become queen, Angoulême would support you over Roland. And if he doesn't?" She shrugged one slender shoulder. "We kill him. Kill Roland, too, because of a certainty, Trollus is better off without our younger brother. Together, no one would be able to stand against us. No one would dare contest our power."

"You are my sister!" And no logic, or reason, or promise of power could undo that fact.

"No one need ever know that."

My whole body went rigid, the warmth of the room doing nothing to chase away the icy prickles of revulsion sweeping my skin. "I'd know!" I screamed the words into her face. "You'd know!"

She didn't even flinch. "If this is about Cécile, be assured that I wouldn't care if you brought her back to Trollus and kept her as your mistress. You'd still be bonded to her, after all. Ours would be primarily a political arrangement."

I could see in her eyes that she didn't care. Even if such a match did disgust her, Lessa was more than capable of pushing such feelings aside in her pursuit of power. Or worse, maybe she wasn't even disgusted by the idea at all. All she wanted was to be queen. It was the only thing that mattered.

"Why do you want this so much?" I wasn't sure why I asked the question. Maybe it was because standing face to face with her, I realized that this was the first time I'd spoken to Lessa as herself. The resemblance between us was undeniable, which made perfect sense, given we shared half the same blood.

She was my sister, and I had always known that, yet rarely had I spoken to her. Never once had I sought her out or tried to learn more about her, because even as a child, I'd known she was seen as an embarrassment to our family. Someone to be ignored. And by the time I'd grown brave enough for defiance, I'd been in the throes of pretending I considered half-bloods unworthy of my conversation.

It hadn't been only my father who'd cast her aside, it had been her whole family. She, perhaps more than anyone, understood the cost of having human blood in Trollus. For that, did I not owe her at least the chance to prove that there was something good, some pure reason behind her sordid plan to become queen?

"Isn't it obvious?" she said, quiet enough that I almost couldn't hear her. "I was cast aside, sold into slavery, all because my mother had a fractional amount of human blood running through her veins. The fact that half my blood was Montigny counted for nothing. I was a bastard. An embarrassment. I should have been a princess, but instead I have *served*." Her voice shook with emotion. "As myself, I will always be denied, but as Anaïs, nothing will be kept from me. Make me your queen, and you will have no fiercer ally in this world."

She was my father's daughter. Any doubt that might have existed in my mind about that was gone after hearing those words. There was no desire to do good pushing her toward the crown. No thought that she might change Trollus so that what had happened to her would never happen to another child. No hope that she might prove that half-bloods were worth as much as any full-blooded troll. Because I saw now that she hated the human part of her more than my father, than Angoulême, than me. Blamed it for all that she had suffered. She'd stolen Anaïs's face to fool everyone else, but more than that, she'd taken it because she well and truly wanted to become the other girl.

Her pursuit of power had nothing to do with overthrowing all the limitations her human blood had placed on her – it was to create a circumstance where she could pretend those limitations didn't exist because they didn't apply to her. She cared nothing but for herself, and Trollus had seen enough of that sort of ruler on its throne.

"No," I said, shaking my head. "A thousand times, no. I will have nothing to do with this madness of yours, and rest assured, I will do everything in my power to ensure you are never crowned. And it is not because you are bastard born or that human blood runs in your veins." I walked forward, leaning in so that we were almost nose to nose. "It is because *you* are not worthy."

The blood rushed out of Lessa's face. "You shouldn't have said that, Tristan. You really shouldn't have said that at all." Before I could so much as blink, a noose of fire wrapped around my neck and jerked me off my feet, stealing my chance to respond. And my ability to breathe.

Anaïs-mask firmly in place, she smiled up at me. "Now I'm going to make you pay."

CHAPTER 31
Cécile

Sabine's face contorted with effort and she spat out the rag shoved between her teeth. Shifting closer, she bit down on the edge of the rag protruding from my mouth, then moved backwards, pulling it out.

"Are you hurt?" she asked.

"No," I whisper-mumbled, my tongue dry. "Fred is helping them – Catherine gave him a spell to put me to sleep. Where's Chris?"

Sabine's face tightened. "He went to find Fred, in the hopes he knew where you were." She moved closer so that both our faces were caught in a faint beam of light. "Oh, Cécile. You heard what they are planning? What are we to do?"

I licked my lips in a futile attempt to moisten them as I considered what I'd learned. My instant reaction to hearing the messenger's plan was fury that he would use me to manipulate Tristan – it made him no better than the troll king. "I need to think."

Lord Aiden hated King Thibault – that much was clear. He'd made promises to the troll that he had cause to regret, and he knew the only way to win free of them was to see the King dead. The only troll who could reasonably accomplish this was Tristan, but only if he was alive. Except his life hung in the balance as the result of some twisted effect of my ongoing failure to fulfill my promise.

Aiden needed to help me take advantage of the loophole for his plan to work. There was nothing to stop him from slitting my throat after the King was dead in order to take down Tristan, but why should he? Another troll would only assume control, and whoever it was would be a complete wild card. Better to keep me alive and a prisoner for as long as possible. It was a clever plan.

And one I could appropriate if only we managed to break free in time. "We need to escape," I whispered. "We need to warn Chris and get the grimoire back."

If we could escape, subdue Catherine, and retrieve the grimoire, I could perform the map spell again. Then I'd have a few precious hours before Aiden realized I'd escaped in which to track down the witch and attempt to take advantage of the loophole myself. It was far from a perfect plan, but it put control back in my hands, and that was where I wanted it.

"Roll over," I whispered. "We need to try to get these ropes untied."

Squirming around in the dirt, we managed to both roll over so we were back to back. Running my fingers over the knot binding Sabine's wrists to see how it worked, I started picking at the rope. It was harder than I'd imagined it to be, working blind, my numb fingers with their bitten-down nails struggling against the well-tied knot.

Sensing my frustration, Sabine knocked my hands back with hers. "Let me try."

She worked silently, but there was no missing the shudder in her breath or clammy damp of her fingers. I thought to say something reassuring, but then Catherine passed across the floor above us, her stride full of purpose. Sabine's fingers froze and I shifted away from her in case the witch decided to check on us. But it was the back door to the shop, not the trapdoor above us, that opened and closed, the bolt turning a second later.

"She's gone!" Sabine's voice was shaking.

"Hurry," I hissed. "We need to catch her!" I was certain she would keep the grimoire on her; it was too dangerous to let out of her sight.

Sabine clawed at the ropes on my hand, letting out an exclamation of triumph when they loosened. Slipping my hands free, I turned on the rope wound about my ankles.

"Go!" Sabine said once I was free. "Catch her! I'll be fine."

"No." There was no way I was leaving my best friend tied up in a cellar. Dropping onto my forearms, I braced her hands with mine, then sank my front teeth into the knot and pulled. My jaw ached with the pressure, but slowly, the knot loosened. Letting go with my teeth, I shoved my finger in the gap that I'd loosened and jerked it free.

"I'll get my own ankles untied and go warn Chris," she said, shoving me forward.

Running to the ladder, I leapt up the rungs and flung open the trapdoor. Dodging through the clutter to the front of the shop, I flung open the door and went out into the street. There were plenty of people walking about, but none were Catherine. She couldn't have gone far. She'd said she needed supplies, which had to mean one of the markets. Snatching my skirts up in one hand, I started running.

I searched everywhere I could think, ignoring the stares of those curious as to why I was running like a madwoman through the streets, but Catherine was nowhere to be found. Sitting down on the edge of a walkway, I let the realization sink in that it was time to make my choice. Because I had not forgotten what else I'd learned: there was another way to break the curse, but only if I wanted it badly enough.

Twisting the end of my braid into a knot, I put not my mind but my heart to the question – did I want the trolls freed? If so, then I needed to attempt to break Anushka's will now. If not, I needs must submit to Lord Aiden's plan and fulfill my promise, if not in spirit, then by the letter, to the troll king and come what may with the results. A hundred thousand times I'd run through the pros and cons, the merits and the costs, and I knew what I was choosing was between a dreadful known and a dreadfully risky unknown.

I knew with painful certainty what would happen if I submitted: the trolls were doomed. But what would happen if I freed them? I wasn't sure. The cost to human life could be beyond reckoning. Or the good I'd seen in Trollus might triumph, and there would be a chance that we could make everything work. That my friends I trusted so implicitly were strong enough to make things right.

Choose.

Squaring my shoulders, I got to my feet and started toward the city gate.

I would take this leap of faith.

"How much for the ox?" I asked, pointing to the aging creature in the feedlot outside Trianon. I had the hood of my cloak up, my face shadowed from the afternoon sun.

The proprietor raised an eyebrow and named an exorbitant price.

"That's outrageous," I muttered. "The creature won't live another year."

He shrugged. "It's what the meat is worth."

I chewed on the insides of my cheeks, knowing I didn't have that amount of coin on me and that I didn't have the time to procure it. Reluctantly, I unclasped my necklace from my neck and held it aloft – it was time I ceased wearing it anyway. All it symbolized was death.

"It's gold," I said. "Take it, and you'll be ahead in the bargain."

The man had played this game long enough to know not to react, but there was no mistaking the covetous way he watched the necklace swing from my hand. "Let me see it."

I dropped the piece of jewelry into his palm. He judged the weight, bit the metal, and nodded.

Jerking my chin toward an ax embedded in a block of wood, I said, "I want that included, and a lantern as well."

Both eyebrows went up at that, but he only nodded. I'd given him enough gold to excuse me from answering questions.

The light was fading into the orange of dusk by the time I reached the beach, the wind howling and cold, and the grey-tossed waves surging in on the coming tide. I led the ox down below the tide line. Whether it worked or not, the water would wash away the physical evidence of what I'd done.

The magnitude of the sacrifice affected the amount of power, which is why I'd chosen the largest creature I reasonably could have. But Anushka had killed a troll king, and I strongly suspected there was nothing I could sacrifice that would trump his death. I hoped to make up the difference by using regular magic as well, so I set up the scene as a ritual, praying that I'd be able draw enough power from the elements. It would have been better to do it on the full moon, but the best I could manage was to time it for the moment of transition at sunset.

Tying the ox to a fallen tree, I worked quickly, gathering up sticks and branches and arranging them in a circle about ten feet above the rising tide. I liberally sprinkled lamp oil on the branches for good measure. Kicking off my boots, I tossed them high on the beach; and retrieving the ox, I led him inside the circle. The wind caught and tore at my hair, but I ignored it, all my attention for the creature in front of me. He was old and tired from years of overuse, but knowing that didn't make me feel any better about what I intended to do. Now was not the time to lose my nerve.

Forsaken Mountain rose up to the south, its sheared-off face higher than all the others. So far away, and yet it seemed I might reach out and touch it. The sun dipped lower and lower, the tide rising higher and higher. Digging a hand into the damp sand, I pulled on the power in the earth, feeling it rise and fill me to the core. As the orange orb of the sun brushed the tip of Forsaken Mountain, I touched the flame to the branches. A circular wall of fire rose around me, and in my periphery, I saw the waves divide, surging around the circle and up onto the beach. The ox sidled around, fear glittering in its eyes.

"Be still," I whispered, and though the wind raged around us, the animal grew quiet.

The magic filling me felt good and clean and pure, but I knew it wasn't enough. Nowhere near enough.

Picking up the ax, I hefted it in my hands, feeling strong and weak at the same time. This was wrong. Nothing about it was right. But I was going to do it anyway.

I swung hard.

There was blood everywhere. The ox collapsed, dying. No, dead. And I fell to my knees with it.

I was flush with magic. A raw, wild, and directionless power than knew no purpose other than my will. My eyes filled with tears and burned from the brilliance of the last sliver of sun, but I couldn't blink, couldn't even move. It was too much. It hurt. It was more than one body could contain.

So I let it go.

But not before I spoke the words. Not before I gave it a purpose. "End Anushka's curse. Set the trolls free."

I felt Anushka's shock as our wills collided, the ground itself shaking from the impact. If I had not already been on my knees, I would have fallen. The surf surged high, spraying and hissing against the flames as I struggled against her, my body aching, exhausted, fighting...

And failing.

The waves doused the flames, slamming into my back and knocking me forward. The icy water closed over my head, catching at my clothing and pulling me back. Coughing and spluttering, I crawled on hands and knees until I was out of the reach of the waves, and then I curled up in a ball, disappointment at my failure carving into my guts.

Anushka hadn't only used the earth's power to bind the trolls – she'd used the dying troll king's magic. And knowing it was so made me realize that Catherine had been wrong when she'd said a name didn't matter. It did. Because Anushka hadn't only cursed the mortal creatures I knew so well, she'd cursed all of their kind, binding the trolls to their city and their immortal brethren from coming to our world for fear of the same. And I did not know what they called themselves, because Tristan had never trusted me enough to say.

But more than that, what I hadn't had was the desire to see the trolls freed. Anushka hated them – had managed to survive all these long years in order to keep them contained. Nothing mattered more to her, and in order to break her curse, I needed to want them free equally as much or more.

But I didn't. At least, not all of them. There was only one who I'd do anything for.

"Let him go!" I screamed the words over and over until I couldn't pull any more air into my lungs, and had to repeat it in my head.

Then, up out of my mind swam a memory or a dream, or the memory of a dream of summer. *What you seek is the name of that which you most desire…*

With all the strength I had left, I pushed myself up on one elbow, my eyes fixing on the fading glow that was all that was left of the setting sun. A moment of transition, and thus a moment of power. "Let Tristanthysium be free of Anushka's curse."

A pulse shuddered through the air, and I slumped back onto the sand. Darkness that was more than night swept over my eyes, but before all the light was gone I whispered one more thing: "Tristanthysium, come to me."

CHAPTER 32
Tristan

Lessa was every bit as powerful as her blood warranted, and the full strength of her magic was directed into the noose choking off my breath and the shield keeping me from attacking her directly. Before she could crush my throat, I shoved power between my flesh and her magic, but there we reached a stalemate. I tried to pull the rope off, but it was intractable, slithering and reforming every time I broke a piece away. I couldn't breathe. I needed air, and spots were forming in front of my eyes as I tried and failed to force aside her magic.

I needed the iron out of my flesh.

But almost as though she sensed my thoughts, another invisible rope bound my wrists to my sides, sending ripples of agony up my arms. My mouth opened in a silent scream of pain, and I turned on her shield, hammering it with all the power I had. The air shuddered with the echoing *boom-boom* of my magic colliding with hers, but it was a struggle to find leverage hanging in the air as I was. I could feel her magic cracking and splintering under the blows, saw her eyes widen as she realized that even now, I was more powerful than her. Except that I could feel myself failing. I had to get through her shields within seconds, or all was lost.

With the strength only desperation could bring, I sliced at the magic rope holding me up in the air. Landing on unsteady feet, I took only a second to find my balance before attacking her shield. The force of it imploding made the stone walls of the palace groan, the noise drowning out the sound of the door slamming open.

Which is why Lessa didn't see Victoria until it was too late. Her fist connected just under Lessa's ribs, driving the air out of her lungs and sending her staggering back. "That's for Anaïs," Victoria shouted, and before Lessa could react, my friend punched her hard in the side of the face, the crunch of bone audible from across the room. "And that's for me."

Dragging in a breath, I lurched in their direction. Victoria had caught Lessa by surprise, but my sister was still more powerful.

But I needn't have worried, because Vincent and Marc had been right on her heels.

Lessa's eyes flicked between them, the crushed bones of her face slowly reforming. "I'm going to make you suffer for this," she said, her voice garbled by her shattered jaw.

"That a challenge?" Victoria asked, smiling as she rubbed her knuckles. "Because if it is, I accept."

"A duel to the death, perhaps?" Vincent added, clapping his hands together. "Everyone enjoys those."

Lessa licked her lips nervously, using the wall behind her as support as she climbed to her feet. "You can't kill me," she whispered. "You can't... He'll punish you."

"Oh, she *is* a liar, isn't she?" Victoria said, voice dripping with uncharacteristic malice. "I'm more than capable of killing you, *Lessa*."

"Let her go." I coughed, my throat itching as it healed the damage the noose had done. *Was it taking longer than normal?* "I'll not stoop to her level." Just yet.

The twins' faces fell, but they let Lessa scurry by without argument.

"What are you three doing here?" I asked, my relief at seeing Marc momentarily chasing away all my concerns. Was he well? Had he forgiven me? I wished I could see his face so as to better judge his frame of mind, but it was hidden by the hood of his cloak.

"Élise saw Lessa enter your rooms and was concerned about what she intended," my cousin said. "She sought me out."

Élise. I owed that girl a thousand times over. "Your arrival was timely."

"I believe 'thanks' is the word you're grasping for," Marc replied, his voice dry.

He sounded normal. Sane. What stroke of good fortune was this? "You're right," I said, my cheeks aching with an unfamiliar grin. "Thank you. There are no words for how glad I am to see you three."

A wave of dizziness hit me, chased away only by the shot of pain that lanced up my arm when I caught my balance on the desk.

"What's wrong?" Marc asked, and all three of them came closer.

"Cécile." I squeezed my eyes shut, trying to find my equilibrium. "Something's happened. She's desperate. More desperate than I've ever felt her." I clenched my teeth together. "She's going to do something."

But what? I cursed my lack of information. My helplessness. If she was acting under this level of desperation, the outcome could be disastrous. Perhaps even fatal.

The finality of the situation hit me, and with it came a compulsion I could not deny. "I must get back to work," I muttered. "I must finish this."

The three of them exchanged meaningful looks suggesting they weren't unaware of my predicament, then fell into step, the twins behind and Marc at my side. "Your father had all of Pénélope's things returned to me," he said. "And he had Vincent switched to the night shift so the twins are together again. I assume it is your doing?"

"No," I said. "I wanted to do something to help you, but I thought I'd only make things worse."

The compulsion to build, to fulfill my word to the half-bloods, was taking over my mind, making it difficult to think of anything else. *Which construction sites would have blocks ready? Where should I go first?* "He made the choice of his own volition." *What was Cécile planning? How much time did I have before she acted? Would it be enough?*

"Then circumstances truly are dire," Marc said. "He does not want you dead, you realize that?"

Did I? I wasn't sure. "He's killing her. I'm not sure she even realizes it."

"But she isn't dead yet. Don't be the one who causes that to change. You need to ration your strength, give her a chance to succeed." He caught me by the shoulder, although he didn't try to stop me. "That's why I'm here, Tristan. The twins, too. We're going to help you build."

I blinked, my thoughts mercifully clear of compulsion for a heartbeat. "Why? Why would you do this for me?" And the unasked question – how was it even possible that he could help me? What had happened to clear the madness from his mind that had resulted from my meddling?

That was the question answered, the twins falling back a few paces to give us space. "I thought about what you said in the mines."

I interrupted. "I shouldn't have…" But he held up a hand, cutting me off.

"You were right. It would have been one thing if my heart had stopped beating when hers did, if the decision had been taken out of my hands. But to choose it?" He inhaled sharply. "She did not wish it. And now, I find I do not wish it either. There is much I would like to see done before I willingly walk toward the end. This," he gestured out at the city lying in front of us. "Saving this is one."

How much better would the world be if it were men like Marc who ruled?

"I am glad to hear it," I said. "Only now I fear it is I who will not see our plans through to the end."

He nodded slowly, both incapable and unwilling to give false platitudes in the face of such a desperate situation. "It may be that the unthinkable occurs, but it has not yet. And until it does, there is hope yet that we might achieve the impossible."

Hope. It was not something I often allowed myself for it had caused me to suffer so many bitter disappointments. But what else did I have now? I'd had the opportunity to kill my father, and I hadn't taken it, foolishly believing that time was on my side. That a better, more prudent plan would present itself. I'd been wrong. Now my only hope was for Cécile to succeed in this impossible task that had been set for her, and perhaps she was the best place for all our hopes to rest. I knew her: she would not hesitate if opportunity presented itself. She would be bold.

"Victoria, Vincent," Marc said, turning to the twins. "You will manage the sites in the north half of the city."

They both nodded, then Vincent gave his sister a sly smile. "You take the east and I'll take the west. Whoever has the most work done by midnight wins."

Victoria grinned back, but I could see her eyes were glistening. "I accept your challenge."

It took a concerted effort, but I stopped in my tracks. "There will," I said, "be extra points for the *quality* of work done."

"We will do it right, Tristan," Vincent said, his voice strange in its solemnity. "You have our word on that."

"You will judge, won't you?" A flood of tears poured down Victoria's cheeks. "You know contests with subjective elements require a judge."

"I…" I wanted to tell her that I would, but the words wouldn't come out, because I didn't believe they were true. "I trust you." Why did I feel as though I was saying goodbye?

Her lip trembled and she bit it hard. Then she bowed low. "We will not disappoint you, Your Highness."

"You never do." I held my ground long enough to watch them disappear into the city, then I met Marc's gaze. "Let's get to work."

We met Tips on our way to the first construction site.

"You look sorrier than a sewer worker after a feast day, Your Highness," he said, pulling off his hat.

"I must look poorly indeed if you are according me a title again," I said, laughing. The motion hurt. Everything hurt.

"Is she..." he started to ask, but Marc made some motion to silence him. They began to speak in earnest, but I didn't listen. I didn't need to hear once more how precariously close I was to the end. Instead, I went to the block of stone sitting next to a growing pillar. It was ready. Bracing my feet against the street, I lifted the massive block up, watching it rise higher and higher until it reached the top of the column. Sweat broke out on my brow, because it was heavy. Had I really once had the power to hold up the mountain over my head? It seemed impossible now, a memory so distant it seemed another life.

Block after block rose up into the air, some with my power and some with Marc's. I became dimly aware that the streets were teeming with half-bloods, as though the entire population of Trollus had decided to go out at the same time. They were grouped in bunches around the columns, the air filled with the sounds of rock being chiseled into shape.

And the half-bloods were not alone. The familiar uniform of the Builders' Guild stood out among the sea of grey-clad forms, each of them holding a roll of parchment and shouting orders. No, not just the Builders' Guild – all the guilds, all of them lending their strength to do my work. Never in my life had I seen such a thing, or even ever believed that such a collaboration amongst my people would be possible.

"Your Highness." I jumped, my attention turning to the Marchioness who was holding a low curtsey in front of me, her crimson silk skirts pooling around her feet.

"My lady?"

She only smiled, rose, and started toward the next column. I watched in silence as she spoke to the uniformed builder, her head tilted as she listened to his response. Moments later, the half-bloods stepped back from a squared block of stone and it rose up into the air, guided by the woman's vast amount of power.

And she wasn't the only one. Near and far, there were

silk-clad ladies and dark-suited lords of Trollus's aristocracy listening to orders from those they had always treated as lesser, lending their magic to the effort.

"Marc, would you give me some light?" I asked, stepping out into the middle of the boulevard so I could see.

Brilliant orbs bloomed into existence high above, filling all of Trollus with their light and allowing me to finally *see*. Column after column reached up toward the rocky ceiling, growing faster than I had ever hoped. It was how I'd envisioned it in my mind's eye during those long hours I'd spent drafting and drawing. And not just the structure, but the people. How they were behaving, the expressions on their faces – this, *this* was what I had dreamed for my city. And it was glorious.

"I thought it was impossible," I whispered to no one in particular.

Marc answered, "And yet it is happening."

I hoped it would never end – that against all odds, I might see this transformation of my city through. And I was a fool for it. The gut-wrenching shock of disappointment hit me like a fist to the stomach, almost doubling me over. Cécile had failed. At what, I could not say, but in her mind, there would be consequences. Terrible ones. I braced myself for what would come next.

Nothing could have prepared me for the sound of my own name. Like a bell rung in a silent hall, Cécile's voice echoed through my ears, *Tristanthysium*.

"Not possible," I breathed. Except that it had happened, and every muscle in my body tensed like a coiled spring as a result, anticipation of what she would ask making me blind to everything around me. I turned, staring unseeing toward the north.

Tristanthysium, come to me.

Yes, my fey nature whispered even as I shouted. "No!"

"Tristan, what has happened?" Marc's voice was tense, his words clipped. "Is it her?"

He thought Cécile was dead, and though her heart still beat

strong and true, he was not far from wrong. "Cécile has called me to her. By name."

"Is the curse broken?"

"No. She has made another choice."

His eyes widened with realization. "Where is she?"

"Trianon."

The word and all that it meant rippled out and away from us, carried on a tide of fear through my people. I started forward.

"No. No, she can't have done this!" Marc caught hold of my arm, trying forcibly to restrain me.

"You know I must go," I said, shoving down the strange urge rising up inside me to attack anything that stood between Cécile and me.

"But the curse... You can't."

"I know." I swallowed hard. "Please go get my parents. Together, they'll be able to..." *Kill me.*

"Tristan..." He broke off. "I'll do everything in my power to finish what we started." He let go of my arm.

"Thank you." The words burned in my throat. "Goodbye, Marc."

I started walking toward the mouth of the River Road. *Run.* I stifled the urge. "Tips, walk with me." The half-blood fell into step beside me, struggling to keep up with my pace.

"So this is it?" His voice was dull. Toneless. "What will you do?"

"I must go to her."

His crutch skidded on the paving stones, but he caught himself before falling. "But you can't. No amount of power can break through the barrier, it's been attempted time and time again."

As if I didn't know that. "I must try." And try, and try until my heart stopped beating. At a certain point, I knew logic, reason, and sanity would abandon me in my single-minded pursuit to obey Cécile's command, and that I would tear all of Trollus asunder in a mad attempt to break free. Word had travelled ahead of us, as through the gloom I could see the guards at the gates mobilizing, preparing themselves for my arrival. Not that they could stop me.

"I've little time," I said. "But there is something I need to say to you before the... the end."

"I'm listening."

It was an effort to collect my thoughts, but as much as I knew the fight was over for me, I didn't want it to be over for everyone else. "For the longest time, I thought this fight was between half-bloods and full-bloods," I finally said. "But I was wrong. It's a fight against a flawed ideology. A fight for a different way of life. What sort of blood is flowing through your veins shouldn't and doesn't determine how or what you think. If nothing else, what we saw tonight proves that much."

I cast a backward glance at my city, taking in the towering columns of stone I was leaving behind. "You have Marc and the twins to help, but I think it's you who needs to unite those who want to see this tyranny overthrown."

"We need you," Tips said, despair thick on his voice. "You are our leader."

"No." I met his gaze, forcing my feet to stop moving for enough time to say what needed saying. "Others will rise up. They already have. This city is desperate for change, my friend, and you don't need me to make it happen."

Tips hesitated for a painfully long moment, and then to my surprise, he bowed low. "It has been a privilege, Your Highness."

He wouldn't give up, I could see it in the square of his shoulders. And somehow, that made it easier. "For me as well," I said. "Goodbye, Tips."

The time for words was over. Turning to the gate, I swept aside the guards and their magic, then tore the steel blocking my way from its moorings, tossing it aside. I started to run, faster and faster down the slick road toward the world outside. Toward her. It was over, and I didn't want it to be. It was over, and I was relieved by it.

Cécile had made a choice. For herself. For me. And it could not be undone.

The fresh breeze full of the smell of salt and life and freedom struck me in the face, the faint glow of dusk appearing ahead of me, and in that moment, I hated her.

I loved her.

The point of impact loomed, and I braced myself. For the pain. *Please let her survive* was my last thought, and then I threw myself at the barrier.

CHAPTER 33
Cécile

I breathed a sigh of relief when I saw Chris standing at the back stairs of the opera house. The safety of my friends was a small blessing in this night of failures.

"Sabine found you and warned you?"

He nodded. "While I was with Fred. Who is, by the way, an even worse liar than you. She didn't call him out on what he'd done, because she was afraid he'd warn Lord Aiden that you'd escaped. I don't think he would, though. I think he regrets what he did. Were you able to get your book back?"

"I searched every market, but I couldn't find her," I said, hating how well I felt, as though my countless sleepless nights had been washed away by blood. "So I tried to break them free another way. It didn't work." I swallowed a lump in my throat, not ready to explain exactly what I had done, how I'd felt her triumph when I failed, and how a fit of madness had taken me and I'd screamed Tristan's name until I'd collapsed in the sand like a madwoman.

"Sabine told me what you two overheard," Chris said. "She's inside, although everything's all chaos because your mother left for the Marquis' country home, claiming she was ill."

"She isn't ill, she's angry at me," I muttered, pressing a hand to my forehead. I hadn't just failed to free the trolls, I'd failed to protect her, too.

"What are you going to do?"

"Wait for the messenger to come find me," I said. "Let him and Catherine help me catch Anushka, bring her face to face with the King, then set her free." I waited for some passersby to move away, and then I continued, "And what will happen will happen. But at least we'll live to fight another day." My chest was tight. "I'm not giving up, Chris."

"Then there's still hope." He squeezed my hand. "How's Tristan?"

I closed my eyes and shoved away the sick euphoria I felt. "Not well." And I was noticing it much more than I had before, which could only mean he was getting worse.

"Cécile, thank heavens you're all right." Sabine came flying down the steps. "We didn't know where you'd gone. We came back here like you asked, but…" She frowned. "Why are you all wet?"

"Long story," I said, grateful that the seawater had washed away the worst of the blood.

"I'd say we need to get you inside, get you warm, but if you go in they'll want you to perform. Genevieve didn't show, and it's closing night. Put anyone but you on the stage, and the audience will be demanding their money back."

Did I dare? It was only a matter of time before Catherine discovered Sabine and I had escaped, if she hadn't already, and then they'd come for me. Was there a better way to spend my last few hours of liberty than on the stage?

"I'll sing," I said, lifting my chin. "Might as well go down with a little flair."

Neither of my friends smiled.

"They won't try to take me while I'm onstage," I said. "It will be afterward, and I don't want either of you to interfere. I'll go along with the first part of their plan, and then later, I'll try to escape." It wasn't a perfect strategy, but it would give Tristan a fighting chance. "If it doesn't work out, please tell my family that I love them." My lip trembled and I flung an arm around both of them. "Thank you for helping me. I couldn't ask for better friends."

"Good luck." Chris's voice was rough. "I'm going to go see if I still have a job."

He trudged away, shoulders slumped.

I grasped Sabine's hand. "I'm afraid."

She squeezed my fingers. "Me too."

Backstage was utter chaos. The orchestra's music filtered through the walls, and I recognized it as from one of the ballets. The dancers were performing to keep the crowd entertained with their graceful limbs and skill, but they could not go on forever.

"Cécile! Curse you, girl! Where have you been?" The stage manager locked a hand over my wrist, pulling me toward my dressing room. "I thought I was going to have to put Justine on. She's wearing your costume. You'll have to change quickly. Sabine, have her ready in ten minutes."

"Yes, monsieur."

Justine was in my dressing room, her brown hair pulled back tight in preparation for the wig she'd need to wear. Her face fell with disappointment when she recognized me, but she swiftly replaced it with a smile. "I'm glad you're here. I did not much care to go on when they were expecting Genevieve."

I didn't blame her. Everyone in the audience was expecting to witness the final performance of Trianon's most famous singer. Justine could have sung her heart out and it would not have mattered. "She's retired now," I said. "Someone will have to step up, and I'll put in a good word to see it's you." What I didn't say was that more than one girl would have the opportunity to move up in the ranks, because tonight would be my last performance as well.

The ten minutes went by in a blur of costuming, makeup, and hair. I warmed up while Sabine worked, methodically pushing myself up and down the scales while letting my mind drift away, a waking dream where I was surrounded by glass flowers and light, and all I cared about was the pair of silver eyes watching me from afar.

For all that I had failed to free him, Tristan felt closer to me tonight than he ever had since I'd left Trollus. His emotions were a tangle in my thoughts, rich and heady, and I didn't try to separate them from my own. I reveled in a dream world of my own creation, where we were together and there were no curses or kings or witches to keep us apart.

And when I stepped out onto the stage, the roar of the full house filling my ears as they realized I was performing tonight instead of my mother, I channeled those emotions. I sang like I had never before, pushing aside all thought of technique in favor of the rawness that I preferred. My throat burned and I shook with fatigue, but I felt alive. And I didn't want to give that up. Didn't want it to end.

But the curtain falls on every performance, and this one was no exception.

"You were amazing tonight," Julian breathed, his eyes bright after we had taken our final bows. "An incredible finale."

And just like that, the magic broke. My knees trembled, and I swayed unsteadily on my feet.

"Cécile?" He rested a hand on my shoulder.

"Can you ask them to give me a few minutes alone?"

"Of course." Julian's hand left my shoulder, his feet making small thuds as he walked off the stage. "Leave her be," I heard him say.

The crowd cleared out swiftly to the grand foyer, where they might well linger for another few hours. The cast would be off to celebrate the end of a successful production run, and I expected the crew would leave what work they could until tomorrow in favor of warm beds or dark taverns. Word would spread quickly that I'd performed tonight, and Lord Aiden would not find it difficult to track me down.

"You can't do this dressed as a harem girl, Cécile." Sabine was standing at stage right.

"I know." I went with her, changing back into my still damp dress, allowing her to remove the thick cosmetics from my face. When she was finished, I hugged her hard. "I love you," I said into her ear. "Now go find Chris and be safe."

Wiping tears from her face, she nodded. "Good luck."

I went back out to the stage and ducked under the curtain. Far above, the flames lighting the crystal chandelier were being extinguished from the access point in the ceiling, while two men slowly worked their way up the aisle, snuffing the wall lamps as they went. The red velvet of the theatre faded to grey, and one of them turned to give me a questioning look before snuffing out the last flame and leaving me in darkness.

It had been a long time since I had been in blackness so absolute, unable to see and entirely reliant on my other senses to guide me. The sound of the audience outside the gilded doorways at the rear of the theatre. The draft crossing the stage from left to right. The lingering smell of sweat and perfume, and the faint scent of salt rising from my clothes. From the sea, I wondered, or from the blood? My unnecessary and worthless slaughter.

I was afraid. I knew Aiden and Catherine would come for me, but I didn't know what they would do once they found me. Would I be trussed up once more and left in a damp cellar? Would they punish me for escaping? How long would I have to wait? Sitting down on the polished floorboards of the stage, I picked up a rose that had been tossed up by the audience and ran a finger over the petals. Such sweet torment that tonight of all nights, Tristan would feel so near. A punishment and a reward in one. It seemed as though if I closed my eyes and reopened them, he would be standing right there.

One of the doors from the lobby to the theatre opened and shut, and a soft exhalation forced its way past my lips. The faint but distinct sound of someone walking down one of the aisles filled my ears, but I kept my eyes closed like a child who believes the monster can't see you if you can't see it. Only I wasn't a child, and I knew I could not hide from what was about to come behind closed lids. So I opened them.

A faintly glowing orb of silver hovered in front of my face, painfully small and faded from what I remembered, but familiar nonetheless. My breath caught in my chest, the rose slipping from my fingers as my eyes searched the darkness. Another light appeared above the seats, growing and illuminating the theatre with its unearthly light.

"Cécile?" His voice was rough, uncertain, but a thousand years from now, I'd recognize it. Time seemed to stand still as I sat frozen, half convinced I was dreaming, and that when I woke up, I'd be alone in the theatre once more. Then I was running, as fast as I could, down the steps, up the aisle, and I was in his arms.

I had no words. But in that moment, I remembered what it was like not to need them. Because he felt what I felt – the whole twist of shock, uncertainty, and elation were as much in his mind as in mine. I buried my face in his neck and cried, because I'd been so afraid that I'd never see him again.

"I can't believe you're here," I finally managed to choke out. "How is it possible?"

"You called me. I had to come."

Something in his voice sent unease creeping down my spine, and I pushed back so that I could see his face. He was thinner than when I'd left Trollus, his hair longer, and his eyes marked with shadows. But some things never changed, and his expression betrayed nothing of what he was thinking.

"I didn't think it worked," I whispered. "I used the wrong magic."

He swayed slightly, seeming unsteady on his feet. "Tristan?" I asked, unable to keep the concern from my voice. My tarnished bonding marks told me he was deathly ill, but knowing it and seeing it were two different things. He didn't answer, only lifted a hand as though to brush the hair out of his face, but lowered it without finishing the gesture. I didn't miss the gleam of metal at his wrists. And it was then that I recognized the smell in the air.

Blood. And this time, it wasn't my imagination.

"God in heaven," I said, choking the words out. "Please tell me those haven't been on this entire time?"

His silence was all the answer I needed.

"I'm taking them off." I reached for his arm, but he jerked away from me, blindingly fast.

"No!"

"Why not?" *What was wrong with him?*

"He'll put four more in their place." He looked away, refusing to meet my gaze. But of course, it made sense.

"How long do we have until they find us?"

His gaze flicked up to meet mine. "They aren't free."

I stared back at him, unable to comprehend what he was telling me. "What do you mean? How is it that you..." I couldn't even form a question.

"I don't know. It could be..." he trailed off and shook his head. "All I know is that I'm the only troll no longer bound by the curse."

Could I have asked for more? It was a circumstance so perfect, yet so improbable that I'd never even dreamed of it. Tristan free, and all the trolls I despised and feared still caged by the curse. The dilemma I'd grappled with for so long seemed solved – I was sacrificing nothing and no one to be with Tristan. Our lives were safe without me unleashing the likes of Roland upon the world. I should feel giddy, euphoric, even. But I didn't. Instead I felt the sense that we stood in the eye of the storm, and that a step in any direction would plunge us back into chaos.

A door slammed, and we both jumped. "We can't stay here," I said. "They know I have escaped and they'll be after me."

"Who?"

"Lord Aiden du Chastelier. He's been running messages for your father." I motioned for him to follow me backstage, noting the way his eyes jumped from lamp to painting to ladder, trying to see everything and yet focusing on nothing.

"The Regent's son." Tristan's voice was toneless, but I felt the dull force of his shock. "Did he relay my message?"

"In a manner of speaking," I said with a shaky laugh. "Though he intended to use it to his own advantage, not mine. And he enlisted my brother to help him."

Leading him up the stairs to one of the windowless rooms where the dancers practiced, I explained Aiden and Catherine's plan. My words were jumbled, and perhaps only half of what

I said made any sense, but he did not interrupt. Tristan was tense beyond measure, but you'd never know it to look at him. His face was smooth with composure as he wandered the room, examining the sparse furnishings. It was not comfortable between us and our reunion was not going as I'd imagined, but to focus on such things now would be foolish. He was rattled, that was all. What I'd done must have come as quite a shock.

Retrieving some toweling from a shelf and soaking one of them with the water can in the corner that the girls drank from, I turned back to him. "Sit," I said. "I'm taking those things off you, since you seem unlikely to remove them yourself."

"I can't…" he started to argue, but I interrupted him.

"Your father isn't here. He can't come anywhere near you now, and there isn't anyone he could send capable of making you put them back on. I haven't survived this long only to have you kill us both out of foolishness."

His jaw tightened, and the reluctance I felt sparked anger in my heart. "Unless you have a very good and very logical reason why they should remain in place, you will sit down and allow me to remove those things."

Tristan stared over my shoulder at the plain wall and its barre. "It's unpleasant," he finally said. "I don't want you to see."

"Not good enough," I said, settling down on the floor and arraying my supplies around me. "Now sit down."

"Fine."

He eased out of his coat, and although I could feel the pain ricocheting through him, he did not flinch. Hiding his weakness from me. He sat down cross-legged, and rested his elbows on his knees. The motion pulled the cuffs of his black shirt back, revealing the steel manacles. Black fabric wrapped around his wrists and halfway up his forearm, but it was damp with blood, the smell of it thick in my nose. Gloves concealed his hands, and my pulse sped as I considered what might lay beneath.

"Lift your elbows," I said, hoping my voice was steadier than I felt. Not that it mattered – he could feel my emotions as much as I felt his. It crossed my mind how foolish it was that we ever tried to hide them from each other.

Spreading a towel across both our knees to catch the mess, I carefully slid his sleeves up to his elbows, then started to work unfastening the knot holding the fabric in place. My fingers brushed the warm skin of the inside of his arm, and he made a soft noise. When I looked up, his eyes were closed. Clenching my teeth together, I started to unravel the fabric. Slowly, I told myself, because I didn't want to hurt him. But in reality, I knew it was because I was afraid.

I was right to be.

The skin beneath grew icy the closer I got to the manacle, the pale luster of his skin turning the grey color of death, the veins beneath black as though they ran with ink, not blood. Sweat broke out on my forehead as I peeled away the sticky fabric to reveal the blackened wound beneath. The only thing I had ever seen like it was severe frostbite, and this was different and worse.

It took every ounce of control I had not to react, not to weep for the horror of what had been done to him, because I knew he would not appreciate it. Pain and shame built in the back of my head as I peeled off his glove, revealing a hand that was dark and immobile. Barely recognizable as the hand that had once made me burn with the slightest touch.

"It's iron rot, if you were wondering." His voice was tight.

I nodded, although he couldn't see through his closed lids. Leaning forward, I examined the steel encasing his wrist. There was no lock on it – only a metal clip holding it shut. That bothered me more than it should, because it meant what had kept them on was fear of something worse.

Holding the manacle steady, I flipped the clasp, and without warning him, I pulled the metal spike out of his wrist. Tristan jerked back with a sharp hiss of pain, pulling his arm out of my grasp. His shoulders hunched around his wounded arm, muscles spasming as he struggled to keep from retching. Then his other arm was in my face, the motion so fast I barely saw it until it was over. "Do the other quickly, before I lose my nerve."

I did what he asked, working swiftly. "Now," I said, warning him this time.

He tensed, and the metal made a sucking noise as I pulled it free. "Bloody stones and sky," he swore, then added on worse, bending at the waist so all I could see was the top of his head.

Anyone else, I would have held. Whispered soft reassurances. But some instinct told me that to do so would only make things worse. It hurt my heart that I could do nothing to ease his pain, but what stung more was that he didn't want comfort from me. I clenched my teeth, waiting for him to master the pain without my help.

When he straightened, I silently set to cleaning one of the injuries, his hand as cold and rigid as ice as I wound a bandage around his wrist. Part of me had thought the wound would instantly start to improve once the iron was out, but it remained the same. What if that meant it wouldn't get better? Should I offer to try to heal them?

"Are you going to be all right?"

"Don't concern yourself over it."

His words stung. Keeping my face low, I bundled up the bloody towels and crusted manacles. "Catherine has the grimoire," I said, needing to cut the tension. "It was part of a spell I was using to track Anushka, and without it, I have no idea how we'll find her. And once they realize you are free and their plans are in shambles, I expect they'll destroy it." I needed to tell him what I'd discovered about my heritage – how Anushka was maintaining her immortality using the deaths of her descendants, but something stayed my tongue.

"I agree," he replied. "We need to retrieve the book now while we have the advantage. Do you have any idea where she might be now?"

His perfunctory tone was unnerving. "Looking for me?"

"And when she realizes she can't find you? Where would she go then?"

"Home. She lives at the rear of her shop in Pigalle."

"Then we go there."

Before I could say another word, the bundle in my hands pulled away and moved to the center of the room where it burst into flames. Silvery blue troll-fire, unnatural and strange in its intensity, incinerated the cloth, and the steel melted in glowing globs that dripped onto the wooden floor. Snatching up the water can, I tossed the contents over the smoking mess before a fire of the natural sort could break out.

"There was much there that could cause harm," he said by way of explanation. "Now let us go find this Catherine before it is too late."

CHAPTER 34
Cécile

I stole a cloak from the costume room for him, and he walked next to me with the hood up to keep his otherworldliness from being recognized as we navigated the streets to Pigalle. The night air was icy and full of stars, the quarter moon bright enough that we didn't need troll-light, though seeing him without one was as strange as me for once being the one who knew the way.

As we walked, Tristan kept glancing upward warily, almost as though he expected one of the stars to fall out of the sky and strike us where we stood. And when he was not looking upward, his attention jumped from the revelers, to the gaslights, to the horses trotting by, to the dog that barked as we passed. Anywhere but me. I felt tense with all that had remained unasked and unsaid, and I didn't need to feel his emotions to know he felt the same.

"Don't react, but someone is following us. Two someones."

My stomach did flip-flops, and I only barely refrained from grabbing his arm. Who else could it be but Lord Aiden and Catherine? "What do we do?"

"Catch them. Quick, turn here." He nudged me around a corner and into the entranceway of a building. It reeked of alcohol and urine, and even in the dim light I saw his nose wrinkle with distaste.

We waited in silence, but not for long. "I don't see them," a woman whispered.

"They went this way," her companion responded. Both voices were deeply familiar to me.

"Oh, for goodness' sake." Skipping around Tristan, I stepped out of the entranceway.

Sabine and Chris both jumped in surprise. "Cécile!"

"What are you two doing following me?"

"We wanted to see where he would take you."

"More accurately, where she's taking me." Tristan stepped out of the shadows. "I'm afraid I'm quite at her mercy in this strange city of yours."

Sabine clapped a hand over her mouth and Chris's eyes bugged out. "Tristan? Is it really you?"

"None other." His attention turned to Sabine, his curiosity apparent. "Am I correct to presume you are Mademoiselle Sabine?"

Expression wary, she nodded.

"It is a pleasure to finally meet you. I've heard fine things about your character."

Her jaw tightened. "I wish I could say the feeling was mutual. You aren't what I expected."

"Sorry to disappoint."

"You know perfectly well you don't disappoint," she scoffed, her lip curling up with disgust. "I'd thought you'd be something I could pity, and that pity would allow me to forgive you for what you did to her. I was wrong."

"Tristan." Chris interrupted the exchange before it could devolve further. "Where are the rest of the trolls? How is it that you are free? What is the plan?"

"I'm uniquely privileged in my freedom," Tristan said, his eyes flicking in my direction. "As to why and how that is the case, you'll have to ask Cécile, as she has not yet graced me with an understanding of how it came to pass. Among other things."

He said it with lighthearted indifference, as though the answer were of no consequence to him at all. But I knew differently, and now I knew why. His name. It was his greatest secret. The one thing he told no one, not even me. Yet somehow I knew it, and I'd used it. The complex twist of strange syllables capable of bending him to my will. And even as I knew the sun rose in the east and set in the west, I knew this would not sit well with him.

"Cécile?" It was Chris who asked the question.

"I..." A gust of wind blew across us, carrying with it the heavy smell of wood smoke. "Something's burning." With the wooden homes packed together as they were in Pigalle, even a small fire had the potential for disaster. But there was something more, a worry that sent prickles down my spine.

"There." Chris pointed and our eyes went to the orange glow in the distance.

"No," I whispered. "No, no, no." Then I started to run, pulling my skirts up in one hand as I sprinted toward the street Catherine's shop was on. As I rounded the corner, I saw the crowd of people, buckets passing from hand to hand in a fruitless attempt to extinguish the inferno engulfing the shop. A shriek filled my ears, and it took me a moment to realize it came from my lips. Clapping a hand over my mouth, I stared for a second, then started running.

I sprinted up to the next road, then down it until I reached the building with the adjoining yard. Tearing open the front door, I ignored the shouts of those inside as I ran through the clutter of cots and out the back. In the yard, I jumped, catching hold of the top of the stone fence and hauling myself over.

"Cécile, what are you doing?" I heard Tristan yell, but I ignored him, dropping into the dirt on the far side. The fire was intense, the heat radiating from it making me flinch away, my eyes stinging and watering. It didn't matter that Catherine had betrayed me. She was involved in this because I'd asked her to be, so if she was in there, I had to help her.

I started to walk toward the flames, the smoke making me cough and choke, then magic locked around my waist, pulling me back.

"Have you lost your mind?" Tristan shouted into my ear, dragging me toward the fence.

"Catherine might be in there." I struggled against his grip, trying to go back to the fire. "I have to help her."

Fingers of magic caught hold of my chin, forcing me to look at him through the haze. "If she's in there, she's dead. There's nothing you can do."

Logically, I knew what he was saying was true, but the idea of leaving Catherine in there to burn was more than I could bear. Tears trickled down my cheeks, cool against my overheated skin. "She has Anushka's grimoire. I need it to find her. I need it to keep my mother safe."

"What are you talking about?"

"I need it!" I screamed the words in his face, my desperation to retrieve the grimoire twisting me into a mindless frenzy.

Tristan swore, and I could hear him talking with Chris over my head, but the words were meaningless. Nothing mattered more than finding the witch. No sacrifice was too great.

Then Tristan was pushing me at Chris and walking toward the fire. "What's he doing?"

Exactly what you asked him to. The realization that I'd just put a book ahead of Tristan's safety slapped me in the face, and I scrabbled forward to catch his coat, but Chris jerked me backwards.

"Cécile, calm down," he shouted into my ear. "He knows how to take care of himself."

The flames crept higher, catching at the buildings to either side, the efforts of the bucket brigade futile against the inferno. Nothing could survive in that heat, and I could hear the splintering and cracks of timbers that told me the roof was on the verge of collapse. Logic told me that Tristan's magic would keep him safe, but instinct made me scream warnings for him to get out.

Then, through the smoke, I saw him walking toward us, a limp form floating ahead of him.

Chris let go of me, and I started to run toward them, but an invisible rope of power caught me, lifting me up into the air and setting me in the corner of the yard. "What are you doing?" I coughed, clawing at the magic. "I can help her."

"She's beyond help." Tristan set her on the grass, but I couldn't make anything out through the haze. "You don't need to see this."

"Let me go!"

Tristan only shook his head, ignoring Chris, who had taken one look and was now retching against the wall. "She's dead, Cécile. Someone slit her throat, and then the fire did its work. It isn't something I want you to see."

I didn't deserve to be protected, I deserved to see what had befallen Catherine because I'd involved her in a plot far bigger than she knew. "What about the grimoire?"

"Not on her. And if it's inside, there's nothing left but ash."

Our only hope was gone. Slumping into the dirt, I rested my cheek against the mossy stone of the wall and watched the shop burn. Then a motion at my arm caught my attention, a soft tongue licking at my hand.

Looking down, I saw the bedraggled form of a dog. "Souris!" I clutched him to my chest, petting his fur, and whispering comforts to him that I wished I could feel. As I held him, part of the roof collapsed with a whoosh of hot air, and the rear door of the building slammed, making me look up.

My hands turned cold, making me long for the returned heat of the fire as I stared, my comprehension coming quick and my reaction slow. "Tristan," I called, my voice ragged. "Chris!"

The tone of my voice made them look over, and with one shaking finger, I pointed to the closed door of the burning house. Any doubt I had about who had killed Catherine was gone.

Painted in thick red across the wood was the letter A. Anushka had killed Catherine, and she had left a message.

And the worst part about it was, I was certain it was for us.

CHAPTER 35
Cécile

We stayed at the fire until it was under control, Tristan creating a sort of magical chimney to keep the flames from spreading any further. Bystanders whispered that it was a miracle the whole quarter hadn't gone up, but it did not appear to cross the mind of any of them that the tall young man watching from the street had anything to do with it.

Chris helped with the bucket brigade, while Sabine and I circulated through the crowd, listening for any hints as to how the fire might have started. No one knew anything. No one had seen anything. But there were plenty who believed the flames that had been chasing the infamous La Voisin these past four years had finally caught up with her. Only the four of us knew how right they were.

We'd lost the grimoire. Whether it had burned in the fire or been taken by Anushka, it didn't really matter. Without it, I had no way to track her, and I felt as though I'd fallen back to where I'd been that night the King had summoned me to the beach. Everything I'd done had been for naught.

Well, almost everything. Lifting my head, I regarded Tristan's lean form walking ahead of me, his head slightly turned as he talked with Chris, pestering him with questions about the city. Not so very long ago, it would have felt like a dream to have him be the only troll free of the curse, but now that dream seemed entirely short-sighted, as all our problems remained. I squeezed Souris to my chest with one arm and pressed closer to Sabine, who had her elbow linked with mine.

"Is there really no way to break this bond between you two?"

"Only death," I said, sighing. "And even if there were a way, I wouldn't take it. I love him."

She was silent.

"You're being awfully quick to judge, given you just met," I said.

"I know enough." Her voice was low. "Just looking at him makes my skin crawl. I cannot understand what you see in that... that thing."

I flinched, but a second later, anger chased away the hurt and I dragged her to a stop. "There were those in Trollus who said the exact same thing to him," I snapped. "Except I was the thing. I was the one who was different. But he didn't see it that way, and neither do I."

Chris coughed, and I looked up to see them both watching me. Tristan's face was hidden in the shadows of his cloak, but I knew he'd heard what I said.

"Tomorrow, then?" Chris said, breaking the uncomfortable silence.

"Outside the south gate."

I frowned, realizing they'd come up with some sort of plan and annoyed that I hadn't been involved.

"Remember what I said about a disguise. In the daylight, no one will believe you're human." Chris jerked his chin at Sabine. "I'll walk you home."

"What plan is this?" I asked once my friends were out of earshot. "I didn't realize we had one."

"We need to find Anushka," Tristan replied, his voice low. "I can see the effects of the promise you made to my father written all over you. I can feel them. When was the last time you ate? Slept? And that was when you had an avenue to find her – an avenue that is now lost to us. We must use another tactic, or we'll both be dead within the week."

His words spoke of concern, but that wasn't what I felt. Tristan was frustrated and angry, and all I heard in his words were blame. My temper snapped. "What exactly would you have had me do? Turn my back and walk away while he had you beaten? Stand silently while he dragged out every individual in Trollus whom I cared about and tortured them? Killed them? I'm well aware that he manipulated me, but what I don't understand is how you think I could possibly have made another choice."

"Cécile…"

"Don't!" I held up a hand to silence him. "You'll barely even look at me, and do you think I don't know why?" Once I started speaking, the words refused to stop. I needed everything out in the open so that it would be over and done, and no more words would hang unspoken. "Do you have any idea what it felt like knowing that in choosing to help you that I had disappointed you? That everything I've done and all the sacrifices I've made have been the exact opposite of what you wanted me to do?"

I squeezed my eyes shut, furious that they seemed intent on undermining my anger with tears. "I feel more allied with your cursed father than you, and just the thought of it makes me sick."

Forcing my eyes open, I searched his face for some sign of what he was thinking. Something that might dull the anger and frustration mirroring my own. But there was nothing. He said nothing.

The snowflakes landing on my face felt blissfully cold against my overheated skin, and I tilted my chin up so that more would land, the little droplets of water running down my face serving as a disguise against any tears that might sneak out. I knew what I needed to tell him, but I was afraid what having it out in the open would mean for us. "A curse is an act of will cemented by power, and tonight I learned it can be broken by an act of will fueled by power. Only Anushka added in another element, one uniquely important to your kind."

"A name." His voice was rough, a statement and a question in one.

"Yes." I stared at the dark sky. "But you never told me what your kind is really called, and ultimately, even if I had known, my desire to see the trolls free is too plagued by doubt to have managed the task." I was circling around what needed to be said. But part of me was scared to put voice to what I knew. To what I had done. Because it was impossible for me to un-know it, and I was afraid he'd never come to terms with me having this much power over him.

Lowering my face, I met his gaze. "When you were taking me through the labyrinth, I had a dream – a dream that I did not remember until tonight. I was in a place of endless summer filled with creatures more colorful than any rainbow. And I met a man who made my eyes burn as though I were staring into the sun, and he gave me the name of that which I most desired." I blinked once. "Your name."

Shock slammed into me like a battering ram, but Tristan barely twitched. "My great-uncle told you? That's impossible."

I shook my head. "Clearly it isn't."

His jaw twitched, and in an instant, everything he felt washed over his face. But before I could react, he turned his back on me. I stared at his slumped shoulders, uncertain of what to do or what to say. He was not all right. I could see it and I could feel it, but I didn't know what I could do to make it right. "Tristan?" I reached out to touch his back, but he only flinched away from my hand, unwilling to accept anything he perceived as pity.

"It makes sense, doesn't it?" I said, trying logic instead. "Someone had to have named you, and it seems fitting that it would be him. And he wouldn't have told me if he didn't think I'd need it. I'm sure he wouldn't have told me lightly."

"How can you be sure of something you know nothing about?" he snapped.

I tried not to let his tone hurt, but it was hard. "If I know nothing that's because you've chosen to keep me in the dark. As you so often do."

"It's the way I am. You've always known that."

Exhaustion settled over me, turning my body and mind

numb. "You're right. I have always known it. But I never said that I'd be content with it."

The words left a burning sensation in their wake as so often the truth does. But once they were out, I felt the relief of knowing that there was nothing more that I could say. I waited a moment to see if he would respond, and when he said nothing, I started walking home.

Normally I resented how quick to tears I was, but as I trudged down the snow-dusted walkways, with eyes dry as sawdust and my chest so tight I could scarcely breathe, I longed for the release sobbing would bring. Instead I felt every sleepless night, every missed meal, every mistake I'd made, and every hurt I'd caused. Never in my life had I felt so hopeless, and the result was that I was ill-equipped to deal with it. No matter how I racked my brain, I could not see a way through, and the realization was crippling.

The lamp in the front entrance was the only light in the empty house, my mother having disappeared to the Marquis' country home and the servants gone for the night. I had walked away from the one person I'd never thought I'd turn my back on, and now I was alone. I stood motionless in front of the lamp, staring at the flame while the snow melted, puddling around my boots.

A knock sounded at the door. I didn't move. I knew it was Tristan, and I knew I couldn't ignore him. He was in an unfamiliar place with nowhere to go, and leaving him out in the cold was cruel.

Turning the bolt, I eased the door partially open and spoke right away so there would be no awkward pause. "I can direct you to where Chris lives," I said. "Or to a hotel. I have coin, if you need some. Whatever you prefer."

He hesitated, looking past me into the house. "What I'd prefer is to be with you," he eventually said, his voice quiet. "Though that I've made you think otherwise indicates I probably don't deserve the privilege."

A sigh of relief ran through me. "Is that supposed to be an apology?"

One corner of his mouth turned up. "I was working my way in that direction."

The need to close the distance between us was almost unbearable, but I held my ground. "Work harder."

The wind swirled, snowflakes melting before they touched his cheeks. It made me think of the time we were on the lake, and I had described the seasons to him until the feel of his lips on my skin had chased away all thought. That was what I wanted now: not to have to speak or listen, but just to feel. I held my breath.

"I am sorry." There was a faint shake in his voice. "I love you above all things in this world or any other, and yet there are times when I think I subject you to the worst of me, and I can't explain why."

I opened the door the rest of the way, then stepped aside so he could come in. The corners of his borrowed cloak brushed against my skirt, pressing the damp fabric against my skin, making me shiver. The foyer was wide, but he remained close enough that I could smell the smoke clinging to his clothing, feel the heat radiating from his skin, see the lamplight glittering in eyes that nothing of this world possessed. Close enough to touch, and oh, how I wanted to.

"I was building it." The words were hoarse, and he swallowed audibly. "The structure that I designed to replace the magic tree, I was building it. With the half-bloods' help, and my father's... well, not his blessing, but his permission."

A million questions sprang to mind, but I bit my tongue.

"I can explain later how I got that permission, but suffice it to say, it was gained by my beating him at his own game. The first time ever, I think." A smile flashed onto his face, then faded just as quickly. "Everything's a mess in Trollus. It's worse than when you left. I made a mistake that nearly caused Marc to lose his mind. The twins are relegated to the mines. The half-bloods can lie. Angoulême has possession of my brother's name. Lessa has stolen Anaïs's life." He shook his head once. "My own mother even tried to kill me."

I heard everything he said, but it was almost too much for me to take in. I'd suspected that much had happened in Trollus, but hearing the names of those I cared about as those who had been harmed, and the names of our enemies as those who were triumphing? My stomach twisted, and I clenched my teeth together to keep quiet.

"But despite everything existing in a miserable mess, I was finally starting to see how all the pieces fit together." His eyes were fixed on me, but it wasn't me he was seeing. "I was starting to see how *his* plan fit together, what *his* motivations were. The half-bloods supported me, the guilds were rallying to our cause, and even some of the aristocracy were openly siding with me. My structure was rising higher and higher, and my people were finally beginning to work together in a way I always dreamed they would. I was so very close..."

He blinked, and his eyes focused on mine. "And then you called my name, and I left everything that I'd gained behind."

I recoiled back against the table. "I'm sorry," I choked out. "All I knew was that you were sick, and breaking you free was the only way I could think to help you."

"Don't be sorry." He lifted a hand as though to touch me, then let it fall back to his side. "This is what I'm trying to explain, Cécile. That I'm angry, but not at you."

I let my gaze drop to his chest. "I ruined your plans."

"No. It wasn't a choice between me answering your call or staying to finish my work in Trollus. It was the choice between answering your call or both of us dying." A warm filament of magic caught under my chin, lifting my face up. "The only solution was an impossible one, and yet here we stand. Alive."

There were countless questions I should have asked, with answers that were important for me to hear and know, but I couldn't seem to remember any of them. So instead I asked, "Is it how you imagined it would be?"

His eyes flickered shut. "There was a time I thought often about what the world outside of Trollus was like; so much so, that I almost convinced myself that I knew. But the reality..."

He broke off. "It is vast."

I knew to him it must be true, but in that moment, I felt the exact opposite. It was as though the world had shrunk down to the size of the front entrance of my home, and that nothing else existed outside the two of us.

"And in truth," he continued, "since I lost you, the only thing I've thought of was what I'd do if I had another chance to be with you again." He inhaled, and held the breath, and I clung to the moment with greedy anticipation. "But I never dreamed it would be this hard. That it would hurt to hold you." He held up one arm, then let it fall limply by his side. "That I wouldn't be able to feel your skin against my fingertips."

He broke off abruptly, and I instinctively knew that it had cost him to admit the weakness. I wanted to tell him that the iron rot would fade away, that he would get better, but I didn't know if it would any more than he did.

"You never lost me," I whispered. "I always knew that we'd…" I broke off, because claiming that I'd had any certainty over the last months seemed like such a lie. "I hoped that…" My breath caught. "I…"

"I know," he said. And then he kissed me, and all my uncertainty about how he felt was chased away in the press of his lips against mine, the taste of his tongue, the heat of his skin as I wrapped my arms around his neck. Rising onto my tiptoes, I pulled myself against him, relishing his soft intake of breath as my body molded against his, the feel of him so familiar and yet exquisitely unknown. Desire burned low in my stomach – a want that I'd been too long deprived of – making me feel dizzy and breathless.

"Cécile…" His breath tickled against my ear and the lamplight faded dark, then burst brilliantly.

I *was* dizzy and breathless.

"Cécile?"

"I'm going to faint," I mumbled, and then my knees buckled and everything went black.

CHAPTER 36
Tristan

Had she always been this tiny? I carried Cécile upstairs, finding a bedroom that was all lavender and lace, which managed to be both tidy and disorderly, and knew it was hers. Laying her on the bed, I removed her sodden boots and stockings, but I paused over her dress. It was damp and reeked of smoke, but I hesitated about undressing her while she was unconscious. I'd seen her in less, it was true, but I wasn't sure she'd appreciate its removal. So I left it on, tucking her under the thick blankets and arranging her tangled hair so that it was no longer in her face.

I did it all without touching her once. Because if I had, all I would have felt was pain.

Removing the manacles had made me feel better, stronger, and no longer at death's door. But the damage they'd inflicted remained, and it did not seem to be improving. Any attempt to move my hands sent stabbing shocks of agony shooting up my arms, but my fingers were numb and unfeeling. Would they get better, or was this how I was to spend the rest of my days? A lesser, broken version of myself? With most tasks, I could compensate with magic, but not with her. Never again being able to feel her skin beneath my fingertips or to hold her against me without pain was not a loss I'd easily accept.

Dropping to my knees next to the bed, I let my light drift over so I could see Cécile's face. The rounded cheeks I remembered had hollowed, her bones now sharp and visible through skin that no longer glowed with health. Golden lashes rested over dark bruises like marks beneath her eyes – and the fingernails on the hand that rested next to her chin were bitten down to the point where some had bled. Asleep and without the force of her personality in play, she seemed fragile. Faded.

"I'm sorry," I whispered, kissing her cheek gently before sitting back on my heels.

I was free.

Through magic and sheer force of will, Cécile had broken Anushka's hold on me. And having been wholly unprepared for the moment, I was still coming to terms with that freedom. It was more overwhelming than I ever could have anticipated.

Closing my eyes, I remembered running down the River Road, faster than the water surging next to me. As fast as I had ever run, as though speed might somehow tear me through the barrier that had bound my people for so long. Terror had lurked deep in my chest as I approached the invisible divide between our world and the outside, knowing it would hurt when I hit it, and knowing that I would do it again and again, with magic and fists until my heart stopped. In that moment, I'd never loved or hated Cécile more, because in one simple command, she'd found a way to end us.

But the curse hadn't stopped me.

I'd felt it snatching and grabbing at me, trying to hold me back. But something stronger pulled me through, and then I was stumbling, falling onto the sand of the beach. Rolling onto my back, I'd looked up at the night sky, more vast, open, and unending than anything I could ever have imagined. I'd been rendered immobile as I stared up at the tiny pinpricks of light scattered across the sky, their number and brilliance growing as I watched.

It was my father's voice that had pulled me back to reality, the edge of panic in it. "Tristan?"

I'd sat up, watching as an expression I'd never seen swept across his face. "Find her," he shouted, and suddenly I was running.

He meant Anushka, I knew, but even if Cécile hadn't called my name, it would have been her I'd gone to first. Like we were attached by a silken string, I was drawn in her direction, my passage down the dark road and into the city a blur I barely remembered. Even before I was close enough, I swore I could hear her singing, the crystal sound of her voice in my ears as I'd walked through the theatre and found her sitting on the stage, surrounded by flowers. There were moments in life that burned themselves into memory, forever vivid in the mind's eye. For me, seeing her again on that stage was one of them.

But it was not an untarnished moment.

I did not doubt that she was telling the truth about how she'd come to have my *name*. I'd heard tell of those who'd dreamed themselves into Arcadia, and it was popular opinion that those who went to sleep and never woke were those whose minds drifted and were caught by winter fey.

But never had I heard of it happening to a human. It made me believe that my uncle was meddling, which was troubling. I was in the debt of the Winter Queen, and knowing that Cécile had incurred a debt to the Summer King made me wonder if this was some game in the endless war between the two kingdoms. What mischief they might bring to this world if they were free to walk here once more. There were fell and dangerous creatures lurking in the shadows of my ancestors' homeland, and I wasn't sure we'd be able to control them as we once had. We were not as strong as we once were.

But believing the truth of Cécile's story did not change the fact that she now had the power to control me. She had not uttered it since, and I did not believe she'd do so idly, but I'd heard it drift across her thoughts, each time it did, my mind going blank of anything other than the anticipation of her command. Her knowing it was what had allowed her to break me free, but there was a large part of me that would have gone eagerly back to my cage to regain the autonomy of my will. And to go back to my work.

Sighing, I climbed to my feet, needing to move. The creature

Cécile called Souris was sitting on the floor next to me, tongue lolling out between sharp incisors, surprisingly canny eyes fixed on me. She had said he was a dog, but I wasn't entirely convinced of the verity of that claim. "Will you watch her for me?" I said to him.

As though understanding my question, the animal made a soft yip and leapt up onto the bed. Pawing at the covers, he rotated in a circle three times before settling down behind her knees. "I'll be back," I said.

The rooms next to Cécile's were devoid of anything other than furniture, but at the end of the hallway, I found the master chambers belonging to her mother.

Genevieve de Troyes' room was very much a boudoir, decorated with ornate furniture, plush burgundy fabrics, and artful clutter. The walls were covered in paintings of women in repose, many of them work I recognized as having originated in Trollus, and all of it expensive. Trinkets of glass and porcelain cluttered the tabletops, and a stack of gilt embossed books sat next to a chair by the fireplace.

I knew well enough how little an opera singer – even a star – was paid, and it came nowhere near close to enough to pay for all this opulence. Her benefactor was a marquis well known to be a patron of the arts, and he must be generous indeed to endow her with all this.

Cécile had only rarely spoken of her mother, and I'd never been able to decide whether she loved the woman to the point of adoration, or hated her. Having never met Genevieve, my opinions were all based on hearsay, but what I'd heard, I hadn't liked. Past and current behavior suggested she was at the least, selfish, and at the most, a narcissist. But that might all be a front, an image cultivated to fit the perceptions of how an opera star should behave. From what I knew, she'd been born into a family of modest means, her father dying at a young age, leaving her to be raised by her songstress mother.

Yet Genevieve walked in circles far above her social status should allow, which suggested that there was more to her than what the gossipmongers whispered. I was intensely curious about her, doubly so given Cécile's frantic plea that she needed saving earlier tonight.

With fingers of magic, I began to rifle through cabinets and drawers, making certain I left everything as it had been. I found little of interest other than stacks of love letters from would-be suitors, and pages of badly written poetry signed by someone with the initial *J*. Her closets were full to the brim with expensive clothes, shoes, and all the accoutrements a wealthy woman was likely to own, the whole of it dominated by a spicy perfume that tickled at my nose.

The drawer in the bedside table I opened, immediately closed, then opened again, my curiosity stronger than my moral fiber as I assessed the collection of silken cords, feathers, and bits of lace. Interesting.

It was only as I was about to close the drawer again that I noticed something was off about the depth of the space. A quick inspection showed me how to pop the false bottom up, revealing a stack of age-darkened letters hidden beneath. A clever place to hide something from high-minded servants.

Turning my attention back to the letters, I skimmed through them. They were from Cécile's father to her mother, all written in the five-year period following their separation, and each and every one of them pleading with her to come join her family. Questions as to why she changed her mind about accompanying him. Words begging her to come to Goshawk's Hollow, describing how much he and their children missed her. Desperate sentences explaining that he would sell the farm and bring the children back to Trianon, if only she would answer his letters.

In the last year, they decreased in frequency, but the plea never changed – right up to the point they stopped. Was that when she finally answered him, I wondered? Was that when she said no? Or, after five years of pleading, had he finally realized it was hopeless? And what did it mean that she had kept these letters all these long years? Were they trophies like the love letters I'd found, or deep down, did Genevieve really care?

I thought about taking the letters to show to Cécile, but something stopped me. How could seeing written evidence of her father's unanswered pleas to her mother do anything but hurt her? She had enough to deal with without me digging up old wounds, so I replaced them in their hiding spot.

Downstairs, I wandered through the great room, the parlor, the kitchen, and even poked my head in the cellar before stepping inside the small, windowless study I found under the stairs. Expanding my ball of light, I started going through the contents of the desk, sorting through uninteresting correspondence, invitations to parties, sheaves of opera music, and stacks of bills, all of which she seemed to pay on time.

Then my eyes lighted on a small safe bolted to the floor in the corner. It was made of solid steel with a modern-looking combination bolt. I was loath to put my ear against the toxic metal, but there was nothing else for it if I wanted to get inside. Ignoring the itching burn, I listened for the sounds of the tumblers falling as I slowly rotated the dial, and within moments, I had it open. I'd expected to find jewelry, but instead my eyes landed on stacks of ledgers. I began flipping through them, my jaw all but falling open at what I found.

Genevieve de Troyes was a wealthy woman in her own right.

I read through the pages detailing balances of her accounts, investments, and property holdings. She owned no less than sixty percent of the Trianon Opera House, and parts of several of the smaller houses in the city. All of it was held through a company of which she was the sole owner, the fact of which seemed to be hidden by layers of lawyers and paperwork. Nearly all of it she inherited from her mother – Cécile's grandmother – who had owned it all as far back as the records went. Genevieve was rich, even by my standards, yet she pretended to be entirely dependent on the Marquis for money. Which begged the question of why?

When Cécile first came to Trollus, I'd had her mother thoroughly investigated by those in my employ, and none of them had turned up this information. Which meant it was an extremely well-guarded secret. So well guarded, in fact, that her own daughter didn't even know. Locking the safe, I retreated back up the stairs to check on Cécile.

She hadn't so much as stirred. The room was warm from the glowing coals of the fireplace, so I gingerly removed my coat, feeling the bump of something heavy in my pocket as I did so. The book. I'd forgotten about it.

Extracting the small volume, I set it on Cécile's desk and settled on the chair. It had been beneath Catherine's body when I'd lifted her up, the only thing that had kept it from burning. At the time, I'd only paid enough attention to it to determine it wasn't Anushka's grimoire before shoving it in my pocket, but now, I decided to take a closer look.

Inside the front cover was a piece of parchment that had been folded many times over. I recognized Cécile's looping handwriting, my eyes taking in a list of names and dates. The most recent was that of Genevieve's mother, but none of the others were familiar. There was also a folded map of Trianon. The fire couldn't have touched it, but there were tiny burn marks all over the map. None of it made any sense to me, but it must have been important for Catherine to steal it away from Cécile.

The book itself was full of spells. I read quickly, grimacing at the dark and bloody nature of the magic, until I discovered a spell intended to find a missing person. A spell requiring a map.

My father's minion had said that Cécile was performing blood magic and I hadn't wanted to believe it. But what I was looking at was undeniable proof that he'd been telling the truth. Picking the map up, I counted the marks. "How many times did you perform this spell, Cécile?" I asked, having felt her wake.

She hesitated. "Once. All the marks came from the same casting." Climbing slowly out of bed, she walked behind a dressing screen, emerging moments later in a green velvet wrap.

"Who are these women?" I asked, watching her walk toward me, flashes of bare leg showing with each step. "What does your grandmother have to do with Anushka?"

She sat on the edge of the desk, knees brushing against mine. "My grandmother was one of her victims." She toyed with the sash holding her wrap in place. "I don't know exactly how, but Anushka used their deaths to maintain her immortality."

I waited, knowing she had more to tell me.

"There are certain spells that are made easier by a close blood bond," she said, letting go of the sash. "These women are my ancestors."

"And her descendants," I finished, the information not surprising me as much as it should. I glanced at the list of names and dates. "That's why you were afraid for your mother – she's next." And then it would be Cécile's turn.

"What about your sister?"

"Josette isn't a witch."

"But your mother is?"

Cécile hesitated. "I... Yes. I think she has the capability, but I don't think she realizes it. Certainly, I've never seen her use magic."

I wasn't certain I agreed, but I refrained from pressing her. The question would keep.

She lifted a hand to her mouth and began nipping at one of her fingernails until I carefully pulled her arm down.

"If we stop her from killing my mother or me, she'll lose her immortality. Then it will only be a matter of time."

Because this mess needed another layer of complication. "For certain, we need to catch her," I said. "What we do with her after... We can decide that later."

"What do you propose?"

"We bait her out," I said. Originally, my plan with Chris had been to use myself as the bait. Anushka would know who and what I was, and I did not think she'd stand idly by while I wandered free. But this was better.

"She needs you and your mother," I said. "If word were to spread that I were involved with you, that I intended to take you two away from Trianon, she'll be forced to act, and in doing so, will reveal herself."

One of her eyebrows rose. "What precisely do you mean by *involved*?"

I shrugged. "This Marquis your mother dallies with is rich, but I'm much richer. What do you say, my dearest wife, of your taking on a patron?"

CHAPTER 37
Tristan

"You're late," I said, stepping out from the copse of trees where I'd been waiting, Souris trailing along at my heels.

"You needn't cry about it," Chris replied, pulling the pair of grey horses to a halt on the road.

I tried to glare balefully at him, but I was certain the effect was ruined by the tears that were in fact streaming down my cheeks. The sun was wickedly bright, reflecting off the patches of snow and searing into my eyes.

"You're like a mole that's lost its hole."

"I don't know what a mole is," I said, opening the carriage door and lifting the dog inside.

"It's an animal that lives underground. Doesn't see too well."

"Then the comparison is apt." I climbed up onto the seat next to him. I'd never ridden on a carriage before, and despite my discomfort, I was excited about the experience. The coats of the horses were shiny, and the mud splattered against their legs did nothing to detract from their sleek beauty. They seemed entirely different creatures from the plodding draft animals that pulled wagons full of grain into Trollus.

Everything was different from the world I knew, the smells and sounds terrible and wonderful in their unfamiliarity. I felt crowded by the press of life all around me, and yet almost glad my vision kept the true scope of the *space* from overwhelming my senses.

Chris flicked the reins and made a sort of clicking sound, and the horses surged forward, their harnesses jingling with each step they took. "I'm a bit surprised Cécile let you go through with this," he said.

"Let me?" The carriage bounced in the frozen ruts of the road, jarring my spine.

Chris snorted loudly and slouched down on the wooden seat, seeming perfectly comfortable. "Don't bother pretending we'd be here if she hadn't agreed to it." He cast a sideways glance at me. "You did tell her where we were going, didn't you?"

"Of course I told her."

"And?"

"She understands the necessity."

Chris chuckled. "Got an earful, I expect."

"I'd forgotten how loud she can be when she's angry," I admitted, bracing a foot against the floorboards to keep my balance. "Souris hid under the bed, and I was tempted to join him."

"And yet here we are."

Here we were, trotting down the road toward Trollus and a meeting that I was both looking forward to and dreading. My freedom should have been an advantage I had over my father, but instead it seemed like the opposite. I felt like I had never had less control, and I didn't like it. I was worried about what had happened in Trollus after I left, about the precarious position in which I'd left my friends and comrades. My father wouldn't harm them out of turn, but if I did not act in a way he wanted, he wouldn't hesitate to use them against me.

"Do you think he'll help?"

I wiped my face dry with an arm, careful not jar my wrists. "I do." I stared up at the vast mountain range to my right, my eyes drawn to our mountain, the sheer peak gleaming with gold in the sunlight. "He could not have predicted this turn of events, but make no mistake, he is pleased with what Cécile has done. To him, it is one very large and certain step toward the freedom of all our kind."

The carriage broke free of the trees that had blocked the ocean from our view, but what stole my attention was the rocky slide blanketing the land between Forsaken Mountain and the coast. It seemed smaller than it had from within, incapable of containing the city that had been my world.

There were numerous artistic renderings of the scene from before the Fall, when Trollus had dominated the valley below the monstrous triangular peak, and the gardens had been full of color instead of glass, and the port had been filled with ships, and Trollus had been the center of the world. Now it was a sea of barren rock, lifeless and insignificant beyond its natural marvel. It was the center of nothing – had been reduced to the inconsequential cage of a sick and dying race. Seeing it this way infuriated me, and for the first time I felt of a like mind with my father.

"That's Esmeralda Montoya's ship," Chris said, pointing to a vessel sailing south, likely headed to Courville.

"How can you tell?"

"Seen it enough times to recognize it." He squinted at the ship. "Have to say, I'm surprised to see her on the move. It's been anchored in the Trianon harbor for at least a month, and I've crossed paths with her a time or two. Though she didn't seem too keen on chatter, if you catch my meaning."

I nodded. Esmeralda had sworn the traders' oaths to my father, and as such, her ability to speak about anything to do with Trollus was limited. But she could still listen. The least I could do would be to track her down and let her know the girls had been well enough when I left. It might ease her mind enough for her to carry on with her business. I did not care to see her come to ruin for fear of missing the chance to enter Trollus should my father reopen the gates.

"Do you want me to come with you?" Chris steered the horses off to the side of the road.

"No." I jumped off the carriage. "Keep watch for anyone coming. This isn't a conversation I want anyone walking into the middle of." I started towards the beach, then paused. "Keep an eye on the dog. Cécile is fond of him, but he makes a mess everywhere he goes." Smiling at Chris's muttered oaths about the consequences of damaging the carriage and the ridiculousness of small dogs, I continued on my way.

The snow was compressed where countless wagons and feet had packed down a track, but I walked along the edge of it, enjoying the way it crunched beneath my feet. There was no snow on the beach, as the water rose high enough to wash away any tracks with each tide, and to the casual eye, the uneven cliff of rock concealing the entrance to the River Road appeared entirely innocuous.

I strode across the rocks and sand and into the shade of the overhang marking the entrance to the tunnel, the river flowing fresh and clean down to the ocean. At high tide, the ocean reached right up to the barrier of the curse, and bits of flotsam littered the path. Ahead, it appeared as though I were walking toward massed boulders from which the water flowed, but I knew it was an illusion. And I knew only a handful of trolls could account for the power lurking just beyond it.

"I hope you at least had someone bring you a chair," I said, stopping a safe distance from the barrier. I was taking no chances at getting caught up in the curse's boundary once again.

The illusion fell away to reveal my father. But no chair. I winced in mock sympathy. "I hope you haven't been waiting long."

"I was admiring the view."

I glanced back over my shoulder. "A bit limited from here."

"Not for long."

I looked back. "How did they react?"

"As expected." He leaned a forearm against the barrier, his expression amused. He had no intention of giving me any information about what was going on inside Trollus. He knew it would drive me mad to be kept in the dark, and he'd use the knowledge to negotiate. His was still the position of power, and both of us knew it.

"It would seem Anushka knows Cécile is hunting her," I said.

"Last night she murdered the witch Catherine and either burned or absconded with the grimoire, which means we've lost any method of tracking her."

My father's brow furrowed, and he was silent for a moment. "Why, if she knows who Cécile is, has she not tried to kill her?"

Of course he saw right to the heart of the matter. But I had no intention of revealing Cécile's familial connection to Anushka just yet. Just as I had no intention of revealing that I knew he controlled Aiden du Chastelier.

"The question crossed my mind," I admitted. "I might have thought it some moral conscience or allegiance to her kind, but she has demonstrated that she's no qualms against killing other humans. Which means there is a reason she hasn't made an attempt against Cécile's life."

"There is something important about Cécile," he said. "The foretelling led us to her, and everything she's done has demonstrated its accuracy. This is only more proof that there is something about her that is significant, something we don't know."

"Something that Anushka does."

"So it would seem." He slipped a finger into his pocket and extracted a gold coin, flipping it back and forth across his fingers as he thought. "You have a plan?"

"Of a sort." I watched the gold flick across his knuckles. "Cécile has explained that the curse is nothing more than an act of Anushka's will made physical by magic. Its very existence is predicated upon her desire to keep us contained. Her hate." I tore my gaze away from the gold. "I can only imagine how infuriating it will be for her to discover a troll has broken free of her will. And not just any troll." I squared my shoulders. "The descendant of the one who provoked her hate in the first place."

Which was part of my plan, if not all of it.

The gold coin stopped moving. "You intend to use yourself as bait?"

I nodded. "She'll feel compelled to move against me. I'm certain of it."

He went very still. Nothing showed in his expression, but that lack of motion betrayed his unease with my proposition. "If you announce what you are to the world, you'll put the rest of us at risk. We are yet vulnerable."

"Which is why I have no intention of revealing *what* I am, only who," I said. "I'll infiltrate their aristocracy – we know she walks among them – and then I'll parade around in front of her until she's driven to act, and in doing so, will reveal herself."

"Risky," my father muttered. "For one, she might actually kill you, and two, you're dependent on a woman who hasn't made a mistake in five hundred years doing just that."

"Do you have a better idea?" I asked.

He sighed. "I assume you'll be needing some gold."

CHAPTER 38
Cécile

Standing on a low podium in only a thin silk shift, I watched in the looking glass as the dressmaker deftly wrapped a tape measure around my waist. Her fingers brushed against the thick scar on my ribs, and I flinched as her hands twitched away from the unexpected flaw on my body. "You're thinner," she said to hide her reaction. "All the gowns will need alterations and the busts will require padding." She wrapped the tape measure around my breasts again, glanced at the measurement, and sighed as her original assessment was confirmed.

Against my will, my cheeks warmed. Her assistant smiled pertly at me, but I kept my chin up and met her eyes. "I'll have another one of those cakes, please." To the dressmaker I said, "You needn't go overboard – I've been unwell, but I'm sure I'll be back to my usual self shortly." Sadly, my usual self would still require the padding.

It was true that I was feeling better. The King's compulsion was still with me, but it no longer felt desperate, no longer consumed me. While I'd be a fool to say we were back in control, our circumstances no longer felt so dire. With Tristan free, Lord Aiden was no longer a threat, and we had a plan, albeit an uncertain one.

Tristan would have stayed up all night plotting, but I'd insisted he rest. He'd not complained about his injuries, but there was no mistaking how much they troubled him. I wanted to offer to try to heal them, but I was hesitant to do so. It would require my channeling his magic, bending it to my will, and I did not think he'd tolerate that, given recent developments.

A night's sleep had done *me* a world of good: my head felt clear and my appetite had returned with a vengeance. All of which made me very uneasy. I wished I could believe it was Tristan's presence that was the cause of my improvement – that having him at my side had cured what ailed me.

But I couldn't even allow myself to think such drivel. I'd no doubt it was his freedom that had eased my mind, but not because he and I were happy about it. It was because the King was happy about it, which meant all was going according to his plan. Tristan had left to talk to his father this morning, and I was worried about how that conversation had gone.

The assistant returned with a slice of cake while the dressmaker was helping me into another creation my mother had commissioned. It was the newest fashion, all layers of petticoats and flounce, the bodice and sleeves tight, and the square neckline low. It was the sort of thing my mother would wear, and I felt uncomfortable. There were six of them waiting for me to try on, all of which must have cost her a small fortune.

I'd a sneaking suspicion that my new wardrobe indicated her desire for me to take my place in the salons of Trianon – at the Marquis' side. There was no other reason for me to have dresses this elaborate and in these dark colors. Their completion was timely, but not for the reasons she thought.

Taking the tiny plate with its cake, I nibbled on it while watching the entrance to the fitting room. Tristan and Chris should have made it to the hotel by now, but I was waiting for word that they were ready before I put my part of the plan into action. The bell on the door of the shop rang, and moments later, Sabine walked into the room. She raised an appreciative eyebrow at my appearance, then, ignoring the dressmaker, stepped up onto the fitting podium and whispered into my ear, "They've taken rooms at the Hôtel de Crillon."

"Is that so?" I murmured, but loud enough for the women to hear. "In a suite?"

"The most expensive rooms." Her breath tickled my ear as she leaned closer. "Chris is all polished up and dressed as a manservant, and he's got his own room. Looks about ready to fly out of his own skin from discomfort, but Tristan seems in his element."

"How exciting." I gave her a wicked little smile. "It's been ages since anyone interesting came to the city, and there are none more interesting than him. Be a doll, and see if you can discover anything about his calendar. We'll go for tea when I'm finished here and you can tell me the details." I kissed her cheek, and watched her leave, hoping my nerves didn't show.

"Have you any performances planned, mademoiselle?" the dressmaker asked around the pin in her mouth. She sounded disinterested, but I knew better. She sewed for the wealthy bourgeoisie and a few of the minor nobility, but what she primarily traded in was gossip.

"A few," I replied, after swallowing my last mouthful of cake. "But I've found reason to keep my calendar open."

"Oh?" She used the one word like a crowbar, prying for information.

"There's a gentleman arrived who has a fine taste for the arts."

"Recently arrived?" She didn't pause in her pinning and tucking.

"Today. Although I'd heard about his impending arrival some days ago. I was fortunate enough to make his acquaintance this summer, and he sent me a letter explaining his intention to take up residence in Trianon."

"From where?"

I handed my plate to the assistant. "That was beyond delicious! Would you be a dear and retrieve me another?" I waited pointedly for her to exit, knowing with absolute certainty that she'd be listening from outside the door.

When she was gone, I leaned down. "From an estate in the

south, near Courville. He's apparently grown weary of the reclusive nature of his family, which is why he's in Trianon." I smiled mischievously, hoping my eyes glittered with the promise of the best of gossip. "He's rich as sin and stands to inherit his family's entire fortune." I licked a bit of frosting off my bottom lip. "He's also handsome enough to drive even the most moral of women to become sinners."

The woman's eyes widened. "Titled?"

I shook my head. "No, but I think that will change soon enough." Which was the polite way of saying he was here to find himself a titled wife. The dressmaker did not miss my point, and I could see the wheels turning in her eyes as she considered which eligible young noblewomen came from families in need of coin – as well as the value of knowing the girl who stood to become said gentleman's mistress, if she was not already.

She turned me to face the mirror, fussing at the lace that dangled from my sleeve. "What is his name?"

I hesitated, telling myself that the pause would increase the drama. But in reality, I was afraid. The moment I revealed Tristan's name would be the moment I painted a target on his back for Anushka. But it had to be done.

"Yes, darling. Who is this young gentleman of whom you speak? And why is it you haven't mentioned him before?"

I froze. Very slowly, I looked over my shoulder and met my mother's piercing gaze. "Mama! Returned so quickly?" Rattled, I turned back to the mirror. I was in a heap of trouble with her, but I couldn't afford to have her curb my freedom now. "Are you feeling better?"

"Much." Her voice was cool. "But don't keep us in suspense, dearest. Who is this gentleman?"

My tongue felt dry, and I fussed with the neckline of the dress. But withholding the information now would seem strange. "His name is Tristan de Montigny."

CHAPTER 39
Tristan

Relying half on Cécile's vague instructions and half on false confidence, I managed to check in at the Hôtel de Crillon without exposing my complete lack of knowledge about such activities. The first thing I did, once I was ensconced in my rooms, was to shut all the draperies against the brilliant afternoon sun. Then I let my disguise go, the warmth of magic falling away from my face.

"Trying to set the mood?" Chris asked, examining the tower of teacakes sitting on one of the tables before selecting one for himself and one for the dog.

"I'm starting to wonder about you, Christophe," I said, opening one of the chests of gold so that I could look at the gleaming metal the servants – no, the *porters* had struggled to carry up. All the coins were identical to those created in the Regent's mint for ease of spending. The mint in Trollus had the capacity to create the coinage of any of the continental kingdoms we traded with, and we paid the merchant and pirate captains in the currency of their choosing. To do otherwise would invite questions, and importing all the food Trollus required without attracting the broader attention of our human neighbors was complicated enough.

I turned back to my co-conspirator. "You called me pretty three times on the drive back to Trianon. I can't recall the last time I received so many compliments in such quick succession."

"Being called pretty as a girl isn't a compliment, you know," Chris said around a mouthful of his third cake.

"And I'm sure if I had a predilection for strapping farm boys, my heart would be broken by your insults." I picked up a handful of coins, the motion sending pain lancing up my arm. I'd regained much of the mobility in my hands, but the wounds in my wrists remained black, seeping, and awful. "Here."

He stopped chewing and eyed the glittering gold. "You think I'm fool enough to take that? Troll gold got for nothing is bad luck."

"It isn't *got for nothing*," I said, dropping the coins on the table. "It's for helping us."

He shook his head and stared at his feet. "I don't make that in a year, much less in the couple of weeks you say this will take."

Stones, but he was honest to the core.

"The work you'll be undertaking with me will be more difficult and dangerous, so it's only fair you be paid more."

"This isn't work," Chris muttered. "I'm not doing it to get paid – that's not what I'm looking for."

"Trolls don't like to be in anyone's debt," I told him. "So if it isn't gold, it's something else. Name it."

He shrugged.

"Teacakes?" I suggested.

He scowled.

"Flowers?"

"I've never met anyone as annoying as you."

I smiled and batted my eyelashes at him. "Kisses?"

Chris scooped up the coins and shoved them in his pocket. "Gold will be fine."

I laughed and sat down in the chair across from him, but my good humor didn't last. "We need your help, Chris," I said. "Cécile and I can't accomplish this alone, and you and Sabine are the only people in Trianon we can trust."

And I did trust him. Which was altogether strange, given

that I did not know him well. I remembered the first time we'd met – both of us had been children, and his father had brought him to Trollus for the first time. We'd had a strong relationship with the Girard family for generations, as they'd sold us not only the bulk of their farm's yield, but were also responsible for procuring grain and produce in the markets in the southern half of the Isle. Christophe stood to inherit the farm and the family business, so his arrival had been expected and planned for.

There had been a bit of a ceremony when he'd given his oaths, and I'd been the one to take them. They'd been the first set I'd received, although there had been hundreds since. It was the King's duty to collect them, as it had the added advantage of protecting him from his enemies. But while it was typical for a King to pass the duty off to his heir once he or she was grown, it had been very unusual for my father to pass the duty to his eight year-old son. Yet it had worked out for me in the end, because it was the only reason Chris was free to speak of us outside the confines of Trollus.

"Aye, well." Chris took a fourth cake. "Let's hope our help is enough." He hesitated. "Do you know what you'll do when you find her?"

Would I kill her?

"I honestly don't know." I sighed. "Nearly everyone I care about is in Trollus. It was easy to desire Anushka to live and the curse to endure when I was in there with them. When I could protect them. But I've abandoned them to the mercy of a handful of very powerful and dangerous trolls, and knowing I've done so eats at my conscience."

Chris leaned back in his chair, expression thoughtful. He spoke simply, but anyone who took him for a fool was one themselves. "You're thinking about going back once you've got Cécile clear of your father, aren't you?"

Reluctantly, I nodded. "I've thought about it. But if I did go back, I'd have to kill my father, which might well kill my mother and my aunt. I'd have to kill my brother. And only then would I be in power, but for how long? Everyone would know that I held the freedom of my people in my grasp and threw it away. They'd hate me for it, and how long until one of them found a way to put a knife in my back? Then it would be a war for the throne, and who can say how many would die. The beginning of the end was five centuries ago when Anushka entombed us in rock, but this I think would see her act through to completion."

"Or you could set them free."

"And entertain an entirely different set of costs," I replied, full well knowing that I'd thought of that option as much as the one of which I'd just spoken.

"Stuck between a rock and a hard place, aren't you?"

I laughed, wishing it didn't sound so bitter. "Every day of my life."

A knock sounded at the door. Chris rose to his feet. "That will be Sabine, I expect."

The blonde girl strode in, kissed Chris on the cheek, then took the seat furthest from me. "I've come from tea with Cécile. She's put your plan in motion, so I suppose we'll soon see if it works." Pouring tea into a delicate china cup, she blew gently on the contents. "Genevieve's returned – she dropped in on Cécile's fitting with the dressmaker."

Chris made a sympathetic noise. "Cécile got a bit of a tongue-lashing, I reckon?"

"Oddly enough, no." Sabine took a mouthful of tea. "She said Genevieve seemed out of sorts and was perhaps not yet recovered from her affliction. She stayed only long enough to see the dresses she'd commissioned for Cécile, and then she left."

"That's a stroke of luck," Chris muttered. "Not like that woman to let a grievance go."

"I doubt she has," Sabine said. "I'm sure she's only waiting for a prime moment to dole out punishment."

"Any sign of Aiden or of Cécile's brother?" I asked. Cécile believed there was little risk of a repeat attempt at kidnapping her, but I was still wary of her walking around the city alone.

"I asked at the barracks, and Fred is on duty at the castle. Neither of them have approached Cécile." Her eyes flicked around the room, eventually landing on me. "I see you've exchanged one palace for another."

"I'm here for a purpose, not for my own comfort."

She sniffed and set her cup on the table. "Oh yes, because I'm sure if left to your own devices you would have settled for second-class accommodations."

"Sabine." There was an edge to Chris's voice. "Don't start."

"Why not?" Her words were clipped. "I'm told you trolls value the truth, so shouldn't that be what you want from me?"

She watched me as though I were some dangerous creature, unpredictable and likely to bite at any moment. Not afraid, no. But wary. And angry. I silently nodded.

Sabine dragged in a breath. "You kidnapped my best friend. Forced her to marry you against her will. Kept her prisoner, and very nearly got her killed." Her fingers dug into the upholstered arms of the chair, white from the pressure. "You ruined her life, and because of this *bonding*" – she spat out the word – "she'll never be free of you. And I hate you for it."

"You're acting like a blasted lunatic." Chris stepped between us. "It wasn't his fault, Sabine. He didn't have any more choice in what happened than she did."

"Oh, shut up!" Sabine was on her feet. "He dresses you in fancy clothes, feeds you cakes, and now you're defending him? I can hear coins jingling in your pockets that weren't there before. You should be ashamed of yourself, Christophe Girard!"

He glared over his shoulder at me. "I told you that gold was bad luck."

"I think this has more to do with you calling her a lunatic than the gold," I said. "But I suppose time will tell."

Sabine shoved past him. "Don't you have anything to say?"

"Goshawk's Hollow raises women with steel for spines."

She lifted her chin. "I'm not interested in your compliments."

"I was merely making an observation."

I created an orb of magic, staring into its depths as I thought. Not using my power was like trying not to use my left leg – possible, but at the same time, no small challenge. Using it now was a small comfort as I remembered the pages of reports I'd read about her riding through woods and fields day in and day out in search of Cécile, all the while blaming herself for her friend's disappearance. It had been an impressive display of love and loyalty, and I'd be a fool to be surprised that such intensity would fuel hate when faced with one of the creatures who had stolen her friend away.

How well would I forgive if it were me who stood in her shoes? Not well. Not at all. Pénélope had died believing I despised her for having bonded Marc, because I had believed her death inevitable, and his loss very nearly so. I let my magic wink out.

"I have nothing to say in my defense."

"Nothing?"

I rose to my feet, resting my arms behind my back so that she would not feel threatened. "I could spend the next several hours explaining to you how I fought against bringing Cécile to Trollus. How my father gave me no real choice in bonding her. How if I hadn't, he'd have sooner killed her than let her go free. But all of that sounds rather hollow, doesn't it? Because explanations cannot undo what was done. They cannot wash away the hurt that was caused to Cécile, to her family, to you – their only purpose is to help me cast aside all culpability, which would be cowardly behavior on my part."

I paused, watching her expression. "There are no words I can offer that will earn your forgiveness, Sabine, but perhaps my actions going forward might prove my worth."

Her eyes narrowed, and she slowly shook her head. "You are too perfect. In the way you look, in the things you say. It does not make me like you, and it certainly does not make me trust you."

I lowered my head so that we were eye to eye. "If you think I'm perfect, then you've really not been paying attention."

A knock sounded firmly on the door, and I gave Chris a pointed look.

"I'm already tired of this," he muttered, but made his way

over, stepping out into the corridor.

Sabine and I stood listening to him argue with whoever was in the hall. "He's resting... Won't appreciate you walking in on him... Just give the blasted things to me!" There was a kerfuffle, and a moment later, Chris came back into the room. "Nosy bastard," he said. "Here."

I took the stack of cards he proffered, opened them and flipped through the invitations. "They're all for tonight, but I don't know who any of these people are," I said, frowning at the names.

"Because you're oh-so-familiar with the inhabitants of Trianon?" Sabine asked sweetly.

"More so than you might think," I said. "The important ones, at any rate."

She rolled her eyes. "Read me the names." I did so, watching as she shook her head or nodded at them. "None titled, but that's to be expected given that you're a relative nobody."

Chris laughed around another cake. Between him and Souris, they were very nearly all gone.

"It isn't as though the minor nobility won't come calling," she said. "But it's rather early for them to show interest without looking desperate."

"How does a girl from a small country village know all of these things?" I asked. I didn't think she was lying, but I was curious why she spoke so confidently about a society of which she was not part.

"My parents own the only inn for miles, and people talk when they're deep in their cups," she said. "And I've been in Trianon for months now – none of this is secret, it's free for the knowing to those who bother to listen."

"A well-made point," I murmured, impressed. "So whose invitation should I accept?"

"Monsieur Bouchard's," Sabine said without hesitation. "He's a banker – not the wealthiest, but he has six daughters. And," she continued, "it isn't just a dinner invitation – it's a party. One that's been months in the planning. There will be any number of important people there."

I was only vaguely familiar with banking as a profession, but I had no intention of admitting it. "Done." Going over to the massive desk, I carefully penned my reply to Monsieur Bouchard and my regrets to the others. "Have these sent off," I said, handing them to Chris, assuming he would know how that was to be accomplished. "And have them send up something else to eat – I'm famished. And you–" I rounded on Sabine. "I need you to tell me everything you know."

CHAPTER 40
Tristan

Our hired hansom cab whisked us swiftly through the lamp-lit streets, the air chill and sparkling with frozen crystals. Chris sat across from me, both of us polished within an inch of our lives and twitching with nerves. Our plan was for me to spend the next several nights immersing myself in Trianon society, and then to begin my pursuit of Cécile. Until then, I wouldn't see her at all, and I hated that.

"How will I know what I'm supposed to do?" Chris asked for the seventh time. "What if I make a mistake?"

"As long as you don't say anything you shouldn't, you'll be fine," I replied for the seventh time. "Do whatever all the other men are doing, which is likely nothing that resembles work. Be sociable, but not so much that you draw undue attention to yourself. We've gone through our backstory, so all you need to do is stick with that." The advice was as much for me as it was for him.

"I'm going to make a mistake," Chris groaned. "Sabine would have been better for this."

"Indeed she would have," I said, refraining from mentioning that I'd asked her to do exactly that. "But I'm bound by your peculiar human social conventions in this, so I have to settle for you. People would talk if I showed up with a ladyservant."

"What's that supposed to mean?" Chris retorted.

315

"It means in Trollus, it wouldn't matter. We don't have separate rules for men and women. Power and blood are all that matters."

Chris examined the polish of his boots, mind momentarily taken off his nerves. "What about the oath we take then – that no human man can touch a troll woman. Why isn't it just that no human can touch a troll?"

"For physiological reasons."

Chris blinked.

I sighed. "If a human man consorts with a troll woman, he can leave without taking responsibility for the consequences. If a human woman cavorts with a troll man and becomes pregnant, she will be physically incapable of leaving Trollus until the child is born. For the most part, that's motivation enough for them to turn aside any advances. But frankly," I said, "it's not a rule that's particularly well enforced. Half-bloods have always been a valuable commodity, and a blind eye is often turned to the introduction of new blood."

"Makes sense."

"Imagine that." It was a relief when the carriage ground to a halt. "I think we're here."

As the footman approached to open the door, I examined the home we'd stopped in front of. It was a relatively large, square, two-story affair made of brick, the windows bright with a yellow glow that far outshone that of the half moon above. Music trickled out to greet me as I stepped onto the walkway lining the street.

"Monsieur de Montigny?" The footman inquired.

"Yes." It was strange to be called such.

"Monsieur Bouchard is expecting you."

I followed the man up to the entrance of the house, my skin prickling with slight pain as I passed through the gate of the wrought iron fence encircling the property. I wondered if they remembered why such fences had come into existence – to keep the immortal fey away. Unfortunately for humanity, it did little to protect them from trolls. Mortality had come with some advantages, not the least of which was a better tolerance of the metal.

The door opened, and I stepped inside. The air was roasting hot and full of the smells of food, perfume, sweat, and smoke – the music and chatter of dozens of voices loud in my ear. My pulse raced. I'd been to countless parties in my lifetime where I had an agenda other than entertainment. I'd pretended to be someone who I was not for years. But never had I been so far out of my element, and the challenge both terrified and intoxicated me.

"Monsieur de Montigny!" A booming voice caught my attention, and I turned, half in the process of handing off my hat and cloak, to see a short, crimson-faced man with an abundance of white whiskers bearing down on me. He stuck his hand out, and though the concept of shaking hands was entirely strange to me, I took it, clenching my teeth into a smile as he jerked my stiff wrist up and down. "François Bouchard," he said, finally releasing my hand. "We are so pleased you could join us at our little fête."

"I was pleased to receive the invitation," I said, following through the foyer. "This is my first visit to Trianon, and I confess to feeling much like a fish out of water."

"Well, you're in good hands now."

A woman dressed in brilliant pink stepped out in front of us, her eyes widening as they met mine. "There you are, my dear," Bouchard said. "Anna, this is Monsieur de Montigny, who's just arrived from the south – from near Courville, if what I've heard is correct?"

Thank you, Cécile.

I smiled, kissed the woman's outstretched knuckles, and said, "Your ears have not failed you."

"Good to know," Bouchard said, and I only just refrained from blocking the arm he raised, reluctantly allowing him to slap me across the shoulders. "One can't count on these things at my age."

"It is a pleasure to meet you, Monsieur," Anna said, keen to get a word in.

"Of a certainty, the pleasure is mine," I replied. "I was half-afraid I was facing a lonely dinner, but instead I find myself here, in your company, which is an improvement far beyond what I might have hoped for."

She laughed, and took a mouthful of wine. "The dark side of bachelorhood, I'm afraid. But you are here now, and it is far past time you were introduced. François will take you on the tour – there are a great many gentlemen who would like to make your acquaintance, and more than a few ladies, I'm sure."

"You're in mining, isn't that right?" Bouchard said, leading me off. "I've a number of clients in the business, so I was surprised not to have heard your name, all things considered."

Those *things* being in fact *one* thing: wealth.

"My father takes great pains to protect the family's anonymity," I said, smiling at a cluster of young women standing together – I did have a part to play, after all. The girls all clutched at each other's arms, heads pressed together as they whispered. "We conduct all of our business through agents known for their discretion. I'd be more surprised if you *had* heard our name."

"Your presence indicates you're not of a like mind with your father," he commented. "He can't be best pleased at your decision to leave?"

"He's been surprisingly supportive of my adventure out into the world," I replied. Supportive as long as I walked down the path he wanted. "He personally ensured I was well equipped to *invest in my future*," I mimicked my father's dry voice as he'd shoved the chest of gold through the barrier. "But now isn't the time to talk business."

Which only made him want to discuss it all the more. I took the glass of champagne he handed me, discreetly looking around the room. Was Anushka here? I thought not. Cécile's argument that the witch was under the protection of the Chasteliers had been compelling, and that would suggest she resided amongst a higher class of people.

"I'd be happy to assist you in facilitating those investments," he said, eyes bright. "Perhaps if you gave me an idea of the magnitude of investment you're considering, I'd be better able to direct your introductions."

The question was crass, but given I was supposed to be some sort of back-country recluse, it was prudent that I not react. I leaned in and murmured a number.

Bouchard's eyes bugged. "Your options are many, Monsieur de Montigny."

"Excellent," I said. "I'll make an appointment with you as soon as it's convenient."

And so it began, a whirlwind of introductions and small talk, with everyone clambering to meet me because I was young, attractive, wealthy, and most of all, new. Even if I'd been dull as a brick, my novelty would've made me shine.

And I felt the same way. I'd spent my entire life surrounded by the same trolls, rarely meeting anyone new; and when I did, the barrier of power and class kept me from truly getting to know them. Cécile had been the only exception, and well I remembered the allure of her differentness. The appeal of knowing that so much about her was unknown. I felt a similar sensation as I walked through the party, full of humans who thought I was one of them, everything strange and different and exciting. It was a thousand times more intoxicating than the wine poured liberally into my glass.

So I danced with all the young women and a few of their mothers, made ribald jokes with the men in the corners, flirted with the girls and discussed politics with their fathers. Time flew, and before long, I found myself in a room dark with tobacco smoke, a brandy in one hand, and cards in the other.

"You're either the luckiest bastard to ever walk the Isle or you're counting, Tristan," one of the other young men muttered, eyeing his cards.

"I'm sure you'd do the same if you only had enough fingers and toes to manage the task," I said, enjoying the laughter of the other men. I was counting the cards, I couldn't help it, but I decided to throw my hand down rather than risk being thought a cheat. "I'm out."

"Well, well, well. Who do we have here?"

Smiles grew on the faces of the other men, and looking over my shoulder, I saw Cécile's mother. There was no mistaking her. Setting my brandy on the table, I rose to my feet. "Madame de Troyes, your reputation precedes you."

Her blue eyes managed to be familiar and foreign at the same time. "I should say the same of you. In the city not half a day, and already you have the gossip mills churning. You'll have no peace."

I shrugged. "The only thing worse than being talked about is being not talked about."

Her mouth quirked, but her gaze was cool. "How clever."

"I'm afraid I can't take credit as the originator. My skill lies in repeating the words of those more creative than I."

"False modesty is unattractive," she said, holding out a gloved hand. "It's how a weak man earns his praise."

"And how does a strong man earn it?" I asked, kissing her fingers and wishing I'd been forewarned that she'd be here.

"With his actions."

"Beautiful and wise, I see." She must have heard Cécile's half-invented story of meeting me in the summer and decided to seek me out. There was no other reason for her presence.

She pulled her hand from my grasp, and then surprised me by running one finger along my jaw, the familiarity of the gesture unnerving. "Do you always run so hot?"

"It's in the blood," I replied. "We Montignys have our curses, but clammy feet isn't one of them."

One tawny eyebrow rose. "I suppose that has its advantages on a cold winter's night."

The room burst into whistles and catcalls. I coughed, reaching blindly behind me for my drink, nearly knocking it over in the process. Genevieve laughed, the sound loud and clear as a clarion bell, and every man in the room echoed her as though on cue. My ears buzzed and my spine crawled with discomfort, which I hid behind my glass as I downed my brandy in a long gulp. Any doubt that Genevieve possessed a witch's powers vanished from my mind, but I remained uncertain of whether she was aware. Cécile had used magic unknowingly, and her mother might well be doing the same.

Her laughter eventually trailed off. "Why don't you pour me a drink."

"What's your pleasure?"

"Surprise me."

I went to the sideboard with its dozen decanters and splashed a generous amount of brandy into two glasses. It was well past time I was away from this party. Something about her made me uneasy, and it wasn't that she'd just one-upped me.

"A song for us, Genevieve?" Bouchard was watching from the corner where he stood with a few older gentlemen.

"Later," she called, taking the drink from me. "If I give it up so easily, you'll lose your appreciation."

"Impossible," he declared. "You are beyond compare, and there isn't a man in this room who doesn't know it. Or isn't about to find out." He winked at me and I raised my glass in response.

Genevieve took my arm, leading me closer to the fire. The room was already hot, and the flames only made it worse. A bead of sweat ran down my back, and my shirt stuck uncomfortably to my skin.

"So tell me," she said. "Why have you come to Trianon?"

"What do the gossip mills say?" The brandy tasted foul, and I wished it were water.

"They say a great many things, but one can never be certain of their accuracy."

I chuckled. "That's what makes it interesting, isn't it?"

She pursed her lips. "You're not going to tell me?"

I shook my head. "If I reveal my true purpose, I might have to follow through with it. I'm not sure I'm ready for that much commitment."

"And yet the rumors say you're here looking for a wife." She sipped at her drink. "Some people say that's the ultimate commitment."

"I think you are not one of them."

She blinked. "You seem to know a great deal about me."

"I make it my business to be informed about the mothers of the daughters who interest me," I said. "Cécile has a lovely voice. I was entranced from the moment I first heard it."

The glass in her hand shattered.

She stared at the blood dripping down her fingers, seemingly as astonished as I was. In an instant, we were surrounded by the other men, Bouchard taking hold of her wrist and pulling her fingers open. The rest of the glass toppled to the ground with a muffled little clink.

"What happened?" he demanded, examining the cut.

"The heat from the fire," she said. "It must have made the glass shatter."

Which was absolute nonsense. I'd intended to lure her in by mentioning Cécile, but I'd gotten much more than I'd bargained for. Anger? Fear? I found her difficult to read, so I wasn't precisely sure. But what I did know for certain was that she wanted me nowhere near her daughter.

"This should be seen to by a physician; it may need to be stitched," he said, holding her palm out for me to see. I nodded in agreement, though I knew nothing about judging the severity of a human injury.

"Nonsense." She retrieved a handkerchief and wrapped up her hand. "I'll be fine. But I'll need another glass." She waved away the onlookers, and then set her replacement beverage on top of the mantel. "Cécile has been quite reticent about revealing the details of where she was during the months of her absence."

"And you thought in seeking me out that I might divulge some of those details?"

"What sort of mother would I be if I didn't take an interest in my daughter's comings and goings. And disappearances."

"An absent one, I suppose," I said with a smile, not sure why I was provoking her when my aim was to win her over. "But that is neither here nor there. I'm afraid I'll not reveal Cécile's secrets. If you wish answers, you'll have to ask her yourself."

Her jaw tightened. "What of your intentions toward her? Will you divulge those?"

"You're forward."

"She's young and naive. I don't want to see her hurt."

"Ah." I handed my empty glass to a passing servant. "Well, rest assured, Madame de Troyes, I'd sooner harm myself than your daughter. Nothing would please me more than to see her onstage unencumbered by such trivial concerns as finances."

"You wish to offer her patronage?" Her eyes narrowed. "In exchange for what?"

"Is not the pleasure of seeing her perform payment enough?"

She snorted softly. "Don't patronize me. You could have that for the price of a ticket."

"Her company, then."

"You're in the practice of paying for your... company? Or is Cécile to be first in a line of many?"

"No," I said, my voice chilly. I did not like this woman. The expression in her eyes was flat and calculating. None of her questions were driven by a desire to protect Cécile, but rather to determine whether the longevity of my interest was worth the investment. "But I am in the practice of using what means are at my disposal to make those I care for happy."

"I see."

Nothing would be gained from prolonging this conversation. I needed to leave, but any excuse would look like an attempt to flee her scrutiny.

I was rescued by an approaching servant, his face dismayed.

Coming close to my arm, he said, "Monsieur, I'm afraid there has been an incident."

I raised one eyebrow. "Of what sort?"

He grimaced. "I'm afraid your manservant has overindulged and passed out in the middle of the kitchen floor. What would you have us do with him?"

I closed my eyes, my expression pained. "How terribly embarrassing." To Genevieve, I said, "I hope your injury does not trouble you long, Madame. Perhaps we will cross paths again soon." I hesitated before adding, "My proposal would benefit you as well. Please think on it."

I followed the servant into the kitchen, where Chris was indeed lying snoring, in the middle of the floor. "Don't know what got into him. He was fine, then all of sudden he set to drinking as though this hour might be his last."

I scowled and nudged Chris with my foot, but he would not rouse. "Two of you get him up."

They took him round the back while I retrieved my hat and cloak, then the four of us went out to where a cab waited, the tired-looking horse standing patiently in the snow.

"Put him in the back."

"It's extra if he vomits," the driver declared.

"The Hôtel de Crillon," I said, not bothering to grace the comment with an answer. I sat silently on the thinly padded bench until we were on our way, and then I said, "That was clever thinking."

Chris sat up, if somewhat unsteadily. "Heard Genevieve had arrived, and it was clear enough that you needed a way to escape." He hiccupped.

"Well, it worked. Did you learn anything of interest tonight?"

"Might be I did." Another hiccup.

"Well?"

"They were gossiping about you and Cécile. Apparently half the reason you're in Trianon is to rekindle your love affair."

"And the other half?"

"To take over the Isle with your frivolous spending of your father's hard-earned gold."

I smiled. "Anything else?"

"I..." Another hiccup, and his face went pale.

"Don't you..."

He summarily threw the liquid contents of his stomach up all over the floor.

"Dare," I finished with a sigh, then dug an extra few coins out of my pocket.

CHAPTER 41
Cécile

I was stirring my breakfast around my plate when a knock sounded at the door. Dropping my fork with a clatter that made my mother start, I bolted to the door before the maid would have a chance to answer it.

"A delivery for Mademoiselle de Troyes," the boy on the stoop said, holding out a box embossed with the name of a popular and very expensive confectioner, along with a card.

"Thank you," I said, the smile on my face threatening to crack my cheeks. "If you could wait a moment, I'll have you deliver a card for me."

Extracting a truffle from the box and popping it into my mouth, I flipped open the card and read.

Dearest Cécile,

I hope this note finds you well and in possession of as demanding a sweet tooth as I remember. I have recently arrived in Trianon, but I find myself unable to enjoy the pleasures of this city for want of your delightful company. I've been invited to this evening's performance of the ballet, but feel I must decline if I cannot attend with you on my arm, for to be in the theatre that is your domain without you would render the experience lackluster. Please say you will find space in your calendar so that I

might retrieve you from your mother's residence at 6pm.
Yours,
TdM

My skin flushed hot with pleasure and excitement – a welcome change from the frustration that had been eating away at me more and more each day. I knew what we were undertaking was serious – that we were deliberately attempting to incite a five hundred year-old witch into attacking Tristan, and in doing so, revealing herself. But it had been five days since I had seen him; I could not help the thrill of anticipation I felt.

I'd never been courted. All the boys in the Hollow had known I was leaving and hadn't bothered, and for obvious reasons Tristan had been unable to do so in Trollus. In my more indulgent moments, I'd felt a bit robbed, and that made me want to enjoy this moment, despite the underlying motivations.

Eating another truffle, I went to the desk and extracted a card.

Monsieur de Montigny,
Your taste in sweets is, as always, divine. It would be
my pleasure to attend the ballet with you this evening. I
shall see you at 6.
Cécile

I gave it to the delivery boy with a coin and instructions on where to bring it. Shutting the door behind me, I leaned against it and closed my eyes, licking the traces of sugar from my lips.

"I certainly hope you declined."

Opening my eyes, I saw my mother standing next to the desk, Tristan's note in her hands. I'd left it there knowing she would pick it up, because as much as this ruse was for Anushka's benefit, it also required luring my mother in. "Of course I didn't. Why should I have?"

She grimaced and was silent for a long moment. "Accepting a last-minute invitation makes you appear eager. Desperate.

Boring. None of which are attractive qualities."

I rolled my eyes. "Don't be ridiculous. He knows me well enough to have made his own judgments."

"Which is rather interesting, given that you've never mentioned him before."

"I didn't think I'd ever have the opportunity to see him again," I said, sorting through the sweets so that I wouldn't have to look her in the eye as I lied. "I met him in Courville this summer. After I was injured, I didn't even have the chance to say goodbye before the Girards whisked me back to the Hollow. I didn't even know he knew I was in Trianon until I received his letter."

"And just how *well* do you know this young man?"

Her inflection and her meaning were obvious and my cheeks burned. "Not *that* well, mother."

Relief flooded her face. "Small mercies."

Catching her by the arm, I led her to the settee and pressed a salted caramel upon her because I knew they were her favorite. "I thought this was what you wanted for me," I said. "You yourself said this is what you had me trained for."

"He is a poor choice."

"Why?"

She set the candy on the table. "After you told me the two of you were acquainted, I took the liberty of tracking him down, Cécile. He is not right for this purpose. He's too young, too handsome, too used to having everything he wants. I've met his kind before: his affections will be fierce, but fleeting. And he will not be discreet. There are better options."

"Like the Marquis." My tone was sour.

She nodded. "He will provide what you need at very little cost to your person. And no risk of heartbreak."

I picked up her candy and ate it myself.

"This young man will only end up hurting you," she said, taking my hand. "He'll eventually take a wife and his attentions will turn to her. And there is no chance of it being you. You are not of the same class, and whether he says so or not, he considers himself better than you. Is that really a path you want to go down?"

The caramel was sticking in my teeth and tasted overly sweet. "What if it is?"

"Then you're making a mistake."

"You don't know that."

She caught hold of my chin, forcing me to look into her eyes. "Are you in love with this man, Cécile?"

I jerked my chin free. This conversation had gotten away from me.

"Well, that explains a great deal."

I got to my feet, retrieving my box of candies and Tristan's note. "This is my life, Mama, not yours. Sometimes I think you forget that. Now I'm going to get ready for rehearsals. It would not do to keep everyone waiting."

The clock bonged six times, and I fought the urge to go to the window to check for any sign of the carriage.

"He's with Bouchard, who is chronically late," my mother said, from where she sat reading a book. She'd switched strategies from this morning, now employing passive-aggressive indifference in her attempt to dissuade me from this path. "Don't fret."

"I'm not fretting," I said, smoothing my lace gloves over the rich blue velvet of my dress. The bodice was both tight and low, revealing the slight curves of my breasts, which were amplified by the added padding. It was one of my new gowns, and I could not help but admire the sleeves, snug to my elbow and loose in a spray of lace that hung to my wrists. The crinoline puffed the skirts out from my hips, the velvet slashed to reveal the lace petticoat beneath.

My shoes were matching brocade with ribbons that wrapped around my ankles, and I wore sapphire and diamond earrings that Sabine had deemed a perfect match to the dress. She'd fixed my hair so it was up, a few curls left loose to frame my face, and rimmed my eyes with kohl and tinted my lips.

A knock sounded at the door, and I leapt up. "I'll answer it," my mother said, rising far too slowly for my tastes and then ambling toward the door. "Good evening, Monsieur de Montigny," she said. "Please do come inside. Winter is truly upon us."

"How is your hand?" Tristan asked, but whatever she answered went unheard in my ears as I adjusted my dress for the umpteenth time. When I glanced up, he had rounded the corner with her, and our eyes met.

His disguise was in place, eyes grey instead of silver and skin altered to a duskier, more human hue. But all else was the same, and even if he had made himself unrecognizable I still would have known it was him. I loved him; so much so that my chest felt tight and my breath short, and everything else in the room seemed wan as a faded painting.

"Mademoiselle de Troyes." He smiled, glanced at the floor and then back up to my face. "Memory, it would seem, is a pale comparison to reality."

"How charming he is!" My mother clapped her hands together and we both twitched. "Best be off. You don't want to be late."

Once we were outside, I said, "Marie's ladies were talking about you at rehearsals today. Of a certainty, she knows you are in Trianon. And if she knows, so does Anushka."

"Good," he said, although it seemed as if he hadn't really heard me. I gripped his arm above the elbow as we walked down the slippery steps, uncertain of the state of his wrists and knowing better than to ask.

"I meant what I said," he added. "You look beautiful tonight. That dress…" he trailed off.

"I'm supposed to be trying to seduce you into giving me all your money."

"Trying?" He laughed. "You have succeeded, and in doing so, quite driven thoughts of anything else from my mind."

"Your focus on our task is admirable," I said, but secretly I was pleased.

"If I am distracted, it is your fault. You have been my undoing since the day we met."

The coachman opened the door to the carriage, and Tristan helped me inside.

"Good evening, Cécile," Monsieur Bouchard said, his loud voice filling the small space. I'd met him several times previously, as he was a subscriber, and the nephews sitting next to him as well. "Good evening," I replied. "I understand I have you to thank for giving Monsieur de Montigny an excuse to see me tonight."

"Glad to oblige." The older man winked at Tristan as the carriage started forward. "I wanted proof that he wasn't all bluster and that you two truly were acquainted."

"Oh, yes," I said, smiling up at Tristan. "We met in Courville this summer. I was ever so pleased when he decided to join society in Trianon."

"And from now on, I shall go to Cécile with all my questions," Bouchard said. "She is far less taciturn than you, Montigny."

I laughed. "He hoards his secrets like a miser does his coin, I'm afraid. I spent all summer trying to pry them out, and I'm quite certain I barely scratched the surface."

"For good reason," Tristan replied. "It gives me an air of mystery. If I told you everything, I'd risk you realizing that I'm really quite dull."

"I doubt that," I said, then the carriage hit a dip in the road, bouncing me sideways against Tristan.

"Steady!" Bouchard shouted, banging on the wall. "Curse these roads. Something needs to be done about them."

Except I didn't curse them at all. Even through the layers of my skirts, I could feel the press of Tristan's hip against mine, the brush of his coat against my neck as he rested his arm along the back of the seat, the way his breath tickled my hair. I wanted to lean against him, but the gleam of amusement on the other men's faces told me I was already skirting the line of what was proper. I wanted them gone so it wouldn't matter, and from the burn of the heat in the back of my head, I knew the same thought had crossed Tristan's mind.

There isn't anything stopping you. The thought that I'd been thinking more and more over the past few days, crept across my mind even as I laughed along at a joke I hadn't even heard. *He is your husband.*

I considered the reasons why our intimacy had been limited before. Certainly a child was a complication we could not afford. Our lives were too much in jeopardy, and I couldn't even bear to think about what would happen to our baby if we were both killed. Half-blood as it would be, if the King got his hands on our child, would he not sell it off as a slave as he had done with Lessa? And that would be if he didn't kill it out of hand. And wasn't there a certain inevitability that the child would have to go to Trollus as long as the curse remained? Would it happen the moment it was born? Before? I shivered at the idea.

The carriage pulled to a stop beneath the domed side entrance reserved for subscribers and other important guests. Tristan stepped out first, then helped me down. "What are you thinking?" he asked quietly, leading me toward the doors the liveried men held open for us.

"The compulsion is getting bad again," I said, because it was true and he needed to know, and I didn't want to admit that the only thing that chased it off was my lusty thoughts.

"Keep in your mind that you are doing what you promised you would," he said softly. "She knows my intent, and she'll come after me sooner rather than later. She has to."

I knew he was trying to make me feel better, but the reminder that Anushka would try to hurt him or kill him did anything but. He was not afraid of her, but I was. There was no one alive who knew more about trolls, and she'd killed one as powerful as him before.

Sensing his words had the opposite effect than he'd intended, he reached up with his free hand and squeezed mine where it rested on his arm. Then he lowered his head, his breath warm against my ear. "I know that wasn't what you were thinking about."

My cheeks flushed, but a smile crept onto my face. "Perhaps not."

My mother had taken me on a tour of the opera house soon after I'd arrived in Trianon, but sometime since, I'd lost an appreciation for how extraordinary it really was. Marble colonnades banded with gilt twisted up to ceilings painted with soft golds and blues, with massive crystal chandeliers hanging one after another to light the long stretch of the grand foyer.

We were somewhat late, and went straight to Bouchard's box on the second level of the horseshoe-shaped theatre and took our seats, the lights already dimmed and the curtain up. Willowy girls in white tulle flitted across the stage, and even though I'd seen them perform countless times before, I could not help but marvel at their grace, lifting up onto their tiptoes in shiny satin shoes, limbs impossibly flexible. Tristan leaned forward against the railing as he watched, his expression captivated. This, like so much else, was not something he'd ever seen before.

My eyes went to his wrists, where the sleeves of his coat and shirt pulled up ever so slightly. Instead of skin between cuff and glove, there was black fabric wrapped around his wrist. I turned my gaze back to the stage before he could catch me looking, but my stomach still clenched. Five days, and still not better. It was past time I ask him to let me try to heal the injuries.

A waiter brought glasses of wine, and Tristan leaned back in his seat and sipped at his, never taking his eyes off the stage. What did he think, I wondered, at this display of humanity? Of the color and the vibrancy, of the filth and the beauty, of the faces and features so wildly different from those in Trollus? Did it change the way he felt about me?

Fingers brushed against mine, and I started, the wine sloshing back and forth in my glass. Never taking his eyes from the stage, Tristan locked his fingers in mine, our hands hidden in the folds of my skirt.

He shifted almost imperceptibly my direction, and, keeping watch on Bouchard out of the corner of my eye to make sure he didn't notice, I did the same. My shoulder brushed against his arm, and heat trickled through my veins, building low in my stomach. I took a sip of my drink, the lights on the stage seeming bright and unfocused. His knee bumped against mine, and I inhaled deeply, feeling my breasts press tight against the bodice of my dress. My skin flushed with desire that had no outlet, slowly filling me until I could think of nothing else. Would he ask me back to the hotel tonight? Should I ask him?

Abruptly the curtain dropped and the lights went up. Tristan dropped my hand as though it were on fire, looking at me in surprise. *Intermission,* I mouthed, and he nodded slightly. We all rose and stepped out into the corridor. As we did, I noticed a wave of bows and curtsies coming in our direction, but I was too short to see which of the peers was in the house tonight.

Tristan was not. A vicious wave of his anger filled me, and I held tight to his arm, rising up onto my tiptoes to see who it was – just in time to watch Lord Aiden's eyes light on Tristan. Fred and one other guard stood behind him, and I watched the expression on my brother's face darken as he realized whom I was with. The men surrounding us bowed low and I dropped into a curtsey, hauling on Tristan's arm as I did. He bowed, but only just.

"You're far from home, Montigny." His eyes went to me. "Well done, mademoiselle. I underestimated you."

"You are not the first, my lord," I said. The corridor had gone from slightly chilly to hotter than midday in the height of summer, and I dug my fingernails into Tristan's arm, praying he would not react any more than that. "And undoubtedly, you won't be the last."

Lord Aiden's gaze went back to Tristan. "I'd have a word with you, Montigny."

"As you like." Tristan's tone was flat.

The other men noticed the lack of honorific and their eyebrows rose. As I followed Tristan back into the box, I met Bouchard's gaze and rolled my eyes as though the tension were nothing more than the posturing of young men, and nothing to be concerned about.

"No interruptions," Aiden muttered to the other guard, but allowed Fred to follow us in.

The door clicked shut, but it was magic that drowned out the voices in the corridor and the musicians tweaking their instruments in the pit. Fred frowned, and his hand drifted to the pistol at his waist.

"Don't," I said, and the flames of the massive chandelier overhead flared brightly. Fred blinked, then turned to me, incredulity written across his face. "And don't you dare look at me like that," I snarled. "Not after what you did."

"It was for your own good," he said. "I was only trying to help you."

My head jerked from side to side in furious denial. "Say you did it because you don't agree with the choices I've made. Say you did it because you wanted to stop me from freeing the trolls. Or because your loyalty is to him." I jerked my chin in Aiden's direction. "But don't you dare claim that you did it *for* me when we both know you did it to *control* me."

"Cécile." He reached for me, voice pleading, but I stepped back. "Is that why you hate our mother so much? Because she didn't make choices you liked? Because she wouldn't change to be the person you wanted her to be?"

It was a low blow, but as I watched Fred blanch, I found I was too angry to care.

"That's not the reason," he stammered. "You've got it backwards. She made me choose between her and Father. And when I wouldn't take her side..." He swallowed hard. "She made me pay for it."

"And now you're doing the same to me." I went to stand next to Tristan, who leaned against the edge of the balcony, feeling my anger fuel his and his fuel mine. No good can come from this...

"What do you want from us?" I snapped at Aiden, struggling with the desire to have my own revenge for what he had done to me, for what he had intended to do to my friends.

"Tell me why you killed her," he demanded. "You could have

taken the book back and gone. Catherine was only a pawn – she didn't need to die."

I frowned, more surprised at his sentiment toward the dead woman than his accusation that we were her murderers. It had seemed to me that he'd despised her – had only allied with her out of sheer necessity. But perhaps I'd been wrong. "I thought you hated her."

He leveled me with a dark stare. "I needed her."

Of course.

"We didn't kill her," I said, not bothering to hide my disgust. "When we arrived, her shop was in flames. Tristan got her out, but it was too late."

Fred's shoulders slumped with obvious relief. "Thank God," he muttered.

Hurt sliced through me. "You didn't honestly believe I'd murdered a woman in cold blood?"

"Some people will do just about anything for the sake of revenge," he replied, staring at the ground. "And I'm not even going to guess at what *he's* capable of." Fred lifted his head to glare at Tristan.

"If I was so quick to kill, let me assure you, His *Lordship*" – Tristan coated the word with mockery – "would have been the first to go."

"Then by all means, get it over with," Aiden snapped. "Quit this pretense at being human, troll, and show your true colors."

Tristan's disguise melted away, and in two strides he was in Aiden's face. "I gave you a chance to do a small good – to help Cécile – but instead you thought only of yourself and pursued a plan as evil as any of my father's. If you had saved her, I would have done what I could to help you, and our future might look very different. But now all you are is my enemy, and you will come to regret that fact."

Fred shifted, and I turned to give him a warning look only to find his brow furrowed and his gaze fixed on Aiden. The Regent's son had not, I suspected, told him the whole of the truth, and my brother would not take well to having been manipulated.

"The only regret I have is that my plan failed, because I lost my chance to see a future unencumbered by your father and the rest of your wretched race of creatures," Aiden snarled. "I swear that I'll never stop until I find a way to see every last one of you on your knees, starving, dying, and begging for the mercy of humanity. But let me assure you, troll, I will show you none."

Tristan's temper snapped, and in a motion almost too fast to see, he lifted Aiden off his feet by the throat and slammed him into the wall. Fred swore and tried to reach for his pistol, but the effects of my compulsion remained and he settled for his sword. I opened my mouth to stop him, but before I could speak, the blade tore from his grip, spinning in a silver blur across the theatre to embed itself in the box across from us. Fred lunged toward the two, but magic caught him, pinning him to the ground.

I stood still, and though everything had happened within seconds, time seemed to slow as I watched Aiden's face darken, the dagger he'd managed to pull from his belt banging ineffectually against magic, his free hand clawing against Tristan's fingers. A cruel and vengeful part of my soul wanted to stand back and let him die. This man who was servant to the King I despised. Who had kidnapped me and tried to use me against those I loved. Who had threatened to kill an entire race of people because of the hatred he had for one troll. What mercy did he deserve?

But what sort of person was I if I did not give it? Even through his fury, I could feel Tristan's hesitation. I knew how strong he was – that he could've snapped Aiden's neck with one hand or worse. Yet instead he let death creep slowly toward the other man, not because he was cruel, but because he wasn't a killer. That he was merciful by nature was what made him different from his father, from Angoulême, from Roland; and for us to have any hope of making a future worth living, he needed to remain that way.

"Tristan, he's baiting you. Let him go." I moved forward, forcing my mind to calm and our mutual anger to temper. "If you kill him, everything will come out. It's what he wants."

Tristan's grip lessened, and with a hiss of disgust, he dropped Aiden to the ground. Casting a black look at Fred, he released him, then went to the balcony to look over the edge.

I knelt down next to the man who was destined to one day rule the Isle, watching as he wheezed and choked, hand pressed against his bruised throat. "You believe yourself better because you are human," I said. "But you are not. You are weak, selfish, and your word means nothing. You are not fit to rule a privy. Get out of my sight, or I'll spell you with an itch upon your privates that will have you squirming for the rest of your days."

Not waiting to see if he listened, I poured two glasses of wine and forced one into Tristan's hand as the door open and closed, both of them departed. "Pull yourself together," I said. "Bouchard and his nephews will be upon us in moments."

He nodded, eyes reverting to grey as they fixed on the people flooding back into their seats below. "They'll never be safe while caged by the curse," he said softly. "They are in danger from within and without, and what can I do to help them? How can I protect them?"

There was only one answer, but I bit my lip and said nothing until I heard the other men come back into the box.

"Is all well?" Bouchard asked, his brow furrowed.

"Everything is splendid," I replied. "I believe the second half is about to begin."

"I didn't realize you were acquainted with Lord Aiden du Chastelier," he said once Tristan had turned around.

Tristan didn't answer, so I kicked him in the ankle.

"We've met in passing," he eventually said. "He knows my father."

I could see another question forming on Bouchard's tongue, but now was not the time for inquisitiveness. "The curtain's rising," I said swiftly. "Best we take our seats."

Whether the girls performed well or not in the second half, I could not have said, for I spent it with one eye on Tristan and the other on my thoughts. King Thibault might believe he had control over Lord Aiden, but we'd seen proof that control was tenuous at best. There were ways around any oath – he only needed to find them. And then what? His hatred of the trolls wasn't limited to those who'd crossed him.

He wanted the entire race exterminated, and I knew that was what troubled Tristan. He'd always known the dangers his people faced from within Trollus, but I wasn't sure he ever really considered what a threat humanity could be if they moved against the trolls en masse. Which might very well happen if Thibault died or Aiden found a way around his oaths.

Then what would we do? What would Tristan do if his people's lives were in danger? How far would he go to keep them safe? I desperately wanted to know Tristan's thoughts, but now was not the time or place to ask them. Regardless of what had happened, we had a strategy in play, and to abandon it would be folly.

After the performance, we went to the foyer to see the dancers. The men all watched them with covetous eyes, except for Tristan, who was examining the portraits lining the room, expression light, and his mind grim. "Where is that necklace now?" he asked me. "Could you use it in place of the book?"

I used it to buy the ox that I slaughtered as part of a ritual sacrifice to set you free.

"I sold it." I'd told my mother that it was with the jewelers having the chain repaired. *Lies, lies, lies.* But I didn't want him to know what I had done.

"What for?"

"Coin."

"Why? You're hardly destitute."

"After I saw them all wearing it, it made me feel strange. I didn't want it anymore."

He stepped closer so that no one would overhear. "That was a mistake. Tell me the pawnbroker you sold it to and I'll get it back."

"It wasn't a shop. It was just a... a man I met in passing. I'll tell you where to find him later."

The magic of his disguise faded for a heartbeat and then his eyes were back to grey. "You know how I feel about lies, Cécile. Especially coming from you, and especially when the lives of my people are at stake. You may have lost our only chance for the sake of money to spend on trinkets and toys."

I knew his foul temper was less to do with me and more to do with Lord Aiden's threats, but it didn't feel that way. All I'd wanted was one night where I could feel normal. One night where I could pretend we had a sure future together. It had been a silly desire, but I couldn't help but feel upset at seeing it torn away from me. One night was all I had wanted. Had that been so much to ask?

"I gave it to a stockman in exchange for an ox, and the ax I used to kill it, as part of the spell that broke you free," I said, and not waiting for his reaction, I turned and walked away.

Moving as quickly as I could without attracting undue attention, I left the foyer and made my way backstage to the crew entrance. There was no one outside, so I leaned against the stone of the building, gulping in mouthfuls of cold air. The moon was very nearly full, and I stared up at it, wishing the power I'd used had come from such a pure source.

"It has been a long time, Cécile," a familiar voice said from behind me. I lowered my eyes from the moon, and fear charged through my heart as I came face to face with the pistol leveled between my eyes.

CHAPTER 42
Cécile

I opened my mouth to scream, but only a pathetic whine escaped.

"Be silent. I know the powers you hold."

"Esmeralda?" I choked her name out. "Why are you doing this?"

Her jaw tensed as though she were trying to speak but could not. The pistol wobbled up and down, but steadied when I took a step back. "I'm sorry," she whispered. "But the favor has been called due."

The shot rang loud, tearing apart the stillness of the night. I'd closed my eyes as though not seeing would somehow protect me from the bullet. I held my breath, waiting for the terrible moment when I'd feel hot blood trickling down skin and the pain of metal rending my insides apart. But instead I felt nothing.

Forcing my eyes open, I stared at the flattened bit of metal hanging inches in front of my face, as though it were embedded in an invisible wall. Then beyond it to where Esmeralda lay on her back, the snow splattered with what looked like ink, but what I knew was blood. So very, very much blood.

The bullet dropped from the air to land silently in the snow, and I turned around to see Tristan standing at the crew exit, one arm stretched out in front of him. My gaze went back to Esmeralda, and moving sluggishly, I knelt down next to her, pushed back her hood, and felt for a pulse at her neck. It was a hopeless effort – I could have fit my fist through the hole in her chest.

"Esmeralda." There was no inflection in Tristan's voice, no emotion, but his shock made my own hands shake.

"A troll made her do this." I pulled away my hand, convinced I could feel her skin already beginning to cool beneath my fingertips. "She owned Reagan a favor, and it was called due."

"I didn't mean to..." His voice was choked. "You need to help her."

"She is beyond help," I said. I did not add that what he'd done to her would have been enough to fell any living thing in this world.

"No!" He fell to his knees, heedless of the pool of blood. "Use magic. Heal her. Fix her. You know how."

"Tristan, she's dead."

He shook his head, expressing utter denial of my words. "Help her." Grabbing Esmeralda by the shoulders, he pulled her up off the ground, and I almost gagged at the sight of the gore beneath her. "Help her!"

I didn't know what to do. Someone would have heard the gunshot, and it was only a matter of time before we were discovered. Never mind that we knelt next to a corpse, there would be no explaining the manner in which she died. We had to get away. "Tristan, we need to go."

Standing up, I caught hold of his arm, trying to drag him up. But he was intractable. Moving him against his will would be impossible. "I didn't mean..." he said. "I didn't know it was her."

He kept trying to say that he hadn't meant to kill her, but the lie wouldn't pass his lips.

"Tristan, it was in defense. Whether she wanted to or not, she tried to shoot me." My feet slid in the slurry of blood and snow, but he wouldn't let go of her. He was covered with blood, and in the distance, I could hear the sounds of horses coming this way. "We have to run!

None of what I was saying seemed to register with him. The notion that now would be an opportune time to use his name crossed my mind, but I shoved it aside. Making a fist like Fred had taught me, I pulled my arm back and swung, using the strength of my shoulder. My knuckles collided with his cheek and pain burst through my hand. Tristan jerked away, but more in surprise than in pain.

He stared up at me. "I don't want to leave her like this."

"We have no choice," I said, wishing I didn't need to be so callous. "We need to flee."

We ran through the blizzard and darkness, my skirts pulled up to my knees with one hand and my heeled shoes in the other. My stockings were soaked through in seconds, and not long after the bottoms tore through, exposing the soles of my feet. I was too afraid to feel the discomfort. The city guard would have found Esmeralda by now, and they did not need to be quick-witted to follow tracks in the snow. We needed to get where other people were and then inside so that we could wash away the evidence. Not that it mattered much. Both Aiden and Fred would know who had killed her, and this might well be the opportunity the Regent's son was looking for.

"This way," I hissed, pulling Tristan toward a main boulevard. When we were closer, I slipped my shoes on my numb feet, dropped my skirts, and took his arm. "Smile," I ordered as we stepped out into the traffic of people on the walkways. There I was able to flag down a cab, neither of us saying anything until the horse was trotting in the direction of the hotel.

"I'm sorry I hit you," I said. "But you weren't listening. You were in shock."

He didn't reply. We passed through the bubble of light from a lamp, and I saw the white of his cravat was stained with blood. Fingers numb and shaking, I untied it, shoving the fabric into the pocket of my cloak. He was covered in blood, I was sure, but everything else he was wearing was black, so hopefully no one would notice. I squeezed his hand, the leather soaked and sticky. "Tristan, are you all right?"

His jaw tightened, and he pulled his hand out of my grip. "I should take you home first."

"I'm staying with you," I said. "I don't care what people say."

"Do what you want."

I bit my lip. His words sounded like an attack, and in a way, they were. But not at me. He was attacking himself. His guilt and grief made my heart hurt, and I knew he was pushing me away to punish himself. "Don't do this."

The cab pulled to a stop. "We're here." He didn't wait for the hotel footmen to open the door, instead flinging it open himself and stepping down. I started to follow, but he blocked my way, his gaze fixed on my feet. "You should go home. I'll pay him to take you there."

I lifted my chin. "No."

"Do what you want. You always do anyway," he snapped, turning to pay the driver and leaving a footman to help me out. Without looking at me once, he offered me an arm and escorted me up the steps into the lobby. It was lovely and grand, with crystal chandeliers and lush carpets, massive framed landscapes and seascapes hanging on walls papered in silk. A man played a piano for a handful of onlookers holding drinks, all of them noticing us while pretending not to as we walked toward the staircase. My presence here with him was scandalous in their eyes, but I was far past caring.

Up and up we walked, my feet burning where my shoes rubbed against scrapes and blisters. My skirts were soaked and I was freezing, but I was far more worried for Tristan than I was for me. He'd let guilt over this consume him.

His suite of rooms took up a third of the top floor, and they were warm from the glow of banked fires and lit with lamps of green and gold glass. Pulling my cloak off, I draped it over the back of a chair to dry. Tristan strode across the room, the fire flaring up with magic as he approached. With vicious jerks, he removed the gloves from his hands and threw them into the flames. His coat and shirt followed suit, then he dropped to his knees to watch it burn, the smell of the smoke acrid and horrible.

"How will I tell Élise and Zoé that I killed their aunt? After all the other hurt I've caused them, and now this?"

He was a dark silhouette against the orange glow of the fire. I stayed where I was, afraid to speak and afraid to stay silent. "Tristan, I was there when Esmeralda made her bargain with Reagan. She did it so that she could talk to me." I squeezed my eyes shut, remembering the moment. "She wanted to tell me about the injustices the half-bloods faced because she believed I was in a position to help them. At the time I was too concerned with myself to appreciate the risk she was taking, but I did not fail to notice how much she cared for her nieces. Helping them was what she cared for most – what she'd dedicated her life to. And you gave her a chance to do that."

"She helped me more than I ever helped her," he replied. "And I repaid that debt by killing her."

"You may have struck the blow, but it was our enemies – yours, mine, and hers – who killed her," I said, clenching the damp fabric of my skirt. "Reagan may have held the debt, but we both know she was acting under orders. He could have sent anyone after me – there are men and women aplenty who would kill for the promise of gold. Esmeralda was chosen, forced to do this against her will, because she was our ally. She was sent to kill me because even if she failed, the action would still land a very painful blow."

"My father didn't do this," Tristan said softly. "He wouldn't send someone to kill you."

I peeled the black lace gloves off my hands, letting them fall to the floor. With one finger, I traced the silver marks painted across my fingers. "I know." I swallowed hard. "I will never claim to understand your father or to support his methods, but I know with certainty that he wants you to succeed him. This was Angoulême's doing."

"Yes." There was a faint shake to Tristan's voice. "And that he was willing to make such a bold move makes me very afraid of what is happening in my home."

A home he felt powerless to protect. The weight of his guilt made my shoulders sag – not only for Esmeralda's death, but also for having left his friends, his family, his entire people to fend against the worst. Picking my way around the furniture, I made my way toward him.

"Cécile, there's something I have to tell you." The words came out in a rush and I froze.

"I didn't have to kill her." His voice was ragged. "I could have stopped her just as easily as I stopped that bullet."

The thought had occurred to me, but I refused to make him feel worse by saying so. "You had only seconds to act before she fired her pistol. You were only trying to save my life."

The only sound was the crackle of the fire, his lack of response making my stomach clench as I realized this confession was not over. "Tristan?"

"I had time enough to think." He turned his head, revealing his profile and the motion of his throat as he swallowed. "I had a barrier in place to keep you safe the moment I saw the pistol. But…" The muscles in his shoulders tensed. "I thought it was *her*."

Shock stole all speech from my throat. There was only one *her*.

"I could tell it was a woman," he continued. "I knew what I was doing when I struck. I was trying to kill Anushka."

I felt as though time had stopped and I had stepped away from my body. Like I was watching a girl who was not me listen to words she had not expected to hear. After everything he had said and done to keep from breaking the trolls free, faced with the chance to end it all, he'd taken it. Without hesitation. I did not know what to feel. I felt everything.

"Do you wish you'd let that horse and carriage take you home now?"

The question was much larger than that. He wasn't asking whether I regretted coming up to his room with him tonight, he was asking me if I regretted our relationship. Whether I regretted loving him.

Closing my eyes, I let our time together pan across my

eyes, right from the moment we'd met. Even though I'd been terrified and in pain, I'd thought he was handsome. Except that wasn't even a strong enough word: he was beautiful in a way that was almost painful. Flawless in a way that seemed surreal, like a figment of imagination. So perfect, it was off-putting, because while it was something that could be worshipped, it wasn't something that could be touched or loved. He'd been snide, nasty, and wicked, and I'd loathed him. Except even then I'd sensed something wasn't right, that there was a mismatch between what I was seeing and hearing and what I felt. It was this mismatch that made him captivating, and even as I was grasping for ways to escape, the need to know more about him had lurked in my heart.

That need had only been compounded when we'd been bonded; the veneer of his exterior cracked to reveal a young man so different from the one he pretended to be. A Tristan whom I was uniquely privileged to know. He became a puzzle I needed to solve – the key, I'd thought, to my freedom.

Except solving him hadn't relinquished his hold on me. I remembered the moment in the empty palace stables where the truth had come out, when I'd finally seen the emotions filling my head written across his face, and the veneer had fallen away entirely. It was then I stopped seeing the troll and began to see him. He became my friend, my ally – and the leader of something I could believe in.

I'd admired him, and yes, lusted after him, but then I'd fallen. Fallen for a man who felt too much and took on too much, who believed if only he worked tirelessly and ceaselessly enough, that he could improve the lives of an entire race of people. And I'd had that depth of passion turned on me – seen it in his eyes, felt it in my heart. He loved me, and I loved him. And I'd love him as long as I lived, and if my soul endured, I'd love him for eternity.

"I forgive you," I whispered, closing the distance between us and falling to my knees at his back, and I saw then that the damage on the outside matched that within. I didn't know why seeing it made my heart hurt as badly as it did, because I'd witnessed the torture inflicted upon him. I suppose part of me was so confident in his strength that I'd believed nothing could mark him permanently. How wrong I'd been.

Silver ribbons of scars from the iron-tipped lash snaked across his back from the base of his neck down to the waistband of his trousers. Puncture marks from sets of manacles had left behind coin-sized scars below both shoulders and above both elbows, and his wrists... There was black fabric wrapped around both to hide the skin between cuff and glove, but he was wearing neither. The injuries had healed, but not without leaving their mark, veins still black and skin a dull grey. A permanent reminder that he was not invincible.

With one fingertip, I traced one of the scars on his back, but he cringed away from my touch. "I don't know how you can stand to look at me."

"How could you say that?" I whispered.

"Because I'm not like I was." He drooped forward, hair falling into his eyes. "Not anything you should have to look upon."

"Is that what you think? That scars change the way I feel about you?" I asked, rising to my feet. My fingers trembled as I reached behind my back, unfastening the buttons that reached from below my shoulder blades to my waist. Letting my gown fall to the ground, I kicked it aside. Then, taking a deep breath, I pushed the straps of my shift off my shoulders, the silk sliding down to catch on my hips and leaving me bare to the waist.

The half of me facing the fire burned hot while the other half prickled with goose bumps, and my bravery wavered. He'd never seen me like this before, and my arms trembled, uncertain of whether to hang at my sides or fold across my chest. I stared straight ahead, too nervous to look down and see how he would react. But not seeing didn't stop me from sensing the moment he turned his head, or hearing the soft intake of his breath. Or from feeling...

"You know I didn't mean you."

My chin jerked up and down once. "I know."

"It's different. You're... I'm..." He stumbled over the words as though his ability to use them had abandoned him.

"It's never going to go away," I said, my knees shaking so hard they knocked together as I visualized the livid red scar running down the side of my ribcage. "For the rest of my life, it's going to be there, so if you cannot bear to look at..."

The heat of his lips pressing against the flaw marring my skin turned my thought into a gasp. I swayed on my feet, but his arms wrapped around my hips, holding me steady. "Don't say it." His voice was muffled. "Do not ever even think it."

Letting my fingers tangle in his snow-damp hair, I finally looked down. Tristan sat on his heels at my feet, face pressed against my side, arms gripping me so tightly it almost hurt. He was half-holding me up, and yet I felt as though he were clinging to me like I was a rock in a storm.

"Part of me would erase it, wipe it away if I could," he said. "Because seeing it makes me remember when I thought I was going to lose you. Reminds me of all the hurt that has come to you because of us. Because of me." Letting go with one arm, he traced the scar from top to bottom with one finger, and I shivered, feeling it in places I should not.

He tilted his face up, his eyes no longer dulled to grey by magic and once again the strange silver pools I never ceased to lose myself in. "But part of me is glad that it will always be there for me to see," he continued, "because it is a sign of how much you can endure and survive. And it makes me less afraid."

His hand caught at the silk hanging on my hips, and I waited for him to pull it up. For him to cover up my skin, and for both of us to back away from a moment that we both wanted and yet always retreated away from. Because it was not wise. Because it could cause complications. Because, because, because.

But instead, his hand drifted lower, fingertips scoring a line of fire against my bottom, the back of my thigh, and the curve of my calf. And before I could breathe, the warm silk of my shift pooled around my ankles. He let his hand drop to his side, and

I watched his eyes take me in.

I let my knees buckle, not because they were weak, but because it was what I wanted. Tristan caught me, pulling me against him, and when he kissed me, he tasted like spilled wine and melted snow, and I drank it in like one who has walked desert sands for days. I buried one hand in his hair, kissing him back hard enough that my lips felt bruised while my other hand skimmed the hard muscles of his back, my nails digging into his skin and teeth catching at his bottom lip.

Then my back was against the floor, the plush weave of the rug rough between my shoulder blades and Tristan's breath hot against my throat. He caught my hands in his, our fingers interlocking, and the fabric wrapped around his wrists all that was left between us.

"Cécile." He lifted his head up so that we were eye to eye, his fingers squeezing mine tight.

"Yes?" His voice was serious, and concern made my heart beat a little faster.

He let go of one of my hands and pushed back the tendrils of hair crossing my face. "I know we shouldn't do this," he said, eyes flicking away from mine, then back again. "There are risks and consequences, and logic, reason, and... and good sense say that I should stop now." He bit at his lower lip, and I held my breath. "But I don't want to. We've almost lost each other too many times, and I don't want to regret not giving you everything when I had the chance."

The flames burned high next to us, the heat leaving half of me hot and half of me chill, but all of me was on fire. The choice was mine, and for once, it was easy to make. Wrapping my arms around his neck, I pulled myself up until my lips brushed against his ear. Then I whispered one word.

"Yes."

CHAPTER 43
Cécile

Tristan lay on the sofa with his head on my lap, one leg bent at the knee and the other heel resting on the arm of the sofa – with the disregard of someone who has never had to scrub upholstery in his life. His silver eyes gleamed like coins, distant and unblinking, his mind a twist of dread and frustration as it raced through scenario after scenario. As we waited to see what or who would come.

Both of us were fully clothed, and had been since I'd woken in the dark hours of the night, silken sheets twisted around my legs and my skin cold from Tristan's absence. My eyes had found him standing at the window, one hand pressed against the glass as he gazed out at the night sky. "My father has sent me a letter every night since I left Trollus," he'd said, sensing I was awake.

"What do they say?" My throat parched and voice hoarse. My head throbbed, though I hadn't had nearly enough wine to account for it.

"Nothing. Everything." He dropped his hand from the glass. "They are reminders that he knows all of what I do."

Reminders that he was in control, I thought, wrapping a blanket around my bare shoulders.

"There was no letter tonight."

"Perhaps it is at the front desk and they are waiting until morning to deliver it."

He shook his head. "Chris has already been down to check."

I bit the inside of my cheeks, realizing that while I'd slept he'd come and gone, without my even noticing.

"Something has happened in Trollus," he said, his voice sharp with trepidation. "Angoulême wouldn't have made a move like the one he did tonight if he was not confident that my father could not retaliate."

I hesitated. "Do you think he's dead?" And as I had said the words I'd realized I was afraid he'd say yes. That the troll I'd wished dead more times than I could count was now the lesser evil – the only man who stood between Trollus and the blackness of Angoulême and Roland from within, and the relentless hate of Lord Aiden without.

"You tell me."

I realized I was on my feet and pulling on my dress, though I had no memory of getting out of bed. My skin burned with tension and my head ached with the single-minded purpose of an addict. And I knew what had pulled me from sleep. "He's alive," I whispered, my fingers pausing on my buttons. "But he is very desperate."

"I don't know what to do."

I lifted my head. Tristan had turned from the window to face me, eyes filled with a helplessness I'd never seen before. This young man who was undeniably brilliant. Who'd been raised on plots and strategies and schemes; who'd faced down the most dire of predicaments without faltering, was looking to me for an answer.

I ran my tongue over my lips, but it was very nearly as dry as they were. "That necklace matters to Anushka. We need to get it back."

That had been hours ago. We'd dispatched Chris with a pocketful of gold to track down the stockman and buy back the necklace. We'd tasked Sabine with discovering what she could about the fallout from Esmeralda's death; most importantly, whether Aiden or my brother had pointed a finger at Tristan.

Neither had yet returned, and after discussing every possible contingency, we'd both drifted into our own thoughts.

Tristan sighed and shifted, and I felt his fingers interlock with mine. Glancing down, I saw he'd pressed his face against my stomach, his eyes closed and lashes black against his fair skin. My heart softened, warmth chasing away the tension and ceaseless pressure of the King's compulsion. I smoothed the disarray of his hair and traced a finger along the curve of his ear, my thumb brushing along the line of his cheekbone.

He relaxed, and a smile curved my lips as I thought of this hard-won gift of his trust. That he'd finally stopped trying to hide his fears and weaknesses, and was willingly turning to me for comfort was worth more to me than all the gold in Trollus.

"I love you," I mouthed silently, and his fingers tightened around mine as though he had heard. It made me think of last night. The way it had felt. The intensity of the moment. But then an unwanted thought intruded. "Anushka was Alexis' mistress," I said, half to myself. "Do you know for how long?"

"Two years. Possibly three. It's not something he would have cared to have documented. Nor would his wife."

I frowned. "What was her name?"

"Lamia." Tristan cleared his throat. "Other than my great-grandmother who ruled Trollus for almost forty years, Lamia is said to have been the most powerful queen in our history."

"Did not help her much," I muttered.

He hesitated before answering. "She may not have cared. Their match would have been arranged by the crown for the purpose of breeding power into the line, and she would have been raised to be... pragmatic."

I considered his words, and they sounded hollow. Even if the troll queen had not cared a whit for her husband, she was still bonded to him. Anushka knew how to mute the connection, but it would have required her slipping the other woman a potion every time she was with Alexis. More likely, the Queen had known about the affair and had lived with those feelings in her head over and over again. It would have been maddening.

"Did she survive his murder?"

"Yes. But when it became clear there was no escape from Anushka's curse, she went mad. Her son had to..." He broke off. "He had no choice. Power and madness are a poor mix."

I met his eye, and neither of us needed to say anything to know he referred to his own brother as much as the long-dead queen.

A knock sounded at the door. "It's me," Sabine's muffled voice called through. "Let me in."

Once inside, she pulled back her hood, snow falling to dust the floor. "I swear this is the coldest winter I've ever known," she muttered, pulling off her cloak and draping it over a chair. "Build up the fire, would you?"

The fireplace burst bright with pale troll-fire as Tristan followed Sabine into the sitting room, his expression intent. "Well?"

"There's nothing," she said, sitting on the chair across from me. "No talk of a murder, much less one where the individual died in an ... unusual fashion. Not even a whisper." Pouring a cup of tea from the pot on the table, she took a mouthful and grimaced and held out the cup to Tristan. "It's cold."

He shot her a black look, but a second later, the cup was steaming.

"I went to the opera house to see if by some chance no one had found the body, but it was gone. There was still some blood under the snow, but it looked like someone had put in a bit of effort to make it appear as though nothing had happened, albeit a sloppy one."

Tristan sat down heavily next to me. "Your father's doing?" I asked.

He gave a slow shake of his head. "If it was his doing, it wouldn't have been sloppy."

"Then who?"

"I've no notion."

Sabine leaned back in her chair. "I stopped by your mother's home. She hasn't returned yet, but she sent word that she'll be back in Trianon tomorrow morning. Apparently Julian's gone to join her."

I grimaced. "It makes me nervous having her running around the countryside, given the danger we know she's in."

The door abruptly flung open, and Chris flew in. "I found him!"

"The necklace? Did he have it?" Tristan demanded.

"No, but..."

Tristan swore and stormed over to the window to rest his forehead against the cool glass.

"*But*," Chris continued. "You won't believe who he sold it to. He said a woman came at dawn with a purse full of gold asking about it. Said it was of sentimental value and that the girl who sold it was a fool."

I winced, because that much was true. "Did he recognize her? Did he describe her?"

"He said she was wearing a hood that obscured most of her face."

The temperature of the room burned hot, and Sabine sat up straight in her chair, eying Tristan with unease.

"I should have gone myself," he growled at the window. "I might have caught her and all this would be done."

"Tristan, I missed her by a good hour," Chris said. "It would have made no difference if you'd gone. But listen to this: the stockman said she arrived and left in a carriage marked in the Regent's colors."

I sat up straight and Tristan swung around to face us.

"There's more," Chris said. "The man at the front desk gave me this when I came back in." Walking swiftly around the chairs, he went to Tristan and handed him an envelope. "It can't be a coincidence."

Tristan broke the seal, his eyes scanning the card. "It's an invitation to Lady Marie du Chastelier's Longest Night ball."

I blinked. "That's where my masque is to be performed. It's the most exclusive event of the year," I added, getting to my feet. "The invitations to this went out weeks ago, and only the upper crust of Trianon nobility will be there. Not bourgeoisie boys riding high on their fathers' wealth."

"It's not addressed to a bourgeoisie boy riding high on his father's wealth," Tristan said quietly, handing me the invitation.

My heart accelerated as I took in the words, *His Royal Highness, Prince Tristan de Montigny is cordially invited to...* "It's a trap."

"Undoubtedly," Tristan replied. "And she's confident enough that she's not even trying to hide it."

"Why take so much risk?" Sabine asked. "There will be countless people there to witness what she does. People who will remember her face and who she was. There are better places to kill you."

"Agreed," Tristan said. "But both Cécile and Genevieve will be there, and I cannot help but think that means something."

Longest Night... I exhaled a ragged breath. "It's the solstice."

Chris, who had learned more about magic in the previous months than he probably ever wanted, nodded. "Witches can draw on more power during moments of transitions like the solstices and..." He broke off, turning toward the window and then back to me. "The full moon. Cécile, tomorrow night is a full moon."

"How often do they occur together?" Sabine asked.

"I don't know." I glanced at Tristan, but he shook his head. "I never spent much time studying astronomy – there wasn't much point. Pierre would without a doubt know, but asking him is obviously out of the question. But what difference does it make? Her magic won't work against me."

An idea began to tickle my mind and with it came fear. "Do you have my map? The list of dead women that was tucked into Catherine's grimoire?"

He silently retrieved the paper from a locked chest and handed it to me. My eyes roved over the names, and the years that they had died. Nearly always nineteen or thirty-eight years apart, with a few exceptions. A weak and baseless pattern. Unless it wasn't. I set the paper on the table and pressed a hand to my mouth. I'd left my mother alone, thinking that we had years before she was in any danger. But what if we'd been wrong?

I dropped my hand to my lap. "We need to know when the last time the full moon and winter solstice were in conjunction. We need to know all the times it has been. And we need a reliable source."

"I know what you're suggesting," Tristan said flatly, "and the answer is no."

"We need to find out if there is a pattern," I said. "This might be the only way we can predict her actions. And frankly, we need to know what is really happening in Trollus."

"How?" He grimaced. "It isn't as if we can waltz into the city and ask. My father's control over Trollus is uncertain, and we can be sure that Angoulême will do everything in his power to thwart us."

"We wouldn't waltz in," I said. "We'd sneak."

Tristan shook his head. "Even if we managed to get into the city, there isn't a chance of me making it all the way to Pierre unnoticed. My magic is too strong – they'll know it's me."

"Which is why I'll go alone."

He leveled me with a chilling glare. "Even if it were worth the risk, it would be impossible. There are two ways into the city, and both are gated and guarded."

"That's not entirely true," Chris said, then winced as Tristan redirected his glare.

I stood up and leaned forward until my face blocked their line of sight. "What are you talking about?"

Chris mumbled something shockingly foul to do with goats and then sighed. "Well, they do have a hole in their roof."

CHAPTER 44
Cécile

We left the horses tied up, in the trees, and started toward the sea of rock concealing Trollus from the rest of the world. I was wearing a grey dress and hooded cloak, my hair expertly tucked under a black wig that Sabine had retrieved from the opera house's collection of costumes. It wasn't a perfect disguise, but I was banking on no one taking much notice of a half-blood girl running an errand for her owner.

Tristan had said little since we'd left Trianon, his attention seemingly focused on guiding his black gelding on the road slick with ice and mud, but I knew better. As much as he disliked the risk we were taking to get this information, he wanted, no, needed to know what was happening in Trollus, and that made him much more reckless than he normally was. I wasn't sure if that was a good or bad thing.

"I thought it would be easier to see," I muttered once we had clambered up. "Do you know which way? It's going to take us hours to climb to the middle." Holding my skirts with one hand, I leapt over onto the next rock, then turned back to Tristan. "It's all right to walk out here, isn't it? It won't, you know…" I moved in an exaggerated wobble from side to side.

"You're standing on a great deal of rock, love," Tristan said, the first bit of humor I'd seen in hours rising onto his face. "You're going to need to eat more chocolate truffles if you intend to finish the mountain's work."

A faintly shimmering platform of magic bridged the gap between the two boulders, and he strolled across, then offered me his arm. "Do you remember the last time we disguised you as a troll?"

"How could I forget," I said, holding tight to his arm and trying not to think about all the rock crashing out from underneath us and how far we'd fall if it did. "Only that time you were trying to sneak me out, not in." My eyes drifted over the grey stones as I remembered when I'd decided to stay in Trollus, the way he'd kissed me, and the feeling that I finally had nearly everything I wanted. How long had it lasted? Five minutes before everything had quite literally crashed down around us.

"Your choosing to stay was the most purely happy moment of my life."

I rested my head against his shoulder. "I've never once regretted that choice." But we both knew what was unsaid – that our moments of happiness were so few and far between, hemmed in on all sides by disaster and tragedy. Then and now. Trying to live and love while the blood of a friend and comrade was on our hands and knowing that worse was yet to come. Did that make us appreciate those precious moments more, or did it tarnish them? I didn't know.

"Here it is."

The moon hole was much larger than I'd thought – perhaps ten feet across, and while from the streets of Trollus it had appeared to me as hope and freedom, from this perspective it seemed like the gate to hell itself. Black, menacing, and deadly. A wave of vertigo hit me, and I swayed unsteadily on my feet.

"How high up did you say we were?"

"I didn't." He pulled me tight against his chest, and I inhaled the clean smell of his linen shirt as I tried to find my balance. "I'm not worried about dropping you; it's what happens when I put you down in the middle of a city full of disgruntled trolls that concerns me."

My plan seemed like a worse and worse idea with each passing moment, and I knew if I delayed any longer that I'd lose my nerve entirely. Standing on my tiptoes, I kissed him hard. "For good luck."

He rested his forehead against mine. "Luck is what poor planners rely upon. As long as you stick to what we agreed, you should be fine. Go straight to Pierre, find out what we need to know, and then go back to the place where I set you down. Don't go looking for Marc or the twins or trouble, or any of the usual sorts of disasters you always seem to find."

I nodded, my heart beating so hard and fast I was sure he could hear it. "Right. In and out."

"The riskiest moment will be when you first go in and your shadow will be visible, so I'm going to move you very quickly. Don't make a sound – I know for a fact that your voice carries well in this cursed place."

"Not a peep." I was shaking, and it had nothing to do with the winter air. Removing my riding gloves, I shoved them into my pocket and wiped my sweating palms on my skirts. Before I could even think to back down, magic wrapped around my waist and hips and I lifted up into the air. I scrunched myself up into a ball, resting my cheek against my knees and gripping my ankles with one arm. With my free hand, I clutched Tristan's magic like it was a rope.

"You really don't need to do that."

"Makes me feel better." My voice sounded high-pitched and strange.

"Ready?"

I wasn't. I really wasn't. But I nodded anyway.

He needn't have worried about me making a sound. The force of being snapped backwards and down stole my breath, and before I could think, much less squeak, I was hanging suspended beneath the rocks, all of Trollus laid out below me. Letting go of my ankles, I clung with both hands to the rope of magic, trying to get my breathing under control.

Although Tristan had assured me that it would be all but

impossible for anyone to see me in the darkness, I still felt utterly exposed, and panic began to erode my self-control. There was no surviving a fall from this height. I'd be nothing more than a splatter of gore against the paving stones, my screams echoing long after my life winked out. A whimper of noise forced its way from my lips.

Sensing I was close to cracking, Tristan began to slowly move me along the ceiling of the cavern. It wasn't simply a matter of setting me down in the middle of the city – he needed to keep me hidden in the shadows, dropping me down where the rock rested against the highest reaches of the valley. But he was working blind, entirely dependent on memory to navigate me not only to my destination, but around the magic columns and arcs and canopies that held the rock off the city. His concentration on the task steadied my nerves, and my mind refocused on what was below me.

Trollus was beautiful. It had always felt like a dream to me, so otherworldly that it seemed impossible that it existed in the same reality as my farm, the Hollow, and even Trianon. Seeing it like this transported me back, made me feel as though I'd never left. The familiar roar of the falls, the water sparkling as it fell from the heights at the far end of the city to explode into spray and foam in the river that drove straight and true toward the mouth of the river road.

The terraced streets rising like steps for a giant's feet up the sides of the valley and bisected by staircases that swept and curved around the pale stone buildings. The palace was massive, white and gold and stately where it sat overlooking the river, the glass gardens lying behind it, black but for the troll-lights that lined the meandering pathways. I wondered if anyone walked those paths now that I was gone, or if the flowers, bushes, and trees had languished in darkness.

But not everything was the same.

Dozens of massive stone columns rose up from the city streets, some grown so high that they seemed almost within reach if I stretched my fingers out. But no one was working on them now, and as I twisted around to see back toward the base of the valley, I could see why. The Dregs, which butted up against the wall of rock, was entirely barricaded in with collapsed buildings and piled debris, and behind those hastily constructed walls, there was a flurry of activity marked by tiny bobbing troll-lights. For there to be that many half-bloods in the streets meant they weren't in the mines, and my heart sped as I considered the implications of what that meant.

Not that I had much time to think about it. I was over the Elysium quarter now, the massive manors of the troll aristocracy gleaming with silvery troll-light as they passed beneath me. After the highest row of homes was a strip of empty space between the walls at the rear of the properties and where rockslide rested against the lip of the valley. It was patrolled once daily for any signs of sluag intrusion, but otherwise it was dark, empty, and the safest place to set me down. I stumbled a bit as my feet hit the ground, my legs feeling like pudding, and I held onto the magic until I had my balance. As soon as I let go, it unraveled from around my waist.

I knew Tristan could feel things through his magic in some fashion, but the effect was still eerily strange, like some great sentient serpent stretched between us. Shivering, I stepped away from where it waited and retrieved the more familiar bit of power that I'd tucked into my pocket.

After a bit of whispered coaxing, my little orb began to gleam softly, and my disguise was complete. I hurried toward one of the narrow lanes between two properties; then, looking both ways to make sure no one was coming, I stepped out onto the street.

Keeping my head low and hidden in the hood of my cloak, I chose a brisk pace fitting a servant on an errand for her mistress and prayed no one would pay me any mind. I hardly needed to worry – the streets of this area of Trollus were quieter than the rest of the city, but never had I seen them so empty. It made me uneasy, and I almost breathed a sigh of relief when I finally passed two half-bloods on a set of stairs. It was short-lived though – they gave me a wide berth, and as much as it reduced my risk of discovery, I knew it wasn't normal.

The tension grew palpable as I descended toward the valley floor, magic thick and hot in the air, full and half-bloods alike all looking as though they expected to be attacked at any moment. No one spoke unless they traveled together and many of them wore bands of colored fabric around their arms. I needed no explanation to know the city was divided.

When I finally caught sight of Pierre's home, it was all I could do not to run toward it. Trotting up the front steps, I knocked once and then went inside.

"Get out!" Pierre's shrill voice made me flinch. "You never take my advice anyway!"

He sat on his little wheeled stool at one of his desks, pen in hand and back to me.

"Pierre?"

The tiny troll froze, then very slowly, he looked over his shoulder. "You hide your face," he said. "But your voice is that of the dearest girl I've ever known."

I flung myself at him, wrapping my arms around his narrow shoulders and squeezing them tight. "It's me, Pierre. It's Cécile. Oh, it is so good to see you are well."

Gripping my shoulders, he pushed me back. "What are you doing here? Is Tristan with you? Is he well?"

"He's well," I said, and Pierre's shoulders sagged with visible relief. "He's up on top of the rock fall waiting to lift me out when I'm ready. He lowered me through the moon hole, and Pierre, I was so terrified that Trollus almost got the first rainstorm it's had in five hundred years."

He laughed. "If I had any doubts that you're really Cécile, they are chased away now." His smile didn't last. "Be a dear and bolt the door; the Builder's Guild has little enough time for me, but we dare not risk one of them arriving unannounced and discovering you here."

I did as he asked, making certain the curtains covered the front windows. "What is happening in Trollus? It feels as though fighting will break out at any minute."

"It already has." He passed a weary hand over his face. "The city is quite divided. After Tristan left Trollus, the half-bloods went to the King to demand their autonomy and for him to reinstate Tristan as his heir, but he refused to receive them. So they revolted and are now refusing to work until their demands are met. They've barricaded themselves in the Dregs, but they can't last forever. Even if they could adequately supply themselves, Angoulême will see them put down. Already there are dead in the streets each morning, and all have been identified as those who support the half-bloods' cause. Consorting with half-bloods not your property has become a dangerous business."

I clutched the fabric of my cloak against the chill drifting across my skin. "Hasn't the King done anything to stop this?"

Pierre shook his head. "He does nothing. He has played the two sides against each other too hard for too long, and now all have turned against him. He has made himself vulnerable by giving up control of the tree, and I think it only a matter of time until his life is forfeit. And with Tristan absent, there is no one capable of contesting Roland's rise to the throne."

"The people want him to come back?" Did he want to come back?

"They are afraid, Cécile. Tristan is their only hope."

I forced my head to nod up and down. "I'll tell him."

Neither of us spoke for a moment, then Pierre broke the silence. "You took a great risk in coming here, Princess, and I think you sought me out in particular for a reason."

"I did. We need your help." Extracting the list of names and dates from my pocket, I handed it to him. Then I explained my suspicion about Anushka's immortality. "I need to know if there's a pattern."

"Alignment of the winter solstice and the full moon," Pierre muttered. Books floated off shelves and charts unrolled to hang in the air. I watched in silence as he flipped swiftly through the pages, eyes flicking periodically to the carefully inked charts, one hand holding a pen, which he occasionally used to jot down a date.

Though I was desperate to know if my theory was correct, I stayed silent and out of the way until he set his pen down. "Well?"

He handed me back my list, along with the page with the dates he'd written down. "Your thesis appears to be correct. Although you are missing one – the most recent."

Knowing there was a chance the unmarked grave in the woods belonged to my maternal grandmother in no way prepared me for seeing it all but confirmed in a single, scrawled date. Now I was certain Anushka was using the lives of her female descendants to make herself immortal, and dread seeped through my veins with the knowledge that tomorrow night would be my mother's last if I didn't stop Anushka.

"Tomorrow night is the solstice," Pierre said. "It is also a full moon."

Before I could say anything, someone pounded at the door. "Pierre! Open up or I'll break it down. We saw the half-blood come inside."

Half-blood? It took a heartbeat for me to realize whoever was outside was referring to me. Whether they'd been watching the house or noticing me had been a coincidence didn't really matter: Pierre didn't own any servants. He didn't have a legitimate reason for talking to a half-blood girl. And he especially didn't have a legitimate reason to be talking to *me*.

The little troll hissed a breath out between his teeth, eyes flashing bright with anger. The room grew warm with magic, and for the first time, it occurred to me that my friend was a far more formidable force than he appeared. "Go upstairs and out the window onto the roof," he said. "It's one of the Duke's men."

"This is my fault," I whispered. "They're here because of me."

He shook his head. "This has been a long time in coming, I fear," he replied, taking my hand and squeezing it with his. "My allegiances are well known."

They were going to kill him. "I'm not leaving you to die," I said, racking my brain for a solution. A blow struck the door and the entire house shook.

"You have no choice. If they catch you, they'll kill you in an instant. Trollus can afford to lose me, but losing you is quite another matter."

"I'll take you with me," I babbled, unwilling to concede. "I can carry you. I'll take you somewhere safe."

Another blow smashed against the door with an echoing thud, and I knew it wasn't stone that was keeping them out. It was magic against magic.

"There is nowhere in Trollus that is safe. You must get away now while there is still time."

He was right, and I hated it. But staying wouldn't just be risking my life – it would be risking Tristan's, and in doing so, I'd be putting the fates of countless other trolls in jeopardy. Flinging my arms around his shoulders, I squeezed hard. "I'm sorry. I am so sorry."

He patted me on the shoulder. "Take care of that boy for me, my sweet girl. He needs you."

"I will," I said, but my voice was drowned out by the thunder of magic.

"Run!"

I sprinted to the stairs, taking them two at a time. There were stacks of books and papers littered everywhere on the second level, and I leapt over them, staggering as the whole house swayed. Ahead was a window looking out over the neighboring home, and I flung it open. There was a gap between the two structures. I was going to have to jump. Climbing onto the ledge, I clung to the frame and slowly straightened. Stone fell and smashed against the street as the front of the house collapsed. Sucking in a breath, I bent my knees and leapt forward.

I landed on my feet, but momentum made me stumble into a fall, ripping my dress and scraping my knees. Ignoring the pain, I clambered up and ran to the far side of the roof. Below was a wall. Falling to my hands and knees, I slid over the edge and dropped onto the narrow edge of stone, but before I could go any further, an explosion shook the air.

Debris and dust sailed through the streets, and if I'd still been on the roof, it would surely have killed me. Screams cut the air, and everyone was running. Slipping off the wall, I joined the ranks of fleeing trolls, running as hard and fast as I could. And I didn't look back. I couldn't. Couldn't bear to see the ruin of Pierre's home and know that he was dead. That I hadn't been able to help him.

My breath tore in my chest as I sprinted up a flight of stairs, and then another, working my way back to where Tristan's magic waited to pull me away from danger. I'd been living soft for too long, and even fear wasn't enough to compensate for the exhaustion numbing my legs. My ribs ached where they'd been broken, and rounding a corner, I ground to a halt and bent nearly double, resting my hands on my knees.

Pierre was dead, and it was my fault. I'd brought them down upon him. Dead for no reason other than that he had not hidden his support for Tristan. Slaughtered for believing the half-bloods deserved a better lot in life. Dead, because I'd been powerless to help him, and because a stupid prophesy had deemed my life worth more than his. I breathed in and out, trying to stay calm, trying to keep my wits about me.

A smell brushed at my nose, and if I'd been a dog, my hackles would have risen. If I'd been standing in Trianon, where upper and lower class alike tossed night-soil into the streets, such a smell would have caused as much notice as salt from the sea. But if nothing else, Trollus was always clean. My eyes fixed on the pale stone cobbles in front of me, I watched as a crimson rivulet of blood ran by the toe of my boot. And then another. And another. My heart in my throat, I lifted my face.

The street was painted with so much blood it seemed impossible that it could have come from only one body. I stared, trying to fit the pieces back together into something – someone – recognizable, but my mind couldn't manage it. Not with Roland kneeling in the middle of the mess, tapping the tip of a knife thoughtfully against one tooth, bright eyes fixed on me.

He doesn't know it's you! But did that matter? It hadn't for the half-blood who was now only the sum of his pieces. Tristan's name rippled through my head as I considered whether to call him down. Except I knew that if I did, it would be no less than a battle to the death. I needed to try to find another way out of this.

"Your Highness." I curtseyed low, holding the position until my knees ached. Even without magic, I had no hope of outrunning him – he was many times faster than me, even at my best. "Is there some way I might assist you?"

He huffed out an annoyed breath. "I'd hoped you might run. The rudeness would have been enough excuse."

Excuse for what?

"I'm afraid I don't understand, Your Highness." My knees were starting to shake.

"No one understands." His voice sounded almost sad.

"Roland!"

Never in my life would I have dreamed I'd be so happy to see the Duke

d'Angoulême. He stalked past me toward the murderous prince, four tense-looking guards on his heels. "Stones and sky, boy! What could possibly have provoked you to do this?"

"He tripped and dropped the new Guerre set Lady Anaïs had made for me. I went all the way to the Artisan's Row to collect it from Reagan, and now it is ruined."

"Why do I suspect his tripping was no accident?" The Duke's voice was acidic, and I could not help but notice he kept a wary eye on Roland.

The Prince climbed to his feet. "He walked behind, so I did not see it happen." The knife he'd had in his hand was gone, and I wondered where he had hidden it. Not that he needed it.

"As though that makes all the difference." Angoulême waved a hand at his guardsmen. "Clean this mess up. And you–" He turned around and pointed a finger at me.

I froze. "Yes, Your Grace?"

"Pick that up and bring it."

My eyes flicked to the box lying in the middle of all that gore.

The last thing I wanted to do was pick it up and carry it into the heart of the lion's den.

"Do it!" Angoulême was visibly upset, and I did not care to think what would happen if I disobeyed. Running forward, I picked my way through the mess of flesh and bone and reached for the box. As I was bending down, I saw Roland's knife hidden in a fold of fabric, and before I could even think about what I was doing, I hid it in my skirts. Taking hold of the box, I heaved it up, afraid for a moment that I wouldn't be able to lift it and would give myself away. But I managed to get it up, my fingers slick with troll blood and worse. Heart in my throat, I followed the two toward the Duke's home, which I knew lay not far up the street.

The walls surrounding the house were higher than was typical in Trollus – as high as those around the palace, and just as well guarded. Armed full-blooded troll men and women watched the street, their expressions those who expect an attack at any minute. Two of them opened the gates for us, but none paid any attention to me.

"Where would you have me put this, Your Grace?" I altered my voice to keep it low, but I could not keep the shake from it.

"In here." Angoulême flung open the doors to a large room, and ignoring my aching arms, I carried the box over to a table. "Open it, and let us see if the damage warranted such behavior."

I did as he asked, flinching when he reached over my shoulder to pluck up one of the little figurines.

"It's gold!" He turned and threw the glittering figure at the wall with such force that it smashed through the plaster. Something crashed in the neighboring room, and I heard an exclamation of disgust. Seconds later, the Dowager Duchesse entered, and my heart sank.

Angoulême rounded on Roland. "Do you have any idea how much that half-blood was worth?"

Shoving me out of the way, Roland went to the box and began pulling out the little figures. "Oh, they are gold!"

"Roland."

My hands and feet felt like ice, but sweat dribbled down my back. I would rather have lain naked in a pit of vipers than spend another second in this room. But I could not leave without being dismissed, and none of the three were paying me any mind.

The boy shrugged. "Well, given the fight he put up, I suppose he must have been expensive." What they were having for dinner probably would have interested him more than the man he'd just murdered in cold blood.

"How many times do I have to explain to you..." Angoulême broke off, his eyes flicking to me. "You are dismissed."

I dropped into curtsies for all three of them, then backed out of the room, keeping my face low. Closing the door behind me, I started toward the front entrance, but then I stopped. If they were about to have a row, wasn't it better that I listen in on it? They had unwittingly invited their enemy into their midst, and wouldn't I be a fool not to take advantage of that?

You'd be a fool to stay, I all but heard Tristan whisper in my ear, but I ignored him. Spying a doorway to an antechamber, I quietly went inside. Pressing my ear to the wall, I listened.

"I enjoy doing it. There is no other reason," Roland snapped, and I could imagine his arms crossed, lovely blood-smeared face petulant.

"You cannot keep killing out of hand, Your Highness. Your father might still reinstate Tristan as heir, and you would not care for that to happen, would you?"

The house trembled. "He will not! I will be king!"

"No one wants that more than I, Your Highness." Angoulême's voice was soothing. "But well you know that we must play this tedious game of politics if we are to succeed. Your brother is a sly creature, and he has turned the people's minds against us."

"You were supposed to have him killed."

"And I will." Glass clinked against glass, and I envisioned the Duke pouring himself a drink to calm his irritation. "As much as I despise your brother, he is a Montigny. Felling him is no easy thing, and his human seems to have nine lives' worth of luck."

"I want him to come back."

"That is the last thing you should want, Highness."

"I want him to be as he was before *her*."

I was fairly certain *her* was me, and if Roland blamed me for his brother's changed behavior, that would explain the intensity of his dislike.

"You know he was only pretending to be that way before," Angoulême said. "He deceived everyone."

Roland did not reply, and I wished desperately that I could see his face. There was something about his tone of voice when he spoke about wanting Tristan's return, something that made me think he actually cared for him in some fashion. It made me realize that I knew very little about the relationship, such as it was, between the two brothers. It made me wonder if there was something worth salvaging in that monster of a boy after all.

"Anaïs is upstairs," Angoulême finally said. "Why don't you bring the game to her? I'm sure it would please her greatly to play with you."

"It would be the kind thing to do?" Roland asked, as though he really was not certain what was kindness and what was not.

"Yes, Your Highness. Most kind indeed."

No one said anything, but moments later a door opened and closed, and I heard the patter of small feet running up a flight of stairs.

"You said you had him under control," the Dowager Duchesse snapped. "Blasted creature is a menace to all!"

"I do have him under control." Glass clinked again. "It isn't as though I can go ordering him about by name in the middle of the street."

"What choice do you have?" Her voice was bitter. "Roland is as mad as any I've encountered – a Montigny mind and power utterly corrupted by iron. If he were anyone other than who he is, Thibault would have had him put down years ago. He feels nothing – cares nothing for anything but his own black pleasures, and while he may not be so clever as his brother, he's wily enough to find ways around your weak controls."

"We need him for there to be any chance of taking the throne."

Both were silent for a long time, making me believe that Damia was in agreement. But then she spoke.

"He has outplayed you, my son." Her voice dripped with mockery, and I felt a moment's pity for him having her as a mother. "Thibault has been playing a longer game than anyone believed, I think. And if Tristan succeeds in breaking the curse, the Montignys will rule in a way that has not been seen since the time of the great kings and queens of old."

"What is it you would have me do?"

"Send Roland to kill his father now. With the boy on the throne, we control Trollus and its gold. With that, it is only a matter of sending every greedy cutthroat at our disposal after Cécile. She is their weakness in every possible way, and she will die for it. And once they are dead, we will play our long-held trump card and the world will bend its knee to us."

I'd heard enough. Rising to my feet, I started to turn when the sensation of power froze me in my tracks.

"And they say there are no rats in Trollus," said a young woman's voice from behind me. "It would appear they're wrong. Hello, Cécile."

CHAPTER 45
Cécile

Anaïs stood behind me, arms crossed and expression much like a cat who has cornered a mouse. Only it wasn't the girl I'd known, but an impostor. It was Lessa.

"Does my brother know you're here?" she asked. "Seems a bit reckless for him."

"He's here," I whispered, stepping back and colliding with the wall. "Closer than you think."

Lessa chuckled. "Not close enough."

Her hand shot out and caught me by the throat. I tried to scream, but I could hardly breathe. She lifted me off the ground in front of her, smiling as I kicked and struggled. Panic flooded through me, and I clawed at her arms, but the scratches disappeared in an instant. She was going to kill me.

Then I remembered Roland's knife hidden in my pocket. Catching hold of the small handle, I jerked it out and sliced it across her forearm.

Lessa hissed in pain and dropped me, but I only had a second to suck in a breath before she lunged at me again. Digging deep for the magic I needed, I choked out the words, "Bind the light."

She stopped in her tracks, false face full of astonishment. But it wouldn't last – she knew what I'd done. And when she dove at me, I held the knife out, my arms shuddering with the impact as it slid between her ribs. She screamed, curling around herself and clutching at the knife. But I knew I hadn't killed her – I needed to run.

The door to the antechamber flung open, the Duke appearing with his mother just behind him.

"Prince Roland attacked Lady Anaïs," I screamed, then shoved between them as though in a fit of terror. Which was not far from the truth. I had seconds. Sprinting to the entrance, I flung it open and dashed toward the gates. "Prince Roland is on a rampage!" I screamed. "He stabbed Lady Anaïs, and now he's gone after the Duke!"

I saw the fear rise in their eyes, but to their credit, every one of them ran toward the house, giving me the few precious seconds I needed to escape. My throat burned where Lessa's fingers had dug in, but I did not dare stop. There were no gaps between properties for me to hide in, no alleyways or passages to turn down. I had to make it to the staircase leading up to the last row of houses before the perimeter or I was a dead woman.

Shouts echoed in the streets behind me, and I heard my name on the air. They knew it was me. They were coming.

Magic wrapped around my waist, lifting me off my feet and dropping me on the other side of a wall before I could speak.

"Be silent." Élise shoved me back against the wall, her hand against my mouth.

Half a dozen sets of feet ran by us, and both of us held our breath until they passed. Then I flung my arms around her neck. When the sound of the waterfall disappeared and I knew our voices were shielded, I whispered. "Thank you. How did you know I was here?"

"I saw you go into Pierre's," she said. "Your eye and skin color was altered, but I'd recognize the faces you make anywhere." She squeezed my shoulders. "Is Tristan here?"

With one shaking hand, I pointed up at the moon hole. "He's waiting to lift me out – I need to reach the perimeter, but I don't know how I'm going to get by everyone who's looking for me."

Élise looked up at the roof, her face filled with a mix of

emotion too complex to pick apart. "I'll distract them. Give me your cloak."

"You can't! If they think you're me, they'll kill you."

She shook her head. "The Duke will want to catch you first – and once they realize it's me, they'll let me go. I belong to the Queen and the Duchesse – no one will dare harm me."

I didn't want her to do it. I'd already lost Pierre today, and the thought of risking another friend's life made me grit my teeth. But her logic was sound, and there was no other choice.

"We need to get you out of here alive," she whispered. "Your husband owes me a favor, and I can't collect on it if he's dead."

Reluctantly, I slid off my cloak and handed it to her. "Please be careful."

"You too." There were questions in her eyes – things I knew she wanted to ask. But we had no time. Pulling the hood up so that it obscured her face, she hugged me hard. "Go through this property – there is a gate at the rear."

Then she was gone.

I stood frozen, part of me unwilling to leave her to our enemies. But that part of me was a fool, because Élise had given me the only chance I had. So I began to pick my way through the dark garden, moving as silently as I could to avoid detection from whatever trolls lived within. The gate in the wall was barely visible in the ambient light of the house and street lamps, and I was closing my fingers on the latch when I heard screams tear through the air. "Élise!" Her name forced its way through my lips, but I didn't turn back.

Flinging open the gate, I ran. Ahead was the narrow pathway leading up to the perimeter, and I sprinted toward it, my boots slapping hard against the stones of the street. They were coming. I could hear them coming. The pathway seemed endless, the rocks marking the boundary of Trollus impossibly far away.

Then I was there. Skidding on the tiny fallen pebbles, I ran next to the stacked boulders of rock, my eyes fixed on the faint glow of the ropes of magic waiting for me.

"There she is!"

Risking a glance over my shoulder, I saw two of the Duke's guards come out of the pathway. It would take them a bit of time to cover the distance on foot, but I knew their magic would span the distance in seconds. Flinging myself forward, I closed my hand around the glowing ropes. *Tristanthysium, get me out!*

Magic closed around me like a cage, lifting me up off the ground and into the sky. Blows slammed against the shield protecting me, silver light exploding all around in sparks. Gone was slowness and stealth, and my stomach lurched as I was jerked across the cavern, the force holding me against the floor of my invisible bubble so that I couldn't move. I was helpless and in full view of countless trolls who wanted to see me dead.

Then sunlight was burning in my eyes.

"Cécile!"

Tristan caught me against him, stumbling back. "You're covered in blood. Are you hurt?"

I knew logically his face was inches from mine, but he seemed far away, his voice distant. Like I was watching him search another girl for injuries, for the source of all the blood. My hands were sticky with it. Soaked in it.

"Anushka's going to kill my mother tomorrow night." I heard the words, but I couldn't feel my lips forming them. "Roland's going to kill your father. Angoulême has Élise. And Pierre..." I fell back into myself, shock receding and leaving a world of hurt in its wake. "Pierre is dead."

Wrapping my arms around his neck, I buried my face in Tristan's chest.

And I wept.

CHAPTER 46
Tristan

I watched Cécile ride somewhat ahead of me, her shoulders slumped beneath the bulk of my coat. What she'd told me seconds after I'd pulled her out had put my head in a spin, but she'd dissolved into hysterics seconds later, so I'd had to wait until I'd carried her off the rocks and calmed her down enough to extract more details. After she'd told me everything, she'd gone quiet. Numb.

And that made me wish for the tears to come back, because at least those were normal for her. I could wipe them away and know she'd be herself soon enough. But seeing her like this, her dull and empty eyes a reflection of what I felt in my head, made me afraid that she'd finally been pushed too far.

That fear had made me want to take her somewhere safe, and before I'd known what I was saying, I'd asked her which way to take to get to her family's farm. Now we were on the road to Goshawk's Hollow, and despite there being countless reasons we needed to be back in Trianon, I knew it was the correct decision. She needed time to recover.

And so did I.

Despite my best efforts, I couldn't shove the pain of Pierre's death from the forefront of my thoughts. I'd known him all my life, and while I'd never burdened him as a confidant, he'd been my friend. My mentor in matters that had nothing to do with politics. I remembered the first time I'd met him. My father had led me by the hand through the city, stopping in front of Pierre's door and kneeling down to speak with me.

"Tristan, Pierre is the most intelligent and learned troll I know. I want you to listen to the things he says and to learn from him, do you understand?"

I blinked away the vision of my father's face and shivered against the cold wind cutting through the thin cloth of my shirt. The Dowager Duchesse's words troubled me deeply. *Trump card*. Trump card. The word repeated in my head, and I knew it could refer to only one thing: Anushka's identity. Angoulême knew who she was, and once my father and I were dead, he intended to use the information to secure his power.

Grinding my teeth, I heeled my horse up alongside Cécile's. She held her reins with one hand, the other curled loosely against her thigh. I took hold of her fingers, and they were cold even through the leather of my gloves. "You're freezing." Pulling my glove off with my teeth, I enclosed her hand in mine, trying to chase away the chill.

"Cécile, are you all right?"

It was a stupid question. I knew she wasn't, but I needed her to say something. Anything.

She turned her head to look up at me. "Will they hurt her?"

Élise. It took a lot of effort not to look away. A year ago, I would've answered without hesitation that Angoulême wouldn't dare cross my family by hurting one of ours. But so much had changed since then, and I strongly suspected that Élise had not escaped unscathed.

"My aunt will do what she can for Élise."

Cécile pulled her hand out of my grip. "That isn't an answer."

"Élise knew the risk she was taking," I said. "You didn't force her to do anything."

"Didn't I?" She shoved her hand into the pocket of my coat. "It was my idea to go to Trollus. My decision to linger in the Duke's home to eavesdrop when I could have walked away without trouble. If I had only left, she wouldn't have needed to put herself in danger." Her face tightened. "I should have listened to you when you told me it was too dangerous. If anything happens to her, it's my fault."

"That doesn't mean it was a mistake. You gained valuable insight that we never would have known if you hadn't made those choices." I said the words knowing they sounded callous. Anaïs would have argued that the reward was well worth the risk. Marc would have said that the choices had been made and that we'd need to live with the consequences. My father would say that hard choices were part and parcel of being king.

But what did I think?

"I know that the last thing you ever want is for someone to be hurt," I said. "I know that given the choice, you'd forfeit your life to save that of a friend. But you know what would have happened if you had interfered when they came for Pierre. If you hadn't let Élise help you escape. If you'd sacrificed yourself for them, what of everyone else? You don't have a thousand lives to live or give; and as much as you might hate to think it, fate and fortune and whatever other powers are at work have made it so that your life *is* more important."

Catching hold of her reins, I pulled both horses to a halt. "A good leader, a good ruler, is willing to lay down her life to save one of her people, but is wise and strong enough to know that she cannot."

Cécile met my gaze, blue eyes bright with anger. "You're the leader. You're the ruler. Not me."

I let go of her reins. "Are you certain about that?"

The only answer I got was her digging her heels into her horse's sides and taking off at a gallop. I gave my own mount a kick, and he was more than happy to take off after Cécile, leaving me with the sole responsibility of not falling off the side. We were through Goshawk's Hollow almost before I realized we were in it, the few people outside giving us startled looks as we flew down the one street. Then we were back in the woods, the boughs of the trees bending beneath the weight of the snow, and the only sound the thud of hooves.

Abruptly, she slowed her horse and veered off into the woods. Dropping into a walk, she wove amongst the trees before stopping next to a snow bowl. "This is the last mark on the map from my spell."

"How do you know?" I asked, glancing around at trees and wondering what distinguished this spot from any other.

"The map is in my mind." Her eyes were still and unblinking. "The parchment with the markers was only a physical manifestation of the knowledge – I didn't realize it at first, but I never really needed it."

It was a hard thing to comprehend, but I didn't ask her to explain any further. I wasn't sure if she could.

"I think the body is my grandmother's."

Given that the body of Genevieve's mother had never been found, it was a reasonable enough assertion. I glanced at the trees, feeling a sense of unease in knowing Anushka had murdered a woman in the very spot we stood. That one day it could be Cécile she pursued through the darkened woods.

"Why was she here?" Cécile muttered, more to herself than to me. "What possible reason could she have had to come to the farm when by all accounts, she detested my father's very existence."

It was a good question, but not one we'd ever have an answer to. Whatever her reason for venturing to the Hollow, Anushka had caught up with her before she could fulfill it.

Without another word, Cécile turned back to the road, and we trotted along in silence before she eventually said, "I haven't had a chance to send word to them about you, so this will come as a bit of a surprise." Eyes forward, she walked her horse down the lane toward a modest-sized home and a larger structure that I expected was the barn. Four dogs with substantially more stature than Souris charged us, barking and baying; and ahead, I saw an older man come out of the barn, hand shading his eyes as he watched our approach. In the whites and greys of winter, there was no missing Cécile's hair.

The door to the house swung open, and a blonde girl leaned

out. She squinted at us for a minute, then went back inside, appearing again wearing a cloak and boots. An older woman followed, wiping her hands on the apron she wore.

This was Cécile's family.

Obviously, I'd known we were going to see them, but it dawned on me now that the meeting might not go well. They knew *what* I was. They knew *who* I was. And they had every reason to hate me.

"Cécile!" The blonde girl barely waited until she was off her horse before throwing her arms around her sister. They rocked side to side in a strange sort of dance.

"We weren't expecting you until the new year," her father said, giving me a curious nod as I dismounted.

I nodded back, at a loss for what to say.

"It's impromptu," Cécile replied. Pulling off my coat, she handed it to me.

Josette's eyes widened. "Is that blood? What happened?"

"Are you hurt?" Her father reached for her, but Cécile held up a hand. "I'm fine. It isn't mine." She hesitated. "Papa, this is my husband Tristan. We'll only be here for the night – I need to be in Trianon tomorrow." She thrust the reins in his direction. "Can you take care of Fleur? I need to get cleaned up." Then with her sister's arm around her, she all but bolted into the house.

Her father and I stared at each other, and I was quite certain I'd never felt so awkward in my entire life.

"You're the troll," he finally said. "The troll that stole my little girl and forced her into an unnatural union?"

I winced, twisting the leather of my reins back and forth. "Yes." Trying to put the blame on my father seemed like the wrong thing to do.

"Am I to guess that the whole Isle is now crawling with you and yours?" he demanded.

I shook my head. "Only me."

"Well, I'm sure there's quite a story behind that." He scowled. "What happened to her?"

"That's complicated."

Reaching forward, he grabbed me by the front of the shirt. "Complicated? After all you've done, you show up with my daughter – visibly upset and covered in blood – and tell me it's complicated? You explain yourself now, boy, or you can get off my property."

I stared at the grizzled farmer who had me by the shirt and realized why Cécile was the way she was. "I'll tell you everything, Monsieur de Troyes," I said. "If you're willing to listen."

Grudgingly, he nodded and let go of my shirt. "You can call me Louie – we don't waste time on ceremony in these parts." He glanced at my horse. "Good-looking animal you have there."

"Christophe Girard selected him for me." But not before first trying to convince me I should learn to ride on a pony.

"Aye? Well, Chris might not know much, but he knows horses."

I led my horse into the stall Louie pointed at. "He has more to offer than people seem to give him credit for," I said, examining the buckles holding my saddle on. "He's loyal, which is a rare thing in my experience. He's also been a good friend to Cécile and Sabine. And to me."

Fleur was in the stall across the aisle, and I noticed Louie already had all of her tack removed and was leaning on the door watching me. "Won't argue with you," he said, scratching his greying head. "You know the first thing about caring for a horse?"

I shook my head.

He came out of the stall and over to me. "How old did you say you were?"

"Seventeen."

"Have to say, I thought you would be older." He shrugged. "Either way, you're well past due to learn a few useful skills. Think you can talk and learn at the same time?"

I nodded, feeling suddenly desperate to prove to him I wasn't useless.

"All right. Best you start from the beginning, then."

With little more than an occasional grunt and the odd word, Cécile's father showed me how to care for my horse while I talked. I didn't start at the beginning of today, or the moment when Cécile arrived in Trollus. I started at *my* beginning, and I told him everything. Revealing so much about myself was entirely at odds with my nature, but I found the story slipping off my tongue as though it wanted to be told. Louie was Cécile's father, and I needed him to know who I was, to prove to him as best I could that despite everything, I wasn't entirely unworthy of his daughter.

We moved from the horses to the cows to the pigs, him asking the occasional question, but for the most part listening in attentive silence. By the time I finished, all the chores were complete and dusk had settled onto the land.

"So you say this witch intends to kill Genevieve tomorrow night?"

"It is a near certainty." We were sitting on the front stoop of the house, and Louie was smoking a pipe, the smell of it both strange and comforting at the same time. "She's been maintaining her immortality by killing her female descendants. Cécile believes she needs the link of the bloodline in order for the spell to work, and that the only time she can access enough power is when the solstice aligns with the full moon."

Louie grunted in understanding, then blew a puff of smoke into the air. "And if she succeeds, then Cécile will be next?"

"Not if I have anything to say about it."

He nodded. "Now you say trolls and humans can..." Wincing, he puffed out a series of smoke rings.

I knew what he was getting at. "Around three-quarters of Trollus's population has human blood running in their veins."

He was quiet for a moment. "How well would this Anushka's spell work if Cécile's girl-children were half troll?"

He'd landed on a notion I hadn't even considered. "Not well at all."

"Then it would appear that no matter what you two decide to do, the witch's days are numbered. Can't say I entirely understand where your aunt gets her prophesies, but it would appear she was right." Climbing to his feet, he knocked the embers out of his pipe. "I've a few last chores to finish up. Why don't you head in and get washed up for dinner."

Instead of going inside directly, I sat for a minute longer, taking in all that was around me. The glow of the sun fading behind the mountain peaks. The cold wind smelling of pine. The sounds of the animals in the barn. One of the dogs came up and sat beside me, brown eyes bright as she surveyed her domain. It was more than just a different life – it seemed like an entirely different world, and I allowed myself a moment to imagine what it would have been like to grow up here. To have a father like Louie. To have siblings who weren't trying to kill me. To spend my days growing crops and raising animals rather than at politics and plotting. It seemed a very grand life, a perfect life, and it made me realize what Cécile was risking to help me.

Inside, I was greeted by the smell of wood smoke, cooking food, and Cécile's little sister stirring a pot on the stove. "Put you to work, did he?"

"We had a great deal to discuss." I tried scraping the mud off my boots, but it seemed like a lost cause, so I pulled them off and left them at the door.

She snorted and set the spoon aside. "You don't say. Thirsty?"

"A bit."

Josette went to a small cask sitting in the corner and returned with a mug of dark ale. "It's this or water."

"This is fine, thank you." I expected her to go back to stirring, but she stood her ground, unabashedly looking at me from head to toe. Josette was quite a bit taller than Cécile, and blonde, but otherwise there was no mistaking that they were sisters.

"She's upstairs with Gran, if you were wondering," she said. "They sent me to finish dinner so they could talk."

"How is she?"

"Upset. Scared." Josette looked at our feet, then back up at me. "She cried for a long time."

"She had reason to," I said. "We lost a close friend today. And another is in grave danger."

"She told us that." Josette lifted her chin, and there was no missing the judgment in her eyes. "Cécile's a crybaby. Always has been. Weeps when she's happy, sad, mad. Last time I saw her cry like this was when Fleur got stung by a bee and bucked her off. But she got back on. My sister always gets back on."

It was a challenge if I'd ever heard one, and I sensed that if I said a thing against Cécile that Josette would spit in my face and stick a knife between my ribs.

"If crying made me half as brave as your sister, I'd fill my pockets with handkerchiefs," I told her. "That she wears her heart on her sleeve is one of the things I love about her most."

She eyed me suspiciously, then nodded. "All right. You can sit if you want. They won't take kindly to interruptions, so it's best you wait for them to come down."

I pulled out one of the chairs surrounding the scarred kitchen table and sat.

"You don't look much like I thought you would," she said, going back to the stove. "Trolls are supposed to be big and ugly and stupid."

"So I've heard."

"Cécile wouldn't talk about you much, but she did say you were the handsomest boy she'd ever met. Of course I couldn't really trust in that, because there isn't much accounting for her taste." Her blue eyes gleamed with amusement. "She kisses the pigs because she thinks they're cute."

"There is something endearing about the baby ones," I said, thinking about the small pink creatures I'd seen in the barn.

Josette laughed wickedly. "I'm not talking about the piglets."

She could be making up stories, but I sensed every word of it was true. "The good thing about setting your expectations low is that you will not often be disappointed."

"Who said I'm not disappointed?" She tasted whatever was in the pot, frowned, then added a pinch of what looked like salt. "She also said you were magic, but the only magic I've seen you do is convince Papa to let you do my chores instead of me."

"She was telling the truth," I said, struggling to keep the smile off my face.

"Prove it."

Laughter burst from my chest. "Are you quite serious?"

"If you hadn't noticed–" She paused to taste her sauce. "I'm always serious."

I extinguished all the light. Lamps, fireplace, stove, all smothered so that we sat in darkness.

"Well, that's clever," she said. "Make it so that I can't see a thing so I won't know if you're doing the magic or not." Her words were light, but I hadn't missed the gasp of surprise.

I obliged her with several dozen little orbs of light that I set to drifting around the kitchen. Her eyes leapt from light to light, reminding me of the first time I'd lit the glass gardens for Cécile.

She reached out a hand to touch one of the orbs, then hesitated. "May I?"

I nodded, watching as she passed her fingers through one of them in an attempt to catch it. While she was distracted, I wrapped a delicate web around her, then gently lifted her up in the air. She shrieked, then laughed. "Higher!"

"I thought it was rude to tell a troll what to do with his magic?" Cécile whispered in my ear, her breath against my skin making me feel things that were not appropriate under the circumstances.

Catching her hand, I kissed her fingers. "I've been known to make exceptions."

Out of the corner of my eye, I caught sight of her grandmother standing by the stairs, arms crossed. In a flash, I had Josette back on the ground, my lights extinguished, all the fires relit, and my feet underneath me.

Cécile took hold of my hand and squeezed it. "Gran, this is Tristan."

"It is a pleasure to finally meet you, Madame de Troyes," I said, more than a little worried what the matriarch of the family would have to say to me.

"Well, at least he knows his manners," her grandmother said. "Have a seat, young man. Girls, get dinner on the table. I can hear your father coming up the steps."

"She won't abide smoking in the house," Louie said, leading me outside after dinner. I sat next to him, drink in my hand, and looked up at the massive moon overhead. It was ominous in its fullness, and I distinctly remembered the last time I had paid it this much attention: the night before Cécile had been brought to Trollus, which I'd spent racking my brain trying to think of a way around being bonded to a human. It seemed like a lifetime ago.

"Can't help but think I might have kept Genevieve safe if only I'd tried harder to get her to come to the Hollow."

I thought about the letters he'd written her, and knew that short of dragging her forcibly, there had been nothing more he could have done. "I'm sure Anushka has her ways of keeping track of her family," I said. "You would have needed to take her far further than the Hollow to be out of her reach. And quite frankly, I've met her – I don't think she does anything she doesn't want to."

"Might be you're right." He puffed on the pipe. "She weren't always this way – her mother's disappearance changed her."

"They were close?"

He laughed. "Furthest thing from it. Genny *hated* her mother. The woman was a dominating old shrew. Was one of the reasons why Genny was so excited to move to the Hollow. She wanted to get as far away from that woman as she could."

I frowned. Something about what he was telling me didn't seem right. "She *wanted* to leave Trianon?"

"It was her idea. She was tired of performing night after night and being away from the children, but after each pregnancy, her mother always convinced her to come back. When my father died, we had to make the decision of whether to take up the reins of the farm or sell it, and she was adamant we go. Sent me ahead with the children while she finished the run of the show she was starring in. I still have the note she sent a couple days before she was meant to arrive, telling me how excited she was for a fresh start. But she never showed."

"I rode to Trianon straight away, certain that something had happened to her. I found her at the Opera – she told me that her mother had gone missing, and that she could not in good conscience leave until she'd been found. I wanted to stay to help her look, but she insisted that I go back to be with the children. Told me that she'd come to join us." Louie rested his pipe against his knee. "She never came."

"Did she give you an explanation?"

Louie sighed. "I went to see her several times, hoping I'd convince her to come home with me, but she always had a reason why she couldn't leave. The law eventually declared her mother dead, but by then, I knew there was no hope. I confronted her directly, and she told me that she'd changed her mind. That her place was on the stage in Trianon, and if I truly loved her, I wouldn't interfere." He rested his head on his hands. "If only I'd gotten her away sooner, then maybe…"

Would it have mattered? It was no coincidence that Genevieve had changed so markedly following her mother's death – a death that was perpetrated by Anushka. I had no doubt that the witch had done something to alter Genevieve's desire to leave Trianon – what other explanation could there be? Another question rose in my mind; one that had been nagging at me since our encounter with Aiden and Fred at the opera. "During an argument your son had with Cécile, he said that Genevieve forced him to choose between you and her, and that when he would not, she took some sort of revenge on him. Do you know anything about that?"

Louie spat into a mud puddle, one hand balling into a fist. "No. I knew something had happened to turn him against her after he went to Trianon, but he refused to talk about it." He sighed heavily. "She was keen to have him – arranged for a position in the city guard, a carriage to collect him from the farm, and a fancy room done up for him in her home. Didn't last – he moved into the barracks in a matter of months." He turned his head to me. "Why do you ask? Cécile is the apple of her brother's eye, if that's what concerns you. Not much he wouldn't do to keep her safe."

I shook my head and made a noncommittal noise, uncertain why Fred's words wouldn't leave me alone. Something about the way each fact I learned about Genevieve painted a clearer, but darker picture of the woman. And it wasn't the portrait of a victim.

"Past time to turn in," Louie said, interrupting my thoughts. "You two still set on going back to Trianon in the morning?"

"Yes." Although what precisely we would do remained to be seen.

"I don't care a whit for Genny," Louie said, climbing to his feet. "But there's nothing more important to me than my children. You keep Cécile safe."

The floor creaked softly, and the door to the bedroom opened. Cécile padded softly on bare feet across the room and climbed under the covers next to me. "I thought you were supposed to be sleeping with your sister so as not to shock your father's sensibilities," I whispered, pulling her close against me. "I'm not convinced he believes our marriage is entirely legitimate."

"It's almost dawn, and Joss won't even notice I'm gone." She rested her head on my chest. "And I couldn't sleep anyway."

I traced her spine from the base of her neck down to the curve of her bottom, then up again.

She sighed, her breath warm against the bare skin of my chest. "I'm not going to let her kill my mother."

I felt her hold her breath, as though she expected me to argue with her. "I know," I said. "We won't let that happen." Even if Genevieve did deserve it.

She lifted herself up onto one elbow, her raised eyebrows mirroring the surprise I felt. "I thought you would argue about putting the life of one human ahead of the life of many."

"She's your mother," I said, watching the tiny ball of light float above us. "Haven't I caused enough hurt in your life without sacrificing your family members to a murderous witch?"

"Your father, and by extension, your mother and aunt, are in just as much danger as my mother."

"I don't care about my..." I broke off, the word *father* catching in my throat. *It's not a lie!* I screamed at myself. But no amount of effort could force the statement from my lips. Whether I liked it or not, I did care what happened to him. "My father will not be unaware of Angoulême's plots," I muttered, annoyed with myself. "And he is far from helpless. What's more, he made this bed – it's his own damn fault if he has to sleep in it."

"And what about everyone else in Trollus?" she asked. "Must they sleep in it too?"

"Don't ask me that." I turned my head sideways against the pillow so I didn't have to meet her gaze.

"Can you imagine what would happen if Angoulême succeeds? It would be a thousand times worse for the half-bloods under his rule than your father. And what's more, he knows who Anushka is. If he catches her and kills her, all the gains you've made will be lost."

I ground my teeth together. "Do you think I don't know all of this?"

"I'm well aware of the fact you know it, but what you seem unable to admit is that you want to see her dead. That your reaction yesterday night wasn't an act of desperation, but a reflection of what you really want."

"You..." I cut off, the sound of footsteps and a loud thud reaching my ears. "There's someone outside."

"The dogs would be barking like mad if anyone came near." She bit her lip, eyes wide. "Oh no."

Climbing off the bed, we both went to the tiny window, Cécile inching the curtains apart. "It's too dark," she whispered. "I can't see anything."

My eyes were better. "It's a large box or chest." Grabbing my shirt, I pulled it over my head. "Stay here."

Cécile didn't pay me any heed, following me out the door and down the stairs.

Louie was peering out the front door, a pistol that looked like it hadn't seen action in years held firmly in one hand. "Whoever it was, they're gone now."

One of the dogs trotted up to the front door, licking its chops. "Baited the damn dogs off," he muttered. "Blasted things wouldn't know a threat if it bit them on the ass."

"Keep her here." I pulled on my boots and went out onto the step, illuminating the yard with brilliant light as I went. There was an ironbound chest sitting in the middle of the yard, but there was something odd about it. It looked bowed out, the wood splintered in places, almost as though something of great strength had been locked inside and had tried very hard to get out.

My heart beat faster as I made my way down the steps toward it.

"Tristan!" I glanced over my shoulder and saw that Louie had Cécile firmly by the shoulders. She looked so young standing there in a childish nightgown, her hair loose and mussed, eyes wide. Whatever was in the chest, I was quite sure I didn't want her to see it.

I stopped a pace away. There was an iron lock holding the lid in place, and I wrenched it off with a squeal of metal. I did not want to look inside. Did not want to see. Because it was not a matter of what I would find. It was a matter of whom.

Drawing in a deep breath and ignoring the icy tightness in my gut, I reached forward, and with one hand, flipped back the lid.

CHAPTER 47
Cécile

The ground trembled and shook, the shutters rattling against the house. The fresh snow around Tristan melted into a muddy soup, spreading out in a circle away from him. The air was as warm as the height of summer, and water gushed off the house and barn in torrents.

"God in heaven," my father whispered, letting go of me with one hand to steady himself.

Tristan fell to his knees next to the chest, holding someone against him. A woman dressed in grey, her long dark hair spilling over his arm. She wore a dark cloak I recognized because she'd been wearing it the last time I saw her.

"Let me go." I choked the words out.

"Cécile, no." My father's fingers clamped tighter around my arm.

"Let me go!" The words ripped from my throat, loud and full of power. Not caring that I'd just compelled my own father, I sprinted down the steps toward Tristan. The mud oozed hot and slippery between my bare toes, splattering up onto the white of my nightgown. But what did any of that matter?

"Élise…" Reaching out with one hand, I brushed back her hair, bile rising in my throat at the sight of her blank and unseeing eyes. "How?"

"Because she is dead." Tristan's voice was thick with a fury that rendered it almost unrecognizable. "And the curse cares naught for corpses."

I let my hand drop to my side, my eyes taking in the chest, the damage done to it telling me all I needed to know about what had been done to her. To my friend, who was so terrified of confined spaces that she could not even bear the mines.

The ground stopped shaking, and a wind blew down from the mountains, wiping the heat of magic away. My skin prickled and I shivered, but not because of the chill of winter. Tristan had turned, and his face was full of vicious fury. I took a step backwards. He looked nothing like my husband. Nothing at all like the boy I'd fallen in love with. And most certainly nothing human. This was a creature I'd unleashed on the world with the power to tear it asunder, and his wrath was a terrifying thing.

"I'm going to burn him alive for this," he said, and my eyes flicked past him to the inner lid of the chest. To the single name carved by the bloody nails of a terrified and dying girl.

Angoulême.

Our minds were connected. I knew what it was like when we were in perfect unison in love. Passion. Sorrow. But in that moment, I let his fury wash over me like water, soaking into every corner of my soul until it was no longer his anger, but mine. And it wanted vengeance.

CHAPTER 48
Cécile

We rode hard back to Trianon, our plan developing as we shouted back and forth to each other over the sound of pounding hooves and gusting wind. Collecting my mother and hiding her away until the night was over and Anushka had lost the chance to perform her spell wasn't an option. For one, the King's compulsion beat in my head like a drum, marching me toward my goal; and two, it might be the only chance we had to catch Anushka. The masque was a trap for us, but that didn't mean it couldn't be turned on her. Her death was long past due.

Trotting our lathered horses through the frosty streets, we stopped in front of the townhouse, and I dismounted, handing my reins to Tristan.

"Stay with her," he said for hundredth time. "Don't let her out of your sight. Anushka won't make her move until the sun has set, and I'll be inside the castle by then." He hesitated before adding. "If something happens before, you know how to get my attention."

I nodded, standing on my tiptoes as he bent in the saddle, his lips brushing mine. "Be careful."

"I will."

I stood on the front steps watching him until he rode out of sight, and then I extracted my key and went inside.

"You're back," the maid said, sparing me a passing glance as she polished the wood of the front table. "We all thought you'd decided to run off again."

I ignored the comment. "Where is my mother?"

"Not here."

My stomach dropped and I swallowed the burn threatening to rise in my throat. "Where is she?"

"At the castle, I expect. Lady Marie sent her very own carriage to retrieve her this morning, and your mother was fit to be tied about your absence when she left. Left a message that you're to join her as soon as possible, though I daresay she's probably given up hope."

They had her. My heart hammered and I struggled to keep the dismay from my face. It's too early for the spell, I reminded myself. But it was cold comfort, because our plans had been disrupted before we'd even begun. The witch had made her move.

And now it was time to make ours. "I'll leave as soon as I'm washed," I said. "If you could please heat me some water for a bath."

Bathing didn't seem a priority, but I had a part to play that did not include showing up sweaty and stinking of horse. Bolting up the stairs, I went to my room to retrieve the herbs I'd hidden in my desk in case I needed them.

My eyes went to the gown hanging freshly pressed from my dressing screen, clearly my mother's selection. My stomach clenched, knowing that when she'd had it hung there, her only concern had been my appearance. How I would be received. She had no idea how much danger she was in, and I couldn't even warn her. As disgusting as the idea was, she was our bait and I could do nothing to jeopardize that.

But I still needed to know where she was.

Hurrying down the hall to her room, I went to her vanity and snatched up a hairbrush. It was as devoid of hair as if it were new. Frowning, I riffled through the rest of her combs and cosmetics looking for strands of hair. Nothing. The maid must have been through, and she apparently did a better job cleaning my mother's things than she did mine.

Turning up a lamp, I went to her closet and began going through her clothes, searching for the gleam of red-gold, but there was none. How was that even possible? The linens on her bed were freshly laundered, and my eyes roved around the room for something else I could use. An object would work, but it had to be something that mattered to her – not some little knickknack she'd bought and not thought about since.

Tristan's plan had seemed so straightforward. I'd go to the castle with my mother, and then I'd track down Marie or something of hers, and steal a memory of Anushka's identity. When I had it, I'd use his name to give him the information, and he'd hunt her down. That failing, I'd remain glued to my mother's arm, and wait for Anushka's approach. There was no place she could take me that I could not call him, no place where he could not find me. And we were banking on her not knowing that fact.

The door opened behind me, and I turned, thinking it was the maid with my bath water. But instead, I found myself facing two grim-faced soldiers dressed in formal uniforms, a sprig of dried crimson berries pinned at their lapel.

"Mademoiselle de Troyes," one of them said. "The Lady du Chastelier requests your presence."

"I'm not ready," I protested, taking a step back. "I haven't even bathed."

"You'll be provided with what you need at the castle. You need to come with us now."

I drew on the earth's magic. I only needed a few more minutes – a chance to select something of my mother's so I could find her. To retrieve my supplies where they sat on the desk in my bedroom.

"Wait downstairs. I'll be with you shortly," I said, forcing every ounce of my power into the words, feeling the force ripple out.

And fall away.

The guard shook his head, coming forward to grab my arm. "Now."

And it was then the meaning of the berries struck me. The memory of Chris telling me the wooden charm he'd purchased would ward a person from magic, and my dismissal of the very idea. Of the strange wooden earrings that Lady Marie had worn, and the sprig of those very same berries pinned into her hair.

Rowan. The witch's bane. And its presence rendered our plans useless, and put Anushka back in control.

If she'd ever lost it.

CHAPTER 49
Tristan

"They refused me entry to the castle," Sabine snarled, her boots leaving tracks of mud across the floor. "Told me that Cécile would not be requiring my services tonight."

"Did they refuse any of the other crew?" I asked, scratching Souris behind one ear because watching Sabine pace was only adding to my nerves.

"No." She spat the word out.

"They're cutting her off from the herd," Chris muttered.

Sabine stopped moving. "That's morbid." I felt her gaze turn on me. "You're awfully calm, all things considered."

I shook my head, picking at a frayed stitch on my boot. My anger was a slow burn, boiling hotter and hotter and threatening to erupt. Every minute seemed to pass interminably slow as I watched the sun track across the sky, and instinct told me to act, to go to the castle and find Marie and extract Anushka's identity from her with whatever means necessary. Only the finest filament of control kept me in my seat, reminding me that only strategy and wit would win us success.

"There's something I need to tell you both. You might want to sit."

Sabine stayed where she was, crossing her arms.

"Cécile's hypothesis about the alignment of the winter solstice and full moon has been proven correct," I said. "If we don't stop her, Anushka will kill Genevieve tonight and perform whatever spell she's been using to maintain her immortality. Even without the cost of Cécile's mother's life, given that we've lost the ability to track her, tonight is our only opportunity to catch her."

"And you've sent Cécile into the lion's den alone?" Sabine's cheeks flushed red with anger. Spinning on her heel, she started to the door. "I'm going to find a way into the castle. I'll swim across the cursed river if I have to."

"Sabine, come back here," I said, jamming the door shut.

She jerked on the handle. "Open it. Let me out."

I briefly considered lifting her up and depositing her in front of me until I was done talking, but I suspected manhandling the girl would not predispose her to listening. "Sabine, sit down and listen. Please."

She grudgingly returned and sat next to Chris, and I proceeded to explain all of what Cécile had seen and heard in Trollus. "Angoulême plans to take control of the city using my brother, and when he does, he'll arrange to have Anushka killed. The trolls will hail him as their savior, and all the world will suffer for it. And I do not think I'll be able to stop them."

"So you plan to kill her instead," Chris said, and it wasn't a question.

I nodded. "There is a chance we could catch her and use Aiden's plan to free Cécile from my father, and then hide her away from the world, but..." I hesitated. "My people are in danger from both within and without, and I have to do what I can to keep them safe."

"And when the rest of the trolls are free? What then?" Sabine's arms were wrapped around her body as though to ward off the chill.

"I will try to take the crown," I said. "And I will spend the rest of my life trying to keep them in check."

"And if you fail?"

I closed my eyes for a moment, my knowledge of life before the Fall marching unwanted across my vision. "I suggest you pray to your God that I don't."

"Is this what Cécile wants?" Chris lifted his head, gaze steely and unflinching.

"So she says." I leaned back in my chair and hooked an ankle across my knee.

Sabine and Chris exchanged weighted looks, and I stared at my boot to give them a moment.

"I understand if you want to try to put a knife in my back or an arrow through my heart. Who could blame you?" I inhaled and exhaled slowly. "Cécile's father intends to warn everyone in the Hollow at midnight tonight – it could not be sooner, because we cannot be certain of the loyalties of everyone in your village." I looked up. "I'll not stop you if you want to leave and go to them now. I'll give you the gold you need to book passage on a ship to the continent, although I cannot be certain how long Trianon will be a safe harbor, so you'd need to leave immediately."

Chris glanced at the water clock and his jaw tightened. Even if they left now, riding in the dark they wouldn't make it home much before when Louie would set out to spread the word. "You can take my horse and Cécile's," I said. "I do not think those in Trollus will act immediately, but the sluag may well venture out under the cover of darkness once they are able."

Rising to my feet, I went to my chest of gold and filled up a sack. "Here." I tried to hand it to Chris, but he shook his head. "Sabine?" I held it in her direction, hoping she would at least have a little sense.

"No." Picking up her cloak and gloves, she donned them. "I need to be with Cécile. I don't know what good I can do, but she needs at least one friend at her side. Help me get in the castle, or at least give me a weapon."

Silently, I extracted the knife hidden in my boot and handed it to her hilt first. She gripped it as though she were not entirely familiar with how to use it, but was more than willing to try. "Don't leave just yet." I turned my gaze to Chris. "What say you?"

"I've been around trolls most of my life," he said. "I know

what you are capable of, and I won't lie and say the thought of your people free to do what they wish doesn't terrify the piss out of me. But it sounds like it's going to happen whether I like it or not, and I'm damn well going to do everything I can to make sure ours is the winning side." He squared his shoulders. "If I'm going to be ruled by a high-minded pretty-faced troll, it might as well be you."

"I'm glad to hear it," I said, trying not to smile. "Who knows what would happen to my ego if you decided to abandon me."

Chris rolled his eyes.

"Sabine," I said, hefting the sack of gold once more. "I'm of a mind to have a pretty girl on my arm at this party, and if she happened to have a knife or two hidden in her skirts, all the better." I tossed the sack her direction. "Spend what you need to play the part."

Climbing to my feet, I went to the window and peered up at the wintery sky, the cold an ominous prediction of what was to come. If all went to plan, more than just trolls would be released onto the world tonight. How long would I have until the Winter Queen's bargain with me came due?

"There is one more person I need to speak to before we set our plans in motion," I said. "I only hope that he's now of a mind to listen."

CHAPTER 50
Cécile

They took me to the castle in a carriage, and if the guards thought it strange that a young opera singer be treated so, they were too well trained to ask questions. Or to answer them.

They took me in a small entrance at the rear of the castle and up to a set of rooms where a steaming bath and an elderly servant woman waited. The white silk costume resplendent with feathers that Sabine had made hung on a privacy screen, but of my friend, there was no sign. Everyone I encountered wore a sprig of rowan berries, and when I enquired of their meaning to the maid, she told me they were in honor of the solstice celebration and to remove them would be bad luck.

I surrendered myself to her ministrations, the whole time my mind a whirl of how I could possibly get around the rowan's effect on magic, which seemed much like the sluag's effect on the trolls. There had to be a way around it, or at the very least, a way to remove its protection from Marie once I found her. I needed to hold up my end of the plan, which is why I hadn't contacted Tristan. He was not in a good state of mind, and I was afraid if he learned our plans were in disarray, he'd come in and take the information from Marie by force. It might to come to that, but I had every intention of doing what I could to avoid it.

"You've led us on quite the runaround."

I lifted my head to watch Marie enter, noting the twisted

branches woven like a crown into her hair. Not something that could easily be removed.

"Why are you doing this to me?" I demanded.

"We both know why, Cécile, so drop the pretense," Marie responded. "You caused us no small amount of grief with your disappearance, and we could not risk you deciding not to show for our little fête this evening."

I swallowed hard, my throat dry. "Where is my mother?"

"You'll see her soon enough. Do not cause any trouble, Cécile. If you do, she will punish you by harming those who matter to you most. The troll included."

"Are you threatening me?"

She shook her head. "I'm warning you."

"I want proof my mother is unharmed." Given it seemed impossible to use magic on Marie, my primary goal was my mother. And stay with her until Tristan found us.

"You will see her when Anushka wills it, not before."

She *was* here. "And here I believed you were the most powerful woman on the Isle," I said. "Apparently I was wrong."

Marie laughed, but the sound was all harsh edges. "When she sings, we all dance to her tune. She might be more devil than woman, but what is the saying? 'The enemy of my enemy is my friend?'" She walked further into the room, and my eyes fixed on a red-gold hair caught on one of her heels. Mine? My mother's? Anushka's?

"Besides, she punished me harshly the last time I crossed her, and I will not make the same mistake again."

"Please," I said, dropping to my knees in front of her as if to beg. "She's going to kill my mother. You need to help me." I pressed my hand against the stray hair, holding it against the ground.

"I wish I could, Cécile," she replied, stepping back and averting her eyes in discomfort. The hair remained under my hand. "But this is the only way to keep the Isle safe. She is the only one who can keep them contained."

My eyes went to the costume still draped on its hanger, and

hers followed suit. "After all this, you honestly expect me to perform?" Closing my fingers around the hair, I sat back on my heels.

"If you want the troll to survive the night, you will do just that." Her face was grim. "Those are Anushka's terms: if you do as she asks, she will return the creature to his cage alive. If you interfere with her ritual, she will see him dead."

My stomach clenched, and I turned away from her, staring at the glow of the lamp until my eyes burned and watered. "You'd have me choose between the life of my lover and the life of my mother?" All of this was just words now. I needed her gone so I could attempt a spell.

"Genevieve's death is not negotiable. Whether you choose to cooperate tonight will not change that fact. All you can hope to gain is the life of your *lover.*" Her voice twisted on the word as though it were some revolting and debauched thing.

"He knows this is a trap," I whispered. "He knows what she plans to do."

"That will not save him." Marie went to my costume, tracing a finger down the silken fabric. "I want you to know, Cécile, I don't relish this task. Harboring Anushka from the trolls is a burden those in my position have borne for five centuries. The duty of protecting the woman our husbands are oath-sworn to hunt down and kill. And she does not make it easy."

The Regent didn't know, and neither did Aiden. That explained much.

"It all makes for such strange irony that you – who are destined to be part of what keeps the curse in place – are responsible for unleashing one of the worst of them upon the world."

"What has he done that is so horrible?" I demanded.

"It is what he can do that is terrifying," she snapped. "Which is why he must be contained or killed. Those are your choices."

I glared at her for a long moment, then let my shoulders slump in defeat. "I will do as she wishes. For his sake."

"You've made the right choice." She went to the door. "Finish getting ready. The guests have already begun to arrive."

I waited until she was gone before wiping the fake tears from my face. Then I peeled the hair off my sweaty palm and examined it. There was no way of knowing who it belonged to, but it was my last chance. Tristan was planning to arrive promptly, and he'd be expecting to hear from me. I wasn't ready to think about what might happen if I didn't deliver.

CHAPTER 51
Tristan

"Eyes up," I muttered under my breath, trying to keep my apprehension regarding Cécile's silence out of my voice. "Remember, you're supposed to be here."

Sabine dutifully lifted her chin, but her death grip on my arm didn't lessen.

"You told me once that information was free for the taking to those who watched and listened," I added. "This is the same. Watch them, and do as they do. They may not know who you are, but that is not same as them knowing you're the daughter of an innkeeper from a town in the middle of nowhere."

"Right."

I nodded at a pair I recognized from one of the many parties I'd attended during my first week in Trianon, introducing Sabine as an old friend of the family, before moving on. I heard their whispered speculation about how I secured an invitation to such an exclusive event, but none of that concerned me. Cécile should have contacted me by now, if not with answers, then at least to let me know our plan had failed.

"Do you see Marie?"

Sabine shook her head. She'd assured me she'd recognize the Lady du Chastelier, and I'd set her to watching the woman to see whom she spoke with. In the worst case, I needed to have the woman within reach in case I needed to force answers out of her the hard way. "But that's the Regent over there," Sabine added.

I let my gaze pass over the direction she'd indicated, easily picking out the Regent by the circle of courtiers fawning about him. He had the look of his son, but with many more years, grey hairs, and paunch around the middle.

"I suppose I shouldn't be surprised that you'd have the audacity to show your face here."

I turned around to find Aiden standing behind me. He was freshly shaven and dressed as befitted his station, yet he looked haggard. A decade or more older than I knew him to be. "My lord." I bowed low. "I take it you aren't the individual I have to thank for the invitation to tonight's fête?"

"Bad enough that I have to suffer you traipsing around my city as though you were…" He broke off, finally realizing the degree of attention we'd garnered from his outburst. "As though you were human," he said. "Not the cursed devil of a creature I know you to be."

"Not cursed any longer," I replied, plucking a glass of wine off a passing tray. "You should really try to keep up with these developments."

His face darkened. "De Troyes said you wanted to make a bargain. I'll hear you out, but then I want you gone."

I shrugged. "As you like." Bending, I whispered in Sabine's ear, "You know what to do. But be careful."

Aiden led me out of the hall, down a few narrow and low-ceilinged corridors, and into a study. "Shut the door," he snapped at Cécile's brother, who had followed us out of the main hall. "I don't want anyone overhearing this."

I selected a seat next to the banked fire where I could watch him pace, careful to keep Fred, and the pistol he had in his grip, in my line of sight.

"De Troyes has told me that you're willing to dispatch your father in exchange for my assistance tonight."

"Anushka is here in the castle," I said. "I've strong reason to believe your mother has been harboring her, although I cannot say whether it is by choice." Aiden opened his mouth to argue, but I held up a hand to cut him off. "The witch has been maintaining her immortality using a spell that involves a specific set of conditions and the sacrifice of her female descendants. She intends to murder Genevieve de Troyes tonight."

Aiden's eyebrows lifted. "But that means that Cécile is..."

I gave a slight nod. "I'd like your assistance in catching Anushka before she completes the spell."

He stared at me in silence for several long moments. "You must think me a fool. If I help you catch the witch, you'll kill her and release your scourge upon the Isle."

"Yes," I said, shoving aside the anger I felt at his terminology. "I will kill her. But what you need to understand is that her death is inevitable. My father's adversary, the Duke d'Angoulême, has discovered her identity. He means to take control of Trollus using my younger brother and then kill her. Which means you have a choice: deal with him or deal with me."

"This is a trick," he whispered. "I won't fall for your kind's duplicity again."

"It's the truth," I said. "My brother is violently insane, and the Duke is an extremist of the first order. If they kill the witch, they will be hailed as saviors of my people, and who can say how much harm they could inflict before that aura fades."

"I'll hear no more of this," Aiden said. "Your words are poison." He made a gesture with his hand, and a second later, I felt the barrel of a gun press against the back of my head.

I didn't move. "I'll give you one last chance to reconsider." But my words landed on deaf ears.

"Do it, de Troyes," Aiden shouted. "What are you waiting for?"

"You're making a mistake," I said, my pulse roaring in my ears. "If we work together, there is hope our people can coexist peacefully."

"The only chance for peace is with your kind dead!" His eyes were wild. "Fred, this is your chance for revenge for what happened to your sister. Take it now."

"No." Cécile's brother stepped out from behind me, his pistol now leveled at the other man. "I'm sorry for this, my lord, but I can't let you make this mistake."

"You are satisfied, then?" I asked, rising to my feet. I'd known Aiden would never agree to my plan, but Fred had needed proof before he was willing to commit what amounted to treason.

He nodded, and I didn't miss the disappointment in his eyes. He'd believed Aiden a better sort of man than he'd proven himself to be.

Aiden's eyes widened as he realized that he'd been played. "You're the one making a mistake, de Troyes. This creature ruined your sister's life – you said so yourself."

"I did," Fred replied. "But I also saw him save her life, and right now, he's trying to save it again. I believe what he says that the trolls will escape one way or another, and I'd rather ally myself with the best of them than take my chances with the worst."

"You'll regret this," Aiden shouted.

"Maybe I will," Fred said. "But for now, I'll be needing your clothes."

CHAPTER 52
Cécile

Keeping an eye on the door, I slipped on Sabine's creation. It was gathered at the bust to give the appearance of more curves than I had. The straps were encased with a gilded mesh that molded against my shoulders, and the skirt hung in a whimsical A-line, feeling light as air against my legs. White feathers trailed from the back, in the suggestion of wings, floating out from behind me as I walked.

It made me desperately wish my friend were here. In all likelihood, she was in the castle and Marie was keeping her from me, but a little bit of doubt chewed at my heart. Tristan would have told her our intention to kill Anushka tonight, and I wasn't entirely sure how she would take the news.

Holding the strand of hair between my fingers, I did my best to ignore the shake in my hand. I'd only have one chance at this, and the results were uncertain. Turning the lamp as high as it would go, I focused on the flame, drawing on its power even as I held the hair above it. It crackled; burning unnaturally slowly and bright as the magic flared and I focused my thoughts. "Show me my mother."

Nothing happened.

"Show me Genevieve," I demanded, hating the desperation in my voice. *Please be alive.*

Nothing.

I pulled harder, magic coming into me from all directions, and then I switched tactics. "Show me Anushka."

An image appeared in the flame, and the sound of my mother singing danced through the air. *Anushka's with her!* Leaning forward, I peered into the fire, but it was like looking through the keyhole of a door. Motion flashed in front of me, black fabric and pale skin, but whoever it was sat too close to the lamp to give me any perspective.

My mother sang her warm-up exercises, and there was nothing in her voice hinting at fear or anxiety. She did not yet realize the danger she was in, but that didn't matter. She was alive, and that was all I cared about.

"We have Cécile. She's getting ready even as we speak." A voice interrupted my mother's exercises, but it was a familiar one: Marie.

Elbows bent and hands clasped in front of the flame, and I held my breath, waiting to hear Anushka speak. "Good. Cursed girl seemed set to ruin everything." My heart skipped – it was my mother who had spoken. Something wasn't right.

"She thinks she needs to protect you," Marie replied, her voice toneless. "She'll play right into your hands and bring the creature along with her."

My heartbeat seemed to slow, each *thump, thump, thump* deafening. Realization was dawning on me, too slowly. Too quickly. The wild sting of betrayal pierced my chest, and my wretched heart prayed that my mind was mistaken.

"You've convinced her to perform?"

"Yes." Marie was silent for a moment. "Is the performance truly necessary? The risks…"

"The ritual is everything. The timing is everything," my mother interrupted. "The last one disrupted both, and look at the cost: I was weakened enough that one of them was able to break free. It cannot happen again."

No, no, no! I was on my feet, rotating around the flame, trying to find an angle where I could see her face. I needed proof that it wasn't her – that I was mistaken. That I'd misunderstood.

"Go out and mingle with your guests, Marie. And make sure you and yours stay clear of the troll. His death is mine, along with all the power that comes with it. Tonight, I will crush what remains of the mighty fey."

I clenched my teeth to keep the threatening sobs from betraying me. Dropping to my knees, I looked up through the flame and saw her face. Her painfully familiar face, and around her throat, the necklace that marked those destined to die. The necklace I should have been wearing.

My mother is Anushka, my mother is Anushka. The words repeated in my head, but even seeing proof with my eyes, it was hard to believe. Shaking, I watched as she picked up a cruel beaked mask that I recognized from when Sabine and I had watched Catherine's memory in my washbasin, tying it to her face with a black ribbon.

"It is time."

The witch's eyes turned to the flame. I ducked under the table before she could see me, releasing the magic and vanquishing the spell. And then I sat shaking on the floor.

It had been hard enough learning that Anushka was my ancestor, but knowing that she was my *mother*– that she'd borne me for the sole purpose of sacrificing me to her immortality. That the woman I'd all but worshipped my whole life was a killer. The thought of it made the contents of my stomach rise, and twisting onto my hands and knees, I heaved them onto the carpet, my muscles straining painfully as though they might rid me of everything I'd seen.

I was the target. I was the one who was supposed to die tonight, and Tristan along with me. And with that power, my friends in Trollus had no hope. I had to warn him. "Tristanthysium," I whispered, and then broke off. If I told him Genevieve was Anushka, he'd kill her. And the thought of her lying as dead as Esmeralda had elicited a reaction in me that I could not have predicted: sorrow. She was the enemy, but though I knew I was a fool for it, I still loved her as I always had. Perhaps if we caught her, she could be reasoned with. Perhaps, there was another way…

Staggering to my feet, I ran to the door. Regardless of my sentiments, Tristan needed to be warned. He was expecting to protect Genevieve – our entire plan was predicated on keeping her safe – the last thing he'd expect would be for her to turn on him. I had to find a way to get to him, explain to him the circumstances. Convince him to at least try to find another way.

The handle turned under my grip, but the door wouldn't open. I slammed a shoulder against it, but to no avail. It was bolted from outside. I sucked in a deep breath, planning to scream until someone came, and then I clacked my teeth together. Marie and Anushka would have planned for that. Planned for me to resist. If I screamed, only people under their control would come, and then they'd drag me off and all hope of warning Tristan would be lost. I had to be smarter than that.

Anushka didn't know I'd discovered her true identity, and I needed to keep it that way. The only way to do that was to play along until a chance revealed itself. "Tristanthysium," I repeated, knowing I needed to say something. "Be wary. One of our friends is foe. Trust no one."

The bolt slid, and I broke off the thought. The door opened to reveal Monsieur Johnson, resplendent with a sprig of rowanberries on his collar. "Ah, Cécile, you look marvelous!" he said, beaming from between the two guards who flanked him. "You must come with me; we are about to begin. Are you ready?"

I nodded, though I wouldn't be ready if I had a thousand years to prepare. This would be the performance of my lifetime.

CHAPTER 53
Tristan

Tristanthysium... My name twisted through my mind, and I tensed, waiting for the answer my people had sought for centuries. But Cécile said nothing more. Which made me very worried.

"Tristan?"

I refocused, realizing Fred had spoken to me. "Pardon?"

"Someone will realize I'm not him." Fred rolled his shoulders uncomfortably, then tugged at the sleeves of his borrowed coat.

"Unlikely," I said, trying to keep my mind on the task at hand. Something had happened to Cécile – something that had shocked and horrified her, and only the knowledge that she was physically unharmed kept me from running her direction. She'd called my name, but given me nothing more. "No one knows such a thing is possible, so why would they suspect anything?"

Fred nodded, but his Aiden-mask betrayed his doubt.

"Make sure the castle is locked down," I said, repeating the plan we'd discussed this afternoon. "The gates closed. No one enters and no one leaves. And above all, keep Marie from interfering."

"All right." He swallowed hard. "I don't care much about what happens to Genevieve, but promise you'll keep my sister safe."

I needed to get back to the ballroom, but I felt the need to understand the nature of the conflict between Genevieve and her son. "What did she do to you to make you hate her so?"

Fred went very still, then he quietly replied, "It's not so much what she did as who she is."

I waited for him to continue.

"I didn't hate her before I came to Trianon," he finally said. "Quite the opposite. I thought she was magical – this beautiful nice-smelling woman who came and went like a dream. And when she told me how wonderful my life would be if I came to live with her, of course I couldn't say no. But…" he broke off. "It wasn't enough for her. She wasn't satisfied with me leaving the Hollow, she wanted me to turn my back on everyone I'd grown up with. Loving her wasn't enough: she *needed* me to hate my father. Not just to see her side, but to take it. There was no middle ground, and when I tried to find it…"

"She made you pay," I finished for him.

Fred nodded. "It seemed every time I tried to make plans to go home to visit, something would interfere. I didn't think much of it at first, but eventually I saw a pattern. That she was orchestrating it. And when I disagreed with her or went against her wishes, something would go wrong. My horse would turn up lame. Possessions would go missing. I'd get sick. But the worst thing was her obsession with my sister. She wanted to know everything about her, and most of all, she wanted me to convince Cécile to come to Trianon."

He shook his head. "There wasn't a chance, and I told her so. Told her I'd do everything in my power to keep both my sisters far away from her. And not an hour after our argument, I found myself halfway to the Hollow dead set on bringing Cécile back with me. Even though I knew that wasn't what I wanted."

Unease weighed me down as I realized the implications of his tale.

Fred rubbed his thumbs against his temples, jaw clenching and unclenching. "I knew what she was, then. And I knew that I needed to get away from her, so I moved into the barracks and refused to see her." He swallowed audibly. "Days later, my horse died. My bunkmate fell ill. And then there was a girl I fancied, and she..." He broke off. "She flung herself off a bridge in full sight of witnesses. For no reason. None at all."

He lifted his face to meet my gaze. "She didn't need me to convince Cécile to come to Trianon, but that didn't matter to her. Anyone who isn't a slave to her will is her enemy, and she lives for taking revenge. And I knew if she caught me trying to stop Cécile from moving to Trianon that the consequences would be disastrous. Next, it could have been my father falling in front of a wagon or Josette... I couldn't risk it."

Gone now was any doubt that Genevieve knew of her powers and how to use them. But more than that, Fred's story spoke of a personality, a way of being, that was eerily familiar. Warnings ran through my head, an idea, a notion that had never crossed my mind before abruptly coming to the forefront. That our target was hidden right in front of us.

But how? Genevieve's birth and life were documented and known with certainty. She was not five centuries old, and that was fact. So she could not be Anushka. It was impossible. It had to be something else – that Genevieve was under Anushka's compulsion. That the other witch was affecting her behavior. But why? What was the point of doing so, when all she needed was Genevieve's life?

Tristanthysium, be wary. One of our friends is foe. Trust no one. Cécile's voice interrupted my thoughts, demanding my attention. I waited, but nothing further echoed in my ears. Swearing, I started down the hall toward the ballroom, but Fred caught my sleeve. "When this is over, promise you'll take Cécile away from *her*. Promise me you'll keep her safe."

If only I could. "I'll do everything in my power to protect Cécile. No one is more precious to me than her."

Although at the moment, no one was frustrating me more than her. Why was Cécile being obscure? Did she mean Genevieve? Was that what she'd discovered? But then why not tell me clearly?

I ground my teeth together. It was almost time to consider my alternative plan of action.

•••

The lights had dimmed in the ballroom, ladies taking seats on the banquettes scattered around the room, gentlemen standing behind them with glasses of dark wine in their hands. Sabine spotted me the moment I entered the room, politely breaking off her conversation with an old woman who was dripping with rubies before strolling in my direction, looking for all the world as if she belonged among these people.

"I was wondering where you'd got off to," she said, taking my arm. "The masque's about to begin. Don't you see how they've turned down the lamps, and how you can hear the actors moving behind the curtains…" She blathered on for a few minutes more until those near to us lost interest and stopped eavesdropping, and then she said, "Marie came in only moments before you, and she does not look pleased. Either the evening is not going as planned, or," she lifted one eyebrow, "the plans are not to her liking."

I eyed Lady du Chastelier over the top of Sabine's blonde curls. She stood next to her husband, her expression studiously neutral, and though she nodded occasionally at the man speaking to them, it was clear she wasn't listening. Her eyes swept the room, her face tightening ever so slightly as she noted Sabine and me, before returning to the conversation. I wondered how hard she'd fight to keep Anushka's secret safe. I did not want to harm her, but if it meant saving my people, I'd do it anyway.

"Everyone believes she's upset that Lord Aiden seems set to miss the masque that was commissioned in his honor – it's all anyone will talk about. Besides you."

"He'll make an appearance shortly," I muttered, but I could barely think for the tension threatening to split my skull. "Something's happened. Cécile's seen or learned of something, and whatever it is, it's driven her nearly to the brink. I don't think we can wait to find her after the performance – we need to know what's happened now."

"Did she give you a name?"

I shook my head. *Genevieve?*

"Where is she?"

"Not far." I stared at the set as though with effort I might see through it. "In one of the rooms just beyond the ballroom. I need to find her."

Sabine tugged sharply on my arm. "You can't. The point of this is to lure *her* in, and if you go to Cécile, you'll be doing the exact opposite." Her eyes went to the stage. "Besides, Genevieve will be onstage in moments, and she is the one who needs your protection. I'll go find Cécile. No one will think it strange to find me back there."

It was my turn to hold her back. "They know you're involved," I said. "Be careful."

I watched her blonde curls bob through the crowd and disappear behind the curtains just as the lights onstage dimmed. Fred chose that moment to reenter the ballroom, a frown on his face as he went over to stand at Marie's elbow, his posture a remarkably good imitation of the choleric Lord Aiden.

Everything was silent but for the odd cough, the rustle of clothing, and the soft whisper of the curtain rising up to the ceiling. The lamps near the stage brightened, and there was a collective gasp from the audience.

The set was cast in the blacks, greys, and reds of some sort of underworld, shadowy figures in monstrous shapes painted against the backdrop and some sort of effect with the lighting making it seem as though flames danced across the stage. Music flooded the hall, dark and sharp and filled with echoing discord, but that was not the cause of the reaction.

Genevieve de Troyes perched on a faux-rock outcropping some six feet up in the air like some dark chimaera from another world. Costumed as Vice, she wore a black gown slashed with crimson, ebony-feathered wings stretched out to either side, and a cruel beaked mask obscuring her face. One hand was braced against the outcropping, and the other reached toward the audience. Both were encased in talon-tipped gloves, the metal winking dangerously.

She was beautiful and terrifying and altogether unnerving, but when she began to sing, everyone leaned toward her as though they were puppets attached to strings and she was their master.

Her song taunted the audience, invited them to partake in all manner of wickedness, captivated their thoughts, and rendered them glass-eyed and staring. Girls costumed as the sins danced on the stage beneath her, but I might well have been the only one to notice. Everyone, from the servants standing near the lamps to the Regent sitting in his high-backed chair, was captivated. No. They were compelled.

My unease returned, crawling up my spine. Enthralled as they were, anything could happen and I doubted any of the humans would notice. I shifted so that my back was pressed against the wall, watching for any sign of motion. Nothing. I glanced back at the stage, starting when I realized her eyes were directly on me. Instinctively, I fell still, mimicking the expressions of those around me, but I knew I had been caught out. But by who? Cécile's mother, or someone far more dangerous to my kind?

The song ended, and motion returned to the hall. One by one the girls sashayed to the front of the stage to proclaim their sins' names, and then cymbals crashed and a drum roll thundered through the room. A young man dressed as a devil sprang out onto the stage and began to sing and dance with the girls in a seductive twist of limbs, while Vice watched from above. The rhythm of the music changed, the girls swinging wildly on each other's arms as Vice and the demon sang of their plot to capture Virtue and her maidens and steal their souls.

Still there was no sign of Sabine.

I ground my teeth in frustration, knowing that Genevieve's half of the performance would soon be complete, and I was supposed to go backstage under a veil of magic to keep an eye on her while Cécile performed. But I did not want to lose track of Marie. She was the only person who knew Anushka's identity with certainty, and I mentally weighed the risks of letting either woman out of my sight.

The final chords of music drifted through the room, and the lights dimmed. Where was Sabine?

Indecision still racking me, I began making my way through the tightly packed nobles toward the stage. My priority needed to be Genevieve, not keeping Marie within my grasp. If anything happened to Cécile's mother because I deviated from the plan in pursuit of my own interests, she'd never forgive me. Then the choice was rendered moot as the curtains to one side parted and Genevieve stepped into the ballroom.

CHAPTER 54
Cécile

The music of the first half echoed through the ballroom, an eerie and haunting accompaniment to my mother's voice. No, not my mother's voice: Anushka's. I knew it was fact, but my mind seemed set on rejecting the truth, on holding me back from the actions I needed to take.

"Cécile!"

At the sound of the hissed whisper of my name, I turned between my escorts – to see Sabine standing only a few paces away. She was dressed in an elaborate evening gown, her hair pinned up and jewels hanging from her ears, and I realized she must have come with Tristan. She started toward me, but one of the guards hurried to intercept her.

"Mademoiselle de Troyes is not to be troubled until after she performs," he said under his breath, pushing her back toward the curtain.

Sabine could warn Tristan; could keep him within the crowded ballroom until I had the chance to explain the truth to him, to temper his reaction. "I want to speak to her."

The guard held me back, shaking his head. "After."

Only then did I realize the music had ceased, and that the grinning courtiers vying for Lord Aiden were pouring off the stage. A hand with spiked fingertips closed over my shoulder, and I turned around to see the wicked mask hiding my mother's face. Anushka's face.

"Are you ready, darling?"

The King's compulsion swiftly and violently took hold. My hands whipped up and caught hold of her wrists with a grip I hadn't known I'd possessed. *Kill her!*

Anushka's jaw tightened beneath the mask, and she tried to pull away from me. "A touch of nerves, I see."

My mind grappled with ways I might kill her, but without a weapon, the guards would stop me before I had a chance. But they couldn't stop Tristan. With a wicked sense of glee, I felt his name rise up in my mind, along with the vision of her dead at my feet.

But it wouldn't end there. It would be chaos. The guards would attack Tristan, and how many would die? I needed to get her alone, and knowing that she planned to kill me tonight, that shouldn't be hard.

I forced my hands to relax and fall away from her wrists. "Dreadfully nervous." I swallowed. "Will you watch me, Mama? Out front where I can see you?"

With one hand, she removed the horrid mask from her face and then smiled. "Of course, dearest. I wouldn't miss it for the world."

I watched her walk to the curtain, before turning to see if there was any chance of speaking to Sabine. But there was no sign of her or the guard who had kept us apart. I prayed that she'd make her way back to Tristan, and that I could get through the next ten minutes of performance with nothing happening. Then I'd go to him, tell him the truth, and hope that...

I shoved the thought aside. Plunking my bottom down on the swing, I arranged my skirts and took a firm grip on the ropes. Then I nodded once to the men who would lift me up. The lights on the stage dimmed, music began to play and I was rising up into the air. The beam supporting the swing rotated me out onto the stage, and once they'd lowered me down a few feet, I kicked my legs to set the swing rocking gently back and forth. On my cue, I began to sing and the lamps were turned up. The audience murmured in appreciation at the stage designed to look like a paradise in the sky in blue, gold, and white.

Two throne-like chairs sat in the front and center of the crowd of nobles, and on them were seated the Regent and Lady Marie. Lord Aiden stood at his mother's shoulder, expression grim. I let my eyes drift slowly over the room, keeping my face soft, kind, and benevolent as the skirt of my costume tickled against my bare feet. Out of the corner of my eye, I could see my mother slowly making her way along the wall, nodding and greeting those who spoke to her as she went. But where was Tristan?

I finally spotted him standing in the shadows, his eyes tracking my mother's progress from the far side of the room. He made no move to go to her, but I felt no comfort. I was playing this too close and risking everything by keeping him in the dark, but what choice did I have? My mother reached the door at the far right of the room and leaned against the wall, crossing her arms and watching. *Not your mother, Anushka!*

Tearing my eyes away from her, I glanced down. Below me, the courtiers came out onto the stage and began to dance an intricate pattern. The girls of my company drifted amongst them, lending their voices as harmony to my own. They twirled and danced, and I sang a song designed to be lovely and pleasing without distracting too much from the would-be wives trying to catch Lord Aiden's attention.

The music ended, and I ceased my swinging, leaning forward slightly as though deeply intent on what my subjects were about to do. Each of the girls danced forward and named her virtue, curtseying deeply to Lord Aiden, who dutifully nodded at each of them. If I hadn't been so blasted terrified about what was to come, the whole spectacle might have been a comedy. Except I knew one of these girls was destined to become Marie's successor, her life dedicated to protecting the woman I was supposed to kill.

Out of the corner of my eye, I saw motion from Tristan's side of the room. I wanted to turn my head and look, but I dared not.

Instead I smiled and nodded as each of the girls took their turn, cursing the very idea that there was so much virtue in the world. Finally they had all finished and returned to their partners. The music struck up, I lifted my head to resume swinging, and I saw Sabine standing by the doors closest to the stage. But she wasn't watching me. Instead, she was facing toward the rear of the room, eyes fixed on my mother, her posture rigid.

Too late, I remembered – Sabine had also seen the mask in Catherine's memory. And it had clearly made an impression.

It was only all my practice and training that got the first line of the song through my numb lips as she began to pick her way toward Tristan. My gloves felt sodden with sweat between my palms and the ropes, logic telling me not to react, but instinct demanding I leap off my swing and stop her.

Julian sprang onto the stage below me, dancing circles around the girls as he tried to tempt away their virtues, but they all spurned him, and he and I dueled until he scampered offstage. Only one more short song to praise the victory and strength of the girls, and then it would be over.

I sang louder than I should, wishing I could feel the triumph of music. But there was no winning in my situation, no choice that wouldn't have painful consequences. No matter what I did, I was destined to lose. And it would happen in minutes. Sabine had only a few more people to navigate around before she reached Tristan and told him the truth. Then he'd try to kill my mother, and there'd be only one way to stop him.

Why should you stop him, the promise whispered. *She's a murderer.*

She's my mother.

He'll never forgive you...

You don't know that.

You gave your word...

The ballroom blurred as I warred my internal argument, then sharpened into focus as Sabine stopped in her tracks, and though the music was too loud for me to hear, the curses were clear on her lips. Spinning on her heel, she ignored the appalled expressions on people's faces and pushed her way back to the exit. My voice wavered as my eyes jerked to where Tristan had been standing moments before, catching only a flash of him as he bolted through another exit.

Panic flooded through my veins, and, not caring if all the audience noticed, I twisted on the swing, my eyes searching, searching for sight of my mother.

She was gone.

CHAPTER 55
Tristan

Genevieve ambled her way along the far side of the ballroom, expression unconcerned as she paused to greet guests, the chatter of the room loud to compensate for the grinding noise of the rotating set. She cast a backward glance at the stage when the lights dimmed, and my eyes went with hers in time to watch the curtain lift, revealing Cécile sitting on a swing high above the stage.

She was lovely. Even with the thousand concerns running through my head, I couldn't help but notice that. She wore a white silk gown that revealed an exceptional amount of pale skin, all of which shimmered with gold dust. Her long crimson hair hung amongst the feathers trailing down her back, and both swayed with the motion of the swing.

Only my unique insight into her mind betrayed that she was not content. She briefly tracked her mother's progress before letting her gaze drift across the ballroom to land on me, her mind a twist of nerves, hurt, and... guilt? I smiled at her, but a flash of unease betrayed my expression.

Something was wrong.
Something was not going to plan.
Where was Sabine?

Genevieve had retreated almost to the rear of the ballroom, stopping in the door well of one of the exits and leaning against the wall with her arms crossed. It was too dark to see her expression, but I took advantage of those very same shadows to watch her openly, my ears picking up on every waver in Cécile's voice through a performance I missed almost entirely.

The music rose into a climax, drums beating and cymbals crashing with deafening noise. It would be over in a matter of moments, and then I was sure Anushka would make her move. But as Cécile's voice rose to the highest note of her range, the door behind Genevieve opened, a hand reaching around to clamp over her mouth. I caught a flash of a blade, but before I could react, her assailant dragged her out into the corridor.

It was happening.

Ignoring the surprised looks of those around me, I sprinted to the door closest to me, instead of drawing more attention to myself by pushing through the crowded room. The hall was empty, and I ran, knowing I could be around in seconds to the door Genevieve's attacker had taken her through.

"Tristan, wait! It's her!" Sabine's voice floated up from behind me, but I didn't dare pause. I had to find Genevieve before Anushka had a chance to kill her and vanish. If I failed, the chance of freeing my people might be lost. If I failed, Cécile might never forgive me for letting the witch kill her mother.

The narrow corridor sped by me in a blur, my boots skidding against the floor as I rounded the first corner. Then the second. The music from inside the ballroom was loud even here, but not loud enough to drown out the piercing scream of a woman. Turning down another corridor, I prayed my ears had not deceived me.

Then heeled shoes clattered, and Genevieve de Troyes was running toward me, one gloved hand clutching a bloodied throat. "Help me!" she whimpered. "Please help me!"

Sliding to a stop, I let her through my magic, keeping my eyes on the darkness she had come from, even as she flung her arms around my neck, the steel claws on her gloves making my skin itch. "She attacked me! Oh, God, I'm bleeding. I'm dying."

There wasn't nearly enough blood for that to be a risk, but I wrapped an arm around the woman to steady her anyway. Not for a minute did I believe Anushka had let her go so easily. This was a trap. "Who took you?" I demanded. "Was she alone?"

"A woman. She was alone, but she had a knife." Her words were garbled with tears. "She cut me – I need help."

Running footsteps came up from behind us, and I whirled around, ready to attack.

But it was only Sabine, her skirts pulled up to her knees. "Tristan," she screamed when she saw us. "Get away from her!"

I looked back over my shoulder, sure an attack was coming, but the hallway was empty.

"It's her!" Sabine slid to a stop a few paces from me. "Genevieve is Anushka!"

The truth of her words ran through me, and my first instinct was to shove Genevieve away from me, to bind her, to kill her, but then I remembered Cécile's warning: *One of our friends is foe. Trust no one.* Had she meant Sabine?

I hesitated for a second, and Genevieve spoke. "Well now, this is a vexing development." The steel of her claws bit deep into my neck, the metal burning and blood soaking into my collar. I shoved her away hard enough that she slammed into the wall, but she only laughed and said, "Bind the light."

A vice far tighter than the steel of my father's manacles clamped down on my power. Frozen, I struggled against the binding, but it was like fighting myself. It was fighting myself, because I realized that, just like Cécile had used my own magic to heal me, Anushka was using it to hold me in check. But that didn't mean I couldn't kill her with my bare hands.

I lunged, but the witch was already moving, dragging Sabine in front of her and holding a pistol to the girl's head. "Now, now, Your Highness," she said. "Do not be so hasty."

She would not hesitate to kill Sabine, and without magic, there was no way to stop her other than acquiescing to her demands. Which was the last thing I wanted to do.

"Do you really believe her life is worth so much to me that I'd let you get away to save it?" I snapped, taking a step forward for every one she dragged Sabine back.

"I do," she replied, blue eyes glittering. "But in case I'm wrong, I've another plan. Just in case."

The hammer on a pistol clicked, and I went very still. Turning my head slightly, I saw the young man who had played the devil – Julian – was standing in the shadowy entrance to a room, his weapon leveled at my head.

She sighed softly. "Five hundred years have passed, and you trolls still have not learned."

"Learned what?"

Anushka smiled. "That you are not invincible. These weapons did not exist when I lived amongst your kind, but knowing what I know, I'm confident that even one of your power will not easily survive a bullet to the head."

I did not doubt she was correct. "Then what are you waiting for," I said. "Do it."

"Not just yet," she said. "I need Cécile first. In." She jerked her chin at the room behind me.

I didn't move.

Anushka pressed her revolver hard against Sabine's head. "If her life means nothing to you, then I see no point in keeping her alive."

Sabine's eyes met mine, and while there was no mistaking the fear in them, they were dry. Determined. She gave a slight shake of her head.

There was a good chance I could move fast enough to disarm Julian and save myself. But there was no chance of saving both of us. I'd told Cécile that rightly or wrongly, some lives were worth more than others. By all the rules of logic, what was Sabine's life worth compared to mine? What consequences would result from her death in comparison to mine?

But all that logic seemed meaningless.

"Too late you realize the cost of allying yourself with a troll," Anushka said softly into Sabine's ear. "They will protect you only when there is no cost to themselves. They have no souls."

"Says the black-hearted bitch who murders her own children."

Sabine lifted her chin. "Don't listen to her, Tristan. Kill her."

Anushka tsked softly. "Cécile will never forgive you for killing her mother. Or for letting her dear friend die."

I inhaled, then exhaled slowly. Cécile had discovered Genevieve and Anushka were one and the same. Had discovered it and hadn't told me, which was no small act of will given the compulsion she was under to destroy the witch. It was something only possible if a greater emotion ruled her actions.

Love.

Though Genevieve had done nothing to deserve it, I knew my wife desperately loved her mother and that she'd kept the information from me to protect her. Cécile was coming our direction, her mind desperate and wild with fear. But was it fear for what Anushka might do to me or of what I might do to her mother? "If I do what you ask, will you let Sabine go?" I'd keep her friend safe – that much I could do.

"No," Anushka replied, a smile creeping onto her lips. "But I won't put a bullet in her skull."

I didn't trust her for a second, but what choice did I have? "Fine." Turning slowly so as not to alarm the devil standing behind me, I walked into the room, ignoring the pistol that remained leveled at my head.

Anushka pushed Sabine in after us, kicking the wooden door shut behind her. The room was a set of living quarters, well furnished and unremarkable with the exception of the heavy chains set deep into the thick stone of the walls and floor. Anushka shoved Sabine. The girl tripped over the heavy skirts and would have fallen if I hadn't caught her.

"Chain him."

"Not a chance," Sabine said, righting herself. "Feel free to do your worst, but I won't…"

Anushka's gun fired.

CHAPTER 56
Cécile

The swing took a thousand years to lower, and I jumped off when it was still several feet above the ground. Ignoring the startled looks, I sprinted toward the exit and into the hall, letting instinct guide me in Tristan's direction, screaming a mental warning to him even as I felt his shock and knew it had come too late. My bare feet made little noise as I ran through the narrow corridors. *If she kills him, it will be your fault,* my conscience whispered, and I knew it was true. I'd thought I could have it both ways, and now I was paying for my mistake.

The sharp bark of a pistol firing filled the corridors, and I tripped on the hem of my skirt and fell, barely feeling the pain as the rough stone floors ripped the palms of my thin gloves. A howl tore out of my chest, and I pressed my forehead against my hands, waiting for the sharp knife of death to carve my insides out and leave me empty as it had the moment I'd knelt before the guillotine.

But it did not come.

Tristan was furious and very afraid, but unharmed. So who had been shot?

Climbing to my feet, I eased cautiously down the dimly lit hall, stopping instinctively in front of a heavy door. Tristan was on the other side, but who was with him? Was it only Anushka, or did she have an accomplice? For all I knew, there could be a dozen of Marie's guards standing in the room with her. Of a certainty, this was a trap, but it wasn't one I could run away from.

But that didn't mean I had to go in blind.

Hurrying down the hall, I tried the door of the adjoining room. It was locked. But the next one wasn't. My heart racing, I ran through the dark chambers to one of the narrow windows on the far wall. It was less than a foot wide, but for once my short stature came in handy as I unlatched the glass and climbed up onto the windowsill.

Icy wind tore at my hair and dress, and my stomach clenched as I looked down. It wasn't a horridly distant drop, but if I fell onto the bare stone below, my injuries would be grievous. The alternative was much worse, so I inched out onto the narrow ledge and cautiously eased my way toward the next window, my bare feet burning.

The snow crunched with each step I took, my fingers digging into the crumbling mortar between the heavy blocks of stone. My pulse thundered in my ears as I reached the window well; and clinging to the edge, I peered in with one eye.

It was a bedroom, both dark and empty, but through an open set of doors, I could see into the sitting room that adjoined it. Julian stood with his back to me, the gun he held leveled at Tristan's head, indicating that Anushka had cut him off from his magic, because otherwise such a threat would be meaningless. My mother stood a few paces in front of him, smiling and gesturing with the silver pistol in her hand. And Sabine...

My throat burned with the hurt of betrayal as I watched my best friend fasten heavy chains to Tristan's wrists and ankles, and then toss the key at my mother. It was only when she slumped to her knees next to his feet and pressed a hand to her shoulder that I saw the dark stain on her dress, and my hurt turned instantly to anger.

I needed to get inside that room.

I pressed a hand carefully against the glass, but it was latched from the inside. I could break it, but there was no chance they wouldn't hear it. A glance over my shoulder revealed the moon shining full and bright. I was running out of time.

Then a flicker of motion caught my eye. Peering back in the window revealed the tiniest glimmer floating just inside the glass. It was my light!

Although to call it such was almost a lie, because it had faded almost into nothingness since my flight from Trollus. But it was now my only chance.

Ignoring the violent shivers threatening my grip on the ledge, I focused on the tiny bit of magic, Tristan's words drifting through my mind: *My magic is what I will it to be. It does what I will it to do...* I'd coaxed it into brightening and dimming before, but never before had I tried to change the purpose Tristan had given it. I envisioned it as a force, like a finger hooking onto the latch and flicking it back. Beyond, I could not help but see Sabine slump against the carpets and feel the flash of panic from Tristan as he stood chained and powerless to help her.

With what seemed like reluctance, the magic drifted toward the metal latch, and my teeth chattered together as I willed it into action. I'd lost feeling in my toes, and my fingers were following suit. If this didn't work, I wasn't sure I'd even be able to make it back to the other window.

Click. The magic winked out, and I knew it was gone forever. But it had done enough.

Pressing my reddened fingertips against the glass, I began to push it in, but then stopped. The wind was howling around the castle, and it was sure to blast into the room. My eyes burned with the pain of the cold, and then the air went still as if the world itself was holding its breath. A prickle of apprehension ran down my spine, but I ignored it and opened the window, sliding in as swiftly and silently as a ghost before carefully shutting it behind me.

"What is it you trolls say?" My mother's voice was mocking. " 'All humans are liars'? You had to know there's no way I'd let the girl live. She knows too much, and I've not endured all these long years through lack of caution."

"As though you don't know a hundred ways to wipe the knowledge from her mind," Tristan snarled. "You did this to provoke me and hurt Cécile, not out of necessity."

"Don't presume to simplify my motivations, Your Highness. The curse I set on your kind required the death of a troll and the sacrifice of a human. With you and her, I will finish what I started five centuries ago."

She jerked her chin at Julian. "He's no danger now that he's chained. Go track down Cécile – there's little chance of her stumbling upon us, and we'll have need of her shortly."

"Yes, love." Julian hid his pistol in the waistband of his costume, and I would have cringed as he kissed her cheek in passing, but my mind was on her words. If she didn't know that I could find Tristan, that meant she didn't know we were bonded, and there had to be a way to use that to my advantage. Keeping to the shadows, I crept closer to the door, hoping Tristan had noticed my presence.

He had.

"Really?" It was Tristan's turn to mock her, and he did it well. "I'd heard you'd a taste and a talent for ensnaring powerful *men*, but I see your predilections are for those young enough to be your son. You've fallen far indeed if manipulating children is all you're now capable of. The great Anushka, guilty of murder, regicide, infanticide, and… the bedding of orphan boys."

He was baiting her, trying to distract her so that I could make my move. Except I didn't have one. Regardless, my mother only laughed. "Oh, don't be ridiculous. Julian isn't for me – he's for Cécile."

Tristan lifted one brow. "Seems it will be a short courtship, given you intend to kill her tonight."

"On the contrary, Cécile will have a long and glorious career with Julian at her side. It's Genevieve whose time has come to an end."

Tristan's confusion mirrored my own, and my stomach tightened, knowing that her plans were not as we had thought.

"All will become clear in time," she said. "But the girl need not suffer for so long as that. The power of her sacrifice will keep."

In a quick motion, my mother caught hold of Sabine's ankle and jerked her away from Tristan. He swore, and the steel chains holding him in place groaned with strain as he pulled against them. "If you harm her, I'll tear the heart from your chest, witch."

"Don't make promises you can't keep, troll." Anushka knelt beside Sabine, and I watched in horror as she pressed the mouth of her pistol to my friend's chest. "I did promise I wouldn't put a bullet in her head," she added with a smile.

I had to stop her, but I didn't know how. I had no materials or time for a spell, and what was the strength of my power against hers?

Her finger tightened on the trigger, and I lunged out into the room. "Stop!" I threw as much magic into the word as I possessed. Her hand froze and her eyes went blank. But only for a second, and then they went wide and overly bright.

"Well, well. It seems you will never cease astonishing me with your resourcefulness, Cécile." She sat back on her heels. "You have a way to find your troll master, do you darling? They are normally reluctant to carry charms and such, but I suppose five hundred years of captivity is enough to change even them."

"Let her go, Mama." Why did I call her that? "Please. She's done nothing to deserve this. Let her go."

"I need her." Her eyes were unblinking. Calculating.

I shook my head, ducking under one of Tristan's chains as I moved closer. "You need *him*. But Sabine doesn't have to die – someone else would serve."

"True," Anushka replied, sitting back on her heels. "But she is here and likely to die from her other wound anyway."

"You don't need to curse the trolls again," I said, desperately trying another tactic as the blood soaked into the carpet beneath Sabine. "I tried to break them free and I failed. I can't do it. I don't want to do it." The lie slipped easily from my lips.

"And yet this one is free." Rising to her feet, she walked

around me to stand in front of Tristan. "Which means it's possible, and a more permanent solution is in order."

Taking advantage of the moment, I dropped to my knees next to Sabine. Tearing a strip of fabric from my skirt, I bound her shoulder as tightly as I could manage. My friend was pale and shaking, and if she didn't get help soon, she'd bleed to death. She smiled bravely, then catching my hand, she placed it on her opposite forearm. Beneath the sleeve of her dress was something hard. A knife. I carefully extracted it, hiding it in the mesh belt of my dress.

"I'm weary of this life." Anushka's voice was soft. "I want the chance to live as I wish. Not to spend my days in fear that the trolls will catch me or that a foolish regent will burn me at the stake. Before, I was too blinded by hurt to see what needed to be done. But no longer."

Kill her! I clenched my teeth against the rush of compulsion. She had the pistol pointed at Tristan, and it might go off if I stabbed her. Still, I edged closer.

She reached a hand to brush the hair off Tristan's face, withdrawing it only when he lunged at her, his face taut with fury as he strained against the chains. "You have the look of Alexis," she said. "But I suppose that's no surprise. You all have the look of each other. Base things that you are."

Turning away from Tristan, she went to a chest and pulled out a jar. Something moved from within. Keeping one eye on me, she set her pistol on a table next to a basin of what looked like lamp oil. Touching a candle to it, she waited for the flames to flare brightly, then she opened the jar and dumped in the contents. I caught a glimpse of a large spider, legs thrashing, and then it was gone, consumed. She murmured some words under her breath, and suddenly I couldn't move, my legs frozen in place and my arms paralyzed at my sides. Helpless.

"You see, Cécile," she said, leaving the pistol where it lay and coming toward me. "That's what they are. Base. To the human eye, they are so very lovely, but to their ancestors, the immortal fey, they are wretched, ugly, and colorless things. Trolls. With his death, I will curse them never to draw another breath, and no one in this world or the next will mourn their loss."

I spat in her face, because it was all that I could manage.

Lifting one black sleeve, she wiped it away. Then she slapped my cheek hard enough to whip my face sideways. "Of all the disobedient daughters I've had over the centuries, none caused me half as much trouble as you."

My eyes watered from the pain and I blinked. "I'm sure if they had known the truth about you, they'd have fought harder."

"The truth?" The look she gave me was ripe with pity.

Going to the window, she pushed back the drapes and eyed the moon. "Time enough." Her heels made muffled thuds against the carpet as she walked back to Tristan. "How did you know Cécile was mine?"

He laughed silently. "You of all people should know that the fey see all they wish to behold."

She cocked her head to one side. "If that is so, why did they wait so very long to help you?"

He lifted one shoulder and let it fall. "What is five hundred years to those who watched time begin and will endure beyond its final hour?"

She snorted. "Which is your pretty way of saying that you don't know. Maybe they wanted to see you suffer?"

"Perhaps." He smiled at her. "But a base creature such as myself has no business speculating about the motives of his immortal betters. Does it unnerve you that, even now, they are watching?"

Her expression tightened. "Let them watch. Let them bear witness to the end of the trolls."

"We'll see," Tristan replied. "Pulling a mountain down on our heads was not enough to destroy us, so we may yet endure your spell."

Recoiling, naked surprise broke across her face. "You think I broke the mountain?" She threw back her head and laughed. "Why would I have done such a thing? And how? Ah, you see, Cécile? They cannot lie, but they are the masters of deception.

What great steps they must have taken to erase the truth and cast blame so that five centuries later, a Montigny prince himself believes such a falsehood to be true."

"You're lying." Tristan's voice was flat.

"No, Your Highness, I am not." She licked her lips, then smiled as though they'd been rimmed with sugar. "The greed of the trolls broke the mountain. You mined the earth too viciously, and it was she who took revenge."

"I don't believe you," Tristan snarled, but I could feel his doubt.

"What if the words came from the one you love?" Her eyes flicked to me. "Would you like to see my memory of that day, Cécile? I know you've meddled in such magic before."

She was talking about Catherine. How much had she extracted from the witch before killing her? "You murdered her."

"She gave me no choice. She should have learned the first time not to cross me, but still she insisted on meddling," she said. "Now do you wish to see the truth? If not, it matters little to me."

Except that I could see that it did. There was anticipation in her voice and an intensity in her stare that betrayed her. I might not have known her true identity, but that didn't mean I didn't *know* her. She wanted me to see what happened, but for what purpose, I wasn't certain. To prove she wasn't a liar? To gloat? Seeing wouldn't change anything, but it would delay her plans, and maybe Tristan would think of a way to get free. I nodded. "Show me."

Going back to her chest, Anushka extracted jars of dried plants that I did not recognize, putting a pinch of each into a basin, along with what I thought was a tortoise shell. On top of it all, she drizzled a dense and foul smelling liquid. With a touch of a lit candle the potion burst into flames, and she set the smoking basin between us.

"Look at me and inhale," she said, and then in a different tone she added, "Remember."

The smoke seared my nostrils, and with the word, magic rose in a torrent, from the earth, the sky, the flames, and the water they burned upon. Infinitely more power than she needed, but it was rich and heady on the air, ready for the taking.

Then the room fell away, and when I opened my eyes, I lay beneath the sun in the heat of summer. This was different from when I'd taken Catherine's memory – then I had been but a witness. Now I was myself, but I was also *her*.

I lounged on a divan, my fingers trailing through grass so lush it felt like streamers of velvet. In the distance, the royal palace gleamed in the sun. It seemed far vaster than I remembered, but perhaps that was because I'd only ever seen it cloaked in shadow.

I – no, Anushka lay in the gardens, but they were not made of glass. Instead, a natural beauty that the trolls would later try to mimic with their art surrounded her. Flowers, plants, and trees all rose up in a wild yet cultivated abandon, and through her eyes, I drank in colors more brilliant than any I'd seen. Tiny creatures with gossamer wings flitted between the flowers, the blooms opening with the touch of their tiny hands. It was a charmed place, as magical as the garden that now stood in its place. Only her eyes were not for the flowers or their tiny gardeners, but for the troll approaching her.

I recognized King Alexis from his portrait, but no painting could capture the arrogance of the man walking toward me. His utter surety that he was the most powerful creature in this world, and by that right, would one day rule it all. Dropping to his knees next to the divan, he caught Anushka's face between his hands and kissed her deeply. My mind clambered back and away from the feel of it.

Anushka turned her face away from his. "Someone might see."

"Let them." His voice was a growl in her ear. "I care not."

"*She* does."

Alexis sat back on his heels. "And since when do you care about that?"

I sensed this was an old argument that had been picked up in the middle, what I'd seen and heard not enough to account for the heat of emotion in Anushka's heart and the flash of annoyance in Alexis' silver eyes.

"Do you love her?" The knowledge that the troll queen had recently given birth drifted into my consciousness, and I knew Anushka was deeply irritated that for all his words, the King was still bedding them both.

"I'm bonded to her," he murmured, nuzzling her neck and nipping at her earlobe. "It's different."

"That is no answer."

Alexis left off kissing her throat and raised himself up on one elbow to look her in the eye. His were nearly identical in color and shape to Tristan's, but their expression was wholly unfamiliar. "My father chose Lamia because of her power and family. I chose you for your beauty and voice, and the delightful little things you can do with magic."

I heard the patronizing lilt in his voice, but Anushka seemed deaf to it. "You do owe me for your early rise to the throne."

"That's our secret." He held up one finger to his lips. "Besides, it was my magic you used to subdue my father and my magic that stopped his heart."

A flicker of annoyance ran through her that Alexis refused to give credit where it was due, but it was tempered by the glee she yet felt over ending the life of the troll who'd chosen Lamia. And besides, Alexis seemed well practiced at distracting her from her thoughts.

The flush heat of desire rose in her as he pulled down the bodice of her dress, his lips brushing against the curve of one breast. My discomfort was intense – I felt like a voyeur. An interloper without the power to close my eyes or turn my head.

"You're supposed to be in the stadium," Anushka whispered, and I felt her reluctance to dissuade him from their lovemaking. "Everyone is here for your birthday. Even some of the fey."

"Lamia's doing," he muttered. "What blasted reason is there to celebrate growing a year older? Find a way to stop the years from extracting their toll, and then I'll have cause to celebrate. That those who do not age are here to *celebrate* is nothing more than mockery."

You should not be so bitter... The words rose in Anushka's mind, but she did not speak them. The loss of immortality was fresh in this troll's mind, and not something she dared disparage. The fey who still walked between worlds would say enough with their clever and cutting words.

"I can think of much I'd rather be doing, but I suppose it would not do to keep the masses waiting." He kissed her again. "Besides, that which I want is currently denied to me."

Anushka's eyes flicked down, and I saw for the first time that she was pregnant and large enough that the child could not be far off. Dismay twisted in my gut, because in all that I had read, nothing had mentioned that Anushka had borne the King a child.

"What will we name him?" Her voice was dreamy as she twisted the all-too-familiar necklace dangling from her neck. And while she did not notice the discomforted way he looked away, I did. "You cannot know if it is a boy or girl, but either way, it will tell you what it wishes to be called in due time."

She did not miss the *it*. "Alexis." Her voice carried the weight of a hundred disagreements that had not gone in her favor.

"I must go." He rose to his feet, but got no further before a deafening crack shattered the air. Pain lanced through Anushka's skull, and she clapped her hands against her ears and screamed.

I screamed too, because never in my life had I heard something so loud, and I knew what it heralded. I knew what was coming.

The ground shuddered and her face jerked toward the massive peak looming above. Half of it was sliding away from the rest, breaking and crumbling, falling faster and faster, and the roar was that of the world being sundered in two.

"Anushka!" Alexis caught her up against his chest and flung a hand up. The mountain slid across the sky like a wave of rock and death, and then there was no more sun. And for some, there never would be again.

CHAPTER 57
Cécile

My heart fluttered in my chest like that of a wounded rabbit, and my hands pressed against my ears from the memory of the pain. Anushka had shown me the mountain, and I believed, as I always had, that its breaking was not her doing. I hated the feel of her mind, and wanted no more of this.

But she wasn't finished.

I fell back under, and this time when I opened my eyes, it was dark and Anushka's body was racked with exhaustion and pain. A candle burned in the lavishly appointed room, but she was alone. Alone and giving birth to a child. I ground my teeth against her pain, my gaze going to the ceiling with hers with every reverberating groan of shifting rocks. She pushed and screamed, and then a baby's voice cried out. A girl, covered with blood but perfect.

"He will keep you safe," Anushka whispered to the infant, clutching the girl against her chest. "He will change everything to keep you safe."

And the words that went unsaid, but which I heard in her mind: *I promise to protect you.*

Anushka plunged me directly into the next memory. She walked through the streets of Trollus, her newborn clutched tightly against her chest. The city was not destroyed, but it had suffered much. Massive boulders rested on the crushed remains

441

of homes, fountains and statues cracked and broken from fallen debris, and dust hanging thick in the air. Far above, the rocks shifted continually, the groaning and grinding incessant and sickening.

But worst of all were the bodies. They lay in the streets or protruded from the rubble, rot and decay caring no more if they were human or troll than the rocks had. The stench was incredible, and she knew nothing was being done to dispose of the bodies – none could be spared. She could practically taste the pestilence in the air – knew that it was claiming more victims with every passing day – but she'd brought the child with her anyway. She hadn't dared leave her alone when there were rumors of humans scouring the streets like dogs, searching for anything, *anything,* they could eat.

She found Alexis standing alone in front of the palace, wearing the same clothes he'd worn the day the mountain fell. His hair was lank and unwashed, face smeared with grime. Little tracks of sweat cut through the filth, and his entire body was tense with strain. "Alexis?"

Dull eyes shifted to her. "You shouldn't be in the streets. It isn't safe."

"I know." She whispered the words, although she didn't know entirely why. "But I wanted to tell you myself that you have a daughter." She held the child out to him, but he turned his head away. Hurt sliced through her, and she hugged the baby tight. "What do you want to name her?"

Alexis grimaced, the first reaction I'd noted from him. "She's half troll – she'll name herself and tell you how she wishes to be called when she speaks. You know that."

Anushka had known that, but also that trolls gave their children baby-names until the child was old enough to communicate its wishes. "What do you think of Lily? Or Rose?"

His lids drifted shut. "I think you should not allow yourself to become attached."

Anushka flinched.

"Go back to your manor and lock yourself in. I've enough to

worry about without you wandering the streets."

She went.

I wanted no more of this. I knew what she was doing, why she was showing me these memories. Anushka wanted me to see what the trolls had done so that I would hate them like she did. So that I'd understand why she'd cursed them and turn against Tristan. Not because she had any intention of sparing my life, but because her desire to inflict as much hurt as she had suffered was insatiable. I struggled, trying to extract my mind from her clutches, but she would not let me go.

"You will see, and you will know," she whispered, and threw me back under.

She was down to her last candle. Lily squalled in her arms, refusing to be soothed and unaware of the danger of attracting unwanted attention. I could feel Anushka's heart as though it were my own, leaping and skittering in her chest with every scream and crash from outside. Worse was the sound of skirmishes outside the windows. The crack of bones and the thud of impacts against flesh. The dull thump of bodies falling to the ground. The rustle of fabric against stone as the corpse was dragged away to be... My mind recoiled at the things she had seen through cracks in the curtain.

There was nothing left in the house to eat, and all that remained to drink was wine, mixed with the stagnant water she'd drained from the fountain in the courtyard. Yet she knew she was lucky, because for the humans and half-bloods outside, it was far worse. Thirty thousand soldiers had returned for Alexis' birthday, and once the task of holding up the rock had been organized into shifts, they'd eaten and drunk all there was to offer. The riverbed was bone dry; the few streams of water that made it through the rock were snatched up by the trolls with the most power.

For that was the way of it. The most powerful took everything, raiding the city stores and taking all, killing anyone who dared try to stop them. A pure-blooded troll could go weeks without food or drink with little effect, but they did not *want* to go without. So they dined on fresh bread daily, while those who needed it suffered, starved, and died. And the fey did nothing to help, all of them fled back to Arcadia or to wherever their fickle hearts desired. What care had they for creatures destined to die anyway?

A fist hammered against the door.

"Shhh, shhh," Anushka whispered to the baby, trying to silence her. She knew a hundred spells to use against trolls, but all required planning, stealth, and one ingredient she did not have. If they came after her directly, there would be no stopping them.

The fist hammered again. "Anushka!"

"Alexis!" His name came out as a sigh of relief. Flying down the stairs, she jerked open the door and flung an arm around his neck. "You're here!"

"Wait outside," he ordered whoever had accompanied him; then he backed Anushka inside.

"Stones and sky, you stink." He pushed her gently away from him.

"Alexis, there is barely enough water to drink, much less to wash with." And yet he was the kind of clean that only comes with a bathtub full of water. I noticed it, and so did she.

"Never mind." He was studiously looking anywhere but her or the baby. "Pack what things you need – I'm moving you to the palace."

Anushka's skin prickled, a thought flickering across her mind that the palace was Lamia's territory, and that she had demanded Alexis never allow her inside. "Why?"

"It's safer."

Anushka shook her head slowly. "Tell me the real reason."

He grimaced and walked over to the banister and leaned his elbows on it. "The Princess's wet-nurse is dead. I need you to feed her, care for her."

"Is there no one else?"

"None who can be spared, and besides, there is no one I trust more than you."

"What about Lamia?" Anushka demanded without thinking.

"Why can't she care for her own child?"

"Lamia is caring for all of Trollus!" In the blink of an eye, he had her by the shoulders, fingers digging painfully into her skin. "Ten thousand are dead and rotting in the street, but how many more would there be if not for her? She does not sleep – spends day and night in the streets holding up rock heavier than anything you can imagine, and yet still you spit out your petty jealousies. What right have you to deny her this when all you do is hide in a house?"

Those were Lamia's words…

"Alexis, you mistake me." The desperation in her voice mirrored that twisting in her gut. "I've barely enough for Lily, much less two of them. They'll both go hungry." But Lily was half human, and would suffer more for it.

"Find a way to make it work."

"It's impossible."

Alexis let go of her shoulders. "Then you must prioritize. And if the Princess does not thrive, you will suffer the consequences."

"Lily's your daughter, too!" The words slipped out, and she desperately wished to take them back, because she knew how he would respond. And she didn't want to hear it. Didn't want the fragile hope that he would change the laws for her sake to fall into pieces.

"The life of a bastard half-blood destined for servitude means nothing compared to that of a princess of Trollus."

Her hope shattered, and she took a step back.

"Anushka, you know I love you." His lips brushed hers, and she cringed. "If you love me, you'll do this. Don't make me resort to threats."

As if she had any choice. Escape was impossible – she was as trapped as they were. The only option was to do what he asked, and then when they dug their way out, she'd flee. Take Lily and as much gold as she could get her hands on, and run as far away from this cursed Isle as she could get. Back to the north, where folk knew ways to resist the fey.

•••

I opened my eyes to find my mother staring back at me. "Has that changed?" she asked, face full of an old sorrow.

I wanted to say that it had, that Tristan was trying to rid Trollus of slavery and oppression, but then I thought of Lessa. "What happened to her?"

"I'll show you."

Anushka sat in the royal nursery, exhausted and afraid, but determination burned in her heart. The trolls were close to freedom – Alexis had told her himself. It was only a matter of time.

For two weeks, she'd nursed the two babies, favoring the Princess as was required, while the hungry cries of her own daughter broke her heart. She plotted her escape; and at every possible chance, she wandered the rooms of the palace, stealing gold where she found it. One more day, he'd said. One more day.

"Freedom is very nearly upon us."

A woman's voice: soft, cultured, and troll to the core. Lamia.

Anushka rose, then curtsied low. "Your Majesty."

The troll queen was dressed in a plain black dress that emphasized an almost painful leanness, her face beautiful, but in a sharp and angular way. She did not look like a woman who often smiled, but I suspected she was not often given cause.

Lamia walked to the Princess's bassinet and ran fingers softly across the girl's forehead. "She appears well."

"She thrives, Your Majesty."

"And in somewhat less than an hour's time, she will no longer be your burden."

There was no threat in the Queen's voice, but Anushka all but shook with terror. Slowly, she edged her way toward where Lily lay sleeping, but an invisible barrier had materialized in her way.

"I know of your spells, witch. I know that he lets you use his power, and he's a fool for it, because you are not half as helpless as you look. I'll not let you near."

"What do you want from me?"

Lamia laughed, a brittle and ugly sound. "I know he loves you. I live every day with the feel of it in my mind, and it is enough to drive me to madness. I tried to make him break off his affair with you – told him I'd kill you myself if he didn't. For what punishment could he possibly dole out to me that I haven't already suffered?"

The Queen leaned a hand against the barrier, the flesh of her face pulled tight as though every muscle beneath it strained. "He told me that he would not live if you were dead. That he'd tear my heart out and fall on his own sword if I harmed you."

Anushka slammed her fists against the barrier. "Then unless you have a death wish, I suggest you let me go!"

Lamia picked up the Princess, cradling her in one arm. Then her eyes drifted to where Lily lay sleeping. "Some punishments are worse than death, would you not say?"

A soft snap. The crack of bone. Anushka screamed and bloodied her fists against the invisible wall, and I cried along with her.

"Enjoy your freedom, Anushka," Lamia said, and her face faded into darkness.

Alexis stood with his back to her, head in his hands. "I am sorry for what Lamia has done. In my worst nightmares, I never dreamed she would stoop to such wickedness."

"Punish her." Anushka's throat was raw from screaming, but she did not feel the pain.

"How?" Alexis asked. He turned around. "I cannot harm her without hurting myself. Is that what you want? Is your need for vengeance so great that you would make me suffer to punish her?"

Yes.

But Anushka could see he would do nothing. Alexis was too weak, too selfish to do what needed to be done. And Lamia was too clever to let Anushka close enough to harm her. There was only one way for her to have revenge, and a plan began to build in the depths of her mind.

"Shame her."

He frowned. "What do you mean?"

"If you will do nothing else, then at least shame her for me in front of your people. I want to be the one on your arm when you step out into the sun. Let me be first in this one thing."

He hesitated long enough that she began to fear he would refuse. "It will be done."

She found him hidden in a half-collapsed house, nearly dead from dehydration. "Do you want revenge on the trolls and the fey for what they have done to us all?" she whispered in his ear.

"Yes." His throat was so dry the word was more motion than sound.

"What would you do to have it?"

"Anything."

She sliced the knife across his throat, and as his life poured out, power like none she had ever known flooded her. "It will be done."

The passage they had carved down to the ocean was narrow and so thick with magic it felt like wading through syrup. She held tight to Alexis' arm, and the knife – still sticky with human blood – hung heavy in her pocket. All the might of Trollus followed behind them, Lamia included. The Queen's gaze burned between her shoulder blades, a hate so intense it felt tangible.

"Father." A young troll stood in front of a boulder, the sunlight filtering in around it framing him. "I thought I'd let you do the honor."

Alexis braced a booted heel, and the rock toppled out and away, splashing into the surf. Sunlight shone in, and the intensity of it burned Anushka's eyes. He turned to her and cupped her cheek with one hand. "You are the first."

"I love you," she lied.

He led her out into the sun.

I blinked against the memory of sunlight unseen for so long, my cheeks sticky with tears and clumped with golden powder. My mother let go of me and took a heavy step back, her own face flushed with spent emotion. Tristan stood unmoving in his chains, his shoulders slumped and face devoid of expression. He had not seen what I had seen, but he had felt what I had felt. And that was enough.

"Do you see why they must not be let free? Why the fey cannot be allowed to return?"

"You suffered a great injustice at their hands," I said. "I cannot blame you for seeking revenge against Lamia, but what I cannot understand is how, after enduring that loss, that you can murder daughter after daughter to make yourself immortal."

"Because there was no other way," she snapped. "Do you think I did not try? The soul needs a bond of blood for the exchange of souls to work."

Exchange of souls?

"That is little comfort for me," I said. "I'll still be dead."

"You'll be free." Her eyes had the too-bright gleam of a zealot. "Do you think the same thing would not have happened to you if I had not intervened? He might keep you as his whore, but that's all you'll ever be to him. I'm saving you from a miserable fate."

"This is about extending your life, not about saving mine."

She laughed. "Is that what you think? That it is such a treat to live in fear of the trolls finally hunting me down? To carry the burden of keeping the world safe from their evil with no help and no respite? Is it so wrong after all these years of living the lives of other women that I should have a chance to live one of my choosing?"

And everything she'd done seemed so clear. How she'd managed to go undetected for so long. The way she'd managed my career and set me up for success. Tonight's masque. She'd been orchestrating my life so that when the time came for her to steal my body, she'd be stepping into the life she wanted.

And once she'd done it, she intended to kill Tristan and Sabine and murder all the trolls along with them. There would be no one left to stop her, to punish her. Quite the opposite, the Regent would probably reward her beyond my wildest dreams for ridding the Isle of the trolls.

"The world owes me this," she said, and then her face softened. "It will be over swiftly, Cécile. I promise you that."

"Is that what you said to Genevieve when you chased her down in the woods?" I said, my voice shaking. "Was that the comfort you gave her when you stole any chance of her seeing her family again? Of raising her children? Of living her own life?" My body tensed with fury. "You're every bit as bad as

Lamia was. Worse, because you've done it over and over to your own blood!"

"Shut up!" She snarled the words and then dissolved into a fit of activity, fetching four small silver bowls, one filled with rocks, one with water, one with lamp oil that she lit with a taper, and one that held nothing at all. Taking out a tiny knife, she sliced across her forearm, allowing blood to flow into each of the basins, and then did the same to me, the pain sharp and fierce.

I watched in horror as droplets floated on top of the water like oil, danced weightless on the air, turned the flames a pure crimson, and sat on the rocks as round and solid as little red marbles. She placed the bowls in a circle around us, and magic surged like waves through the room, tearing at my hair. I tried to struggle, but the strength of her magic kept me frozen in place, my jaw locked shut so I couldn't even scream for help.

Grasping my arm so that our blood ran together, Anushka met my gaze. "The tie that binds our souls to our bodies is a tenuous thing, dearest," she whispered. "And once it is broken, there is nothing to hold your soul in this world. It will be gone in an instant, disappearing to a place where no more harm can come to you." She extracted an oleander blossom from a velvet bag, and without hesitation, held it over the candle flame. The petals singed and burned, smoke floating up on the air. "Goodbye, Cécile," she said, and blew it into my face.

My heart beat like a drum, and then it stumbled. And stopped. Pain bloomed through my chest, and I fell backwards to the ground, the sound of Tristan's screams filling my ears. Then there was nothing. No sight, no sound, no smell. All my senses were gone, leaving me with nothing but... awareness. I was dead. I knew that much – knew that Anushka had killed me and was waiting for my soul to abandon my body so that she might infiltrate with her own. But she'd been wrong to believe that nothing bound my soul to this world, because though I had no senses, I could still feel the ties that bound me to *him*. And they were not ready to break.

A blow struck me on the chest, and I gasped, light filling my eyes even as air flooded my lungs. Anushka leaned over on top of me, face white with panic and the weight of her failure. "Impossible," she whispered, recoiling away from me.

Her power had been expended, and I felt the weight of all her spells fall free from me. Struggling upwards, I watched her warily even as I pulled the white gloves off my hand to reveal the bonding marks brilliantly bright against my skin. "Not impossible. You cannot vanquish my soul and steal my life, because they are bound to him. Just as his are bound to me."

"They do not bond humans," she whispered. "They'd never lower themselves."

"Sometimes, one must do the unthinkable," I said, "for it is the only way to accomplish the impossible." Taking advantage of her shock, I snatched up the pitcher of water and poured it down Tristan's neck, washing away the spell. Anushka bolted for her pistol, snatching it up even as the metal manacles on his wrists shrieked apart, and for a moment, I thought he'd kill her. Bore a hole through her chest and end the curse here and now.

But he did not.

Instead, Tristan lifted her up in the air and deposited her back in front of me. Picking up Sabine's knife from my belt, I turned it over in my hand, barely managing to contain the desire to embed it in her chest.

"Cécile, have mercy." She sobbed. "I'm your mother. I bore you, and I cared for you as a baby. Brought you to Trianon and made all your dreams a reality. Please."

And this was it. The future the prophesy had foretold. By binding me to Tristan, it was ensured that Anushka could not strip away my soul and use my body as a vessel for her own. Any of her descendants before or after me could have done the same, but some twist of fate had made the fey decide that now would be the time for them to reveal the knowledge they had gleaned from watching the world. And so the task fell to me.

My eyes sought Tristan's.

"I'm not going to kill your mother, Cécile," he said. "At least, not unless that is what you want."

I let my eyelids drift shut, not wanting to see him or her while I thought. The end of the curse was no longer an if, but a when. The body she possessed was yet young – she might live another thirty years. Three decades more for the world to be kept safe from the dark power of those like Angoulême, Roland, and Lessa.

But what of those in Trollus? My friends, the half-bloods,

and all of those who were desperate for a better life? How many of them would end up like Élise? How many dead friends would arrive in caskets at our door while Anushka lived out the rest of her years? In my heart I knew Trollus existed in a fragile moment when change was possible, but that it would not last for long. The trolls' freedom was inevitable, and not acting on it now might well cast a blacker cloud on the future.

"Let her go."

Tristan sighed, but I ignored the twist of crippling disappointment that writhed through my skull; instead I watched as Anushka's feet settled on the ground and her arms were freed.

"You are making the right choice, Cécile," she said, and then the arm holding the pistol rose, and I knew she intended to kill me, and for my death to kill Tristan. For history to repeat itself once again.

But I moved faster.

She stumbled backwards, fingers dropping her pistol to clutch at the wound in her chest. But it wasn't deep. Wasn't enough. Knife slick in my hand, I went after her, and stabbed the blade into her again, feeling it grind against bone. Leaning over, I met her wild gaze and swallowed the lump in my throat.

"You are not my mother. You are her killer."

Anushka gasped out one breath. Then another. And then she whispered, "If the world burns, its blood will be on your hands."

She said no more.

A dull echo reverberated through the air, and the ground shuddered and shook. Tristan caught me against him, holding me steady, and then the earth stilled. "She's dead," I said, my toneless voice at odds with the cacophony in my head. The curse was broken, but the implications of that had yet to settle in my mind.

"Cécile?" Sabine's voice was weak, snapping me out of my thoughts. Rushing to her side, I used the bloody knife in my hand to cut away her dress.

"The bullet's still inside," I muttered. "Can you get it out?"

"Yes." Tristan's face tightened in concentration, but as Sabine screamed and fainted, the shards of metal pulled free of her wound.

"Keep pressure on it," I said, pressing his hand against her shoulder.

Then I ran to the chest where my mother had the ingredients

for her magic. My hands shaking, I dug through them, searching for what I needed for a healing spell. Tiny bottles clutched in my arms, I dropped them onto the carpet next to Tristan, and then, relying on my memory of the time I'd helped Tips, I started mixing them in the basin.

"Fire," I ordered, holding out a scrap of paper, waiting for the flames to turn from silver to yellow before touching it to the potion. As the fire flared up, I said, "Heal the flesh."

Magic came from all directions, intensified by the moon and the solstice, and I pressed my hand to the injury, feeling the power flood into her and the wound knit beneath my hand.

Then it was over. Sabine remained unconscious, but her breathing was steady and her pulse even. Wiping my hands on my ruined costume, I slumped against Tristan, fingers gripping his shoulders as my emotions threatened to overwhelm me.

"Why did you do it?" Tristan's heart beat rapidly where my ear pressed against his chest, and one of his hands slipped up into my hair, gently cupping the back of my head.

"She was going to kill me in the hopes you'd die too."

"That wasn't my question." He caught my face in his hands and tipped it up. "I could have stopped her without killing her. I would have."

"I know." And I might still come to regret the choice. "Anushka was telling the truth when she said she didn't break the mountain," I said, seeing my memory of her memories though my eyes were wide open. "It was the mines, and the trolls knew it."

"Then..."

"Alexis treated her better than he did his own wife." I turned my head so I could see Anushka. She was a murderer, but then, so was I. "She had his child within days of the mountain's collapse; and I think until that point, she believed none of the laws, customs, or beliefs of the trolls applied to her. That she was queen in his eyes, so their daughter would be a princess, or at least treated like one."

My eyes burned as I remembered the way he had looked at the baby. *The life of a bastard half-blood destined for servitude means nothing...* "That was not how it came to pass."

"She plotted and planned to flee with the child once there was a way out of Trollus, but Queen Lamia had other plans for her. She hated Anushka. When they were hours away from freedom, Lamia killed the baby right in front of her."

Tristan's breath caught in his chest, but he said nothing.

"Alexis refused to do anything to punish Lamia. Not because he didn't think she deserved it, but because doing so would harm himself. She killed him for his weakness, but she cursed the trolls as revenge against Lamia. What the Queen wanted more than anything was to see her children rule the world, and all Anushka wanted was to take that dream from her." *Some punishments are worse than death...*

"You think she was wrong to kill them?" There was incredulity in Tristan's voice.

I shook my head. "She deserved that revenge, but..." I struggled to find the words to explain what I'd seen and how I felt. "She is not a god to condemn an entire race for an injustice she alone had suffered. And I could not live with myself for leaving our friends to die because I was too weak to do what was needed."

My words were strong, but my skin already crawled at what I had done. A decision made in an instant that would change life as we knew it. *If the world burns, its blood will be on your hands...*

A slow, measured thud filled my ears like a vast drum beat by giant hands. *Thump. Thump. Thump.*

Tristan's whole body stiffened, his arm tightening around me and making it hard to breathe. "No. Not yet."

"What is it?" I demanded, his fear ratcheting up my own.

A scream like nothing I had ever heard rent the stillness of the night, piercing my ears and making my heart beat in the rapid, primal way of the hunted.

Clambering to his feet, Tristan pulled me along with him to the window and we both stared out into the night. A strange shadow flew across the sky, pausing in front of the glowing moon on wings as vast as a ship's sails. Something so vast it defied reason. A creature that could not possibly exist outside of fairy tale and legend.

Just like the trolls...

Horror flooded my veins as I watched the dragon furl its wings and dive toward Trianon, and seconds later, all too real human screams cut through the night.

What had I done?

CHAPTER 58
Cécile

Swearing under his breath, Tristan went back to the other room and scooped up Sabine, depositing her on the bed. "She'll be as safe here as anywhere," he said. "The castle walls are rimmed with steel – the dragon won't be able to breach the perimeter."

"What do we do?" I said, pulling one of the blankets off the bed and draping it over Anushka's corpse, more to spare Sabine the sight than out of any sentiment. The woman was nothing to me. "How do we stop it?"

Tristan picked up the knife and pistol from the blood-soaked carpet and handed them to me. "*We* don't. I do. Keep a steel weapon on you at all times – those who come will have even less tolerance for the metal than a troll. Stab one while it is corporeal, and you'll likely kill it."

"I don't know what that means." I followed him into the corridor, trotting to keep pace with his long stride.

"If it takes a shape." He stopped in his tracks and gripped my shoulders. "I should have told you more before, but I did not believe they'd come so soon. They must have been watching." He took a deep breath. "There is too much to explain, and we've no time for it. Stay within the castle walls, and you'll be safe."

I nodded in understanding if not agreement, as I had a sinking suspicion that he had no intention of remaining safely behind walls.

We ran toward the front of the castle and out into the darkness of the night. The torch flames danced wildly with the force of the wind, the sudden thick snow descending from the sky, carpeting the ground. It was painfully, unnaturally cold, and I would have retreated back if not for the warmth of Tristan's magic wrapping around my body.

The gates were closed, and the walls were lined with guards too fixated on the monster flying above the city to notice anyone coming up from behind them. "Open them," Tristan demanded once we reached them.

"Are you mad?" one of the guards replied, eyes wild. "Do you know what's out there?"

"Open the gates!"

I turned to see Lord Aiden striding towards us, but there was something about his voice that seemed... off. "Cécile," he added under his breath, and gave me a wink as he passed. It was my brother, disguised as Aiden with troll magic.

"But, my lord, there's a..."

The look my brother gave him, using Aiden's face, sent the man scampering to the mechanism that opened the steel portcullis.

"I trust you can kill that thing," he said under his breath.

"We'll find out," Tristan replied. "Either way, I'll be needing your sword."

In grim silence, we watched the heavy steel rise in its stone casement, the screams of the terrified people running in the city streets sending chills down my spine. The dragon wheeled and dove, coming up with victims in its mouth, their blood freezing into ice before it reached the ground. Frost billowed from its mouth with each roar, coating the city with ice.

"Do not step beyond the walls," Tristan said once the gates were open, and then he walked out onto the bridge.

"Anushka is dead," I whispered, gripping my brother's arm.

Fred tore his gaze from Tristan. "The curse is broken?"

I nodded. "Fred... There's something I need to tell you." I didn't know how to say it. How to tell him that our mother was dead, and that I'd been the one who killed her. But before speak, Tristan shouted in a language not of this world, his voice amplified by magic so that the creature would hear.

"Whatever it is can wait," Fred replied, and I nodded in silent agreement.

The dragon drifted in lazy circles around the castle, listening to whatever Tristan was saying. It was enormous – easily the size of a ship, and I could not fathom how Tristan intended to kill it.

Tristan ceased speaking, and the dragon came round to hover above the bridge, massive wings sending blasts of wind that tore the banners from their moorings.

Thud, thud, thud.

Then the creature opened its maw, and a blast of ice hurtled through the air toward him. And smashed up against a wall of magic. Chunks of ice crashed onto the bridge and into the raging river below, and then the dragon jerked down. It shrieked in fury, trying to retreat up into the air, but invisible ropes of magic held it in place. The bridge shivered and the walls shook as Tristan bound the creature to them, drawing it down and down until it crashed into the bridge, knocking the railings into the river.

Tristan spoke again, and though I could not understand the words, from his tone, I knew he was giving the dragon one last chance to retreat. One last chance to live.

But it only roared in defiance.

Lifting Fred's sword, Tristan swung, the blade whipping through the air to slice into the dragon's neck, and then its head was falling. But before it could hit the ground, it turned to snow indistinguishable from that which fell from the sky. The body also turned, looking for all the world like a giant snow sculpture soon to be eroded by the wind. The blizzard died down, and the unnatural chill left the air.

"God in heaven," Fred whispered. "How is such a thing possible?"

Lowering the sword, Tristan turned back to us. "It was a test, the real threat is..."

Horns blasted from the south, drowning him out. Over and over again they echoed off the mountain peaks and through the valleys, the tone ominous and threatening. The sound of war.

"They have discovered their cage has been broken," Tristan said, and taking hold of my hand, he led me back to the castle.

The courtyard was full of the nobility who had spilled out to watch, and at their head stood the Regent and Lady Marie.

"Anushka is dead and the curse broken," Tristan said. "The trolls are free, and our immortal brethren are returned to this world."

He hesitated, and no one said a word, the nobles, guards, and servants all waiting to see what he would say. Some few knew about the trolls, but all had seen the dragon, and that was enough to lend truth to his words.

"I am Prince Tristan de Montigny, and my father is King of the Trolls. In his mind, King of the Isle of Light, and in his heart, the future ruler of all the world. He is coming; and mark my words, he will show no mercy to those who do not bend their knees before him."

"And you are his forerunner." The Regent's voice was bitter. "Here to prepare the Isle to receive its new king."

Tristan shook his head. "I'm here to fight with you, and with your help, to take the crown from my father. To find a way for your kind and mine to live in peace, and to protect you from those who would see a return to the days of old when humans were our slaves."

I watched as the crowd exchanged worried whispers, and my heart sank. We didn't have time for this – the trolls were free, and too few of those here understood the magnitude of their threat. Roland, Angoulême, and Lessa – they were coming...

"Why should we trust you?" the Regent demanded. "I know your kind. I know your ways."

"Because I am your only hope," Tristan replied. "You are not fighting for dominion over this Isle or even for your own sovereignty. When they come, you will be fighting for only one thing – survival."

In the distance, the horns blared once more.

They were coming, and I had no idea how we'd stop them.

Acknowledgments

Completing a novel is often considered a solitary pursuit – success and failure attributed to what occurs in those long hours where a writer is alone with her keyboard. Far less consideration is given to the impact of the hours spent away from the manuscript, which means the individuals who influence those moments are rarely given their due. The fact of the matter is, none of my books would have been written if not for the support of those who are part of my non-writing life. The majority of *Hidden Huntress* made its way onto the page while I was working out of town, and as a result, I was reliant on a somewhat different group of people than I have in the past. Endless thanks to Carleen, Joel, Cohen, and Camdyn for being my family while I was away from mine. To Brenda, for keeping me employed and for teaching me a whole new set of text message acronyms. To Bob, for always making sure there was Starbucks waiting on the island for the hermit in your basement. To my friends at Campus, especially Shannon, Katie, Jessica, Melissa, Kathyrn, Meaghan, Shaylea, Amber, Sunme, Kaitlyn, Carolyn, Destiny, Brianne, Shelby, Precious, and Kelvin, thanks for the endless entertainment. You guys rule! And for the moments I was in Calgary, so much gratitude to Donna for all the lunches and for listening to my drama.

A thousand thanks to my amazing agent, Tamar Rydzinski, for your endless support and hard work – I'd be lost without you! To Laura Dail for being there when things went sideways, and interns Cassie Homer and Emily Motyka for finding my typos. To the crew at Angry Robot – Caroline, Marc, Phil, and

Mike – thanks for keeping me around and for all the work you put into this book; looking forward to going for round three with you.

Hidden Huntress wouldn't have seen the light of day without the ceaseless support of my family. Huge thanks to my mom for being the greatest book-pusher (though not as good as Sandy, Brenda, and Edith!) a daughter could ask for – I'm not nearly as ungrateful as I pretend. To my dad, for endless editing and not complaining when I ask you to do it last minute. To my brother, for selling my books to your co-workers like they are Girl Guide cookies. And to Spencer, for making sure my life never suffers a dull moment – love you!

Finally, I owe a huge debt of gratitude to the book bloggers and readers who supported *Stolen Songbird*. It is very much thanks to you that *Hidden Huntress* is hitting the shelves too, and for that, I am eternally grateful.

About the Author

Danielle L Jensen was born and raised in Calgary, Canada. At the insistence of the left side of her brain, she graduated in 2003 from the University of Calgary with a bachelor's degree in finance.

But the right side of her brain has ever been mutinous; and in 2010, it sent her back to school to complete an entirely impractical English literature degree at Mount Royal University and to pursue publication. Much to her satisfaction, the right side shows no sign of relinquishing its domination. Her next book will be *Warrior Witch*.

danielleljensen.com • *twitter.com@dljensen_*

Love before duty and honour… to the death.

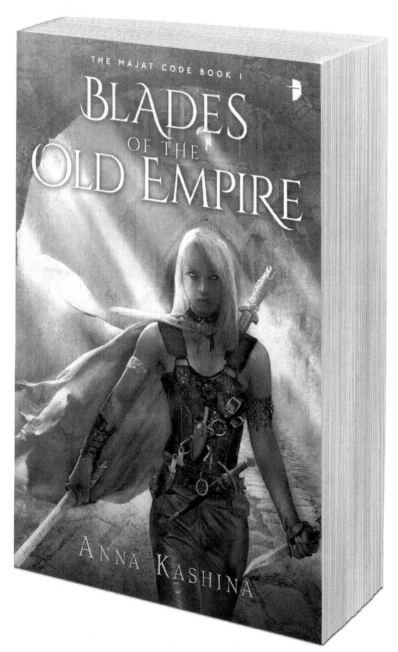

THE MAJAT CODE BOOK I

BLADES
OF THE
OLD EMPIRE

ANNA KASHINA

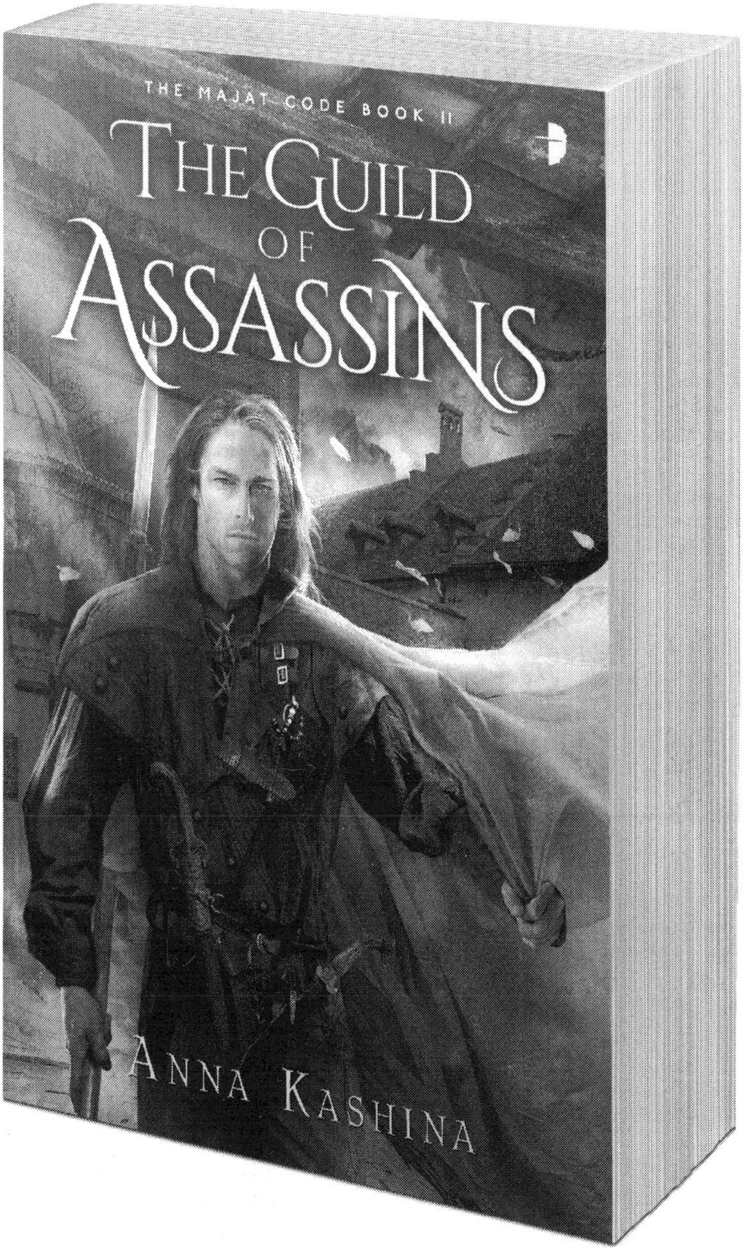
THE MAJAT CODE BOOK II
THE GUILD OF ASSASSINS
ANNA KASHINA

SOMETIMES, ONE MUST
DO THE UNTHINKABLE...

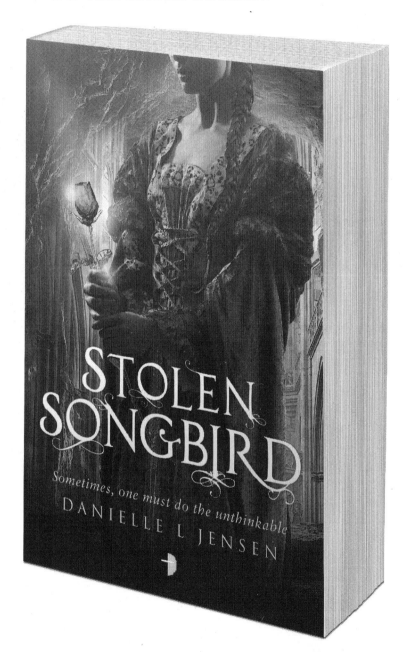

STOLEN
SONGBIRD

Sometimes, one must do the unthinkable

DANIELLE L JENSEN